A Gift for Dying

M. J. Arlidge has worked in television for the last fifteen years, specializing in high-end drama production, including the prime-time crime serials *Torn*, *The Little House* and *Silent Witness*. Arlidge also pilots original crime series for both UK and US networks. In 2015 his audio exclusive *Six Degrees of Assassination* was a Number One bestseller.

His first thriller, *Eeny Meeny*, was the UK's bestselling crime debut of 2014. It was followed by the bestselling *Pop Goes the Weasel*, *The Doll's House*, *Liar Liar*, *Little Boy Blue*, *Hide and Seek*, and *Love Me Not*.

A Gift for Dying

M. J. ARLIDGE

MICHAEL JOSEPH
an imprint of
PENGUIN BOOKS

MICHAEL JOSEPH

UK | USA | Canada | Ireland | Australia
India | New Zealand | South Africa

Michael Joseph is part of the Penguin Random House group of companies
whose addresses can be found at global.penguinrandomhouse.com

First published 2019
001

Copyright © M. J. Arlidge, 2019

The moral right of the author has been asserted

Set in 13.5/16 pt Garamond MT Std
Typeset by Jouve (UK), Milton Keynes
Printed and bound in Great Britain by Clays Ltd, Elcograf S.p.A.

A CIP catalogue record for this book is available from the British Library

HARDBACK ISBN: 978–0–718–18788–0
OM PAPERBACK ISBN: 978–0–718–18789–7

www.greenpenguin.co.uk

For Jennie,
whose gifts are real

Nothing in life is to be feared;
it is only to be understood.

Marie Curie

Book One

I

The shock of the impact, then an act of kindness.

It was rush hour and North Michigan Avenue was teeming with souls. The sidewalk was clogged with office workers, shoppers and tourists keen to experience the magic of Chicago's 'Magnificent Mile'. Progress was faltering and Kassie kept her head down as she barged her way through the crowds. She seldom braved central Chicago – venturing north only to shoplift clothes and cosmetics from the upmarket stores – and she was keen to get back to the familiar sprawl of the southern suburbs.

Her eyes were glued to the floor – seeing feet approaching, then dodging them at the last minute – but her concentration must have wavered for a moment, because suddenly she hit something hard and unyielding. Such was the force of the collision that she was thrown backwards. Her satchel slid off her shoulder, the stolen clothes tumbling out on to the sidewalk, even as she crumpled on to the bubblegum-smeared concrete. She landed on her backside, her tailbone connecting sharply with the ground, the shock robbing her of breath and making her feel light-headed.

She sat there for a moment, aware of how ridiculous she must look, yet seemingly unable to move. To her shame, she felt tears prick her eyes.

'Are you ok?'

The voice sounded far away, but still cut through the noise of the taxi horns on the busy avenue.

3

'Totally my fault. I didn't see you . . .'

Kassie became aware of a man crouching down over her.

'Sometimes I'm so in the zone, I don't notice what's right in front of me . . .'

His voice was warm, calm. Kassie felt more foolish still – if the collision was anyone's fault, it was *hers*. Her mother always said she was clumsy.

'I hope I didn't hurt you,' the voice continued. 'If you need to get checked ou—'

'I'll be fine,' Kassie replied quickly. 'I don't want to hold you up.'

She hadn't looked up at him, but she could tell by his immaculate brogues and expensive suit that he didn't belong in her world. He clearly had status, money and presumably little time to be assisting high-school truants.

'Here, let me help you.'

A hand was offered to her. Strong, confident, open. Gratefully, she grasped it and was soon back on her feet. The pain had gone now and she was keen to be away, fearful that one of the many police officers who patrolled North Michigan Avenue would take an interest in the items scattered on the ground.

'Thank you,' she muttered, keeping her eyes fixed on the floor.

'Now, are you sure there's nothing I can do for you? How about a cab . . . ?'

His voice was so nice, so reassuring, that now she couldn't resist. She looked up, taking in the strong, clean-shaven chin, the thick, brown curls, his deep, hazel eyes. The man was smiling, his eyes sparkling with good humour, but suddenly Kassie froze.

She'd been hoping to find kindness, even serenity in his expression. Instead, she was looking death in the face.

2

He was descending into the underworld.

Cook County Jail was imposing from the outside, with its towering walls and concertina wire, but even more unnerving on the inside. The subterranean tunnels that led to the cells were deliberately labyrinthine, the signs and directions having been removed to hinder escape attempts, and even regular visitors lost their way. Furthermore, the din that accompanied your progress – the catcalling, screaming and hollering – was incessant, only serving to amplify your anxiety about what might be waiting for you at the end of your journey. It wasn't pleasant, it wasn't right, but this was the daily reality inside America's largest unofficial mental health facility.

Adam Brandt had been coming here for years. An experienced forensic psychologist, he had always worked closely with the Sheriff's Office. Harvard-educated, double-boarded for adult and paediatric psychology, he could have made a small fortune attending the clients who visited his private practice in Lincoln Park. But he'd never forgotten his humble origins; nor could he ignore his conscience, which is why he regularly found himself in the bowels of the earth under Cook County Jail.

The faces in the holding cells were depressingly familiar and Adam had been concerned to find himself opposite Lemar Johnson once more this morning.

'I can't be here, man. I can't be here . . .'

'I understand that, Lemar, and I'm going to try to get you out. But I need you to look at me. I can't communicate with you, if you don't look at me . . .'

The 21-year-old was rocking back and forth in his chair, his face concealed by his massive, scarred hands. His life had already been blighted by violence – his father murdered, a cousin gunned down in a drive-by – and his mental health had always hung in the balance. He was bipolar, suffered from PTSD and regularly used heroin to help him sleep. The last time their paths had crossed, Adam had managed to get Lemar referred to a mental health outreach unit and he'd been doing well following his release – with a little help from Prozac and hydroxyzine. Adam didn't exactly approve of the drugs, but they seemed to be working – until last night at least, when Lemar had threatened a man with a knife in a chicken shop in South Shore.

'Have you been taking your meds?'

'Sure, sure . . .'

'Look at me, Lemar.'

'Shit, I ran out,' the young man replied, not looking up.

'Why?'

'They said I had to wait four months for an appointment, a follow-up.'

Adam's heart sank. This kind of complaint was common, given the recent cutbacks to mental health provision and the Capitol's scandalous inability to agree a State Budget. The intransigence on both sides made his blood boil – it was never the politicians who suffered when they played politics.

'I tried to make them last. One day on, one day off, but it was making me crazy.'

'When did you run out?'

'Two weeks ago.'

6

'You should have contacted me. Contacted the Center.'

'I tried, man.'

Adam let the lie go. Lemar had clearly been in a manic phase – socializing wildly, spending what little money he had, so he hadn't a hope of posting bail – but was now beginning the steep decline into depression.

'Ok, we're going to get you some meds, then I want you to tell me exactly what happened. You've got your arraignment tomorrow and I want your attorney to have everything she needs to argue that a short stay in a residential mental health unit is what's needed. I take it you'd prefer that to staying here?'

Lemar stopped fidgeting long enough to nod his head briefly.

'Good, then let's talk.'

An hour later, Adam found himself back in the prison's parking lot. He strode over to his Lexus SUV – an extravagance he'd convinced himself was acceptable, given the imminent arrival of his first child – checking his watch as he went. Lemar had been reluctant to talk and it had taken a while to get a coherent summary of events from him. It was pushing 6 p.m. now – he would have to pray that the traffic wasn't too bad, if he were to call in at the office *and* make it home at a reasonable time. Upping his pace, he zapped the car, opened the driver's door and flung his bag and jacket inside. As he did so, however, his cell phone began to vibrate.

Calls at this hour were never good news and Adam was not surprised to recognize the number. The caller was Freddie Highsmith, Superintendent at Chicago's Juvenile Detention Center.

'I'm just on my way home, Freddie,' Adam said cautiously.

'I know, I know,' Freddie responded brightly. 'But when you need the best in the business . . .'

'Flattery won't get you anywhere –'

'. . . plus there's no one else available. I've rung all the usual suspects, but everyone's under siege. Look, I know you're running on empty . . . but I can't give this one to a college grad.'

Freddie paused now, his jovial manner evaporating as his anxiety punched through. Adam said nothing, suddenly concerned, listening intently as Freddie concluded:

'We've got a live one here.'

3

Jacob Jones drained his Goose Island, then banged the empty glass on the wooden counter, signalling to the bartender that he needed another. The condensation was still thick on the glass and the harassed server snatched it up, arching an eyebrow at the speed of Jacob's consumption. Jacob didn't react. His mind was elsewhere and, besides, neither the bar nor the bartender was familiar to him. Greene's Tavern was one of several old-fashioned drinking holes in the area that harked back to the Prohibition era. Tourists liked to come here to wallow in nostalgia, to take photos of themselves supping beer under the watchful eye of Al Capone, but to Jacob this place was a short-term sanctuary – a port in a storm.

The bartender marked up his tab and slid the glass towards him. Froth spilled over the sides, but Jacob swept it up, raising it greedily to his lips. As the lager slid over his tongue, hitting the back of his throat, he realized that his hand was shaking and he quickly replaced the glass on the counter. Suddenly he felt emotion ambush him – his heart pounding once more – and he had to lower his face towards the floor to hide his tortured expression.

'Get a grip,' he muttered to himself, hoping that the noisy cabal of British tourists nearby wouldn't hear him.

He knew he was over-reacting. In the course of his work, he had encountered many shocking events, though he had seldom been the one at the centre of the storm. Even now, an hour or more after the confrontation, he was trying to process exactly what had happened.

He had been so intent on getting home that he hadn't seen the girl until he'd dumped her on her ass. He had played college football back in the day and often put this to good use on the busy Chicago streets, leading with his shoulder as he parted the crowds. This time, however, he had misjudged his line of attack and taken out the startled teenager.

Determined as he was to get back to West Town, he'd been raised to put his hand up when he was at fault. So he'd checked that the girl was ok and helped her to her feet. He'd then tried to engage her in conversation and she'd seemed all right at first, muttering her thanks through her embarrassment. Then the whole thing kind of went *off*. What had he been expecting? Gratitude? Apologies? A girlish blush? He knew he was an attractive guy – tall, well-built, with a kind face – and on other occasions women had become pleasingly flustered on finding themselves talking to him. But there was no engaging bashfulness in this teenager's expression – she looked *horrified*.

He'd carried on talking to her, but she had just stared at him, shaking and speechless, so in the end he had cut and run. Disconcerted, angry at her lack of gratitude, he had hurried on his way. Nancy wasn't home – she was at a conference in San Francisco – but still he'd wanted to get back to the house, to put the whole strange incident behind him.

But as he'd charged down North Michigan Avenue, dodging the ponderous tourists, he became aware of something. Someone shouting, then footsteps coming up fast behind him. He'd turned suddenly – expecting what exactly? – just in time to see the girl throw herself at him.

Jacob raised the glass to his lips once more, draining

another half-pint. What had happened after that still seemed like a blur. The girl had clasped his right arm, then his lapels, trying desperately to grab hold of him. He had attempted to extricate himself, even as the words – manic and confused – tumbled from her lips. Still she'd clung on, so he'd pushed her forcefully away, but this only seemed to anger her further. She started screaming – threatening him, if you could believe it – and instinctively he'd freed his right arm to strike her. Thankfully, this had proved unnecessary as a couple of police officers now intervened, hauling the girl off. Still she didn't relent, screeching at Jacob, even as she was dragged to the waiting patrol car.

Tugging his suit jacket back into shape, Jacob had turned away, unable to watch the sorry spectacle any longer. The young girl hadn't looked angry or aggrieved any more.

She'd looked deranged.

4

'How long's she been doing that?'

Adam peered through the window of the supervision cell. A teenage girl was pacing back and forth, shouting and gesturing at the door.

'Since she came in,' the custody officer drawled. 'First, she was demanding to be let out. Then she was trying to rip the door off. Now she's happy just handing out abuse.'

Adam digested this information, his eyes never leaving the pacing figure. Half an hour ago, he'd been looking forward to finishing up his paperwork and heading home to see Faith, but already the clinician in him was taking over. This teenager – she was fourteen, fifteen at the most – was clearly in the middle of some kind of mental health breakdown.

'She was brought in an hour ago. Tried to rob some guy on North Michigan. Right in front of the cops. She had an ounce of skunk on her apparently, so I don't know what sense you're going to get out of her.'

Smiling politely at the officer's warning, Adam took the paperwork from him and leafed through it. Juveniles in detention are routinely screened before facing a detective, and it was the duty of psychologists like Adam to decide whether they were fit to be questioned.

Kassandra Wojcek. She was obviously of Polish origin, with an interesting rap sheet. Possession of Class B drugs, theft, resisting arrest, assault, acting under the influence and, according to the accompanying school paperwork, an impressive record of cutting class. She hailed from Back of the Yards, a southern suburb near the old stockyard which had once been popular with Polish workers, but which had now been abandoned to the Puerto Ricans.

'Mother? Father?' Adam asked.

'Father's deceased. We've tried to contact her mother, but . . . Hopefully we can raise her in time for questioning –'

'Let's see if it gets that far,' Adam interrupted, gesturing for the officer to open the door.

The officer looked at him, clearly marking him down as a candy-assed liberal, before unlocking the door. Adam stepped inside, placing the girl's file gently on the chair, before turning to his charge.

'Hi, Kassandra. Do you mind if I join you?'

The teenager said nothing, but finally ceased pacing.

'My name is Adam. I'm a psychologist and I'd like to talk to you. Is that ok?'

A grunt was all Adam got by way of response. Already he had the feeling that the girl didn't have much time for shrinks.

'Now what should I call you? Kassandra? Kass—'

'Kassie,' she answered, still hiding behind her fringe.

Adam nodded, taking her in properly for the first time. She was a strange-looking girl – tall, gawky, but not unattractive, with long auburn hair fringing her pale face. She was dressed in torn jeans, a faded Motörhead hoodie and battered sneakers. It was hard to tell if this dishevelment was a teenage fashion choice or the product of deprivation, but, given her background, Adam suspected the latter.

'Ok, then, Kassie,' Adam continued, shifting slightly to get a better look at her narrow, freckled face. 'I hear you had a bit of trouble today. The police have already told me their side of the story – I'd love to hear yours.'

13

His tone was open and encouraging, implying sympathy for the incarcerated. Curious, intrigued, the girl now chanced a quick look at him. And immediately Adam clocked a reaction. She looked surprised, even shocked, by his appearance, and immediately began to withdraw, turning from him and retreating to the corner of the room.

'I know you're scared, confused even,' Adam continued soothingly. 'And that's fine. Nobody likes being put in a police car, being brought down here. I just want to make sure you're ok, so we can sort this out and get you home. Will you help me do that?'

A long silence, then the briefest of nods.

'So, you were on North Michigan Avenue. Heading home? Heading to the "L"?'

'Home.'

'What happened next?'

Another lengthy pause. In the distance, Adam heard footsteps, but tried to ignore them, focusing on Kassie instead.

'I bumped into this guy . . .'

'Physically bumped into him?'

'Uh-huh.'

'Someone you knew?'

'No.'

'And then?'

The girl hesitated to answer. The footsteps were getting louder now, so Adam pressed on.

'Kassie . . . ?'

'He helped me up . . . then he took off.'

'Did you talk to him?'

'Not at first . . .'

'So, later . . . ?'

She nodded.

'Why was that? Why did you go after him?'

Another pause, as if the girl was making a decision, then:

'I wanted to speak to him.'

She had clearly done much more than that, having to be dragged off the protesting victim.

'Why? What did you want to say to him?'

Kassie hesitated now, even as the footsteps came to a halt outside the door.

'I wanted to . . . warn him,' she breathed quietly.

'Warn him about what?'

The door swung open and the custody officer stuck his head through the door.

'We've got hold of Mom. She'll be here in twenty minutes.'

The door slammed shut again. Adam turned back to his charge, but Kassie had turned away, curling herself up into a ball, clearly alarmed at the prospect of her mother's arrival.

'Why you were concerned for him, Kassie?'

It was said brightly, but he could see that he was losing her – the fragile trust between them shattered by the custody officer's clumsy intervention.

'You said you had to warn him,' Adam persisted, taking a small step towards her.

Still the teenager didn't move, staring resolutely at the wall. So Adam made one last attempt to reach her:

'Please, Kassie. What did you want to warn him *about*?'

5

'I don't want to press charges. I just want to forget the whole thing.'

Jacob Jones stood in the gloom of his hallway, the phone pressed to his ear. He had only just got home and the landline had been ringing as he unlocked the door. Hurrying inside, he'd snatched it up, expecting it to be his mother, who often called when Nancy was away. But it was only a follow-up call from the Chicago Police Department, after the earlier incident.

Jacob's immediate concern was that he sounded intoxicated. He'd had three beers in quick succession – he'd needed them to steady his nerves, but now chided himself for his weakness. Putting on his professional voice, he answered the police officer's questions soberly, making it clear that he didn't want to take matters further. The officer seemed disappointed, not surprisingly perhaps given Jacob's profession, but he wasn't going to push it.

'It's your decision . . .'

'Absolutely. And thanks again for the call. I really appreciate it.'

Jacob was a practised liar and the officer rang off happily enough, bidding him a cheery goodnight. Shaking his head at the craziness of the last few hours, Jacob replaced the receiver and belatedly shut the front door, locking it behind him. He had the place to himself tonight and was looking forward to watching the White Sox game – perhaps with another cold beer.

Dumping his bag and coat on the floor, he flicked the light switch. To his surprise, nothing happened. Just about keeping his temper – *another* light bulb gone – he marched into the kitchen, switching on those lights instead. But again, nothing happened and he remained in darkness. He flicked the switch back and forth – once, twice, three times – without success.

'Jesus . . .'

Hurrying over to the window, Jacob peered out on to the quiet suburban street. All around him, the pretty houses twinkled, brightly illuminated from within.

'Of course, it's just me,' he muttered, his resolute good humour finally evaporating.

Turning on his heel, he marched back across the hall and pulled open the door to the cellar. A flashlight hung on a hook just inside and Jacob turned it on before descending into the gloom. Dust danced in front of the flashlight beam, as he walked carefully down the rickety steps. He seldom visited the basement – and Nancy *never* ventured down here – and he was quite certain he'd miss the final step or stumble on some forgotten piece of junk. His work schedule was too blasted to accommodate a foolish injury, so he proceeded with caution, eventually making it to the basement floor.

He cast around for the fuse box, eventually locating it on the far wall. He made for it, dodging boxes of high-school yearbooks and mouldering sports gear, remarking to himself how large this space was. They should do something with it – an extra room could add thousands to the value of the property – but not today. Today, he just wanted to download and unwind. So, opening the fuse box, he searched for the master switch.

It was facing down, as it should be, and investigating

further Jacob now realized that none of the individual switches had blown.

'What the –?'

Was he going to have go call someone out? At this hour? Grasping the master switch, he yanked it up, held it for a second, then pushed it firmly down. Still he remained swathed in darkness. So he tried again. And again. The same result. Resting his weary head on the fuse box, he swore quietly to himself.

And now he became aware of something else. The sound of someone breathing.

It couldn't be, could it? The house was secure, there was no sign of –

Now he heard someone coming towards him. Panicking, Jacob swung his flashlight around.

To see a man in a ski mask descending upon him.

6

The Union Stock Yard had always reeked of death. Located in Back of the Yards, it had been a magnet for immigrant workers, who'd flocked to the slaughterhouses in their thousands. Back in the day, when Chicago was the hog-killing capital of the world, the work had been plentiful, over a billion animals passing through its gates on their final journey. But the yard was now derelict, long since mothballed, superseded by more efficient operations elsewhere.

Kassie and her mother walked past it in silence. Kassie's father, Mikolaj, had worked and died in the stockyard and the sight of it always brought their conversation to an abrupt halt. Not that this was a problem today – Natalia hadn't said a word since collecting her daughter from the Juvenile Detention Center. The call had come just after she'd finished work, which was one small mercy, but clearly not enough to buy Kassie any slack.

They turned the corner on to South Ada Street, passing a couple of boarded-up properties as they walked the last hundred feet together. The house that had been Kassie's home for the last fifteen years stuck out like a sore thumb. It was a small but pristine brown-brick bungalow. The tiny strip of grass out front was neatly clipped, the steps up to the porch were clean and the ornate metal grille protecting the front door was freshly painted. Say what you like about the Wojcek home, it was never less than immaculate.

Kassie stared at her dirty sneakers, as her mother unlocked

the grille. To many, Natalia's high standards were admirable, but Kassie had always been slightly embarrassed by them. They harked back to a bygone era, when the suburb teemed with good Catholic families, all competing with each other to display their new-found prosperity. But the other Polish families had moved on now, as other communities settled in the neighbourhood, most of the incomers choosing more desirable streets than their own. There were several abandoned properties in the road – realtors couldn't shift units round here – but it was as if Natalia hadn't noticed. As if she were still a young woman fresh off the boat, full of hope and dreams.

Life had not been kind to either of them, and Kassie felt her heart sink as they entered the quiet bungalow. Kassie – Kassandra Alicja Marta – was Natalia's only child and as remarriage was out of the question for a respectable widow, it had remained just the two of them, circling each other in this gently old-fashioned family home year in, year out.

Natalia walked into the kitchen, depositing her purse on the table with a heavy thump – a thump which Kassie knew was aimed at her. Normally Kassie would have headed straight to her room, but she lingered in the doorway watching her mother. She knew she was in trouble, but the truth was that she was still upset by the afternoon's events, and was hoping for some small sign of a thaw, some crumb of comfort.

Natalia opened the refrigerator, removing from it a small china plate with half a sausage and a fresh tomato on it. Without looking at her daughter, she moved into the living room, switching on the TV as she settled into the easy chair. Kassie turned to look at her, realizing how small her mother seemed in the large room that framed the ancient television set and the numerous photos of Pope John Paul II. They had played this scene out many times before, her mother pretending to watch television, while actually taking nothing in. The food sat unmolested on her lap and the TV anchorman talked pointlessly to himself, as Natalia fiddled with the rosary beads she'd inherited from her grandmother. It was a ridiculous tableau but it made its point forcefully. Kassie would not be fed tonight, nor would she be comforted.

There was no forgiveness here.

7

The traffic was light, 'November Rain' was playing on WKSC, and already thoughts of a challenging day were receding from Adam's mind. Though his journey from south Chicago to leafy, middle-class Lincoln Park was often accompanied by a pang of guilt, it always relaxed him, the view of Lake Michigan never failing to raise his spirits. It looked particularly beguiling tonight, the sun reflecting off the water, as the numerous birds who nested here each spring circled lazily above. But his drive along Lake Shore Drive meant more to Adam than just pretty scenery. It meant he was going home.

Home was a beautiful three-storey row house. They had bought it last year – at considerable expense – and they'd never regretted it. Their new home had four lovely bedrooms, space for them both to work if necessary and, best of all, lots of outdoor space. Adam already had visions of his first-born toddling around the backyard, taking his or her first steps – it had been worth mortgaging themselves to the limit. This was what you did after all – studied hard, worked hard, so you could buy a nice house and play at being grown-ups.

The song had now changed to a forgettable Bryan Adams track, so, flicking the radio off, Adam turned on to North Lincoln Avenue and moments later pulled up outside the familiar greystone building. In his fantasies, he'd sometimes imagine Faith standing in the doorway to welcome him home with a cocktail, but in practice this never happened. Faith was busy and, besides, that was far too suburban an image for her. Adam had always known this – in fact it was one of the reasons he married her.

Closing the front door behind him, he deposited his bag on the floor and poked his head into the kitchen. It was empty, but Adam was amused to see the newspaper lying open on the counter at the horoscope page – his wife's guilty pleasure. Leaving the kitchen, he hurried past the living room, past the guest bedroom, towards the studio that looked out on to the backyard. This was Faith's kingdom and he entered reverently, teasing open the door and tiptoeing inside. To his surprise, his heavily pregnant wife was sitting on her stool, her back to her painting, staring directly at him.

'As subtle as a brick, as quiet as an elephant . . .'

Faith looked at him admonishingly, but there was a smile behind her eyes. She was British and Adam loved the way she expressed herself. Despite the fact that they had been together over ten years now, she still came out with phrases or words that surprised him.

'Still, it's nice to have you back,' she continued, turning back to her painting. 'I'd almost given up on you.'

It was done for effect and Adam didn't break stride, walking up to her and sliding his arms around her bump, pulling her in close.

'Long day,' he muttered, kissing her neck.

'Is it ever anything else?'

'Whenever there's need . . .'

'My hero. Talking of which, I'm lazing for two right now, so I haven't had a chance to fix dinner.'

'I'm on it.'

'You *are* my hero,' Faith replied, as Adam kissed her neck once more.

She resumed painting and, disengaging, Adam stared at

her for a moment. He had been dazzled by her when they first met – in the waiting room of his swanky new office – but he was utterly conquered by her now. Her warmth, her wisdom, her talent, her grace. He loved to watch her paint, applying brushstrokes with practised ease, utterly focused on the task in hand, lost in the moment. It made him feel that all was well in the world. It made him feel love.

Retreating to the door, he paused to take one last look at her. It was times like these that made him feel like he was the luckiest man alive.

8

Jacob came to with a start, suddenly aware of how cold he was. His head was pounding, his neck ached, but it was his shivering limbs that demanded his attention. He could feel goose bumps on his exposed forearms and moved to rub them away . . . only to discover that his arms were secured behind him. He tried to stand, but his bare legs were similarly bound. To his horror, he realized that he was tied to a metal chair, naked, vulnerable and alone.

Now it started to come back to him. The cellar. The masked face. That awful feeling of suffocation. A terrified whimper escaped from his lips and, realizing there was nothing over his mouth, he cried out:

'Hello?'

He was met by silence. He scanned the dingy room, but it appeared to be empty.

'Please . . . can anybody hear me?'

The sound rebounded off the walls, but there was no response. Wiggling his frozen toes in a feeble attempt to keep warm, Jacob now noticed something else. There was something beneath his feet. It was cold and smooth, and crinkled noisily when he moved. Confused, he looked down. And now his blood froze. The chair he was tied to was positioned in the middle of a large plastic sheet.

Panicking, he started to buck furiously, trying to move the chair forward. Terror drove him on and he strained and hopped violently. The chair moved forward an inch, then another – then suddenly his head snapped sideways. For a moment, he was dizzy and disoriented, unable to comprehend what had happened, but as he righted himself, he realized that someone had struck him hard on his right cheek.

'Sit still.'

The voice was calm, sending fear arrowing through him. It was coming from behind him and Jacob strained to get a glimpse of his attacker. But with his arms and shoulders firmly secured, he couldn't turn far enough around.

'Please,' Jacob gasped. 'I'll give you whatever you want –'

'I have everything I need,' the voice hissed quietly.

The man came to a halt behind him. Immediately Jacob stifled his moaning – something cold and smooth had come to rest on the side of his neck. Slowly it inched upwards, then stopped, turning on to its side. A second later, Jacob felt a short, sharp sting, then a warm feeling, as blood started to trickle down his neck.

'Please don't do this,' he begged, tears pricking his eyes. 'I'm going to be married . . .'

A firm hand gripped his shoulder. Jacob bucked again, desperately trying to move his chair, but he could make no progress. And now he felt that awful sensation once more . . . cold steel caressing his skin.

9

Kassie crept down the hallway, casting a nervous glance behind her.

She had endured her mother's stony silence for a couple of hours, but eventually exhaustion had come to her aid. Natalia worked three jobs to pay the bills and often fell asleep in front of the TV. On a couple of occasions, Kassie thought she'd gone – her mother's eyelids flickering, then drooping to a close – only for Natalia to rouse herself, casting around the room suspiciously, as if expecting foul play. Eventually, however, she'd given up the fight, the low sound of her snoring filling the spartan room.

Easing herself out of her armchair, Kassie had hurried towards the back of the house. A short walk down the gloomy hallway, avoiding the floorboards that creaked, then she was in the back room, a small utility area containing a sink, a washing machine and numerous boxes of cheap detergent. Hurrying over to the sink, Kassie yanked open the cupboard doors beneath it. Crouching down, she delved inside, pushing aside bottles of bleach and industrial cleaner, to reveal an ancient tin of silver polish. Turning the lid, she removed it, before retrieving a small package from inside. Sliding the package into her pocket, she sealed the tin once more, carefully returning all the bottles to their original positions. Then, checking that nothing was out of place, she closed the cupboard doors and moved away.

Darting a look at the ancient clock – it was already past

eleven – Kassie unlocked the back door. Cold air rushed in to greet her and she pulled her hood up, concealing her features from the night. In the distance, a dog barked and Kassie turned to check if her mother had been disturbed. But there was no sign of movement and Kassie could still make out her gentle snores.

Relieved, Kassie hurried outside, disappearing into the darkness.

10

Detective Gabrielle Grey marched up to the giant, red-tiled building and pushed inside. It was early morning, but already the Chicago Police Department's headquarters on South Michigan Avenue was busy – police officers, analysts, media liaison and support staff criss-crossing Gabrielle's path as she strode towards the security barriers. Some she recognized, some she didn't, but there was one face that was almost as familiar as her own – Norm, the duty officer who had manned the front desk for as long as she could remember. The CPD had moved into its new offices in Bronzeville in 2000 and since that time Gabrielle had never once seen Norm on his feet, a characteristic which formed the basis of many station jokes. Justice never sleeps, her team were fond of saying of Norm, it sits.

'Morning, Norm. What's up?'

'Nothing much. Hoskins is chairing a crisis meeting in the Command Center –'

'Another one?'

'Same old, same old. Other than that, the sun is shining, the sky is blue and the Cubs are the greatest –'

'– team in the world,' Gabrielle concluded, to Norm's evident pleasure.

Buzzing herself through, Gabrielle took the elevator to the eighth floor. From there it was a short walk to the Bureau of Detectives, the most prestigious department in the building and her personal fiefdom for the last three years.

'Morning, boss.'

A number of junior officers greeted her as she strode towards her corner office. She returned their greetings, retrieving her bagel from her bag as she did so. She was ravenous, having skipped breakfast to get the boys to school on time, and was keen to sink her teeth into her BLT, but the sight of three new photographs on the incident board made her pause. Her deputy, Detective Jane Miller, was already out on a job, so Detective Suarez now hurried over to her. Suarez had worked with Gabrielle for over five years and was a dependable, effective detective.

'What've we got?' Gabrielle asked, casting an eye over the faces.

'One fatality in South Shore,' Suarez replied, indicating the Caucasian male in the first photo. 'Gang murder. Three gunshot wounds to the head and neck while sitting in his car. Shooter took off on a motorbike.'

Nodding grimly, Gabrielle gestured to the others.

'And the others?'

'Double fatality in South Lawndale. Two shooters, we think, with semi-automatic weapons. Took place in a popular late-night burger joint, but, guess what, nobody saw a thing.'

'Get extra officers down there anyway,' Gabrielle replied. 'See if we can find somebody with a conscience –'

'Someone with *cojones*,' Suarez corrected her.

'And speak to local religious leaders and social workers,' Gabrielle continued. 'They're bound to know *something* . . .'

Suarez headed off to do her bidding, pulling in a couple of fellow detectives to join him. Gabrielle watched them go, casting her eye around the denuded office. Gabrielle had a large team – the largest in the CPD – but even so they were constantly short-staffed, given the sheer volume of gun-related homicides they had to deal with. The Mayor had promised to crack down on the gangs — providing extra state cash for police officers, as well as social and youth initiatives — but there was little sign of progress so far.

Gabrielle stared up at the photos. Three men gunned down in cold blood — for what? Belonging to a rival gang? Straying into the wrong territory? Disrespecting someone on Twitter? People had been killed for less. It was Gabrielle's duty and that of her team to bring their killers to justice, but she knew the odds were stacked against them. Communities too scared to talk. Drugs lords willing to do anything to survive. Police officers and detectives ground down by the constant bloodshed. Nevertheless, they would do — *she* would do everything in her power to see that justice was done for the families, fired only by her sense of duty, her resolve and a cold BLT. As Gabrielle continued to gaze at the photos, she was reminded of something Superintendent Bernard Hoskins had said to her on her first day in the job.

Nobody becomes a detective in Chicago for an easy life.

Adam awoke to the smell of pancakes. Faith was a good cook, when she could be bothered, but mornings were never her best time, and the aroma of crisping batter meant only one thing. Christine.

Unlike many men, Adam was quite fond of his mother-in-law. She was warm-hearted, thoughtful and foolishly generous. However, her habit of letting herself into their house was a little unnerving, however pleasant the end results might be. As Faith's due date drew nearer, Christine's unexpected appearances had increased in frequency and now not a day went by when Adam didn't encounter his mother-in-law – usually when he was half dressed or dog-tired. If she had a fault it was that she was *too* attentive, but even this could be forgiven. She lived alone – her worthless husband now a distant memory – and the birth of her first grandchild was always going to be a big deal.

Rolling over, Adam was surprised to find the bed empty. Faith often hid from her mother, feigning sleep, until she was ready to be quizzed about her plans for the birth. Grabbing his dressing gown, he stumbled into the kitchen and was surprised to find his wife dressed and ready to go, finishing off a healthy breakfast under the watchful eye of her approving mother.

'Have I forgotten something?' Adam murmured, as he poured himself some coffee. 'The baby's not due today, is he?'

'*She*'s not due for another couple of days,' Faith countered. 'But Mum's going to help me finish painting the nursery.'

'The clock's ticking,' her mother chimed in, scarcely able to contain her excitement.

'Unless *you*'d like to help out?' Faith continued.

'Love to, but I've got a full diary . . .'

It was true. One of the great things about America was that there were always people in need of a shrink. With a final, jovial insult about his lack of practical skills, Faith departed with her mother, leaving Adam to consult his diary, as he wolfed down his pancakes. It was a full roster with some fairly challenging cases. Yet, in all honesty, Adam's mind was elsewhere. He had spent a disturbed night, his mind endlessly replaying his interview at the Juvenile Detention Center. You work in one field long enough and any job becomes routine. He was as familiar a visitor to the Juvenile Center as he was to Cook County Jail, but Kassie had surprised him. He couldn't shake the image of that look on her face when she saw him – was it shock? Horror? Fear? – nor what she'd said to him afterwards. He'd expected the teenager to make excuses for attacking her victim – perhaps even blame him for attacking *her*, as so many of them did. But she'd said she was trying to warn him and, even though she'd subsequently refused to elaborate, she'd said it with such conviction that Adam couldn't help but be intrigued. What had she meant? Why did she feel he was in danger? More importantly, was that danger real?

Adam was worried about her. Was she hallucinating? Gripped by some form of 'magical thinking', in which her fantasies somehow became manifest? Or did she know something about this guy, about some unseen threat to his well-being? These were the questions that continued to spin around Adam's head, even though he knew they were pointless, idle thoughts.

In all probability, he would never see the intriguing Kassandra Wojcek again.

Kassie marched along the road, ignoring the curious looks of the stroller moms. She was tall for her age, but still looked too young to be out of school this early in the day. Lowering her face to the floor, she pressed on. The curiosity and censure of middle-class moms she could handle – running into a police officer would be a different matter entirely. Besides, she only had a brief window before the school secretary called her mother, so she had to work fast.

West Town was busy as usual, the sidewalk clogged with affluent shoppers and smartly dressed toddlers and their carers. Kassie had to keep her wits about her as she wound her way through this well-heeled human traffic, but her progress was swift and soon she was standing outside Jacob Jones's modest home.

The suburban villa in front of Kassie was lifeless – the curtains drawn, lights extinguished, the front door shut and locked. This popular, upmarket street was the kind of place where you were likely to encounter security-conscious curtain-twitchers, so Kassie didn't linger, heading down the passageway at the side of the house. She tried the French windows at the back, then the side entrance to the utility room, but both were secured.

On further investigation, however, she found a side window that would suit her purpose. It had only a single, flimsy latch – no bolt lock – so Kassie didn't hesitate, ramming her elbow through the glass. She had done this before and knew that a short, sharp blow lessened the chance of injury. Removing her arm and dusting off the glass, she was pleased to see a large hole in the window. Sliding on a pair of woollen gloves – inappropriate given the warm, spring weather – she slipped her hand through the hole and gently lifted the latch, before opening the window and clambering inside.

Moments later, she was standing alone in the hallway. Her heart was beating nineteen to the dozen and once again she questioned the wisdom of coming here. She had nearly turned back a number of times, given the trouble she risked landing herself in, yet here she was.

She passed through the ground floor rooms quickly – she didn't expect to find anything here – then moved upstairs. She had entered the house as quietly as possible, hadn't wanted to announced her presence, but still she half expected Jones's fiancée to come hurrying down the stairs, demanding to know what she was doing there. But the house was as quiet as the grave, the lonely creak, creak, creak of the floorboards Kassie's only companion as she crept along the upper landing.

Teasing open the door to the master bedroom, she peered inside. It appeared to be empty, so she walked briskly through it, running her hand over the satin coverlet on the king-size bed, before passing into the walk-in closet. This too was uninhabited, so she passed on to the guest bedroom. This was undisturbed, as was the study, and as Kassie descended the stairs to the hallway, she began to worry. Had she risked a whole heap of trouble for nothing?

She stood stock still, perplexed and angry, pondering her next move, when her eyes alighted on another door. A door which was slightly ajar. Crossing the hallway, she tentatively took hold of the handle and inched the door open. Immediately a draft of cold air hit her, as she took in the dusty flight of stairs leading down.

Kassie arrowed a look back down the hallway, as if fearing ambush, but all was still, so she returned her attention to the staircase. Feeling on the side of the wall, she located a hook, which had presumably once had a flashlight or similar hanging from it, but there was nothing there now, so pulling out her iPhone Kassie hit the flashlight app and stepped inside.

The first thing that hit her was the smell. Musty, rotting, unpleasant. Putting her sleeve over her mouth and nose, she took in her surroundings, her eyes becoming accustomed to the gloom. The dust on the stairs had been disturbed recently, but it was hard to tell when. Should she tread on the faint footprints to conceal her presence here, or should she leave them be? Opting for the latter, she started to descend, keeping her feet as close to the edge of the stairs as possible, to minimize her trail.

One step, then another, then another. Kassie's heart was in her mouth and she had to will her legs forward. Her flashlight was powerful, but its range limited. She could only pick out parts of the cellar and was unnerved by the eerie shadows that the flashlight's beam threw on to the walls. On she went, convinced that at any moment she would discover a scene of butchery, hoping her nerve would hold when she did.

She had reached the final step and carefully stepped down on to the cellar floor. Her chest felt so tight now that she almost couldn't breathe. She knew exactly what she would find here and part of her wanted to turn and run. But Kassie was no coward. She had come this far, so now with a sudden movement she swung her flashlight beam across the cellar floor. She gasped, put her hand to her chest . . . but there was nothing there. The room was deserted, devoid of human presence, a quiet repository for high-school yearbooks and aged sports gear.

Crunch.

As she stepped forward to investigate further, her foot crushed something. Bending down, she was surprised to see small shards of glass littering the floor, sparkling like diamonds as her light swept over them. Confused, Kassie widened the range of her beam and now she spotted a flashlight lying partly concealed under the lip of a cardboard box. Using the toe of her sneaker, she rolled it out of its hiding place. As she'd suspected, the glass face was broken, the bulb too.

Her heart skipped a beat. Obviously, there were innocent explanations for the presence of the broken flashlight – Jacob had dropped it perhaps and been unable to find it in the darkness – but Kassie instantly dismissed them. Suddenly, for reasons she couldn't fully explain, Kassie knew that this was where it had happened.

This was where Jacob Jones's fate was sealed.

13

Patrolman Dwayne Reid let out a rich belch, as he watched the cars roar by. His partner – a tight-assed vegetarian called Lesley – sighed heavily but he ignored her, letting the flavours of his snack roll around his mouth. Every morning he visited Taco Bell for a sausage and cheese biscuit. This was partly to satisfy his growling stomach and partly to annoy his partner. Even if he hadn't loved the greasy, spiced sausage and thick, rubbery cheese, he'd still have bought one just to get a reaction. With any luck, her patience would soon snap and she would apply for a change of partner.

Nothing would please him more. Patrol work was boring – hour after hour cruising the traffic hotspots, looking for incidents – and a good wingman was essential. Patrolman Michael Garvey had been just that – funny, noisy, politically *incorrect* – but they'd been separated after some unfounded reports of them abandoning their posts during work hours. Which is why he now found himself in the company of Miss Goody Two Shoes.

'Doing anything interesting tonight, Lesley? Got a date?'

'Don't be a jerk, Dwayne. You know I'm married.'

'Don't knock it till you've tried it. How else you s'posed to keep things fresh in the bedroom?'

Lesley shook her head wearily, but said nothing.

'Tell me,' Dwayne continued. 'Have you always liked guys? Or did you ever go with a girl?'

'For God's sake.' She turned to him, visibly annoyed now.

'Do you really think I'm going to share my sexual history with you?'

Dwayne was about to respond, encouragingly and in the affirmative, when something caught his eye. A black Lincoln Continental had just sped across the junction in front of them, running a red light and narrowly missing a truck.

'Wagons roll,' Dwayne shouted cheerily, firing up the sirens and pulling away from the kerb.

The chatter ceased now, as both officers focused on the car in front of them. Most pursuits ended quickly, the horrified middle-class motorists or terrified teens pulling over as soon as they saw the blue flashing lights. But the Lincoln showed no signs of stopping – in fact it was speeding up, running another red light as it raced away from them.

'Officers in pursuit of a black Lincoln Continental, heading south on the Dan Ryan Expressway. Registration plate H23 3308. Request backup and intercept.'

Lesley's voice was clear and crisp – even Dwayne had to admit she was good in a situation like this.

'See if they can scramble the chopper,' he tossed in. 'These guys aren't playing around.'

Lesley radioed in her request, which was answered in the affirmative. There had been too many hit-and-runs recently, too many fatal pursuits, not to deploy all available resources.

Dwayne kept pace with the vehicle, silently praying they would pull off at the next exit. If they kept heading straight it might be a long pursuit, given the impossibility of shutting down the expressway at this time of day. Surely it would seem sensible to them to try and throw off their pursuers by changing direction? But, no, it looked like they were continuing straight ahead.

'No-good, knuckle-headed gangbangers –'

Suddenly the Lincoln lurched across a couple of lanes, careering off the road and away down the exit ramp.

'That's my boy!' Dwayne roared, yanking the wheel round to follow in the Lincoln's path.

He knew the fight was over now and, sure enough, as they neared the bottom of the ramp, he saw that the Lincoln had come to an abrupt halt, its path blocked by two supporting patrol cars. Already the driver's door was springing open and Dwayne didn't hesitate, stepping on the gas before skidding to a halt just in front of the fleeing suspect.

'Hands where I can see them.'

Lesley was already out of the car, training her firearm on the suspect, who slid to a juddering halt. Dwayne followed suit, bursting from the car and training his weapon on the driver's companion, who was also considering a bid for freedom. Both were young, Puerto Rican and highly agitated.

'Easy now, Diego. Don't be another statistic . . .'

Seeing that it was hopeless, the suspects now relented and moments later their faces slammed the hood, as handcuffs were applied.

'Good choice, boys. Now let's see what you've got.' Dwayne crowed as he began to pat them down. 'Fifty bucks, some cigarettes . . . and one firearm.'

'It's not loaded, man.'

'Not sure the judge will care about that,' Dwayne replied, dropping the battered Smith and Wesson into Lesley's evidence bag. 'Anything else I should know about?'

The suspects both shook their heads and, after Dwayne had ascertained that they were telling the truth, he moved on to the interior of the car. Pulling open the glove compartment, he surveyed its contents.

'One packet of Lifesavers, one map of Illinois and . . .'

He pulled a book from the compartment.

'. . . *Fodor's Guide to Romantic Hotels in Montana.* Guys, are you *sure* this is your car?'

'We're borrowing it,' the driver muttered darkly.

'Sure you are,' Dwayne chuckled, casting an eye over the footwell, before turning his attention to the rear of the car.

And now he paused. The trunk remained closed, but there was a dark-brown stain on the handle that grabbed his attention. Lesley was looking at him, intrigued by his serious expression, so he didn't delay.

'Right then, boys, let's see what you got in here . . .'

Releasing the catch, he yanked the trunk open.

For a moment, time seemed to stand still. He didn't move, nor did he react at first, stunned by the sight in front of him.

'What is it, Dwayne?'

Concerned by the expression on his face, by his sudden silence, Lesley took a step in his direction, hoping to see what was bothering him. But before she could do so, Dwayne Reid turned abruptly away from the car and regurgitated his breakfast on to the cold tarmac.

14

The smell of decay was overpowering. Kassie tried to shut it out, to find a breath of fresh air from somewhere, but it was impossible. The atmosphere in the Lake View Care Home was stifling – overheated, stale, rich with the scent of urine. The many eyes that clung to her belonged to the helpless and the hopeless.

Attempting to block out their scrutiny, Kassie kept up a constant chatter. She had hurried here straight from the Jones residence, too unnerved by her experiences to return to school. Now she needed to be with someone who loved her.

'I'm trying harder at school,' she said quietly. 'You know, to get better grades. And my English teacher – Miss Wilson – says I have potential . . .'

She looked up at her grandmother, hoping for some kind of reaction, hoping to see that familiar twinkle of affection in her eyes, but the old woman didn't respond. Wieslawa had been in the home for nearly ten years now, written off as senile and delusional, and had little in the way of stimulation or visitors to engage her enfeebled brain. Kassie tried to come once a week, in part to make up for her mother's refusal to visit, and occasionally she thought she *could* see the old woman responding. Then Kassie was transported back to happier days when Wieslawa, who had always been a woman of a certain frame, used to envelope the young Kassie in her generous embrace, whispering little confidences to her and plying her with chocolate mice and candy. Today, however, Kassie was getting nothing back.

'But it's hard, you know . . .' Kassie continued, falteringly. 'I can't concentrate . . . there's so much going on around me . . .'

She looked into her grandmother's deep-blue eyes.

'I try to block it out, but I can't. The things I see keep . . . keep spinning round and round in my head . . .'

The old woman's face crinkled a little, as if she were taking in Kassie's words and formulating a response. Encouraged, Kassie continued:

'What am I supposed to do, *babcia*? Tell me, please. Should I ignore it? Or face it? I don't know what to do for the best.'

Now the old woman's mouth crept open. She ran her tongue over her lips slowly, moistening the cracks that pitted them. Kassie looked at her intently, hoping for some kind of guidance, but to her surprise her grandmother now started to sing.

'*Kosi kosi łapci, pojedziem do babci. Babcia da nam mleczka, a dziadzius pierniczka . . .*'

Tears filled Kassie's eyes. She had heard the nursery rhyme many times as a child – her grandmother would sing it to her whenever she was allowed to visit – and previously it had comforted her. Now it underlined how far her beloved, witless grandmother had retreated from the world. This saddened and scared Kassie in equal measure, and after twenty minutes more of faltering, one-way chatter she rose and kissed Wieslawa goodbye. Her grandmother barely noticed, singing quietly to herself all the while.

Picking her way past the lonely, upturned faces, Kassie slipped out of the French windows into the gardens. The care home was situated on the edge of Lake Michigan, commanding fantastic views of the water and beyond it the metropolis of Chicago. In summer, it was almost pleasant to be here, taking the sunshine while revelling in the view, but today the lake looked grey and lifeless, save for the visiting birds who circled above.

The wind was picking up and suddenly Kassie felt cold and desolate. Pulling a half-smoked joint from her jacket pocket, she lit it and inhaled deeply, the powerful, aromatic skunk filling her mouth and nostrils. Her life had never been easy, never straightforward, but today she felt as if she were in a deep fog. She needed help, needed guidance, and had come here hoping that her *babcia*, the only person who had ever really understood her, would provide them. But her grandmother was lost to her now, driven mad by a lifetime of trauma.

There were no answers here.

15

Gabrielle Grey pushed her way through the gathering crowds and ducked under the police incident tape. Flashing her ID at the nearest uniformed officer, she marched towards the black Lincoln, which was partially shielded by the CSI team. Detective Jane Miller hurried over, falling into step with her.

Her deputy was a fast-tracker, still youthful and occasionally over-enthusiastic, but intelligent and industrious. She had turned down offers from other departments to work under Gabrielle and the latter was glad to have her – no one worked harder than Miller when a big investigation was in play. Slim, with neat, cropped brown hair, she would be a good catch, Gabrielle thought, for some lucky guy – or girl – but she appeared to be married to her job. She brought Gabrielle quickly up to speed now, in her usual efficient manner.

'White male, thirties, possibly forties, discovered by officers in the trunk nearly an hour ago. Two men of Puerto Rican origin are in custody – Edmundo Ortiz and Pancho Martin. We think they run with a crew from Humboldt Park, but we're checking that out.'

'They say anything?'

'Not a word.'

'And do we have an ID for the victim?'

'Not yet, though the car is registered to a Jacob Jones, an assistant state's attorney. I already called his office – he was supposed to be early in today for a conference call, but never showed up.'

Gabrielle felt a knot in her stomach. A state's attorney murdered and dumped in a trunk? She hadn't been expecting *this* when she got the call.

'Do we have a photo? Something to give us a preliminary ID? Jones could be the perpetrator, *not* the victim.'

'Well, we do, but . . . I think you'd better take a look.'

Gabrielle now noticed how pale her deputy looked. The latter stepped aside, allowing Gabrielle to proceed. As she walked up to the car, the crowd of CSI operatives parted to allow her a clear run, having completed their initial forensics and photography.

Gabrielle let out an involuntary gasp. Someone lay inside the trunk, enclosed in a plastic sheet, though it was hard to call the victim a 'man'. Rather the victim was what *remained* of a man. All the relevant body parts were still there, though the arms and legs jutted out at such unnatural angles that there was no way they could be in their natural places. All the toes and fingers appeared to be missing, the victim's torso was heavily bruised and most sickeningly of all, the man's throat had been cut back almost to his spine. His head lolled back hideously at a right angle to his body, his lifeless eyes staring at the interior of the trunk. Gabrielle stood in silence for a moment, taking in what was unquestionably the worst thing she'd seen in her twenty years as a detective. This man had not been killed, he had been *destroyed*.

Turning, she glimpsed the ashen faces of the CSI team and beyond them the growing crowd of bystanders, gathering at the police barriers, camera phones at the ready. Sickened, furious, Gabrielle turned back to the car and slammed the trunk shut.

16

Faith gently closed the door and stepped inside her studio. This was her space – quiet, ordered, soothing – and she needed it now. Putting the final touches to the nursery had been fun – no, it had been more than that, it had been significant, moving even, given her long battle to conceive – but several hours of her mother fussing and getting under her feet was more than enough. She needed some time alone, so predictably had retreated to her sanctuary.

She had almost finished her self-portrait – an elegant, modern image in greys and blacks – and was keen to get it done before the baby arrived. It was already promised to the Fourwalls gallery, and as they had been so good to her, she didn't want to let them down. If it wasn't for them, she would never have broken through in Chicago, let alone nationwide.

Many of her girlfriends who'd had kids had often talked about carrying on with their careers after the birth, but in reality few had found the time. She didn't want to be one of those women who made promises they couldn't keep, and, besides, that wasn't how she wanted it to be. She wanted motherhood to be all-consuming, having waited so long to enjoy it. She loved being an artist, it gave her life meaning – had saved her from herself – and she loved the people she met through her work. But she was thirty-seven now, Adam nearly forty-two, and it had taken them three long, distressing years of IVF to get this far, so why wouldn't she want to immerse herself fully in the experience?

Right on cue, baby gave a small kick. Smiling to herself, Faith laid one hand on her bump, even as she raised her other hand to paint. Feeling the life inside her with one hand, she tried to bring the illusion of life to bear with the other, gently guiding the tip of the brush down the contours of her alter ego's face. Painting this portrait had been the most significant artistic experience of her life, because the picture had changed so much during the process. She had set out to paint one thing – woman without child, the last vestige of herself before motherhood – yet somehow the baby had intruded. Not physically, or at least not obviously physically, as the portrait was only head and shoulders. Was it then the fullness of her face, the expression in her eyes, the serenity of her gaze, that gave the game away. Perhaps it was all three, she couldn't say for sure, but the truth was that the painting had changed because *she'd* changed. Ten years ago she had been lost – bent on a path of self-destruction – but first Adam and now the baby had healed her wounds. Had helped her *grow*. How glad she was of their intervention now.

Putting her brush back on the palette, Faith placed her other hand on her tummy, cradling her bump. There was no fighting it – the love she had for her baby, for her new life, was fierce, consumed her totally. It was like nothing she had ever experienced before.

Such was the bond between a mother and her child.

17

'What the hell are you thinking? Do you *want* to get me fired?'

Kassie stared at her mother, angry but also a little ashamed.

'I had to leave work early. That's the *third* time in two weeks. My boss won't stand for it.'

'I know, Mama. And I'm sorry –'

'What happens if I lose my job?' Natalia continued, ignoring her daughter's apology. 'What then? Will *you* put food on the table? Pay the bills? Buy new clothes?'

'What new clothes?'

Natalia's hand shot out, connecting sharply with Kassie's left cheek.

'Don't talk back to me. If it wasn't for me, you'd be out on the streets.'

Kassie raised her hand to her cheek, regretting her sarcasm. She hated her mother when she was like this, but it was true – she had good cause to be angry. Kassie had been too distressed to return to school after her visit to her grandmother and, following a call from the school secretary, Natalia had eventually found her daughter at home, the scent of skunk still fresh on her breath.

'You're lucky you still have a place at school. I had to beg Principal Harrison to give you one last chance, said I would talk to you about your behaviour. But he's a proud man, a *smart* man, he won't be taken advantage of.'

'I know, I'll apologize to him in the morning –'

'And your teacher. And the other students. For all the trouble you've caused.'

'Ok, ok . . .'

'It's a good school. You're lucky to be there, *kochanie* . . . Why can't you just settle down? Study? You're not a stupid girl, you could make something of yourself.'

Her tone had softened now – regret and sadness undercutting her anger – which made Kassie feel even worse.

'I'll try . . .'

Her mother's expression told Kassie what she thought of that.

'I mean, I will . . .'

'Where were you anyway?'

Kassie paused, unsure what to say.

'Well?'

'I went to see Grandma.'

'All morning?' Natalia replied, scarcely containing her scepticism. 'The old woman can't string two words together.'

Kassie wasn't sure what to say. Was it better to lie or tell the truth? Her mother was staring intently at her, scenting – expecting? – deception, so eventually Kassie mumbled:

'No, before that I went to West Town. I wanted to see that man . . .'

'Who?' Natalia demanded.

Kassie took a deep breath, then continued:

'The man I bumped into on North Michigan Avenue.'

Her mother's face drained of colour and she turned away from Kassie, shaking her head.

'Mama . . .'

'Why would you do such a thing?' Natalia demanded, turning to face her daughter once more, disbelief written all over her face.

'You know why.'

Natalia's hand shot out again, catching Kassie by surprise. The young girl stumbled slightly, tears pricking her eyes, but her mother looked unrepentant.

'Enough, Kassie. I've warned you about this.'

'I can't help it.'

'Of course you can.'

Natalia grabbed her by the wrist, dragging her in close.

'You do it because you *want* to.' She was in her daughter's face now, whispering savagely. 'Because you want to hurt me, to torture me.'

'No, no, I don't want this to happen, it just does.'

'You dream it up, just like your grandmother.'

'It's what I am —'

'No, it's what you *choose* to be,' Natalia spat back, her voice loud and harsh. 'And I will not stand it any longer.'

'None of this is my fault, Mama —'

'Oh, it's all your fault, Kassandra. You have always been a deceitful, attention-seeking child, but it stops *now*. I will not be humiliated like this any longer, not after all I've done for you.'

Natalia was glaring at her daughter, her eyes blazing.

'So, get this into your thick head. No more cutting class, no more drugs . . .' She pulled Kassie in close, as she concluded: '. . . and no more lies.'

18

'I din' do nuttin.'

Gabrielle Grey leaned back in her chair and shook her head sadly. Edmundo Ortiz was the same age as her eldest son, but the seventeen-year-old gang member couldn't have taken a more different path in life. High school was already a distant memory; he'd been in and out of foster care for years. The only real 'family' he'd ever had was the hoods he ran with in the Spanish Cobras – a well-resourced, high-profile drugs gang, currently fighting the Latin Kings for power and influence on the West Side.

To Gabrielle, he looked like so many of the angry young men she'd seen tearing up Humboldt Park. The sullen, hooded expression, the tattoos marking gang allegiance, the pants hanging halfway down his ass to denote that he'd done jail time – if he'd ever had a belt it was now the property of the CPD. He was still wearing the black and green T-shirt he'd been picked up in – another marker of his clan loyalty – a small detail which depressed Gabrielle further. During her early years as a communities liaison officer, she'd seen kids in kindergarten colouring pictures of Mickey Mouse in in gang colours – stark evidence of how early the gangs started to warp young minds.

'I think we both know that's not true, Edmundo,' Gabrielle replied. 'We've got you for possession of a firearm, automobile theft, murder . . .'

'Not me, man.'

'That's not what your buddy says. Pancho is being *very* co-operative.'

But Edmundo just shook his head.

'He ain't sayin' nuttin'.'

He was right, of course. Pancho had confessed to jacking the car, but nothing else. To do more than that would be suicide.

'Look, it's your funeral,' Gabrielle continued doggedly. 'But I'd suggest you start talking. You got a little sister, right? What'll happen to her when you're inside?'

'She threatenin' me?'

Edmundo addressed this last question to his attorney, a beleaguered state official who looked thoroughly depressed by the whole affair.

'She knows better than to do that,' the attorney replied dolefully.

'Good, cos she don' wanna be steppin' up to me –'

'And nor should you,' the attorney continued, staring down his client. 'We're just having a friendly conversation.'

'About a murdered state's attorney who was found in the trunk of the car *you* were driving,' Gabrielle cut in.

'I never saw the guy, don' know who he is.'

Unfortunately, Gabrielle did. Dental records had now confirmed that their victim as Jacob Jones, an attorney living in West Town.

'You're going to have to do better than that, Edmundo. Because the CPD, the Mayor, and the wider law enforcement community will not rest until *someone* is charged with this crime. Whoever did this can thank their lucky stars we don't have the death penalty in this state.'

If Gabrielle was hoping this would be a sobering thought for Edmundo, she was disappointed. The teenager continued to pick at his nails, avoiding eye contact.

'Look, we can play this game today, tomorrow, the next day, the day after that,' Gabrielle continued, deliberately dragging her words out. 'But we're going to keep coming back to the same problem. The victim was found in a car *you* were driving. There are no other suspects – it's just you and Pancho – and sooner or later I'm going to have to charge *someone*. And when it comes to trial, who do you think the jury will believe? A decorated Chicago police detective? Or a couple of Cobras And the judge – do you think he's going to be lenient? With the newspapers going crazy, the Mayor talking tough? Whoever did this is going away for the *rest* of his life.'

Gabrielle stared intently at the young suspect, awaiting his response.

'Ok, maybe I took the car. *Maybe . . .*'

''Course,' Gabrielle responded genially, pleased to finally be making some progress. 'It was taken from the southern border of Logan Park, a short stroll from your place in Humboldt Park.'

'I said *maybe . . .*'

'And that's very sweet, but we have your prints on the driver's door, on the dash, the steering wheel. I think auto theft is a gimme here, Edmundo, so let's talk about the rest –'

'Nah, man.'

'Where d'you and Pancho take the car from?'

'Lyndale,' came the muttered response.

'West Lyndale Street?'

Edmundo nodded and Gabrielle scribbled a note on her pad. Pancho had also named West Lyndale Street as the pickup site.

'Did you follow the owner there?'

'Nah.'

'Did you attack him?'

'What you talkin' about?'

'The lock hasn't been forced, the windows are intact. This looks a lot like a car-jacking to me.'

'It wasn't locked.'

'Come on, Edmundo, this is a luxury vehicle. Do you really think the owner –'

'It wasn't locked. We'd tried some others first, skipped the ones that had alarms, but this one was easy.'

'So you just jumped in and drove off?'

'Sure. Sell that kind of car for ten grand.'

'Keys in the ignition, were they?'

'Right.'

'It sounds nice and easy, Edmundo,' Gabrielle replied, leaning back in her seat. 'But I don't like it. Who told you to do it? Who told you to kill him?'

'*Nobody*. How many times you gotta be told? – I don' know the guy.'

'The victim was a federal prosecutor, Edmundo. He's put several of your compadres in prison over the years. It's all here in black and white.'

Edmundo shifted in his chair, darting a nervous look at his attorney.

'So, you can see what I'm thinking,' Gabrielle continued. 'Payback time . . .'

'This is fucked up.'

'Did you think that we would just let this *go*? You don't get to go around wasting state's attorneys.'

'You got it wrong.'

'According to the forensics guys, the car had fresh mud on the tyres. Did you take him somewhere?' Gabrielle persisted, keeping up her assault. 'Somewhere out of the way where you could torture him, kill him?'

'Do I gotta listen to this?'

The question was once more directed at his attorney, but Gabrielle cut in.

'Let me show you why this isn't going to go away, Edmundo. Why this is going to play *badly* for you . . .'

As she spoke, she pulled the crime scene photographs from a slim file.

'Jacob Jones was a handsome, successful guy. He had a nice house, a beautiful fiancée . . . And this is what he looks like now.'

She slid the first photo across the table, but Edmundo turned away.

'Look at it.'

Edmundo angled a glance at his lawyer, who shrugged uninterestedly.

'LOOK AT IT!'

Reluctantly, Edmundo dragged his gaze to the awful image in front of him.

'This is from another angle,' Gabrielle carried on, sliding another horrific photo across the battered plastic surface. She was watching Edmundo closely – he was sweating and shaking his head.

'And *this* is a close-up . . .'

Had she been expecting a confession? A fervent protestation of innocence? She got neither – for as she pushed the final image towards the suspect, Edmundo Ortiz fainted, sliding off his chair and tumbling on to the hard floor.

Half an hour later, Gabrielle pulled up outside the Jones residence.

The quiet suburban street was now a hive of activity. Crime scene officers traipsed in and out of the house carrying evidence bags, while uniformed officers continued their inquiries on the street. Jones's broken fiancée, Nancy, would be arriving from San Francisco soon and Gabrielle fervently hoped that she would be able to shed some light on this strange and brutal crime.

'How'd it go?'

Jane Miller had broken away from the melee.

'Early days,' Gabrielle replied evasively. 'What have you got?'

'Nothing much in the house – no sign of a struggle, no obvious forensics – but it looks like someone cut the power – the external supply cable was cleanly severed at the rear of the property.'

'Interesting.'

'Plus, we have a witness with some potentially valuable information . . .'

Miller gestured to an elderly woman, flanked by a couple of detectives, standing just across the road.

'And?'

'Well, it doesn't exactly fit with the narrative.'

'Meaning?'

'Well, she says that she was watering her plants this morning,' Miller continued quickly, 'when she spotted someone leaving the Jones residence, dropping down from a back window before hurrying away.'

She had Gabrielle's attention now.

'Can she describe this person? Clothes, hair, build . . .'

'Sure, her eyesight's pretty good . . . but you're not going to like it.'

Gabrielle stared at her, alarmed by her tone, as her deputy concluded:

'She says the intruder was a tall, teenage girl with long, red hair.'

19

Adam Brandt looked up, as the door swung open. He'd been waiting in the relatives' room for half an hour, his nerves increasing minute on minute, but finally they were here. Rising from the battered sofa, he hurried over.

'Hi, Kassie. I'm Dr Brandt, we met yesterday.'

The teenager nodded, but didn't look up at him. She appeared cowed by her surroundings, a little scared even.

'And you must be Mrs Wojcek,' he continued, turning his attention to her mother. 'I'm a forensic psychologist assisting the Chicago poli—'

'I know who you are.'

It was hard to tell who her hostility was aimed at. Him? The police? Her daughter? Possibly all three.

'Let's sit down, shall we? I've got coffee, water, cookies . . .'

He ushered them towards the faded green sofa and coffee table which dominated the room. He had taken the call from Detective Grey an hour ago, just as he was saying goodbye to his last client. Grey sounded agitated, explaining that a teenage girl Adam had interviewed yesterday was now the prime suspect in a murder case, having been seen by police officers as she was confronting the victim shortly before his death. She'd asked if Adam could attend CPD headquarters asap, and Adam had agreed to help out, but he'd made it clear that he wanted to meet Kassie and her mother in the relatives' room, which was less austere, less intimidating than the interrogation suite.

'Now, I know you've already had a long chat with Detective

Grey . . .' Refreshments had been declined, and Adam got straight to the point. '. . . So I won't keep you long. But I would like to unpack a couple of things you mentioned to Detective Grey during the course of your questioning.'

Still Kassie didn't look up, but the narrowing of Natalia Wojcek's expression was unmistakable.

'I believe you told the detective that you visited Mr Jones's house this morning.'

Kassie nodded.

'How did you know where he lived?'

'I saw his name and address on the paperwork when I was being booked yesterday. The desk sergeant wanted me to know that this guy worked in law enforcement, that I was in deep shit.'

'And *why* did you go there? Can you tell me that?'

'We've been through this already,' Kassie's mom interjected impatiently.

'I understand your frustration,' Adam replied. 'But it's really important, so, please . . .'

He turned his gaze to Kassie. The teenage girl took a deep breath, then mumbled:

'I wanted to see if he was ok.'

'You thought he might have come to some harm?'

'Yes.'

'What did you think might have happened to him?'

'For God's sake, we've just been through this charade. Why must you make us do it again?'

All pretence at politeness was now gone.

'We *need* to get home,' Mrs Wojcek continued urgently. 'Kassie has homework to do. All this disruption, all these questions, they only make things —'

'I wonder whether it might be better if you waited outside,

Mrs Wojcek?' Adam replied, politely but firmly. 'If that's ok with Kassie, of course?'

He turned to Kassie. Her mother did likewise, just in time to see her daughter give a small nod.

'Kassandra . . .'

'I'm fine,' her daughter whispered back, her voice shaking a little.

A look of shock, then angry resignation passed over the middle-aged woman's face, then she rose stiffly and walked to the door. Adam waited until she'd departed before turning to Kassie once more.

'In your own words, Kassie, tell me what you were concerned about.'

Another long pause. Still the teenager refused to look at him – Adam was reminded of her reaction to him on their first meeting.

'Kassie?' he prompted gently.

'I was worried,' she replied, haltingly, '. . . that he'd been attacked. Killed . . .'

'I see. And why did you think that?'

Again, the teenager paused.

'You told me before that you didn't know Jacob,' Adam offered. 'So, had someone said something to you? Had you heard about some threat to him?'

'I saw it.'

'Saw what?'

'His death.'

Now it was Adam's turn to hesitate, Kassie's answer taking him completely by surprise. Was this the start of a confession? Was this slight teenager somehow *involved* in this man's murder? Adam's heart was beating fast now, but he kept his voice as calm as he could, as he replied:

'When was this?'

'When I bumped into him on North Michigan Avenue,' she replied, as if this was obvious.

'I'm sorry, I don't understand. He was fine when you left him there, so how could you have –'

'I can see death . . . before it happens.'

Adam remained silent, wondering if he'd misheard. But Kassie showed no inclination to elaborate.

'I'm sorry, you say that you can . . . ?'

'I look at someone,' Kassie continued quickly, 'and I see how their life will end. *When* it will end . . .'

Adam stared at her for a moment, before he eventually replied:

'And this happened with Jacob Jones?'

Kassie nodded, staring at the floor as she continued:

'I looked into his eyes and I saw it.'

'Describe it to me,' Adam responded calmly.

'It was a rush of images, of feelings. A terrible coldness at first, then the most awful pain . . .'

Her hand drifted up to her throat, but she seemed not to notice.

'And then this . . . this horrible, suffocating fear – like he knew he was about to die – and then . . . nothing.'

Kassie shuddered, wrapping her arms around herself. It was almost as if *she* had been the one suffering, such was the effect of her testimony on her.

'And that's why you went after him?'

'*Yes.*'

She gasped the word gratefully through her distress, as if relieved that finally somebody *understood*.

'That's why I followed him. I needed to warn him . . .' She gulped, drawing breath, before concluding: '. . . that he only had hours left to live.'

20

'So, is she nuts? Or is she playing us?'

Adam Brandt was alone with Gabrielle Grey in her office. The door was firmly shut, cocooning the pair of them inside.

'Is she a genuine suspect?' Adam replied, turning the question back on Grey.

'No, we haven't got enough to hold her. Yes, she's a person of interest.'

'What about the others? The two guys who were driving the –'

'We've been over the trunk three times, same with the plastic sheeting, can't find their prints on either. Plus, it looks like their alibi's going to check out. A security guard coming home from work saw Jacob Jones's car drive away from his house at around nine p.m. Edmundo and his sidekick were still at a pizza joint in Humboldt Park at midnight. We're pretty sure Jones was abducted from his house – his phone, his wallet, his ID were there – so unless they've learned to time-travel, we're going to have a hard time making the charges stick. So how about you answer my question, doc?'

It was said with humour, but Adam could feel the tension underneath.

'Kassie is clearly troubled.'

'No shit.'

'She's vulnerable, isolated, lonely. It may be that she's a confused child trying to get some attention.'

'But . . .' Gabrielle replied, sensing there was more coming.

'But it may be more complicated than that. She's a drug user – her records suggest that she's been smoking skunk since the age of eleven. Prolonged exposure to the harder forms of skunk can make you paranoid, delusional even. If you factor in clear evidence of a history of mental illness in the family –'

'So, she *is* crazy?'

'I said she's *troubled*. But she is also lucid and precise. She doesn't seem to be in the middle of a mental health crisis – she's aware of where she is, why she's being questioned, understands why you're suspicious of her. That level of comprehension is unusual in someone who's experiencing psychosis.'

'Could she be faking it?'

'It's possible, but, if so, it's an impressive performance.'

'Did you detect any animosity towards Jones? Any reason why she might have wanted to harm him?'

'Quite the opposite, she says she wanted to protect him.'

'And you buy that?'

'I don't know yet.'

'She confronts the guy the day he goes missing. A day later, after his body's been dumped, she's seen leaving his house. She knows *something* . . .'

'She says she went there to find out if her fears were justified.'

'Come off it.'

'Why would she need to break into the house? If she'd abducted him the night before?'

'Maybe she went back to clean up the scene, make things right.'

'Meaning what? That Jones willingly let her in the night before? Did they *know* each other?'

'We're still chasing down potential connections, but never say never . . .'

63

Adam let this slide. It was unconvincing, but in truth neither of them really knew what they were dealing with.

'You said the victim was driven somewhere,' he eventually continued. 'Then mutilated, killed . . .'

'Right. There was black mud on the car's tyres.'

'Do you really think Kassie's capable of all that?'

'So maybe she's got an accomplice? Maybe it's . . . what do you shrinks call it? . . . a *folie à deux*?'

'And you've got evidence to support that?'

'Do I detect sympathy for our suspect?' Grey replied, a little riled now.

'I'm concerned about her.'

'You going to see her again?'

'I've offered to help her and she's promised to think about it. I *have* managed to get her to agree to enrol in a teen NA programme, which is something. There are some good ones locally, specifically designed for teenage drug users.'

Grey nodded, but seemed deflated, rather than cheered, by this news.

'Look, we can't hold her, so tell me what we're looking at here? She's obviously an inveterate liar.'

'That's not fair –'

'Look at her record. She's repeatedly lied to the police, she's lied under oath.'

'And maybe she *is* lying. Because she's involved . . . or because she wants to matter for once. Or it might be something more complex.'

Grey was silent now, watching him curiously.

'My feeling is that she believes what she's saying, that it's real to her . . .' Adam was almost talking to himself, as he concluded: 'The question we need to answer is *why*.'

21

Kassie and her mother walked to the car in silence. They had had to park some way from the police station, which only made things worse now. Kassie wanted to be at home, in her room, as soon as possible. Anything to escape her mother's fury and disappointment.

Faces passed by, but Kassie didn't look at them, sidestepping them even as she kept pace with her mother, as if tied to her with an invisible cord. It was the only thing she could think of to do to show that she wasn't being wilfully difficult, that she didn't want to cause her mother embarrassment or pain. But it clearly didn't register – her mother strode along the sidewalk, barely acknowledging her presence.

Eventually they made it to their battered station wagon. Her mother slid the key in the lock and Kassie waited dutifully for her to lean over and unlock the passenger door. There was a moment when she thought her mother might not bother, might drive off, leave her standing in the road. But, no, Kassie thought angrily as her mother leaned over, that would be too easy. Her mother was too much of a martyr to let this opportunity go.

Kassie climbed into the car and settled down for the long, silent journey home. But her mother didn't move, didn't even raise the key to the ignition, and as Kassie now turned to her, she was surprised to see that she was crying.

'Oh, Mama . . . please don't cry . . .'

Guilt-stricken, Kassie reached out a hand, but her mother

batted it away. Kassie sat in her seat, holding her smarting hand, feeling utterly hollow. She wanted to do something to ease her mother's pain. Wanted to say something to let her know that in spite of everything she *did* love her. But as she tried to speak, tried to find the right words, her mother's response was brutal and crushing:

'You're a stain on this family.'

22

The sauce dribbled down his chin, but Adam managed to catch it just before it made contact with his pristine white shirt.

'He really is a pig. I don't know why you married him . . .'

Faith shrugged and rolled her eyes, before winking at her husband. Adam was a sucker for a hot beef sandwich – he always maintained that Chicago's were the finest – and he and Faith visited Al's Shack as often as they could. This time they had been joined by Adam's best friend – and best man – Brock, and his wife, Fernette. Brock was a former college roommate. He was also a model train enthusiast, birdwatcher and IT geek, but Adam liked to joke that he didn't hold that against him. They saw each other once, sometimes twice, a week without fail. Fernette, his long-term girlfriend who'd eventually become his wife, often attended too – her ready wit always enlivening their evenings together.

'Look, I know he's cute,' Fernette continued. 'And smart and *loaded*, but, really, how can you bear to watch someone do that. I mean it's like he's going to swallow it in one mouthful –'

'Never come between a man and his hot beef sandwich,' Faith intoned, just about suppressing a smile.

'Wise words, Faith,' Brock agreed, taking a healthy bite of his own. 'This man's on the case all day, every day. He needs brain food –'

'And lots of it,' Fernette butted in, to general agreement.

Adam played along – happy to be the object of their gentle

jokes. It was good to kick back at the end of what had been a very disorienting day. Kassie's testimony had unnerved him, as had his subsequent interview with Gabrielle. She had always been one of the saner, more reasonable officers, keen to use his services and follow his directions. But today she had seemed ill at ease, suspicious even, as if she feared having the wool pulled over her eyes.

For an hour or two afterwards, Adam had struggled to shrug off his anxiety, but slowly good food, better company and a couple of craft beers had lowered his blood pressure. He loved the resolute, light-hearted optimism of his friends, but most of all he adored spending time with Faith. He had always done so, but even more so now, when all he had to do was look at her and her perfectly rounded bump to make him smile.

'You think I've had enough?' Faith said, gesturing to her bump, then to her half-eaten sandwich. 'You worried I'm getting fat?'

Adam snapped out of it, realizing he'd been caught staring.

'Because if so, you know where you can go . . .'

It was said with a twinkle and, wiping the remnants of sauce from his chin, Adam leaned in close to her, nestling his nose in her thick curls.

'I love you,' he whispered, kissing her gently on the cheek. '*Both* of you . . .'

'For God's sake, get a room,' Fernette complained.

'Yeah, you're making the rest of us look bad,' Brock chimed in.

The conversation continued in this vein until they departed for Navy Pier. Chicago's premier tourist attraction was thronging with revellers and normally Adam would have avoided it like the plague. But Faith had decided she wanted to go on the

Ferris wheel for one last time as a couple. It was goofy and romantic, and, of course, Adam couldn't resist. So they made their way towards the huge wheel, mentally preparing themselves for the steep ticket prices, but loving the idea just the same.

For the first time during what had been a difficult day, Adam felt at peace. Grasping his wife firmly by the hand, he strode along the pier cheerfully, losing himself in the busy Friday night crowds.

23

It was early morning and mercifully the roads were clear. Breakfast had been a long-drawn-out affair – why was it that Eden and Zack were such daydreamers? – but still Gabrielle had been on the road before eight. She drove in silence – the morning bulletins had been full of sensational reports about Jacob Jones's murder and she had no wish to listen to the ill-informed speculation. Instead, she watched the world go by, noting the change in vista as she left her house in Albany Park and journeyed to West Town. Her neighbour-hood was a little way from the city centre and had always been incredibly diverse, with large Korean, Mexican and African American communities. West Town might have been like that once, but not now.

Driving along West Chicago Avenue, Gabrielle took in the affluent moms breakfasting in gym gear and the hipsters drinking coffee outside the vinyl stores, marvelling at how one city could have so many faces. When she first moved to Chicago, nearly ten years ago now, she'd had a fond notion that she might live in a place like this. But one look at the realtors' websites had put paid to that. She only visited these parts of town in her professional capacity nowadays.

Swinging off the main avenue, Gabrielle found herself once more on West Erie Street. The police tape remained in place, sealing off the Jones residence, and flanking it were several press trucks. The local reporters were busy, collaring local residents for expressions of sympathy and tidbits of information about the deceased. Deciding on the direct approach, Gabrielle drove right up to the tape, the uniformed officers raising it for her second-hand Pontiac to crawl underneath on to the drive.

'Detective Grey, do you have anything to add to last night's statement? Have you made any arrests? What's your working theory?'

Gabrielle climbed out of her vehicle to be greeted by a cacophony of familiar voices, but she ignored them, heading into the house swiftly. Closing the door behind her, she took a moment to enjoy the silence – the cries of the hopeful reporters fading outside – then got down to business. She had seen the property yesterday, but it had been so full of activity, of bustle. She wanted a moment to take it in by herself.

It was exactly what you would expect a successful attorney's house to be: tastefully decorated, expensively furnished and immaculately tidy. As Miller had indicated, nothing appeared to be out of place and there was no obvious sign of a struggle. Kassie Wojcek had confessed to breaking the side window, which meant the only other hints of a disturbance were the broken flashlight and disturbed dust patterns on the floor of the basement. Other than that, the house was exactly as it should be. Framed pictures of Jacob and Nancy decorated most of the surfaces and many of the walls – a loving couple with their whole life ahead of them. How cruel those images seemed now.

Flipping open her notebook, Gabrielle consulted her timeline. Jacob Jones had returned home the night before last – taking a call from a CPD officer at around 8 p.m. – and an hour or so later had vanished. Kassandra Wojcek was their only viable suspect – she clearly had some sort of animus against Jones and her alibi was weak, her mother having confessed to falling asleep in front of the television early evening – but was it possible that she had spirited away a grown man, a former college football player?

Lost in thought, Gabrielle wandered through the kitchen to the access door that led into the garage. Jacob Jones's Lincoln had been driven from here the night before last, presumably with the man himself inside. Bound? At gunpoint? And from there he was driven . . . where? The black mud on the tyres suggested proximity to water – one of Chicago's many rivers perhaps? The lake? It was impossible to say. The car, like the man himself, had simply disappeared until Edmundo and Pancho had stumbled upon it.

Frustrated, Gabrielle headed back into the house, but, as she did so, her phone buzzed. Pulling it from her pocket, she saw that it was Detective Montgomery.

'What you got for me, Detective?'

'Just some context, boss, but it's interesting.'

'Go on.'

'I've been going back through Wojcek's court history. Six months ago, she got a suspended sentence for assault and acting under the influence. She blamed her behaviour on medication she was taking, but the prosecutor didn't believe her and neither did the judge. She was given a large fine and only escaped a custodial sentence because of her age. Apparently, the prosecutor tore her testimony to shreds. The state's attorney that day –'

'Was Jacob Jones,' Gabrielle said, completing her deputy's sentence.

'Exactly. I've put the file on your desk.'

'Thank you. Good work, Detective.'

Gabrielle hung up, feeling energized once more. They had been struggling to make sense of this brutal murder – struggling to find a possible motive – but finally they had a concrete connection between Jacob Jones and the mysterious Kassie Wojcek.

24

'Does your mother know you're here?'

Kassie looked up sharply.

'Because, if so, I might need to organize some personal protection. I'm not sure she *likes* me very much.'

Adam was pleased to see that this earned a sheepish smile from Kassie. It was their first proper session together at his office and it was crucial to establish a relationship – a basic trust – before they could begin. Kassie was clearly still on edge and he was keen to put her at her ease.

'I'm not sure she likes me either,' Kassie responded quietly. 'And, no, she doesn't know I'm here. I told her – told school – that I had a doctor's appointment.'

'Which you do,' Adam responded, smiling. 'But we don't need to let your mother know what *type* of doctor, do we? If we're the only two who know about our chats, then that's fine by me.'

Kassie nodded quickly, looking pleased – perhaps surprised – that she had an ally. Adam was beginning to get a sense of just how isolated this young girl was. She had no father, no siblings, no friends to speak of – she had moved around schools, often being asked to leave after cutting class repeatedly or for rebellious, even violent, behaviour. At first, he'd assumed that this was the outcome of undiagnosed mental health problems, but now he was beginning to wonder if Kassie had deliberately sabotaged her attempts to fit in, whether she had *sought* solitude, rather than had it imposed upon her. This intrigued him, as it inevitably threw her back on her mother's company – someone she clearly had a difficult relationship with.

'Now what can I get you to drink? Coke? Sprite? Water?'

'Coke, please.'

Nodding, Adam crossed the hardwood floor to the fridge. Pulling a cold Coke from the fridge, he paused briefly to look out the floor-to-ceiling window towards Lincoln Park. This huge swathe of green space, which contained the city zoo, baseball pitches and much more besides, looked particularly beguiling in the morning sunshine, framed by Lake Shore Drive and beyond that Lake Michigan itself. Affording himself a brief moment of self-congratulation – this office really had been a find – he crossed back to Kassie.

'Here you go,' he said, handing the can to her. 'I'd join you, but it gives me terrible gas.'

Kassie laughed – the first time he had seen her look happy. He suddenly realized how pretty Kassie was – when she didn't appear so damn haunted.

'Seriously, my wife bans me from drinking it with clients for precisely that reason.'

This seemed to amuse Kassie – the idea of a figure of authority embarrassing himself – which made Adam wonder how many austere doctors, police officers and teachers she had faced during her short time on earth. Settling himself into his chair, he turned to face her.

He was pleased by what he saw. When she'd arrived, she'd been monosyllabic and anxious, avoiding eye contact and generally looking like she'd rather be anywhere than here. She had sat scrunched up, her legs tucked in, her arms folded, as if trying to make herself as small, as closed, as possible. Now, however, she appeared to have relaxed a little. She still wouldn't look at him, but she was perched on the edge of her comfy seat, swinging her legs back and forward, looking around the office with undisguised interest. He watched her for a moment, before eventually breaking the silence.

'So, Kassie . . .'

She ceased swinging her legs.

'I asked to see you again because I'd like to talk further about Jacob Jones. As you know, I'm talking to you now in my capacity as a psychologist and anything you say is strictly confidential. I am not acting on behalf of the Chicago Police Department – my only interest is in helping you.'

'Will I have to pay?'

'Only if I put you on my books, which I'm not minded to do yet –'

'I'm not a charity case,' she interrupted, the first signs of attitude surfacing.

'I know that,' he responded calmly. 'And that's not what this is. If I contact your health insurer, then inevitably your mother will have to become involved and I'm not sure either of us need that right now.'

Again, a small smile from Kassie.

'I'd like you tell me more about your experience with Jacob on North Michigan Avenue. What you felt, saw, sensed . . . ?'

He deliberately avoided words like premonition or vision. He knew they wouldn't be helpful – would perhaps reinforce Kassie's own analysis of her experiences – and he wanted to keep things grounded.

'Well, I bumped into him, like I said. He actually hit me quite hard, so I ended up on my ass.'

'Was he apologetic?'

'Sure. He helped me back up, asked me if I was ok, if I needed a cab.'

'And then?'

'Then I looked up at him. Which is when it happened. That's when it *always* happens . . .'

'So this occurs regularly?' Adam queried, intrigued now.

'Every day of my life.'

Adam noted her weariness. With life? With herself? He made a quick note, then continued:

'How exactly does it happen?'

'If I don't look at them, then it's ok. But if I look at them, if I look into their eyes, then I see it.'

'The eyes being the window to the soul?'

'Something like that,' Kassie said sharply, as if fearing she was being made fun of.

'And what did you see this time?'

'The images came in a rush. It was somewhere dark and gloomy. I could smell paraffin . . . or something like that. It was a basement perhaps . . . Or a workshop . . . There were these shadows dancing around me . . .'

She was checking his reaction as she spoke, darting quick looks at him to see if he had reacted with disbelief, even amusement. But Adam's facial expression was deliberately neutral and she lowered her gaze once more, seemingly satisfied that she was safe from ridicule.

'But it wasn't what I could see,' she continued. 'It was what I *felt* . . .'

'What did you feel, Kassie?'

'I felt cold. Really, really cold. My feet were pressing against something smooth and lifeless. I couldn't tell what it was, but I didn't like it at all.'

Adam's mind leaped to the plastic sheet that Jacob Jones had been found in, but he pushed the thought away. He knew better than to jump to conclusions.

77

'And then?'

'I felt someone's presence in front me, then something cold and hard pressing against my skin . . .'

Kassie had her eyes clamped tight shut now – she was talking so fast that Adam struggled to keep pace with his note-taking.

'Then . . . I couldn't breathe. It was like I was drowning . . .'

Adam paused in his note-taking to look at her. Even though Kassie was describing someone else's pain, it was as if it was actually happening to her.

'And I was scared . . . so scared . . . my heart felt like it was going to burst, because I knew this was it . . . that I was dying and then . . .'

Her hand went up to her mouth and her eyes opened suddenly.

'And then I could hear laughter. This horrible, high-pitched laughter . . .'

And now for the first time she looked up, as if finally emerging from the horror.

'Poor guy, he died like that,' she gasped, cradling her face with her hands and staring straight ahead. 'He died with that terrible laughter ringing in his ears.'

25

The remains of Jacob Jones were spread out before her. Aaron Holmes, the burly Chief Pathologist who'd haunted the city morgue for as long as anyone could remember, had arranged the victim's torso and limbs in their anatomically correct positions, but even so the sight of him struck Gabrielle as deeply perverse and horribly wrong. He was more jigsaw than man now.

Swallowing down her disgust, she turned her attention to Holmes once more. The gruff, bearded South Sider fielded three, four, five bodies a day and was not prone to emotion or histrionics, outlining his findings in a steady, dispassionate monotone.

'Small stuff first,' he muttered, pointing to the blotchy torso in front of them. 'Significant bruising to the torso and also the side of the neck, suggestive of strangulation.'

'Ligature or hand?' Gabrielle replied evenly.

'Hard to say, but I'd guess your killer had the victim in some kind of hold. The arm would have looped round the neck and then look here . . .'

He pointed to a series of evenly spaced purple dots on the victim's cheek.

'What do they look like to you?'

Gabrielle moved in closer.

'Judging by their size and spacing, I'd say they were the fingertips of a hand.'

'Exactly. With an arm round the neck, perhaps your killer

grasped the victim's face to get a proper grip. The harder he or she squeezed, the quicker the oxygen supply would be cut off.'

'Why are the fingermarks purple? Is that due to the pressure?'

Holmes shook his head.

'If you look at them closely, you'll see the skin is raised slightly, suggesting an allergic reaction. Your killer was probably wearing gloves – there's no DNA or secretions on the victim – and my guess is that the victim was allergic to whatever they were made of.'

'Leather?'

'Leather, latex, suede . . . I'll have to run more tests to know for sure.'

Gabrielle digested this, then continued:

'Is that what killed him? The strangula—'

But Holmes was already shaking his head. He gestured to the victim's blood-caked mouth.

'You can see for yourself that he had his tongue cut out.'

Gabrielle shuddered as she took in the bloody stump.

'Also, his fingers and toes were severed. From the amount of blood loss, we can tell that these amputations were carried out while the victim was still alive. The general dismemberment – the severing of the arms and legs from the torso – was done *after* death.'

Immediately, Gabrielle's mind was turning. Was the dismemberment designed to aid transportation or for some darker reason? Did this brutal killing have a ritualistic element?

'What actually killed him,' Aaron persevered, 'was *this*.'

He indicated the long, deep cut that had nearly severed the head from the body. Once more, Gabrielle moved in to get a closer look.

'The larynx has been crushed, the windpipe severed, several major arteries compromised. The blood loss would have been catastrophic, the withdrawal of oxygen complete, so death would have occurred in under a minute.'

This was one small mercy perhaps, Gabrielle thought to herself. But how much had he suffered before this coup de grâce was delivered?

'How was it done? Was he struck several times or –'

'No, it was one clean chop wound. Like an execution, but from the front.'

'Is it possible . . .' Gabrielle hesitated a moment before completing her question. '. . . that a teenager could have inflicted an injury like that? A teenage girl in particular?'

'It's not impossible,' Holmes replied calmly. 'But I'd say it's unlikely. This was a blow of considerable force. Take into account the span of the fingermarks on the victim's face and I'd say that it's odds on your attacker is an adult male.'

Gabrielle continued to chew on Holmes' words as she left the morgue clutching his preliminary findings. Wojcek was their only suspect, yet it seemed unlikely that she was responsible for the inhuman brutality meted out to the unfortunate Jacob Jones. She lacked the strength, plus there was no evidence that she could drive, nor that she possessed the experience or guile to carry out such a flawless abduction and murder. She had a possible motive, however, and was clearly involved in some way, which raised an interesting question in Gabrielle's mind.

Was it possible that the troubled teen had an accomplice?

26

'You say you have these experiences daily?'

Adam had deliberately chosen an uncontroversial question to resume their discussion. After her description of Jones's 'death' Kassie had become agitated and they'd been forced to take a break. Another soda on the balcony had helped, but, none the less, when they returned to their session, Kassie's legs were pulled up underneath her and she fiddled constantly with her cuffs, her body language screaming anxiety and retreat. Adam knew he would have to proceed carefully if he wasn't to lose her and had decided to keep his questions general.

'Three or four times a day . . . on school days. At the weekends, I can keep myself to myself.'

Adam already had 'tendency to self-isolate' scribbled on his pad and he underlined it now.

'And is the . . . content similar? Do they *feel* the same?'

Kassie was already shaking her head.

'The more imminent the death is, the more I feel it. The more *painful* the death, the more I feel it.'

'So the intensity of the experience varies?'

'Sure. Some people pass away painlessly in their sleep. I barely feel their deaths, especially if they have a long time left. Others get hit by a car, so it's painful but quick. Others *really* suffer . . .'

Kassie shuddered, before continuing:

'. . . but they all start the same. I get this . . . shortness of breath, a dizziness, then it hits me. Afterwards, I feel an emptiness, a hollowness . . .'

Despite himself, Adam felt a rush of sympathy for her. Whatever psychosis she was in the grip of, this girl clearly felt surrounded by death. It was a horrible place to find yourself.

'And these memories stay with you?'

'Of course. Though I'd be lying if I said the blow didn't help . . .'

'We've talked about that,' Adam replied, keeping his tone friendly.

'I *know* and I've said I'll do the treatment,' Kassie moaned. 'But it's hard. You don't know what it's like . . .'

'You're right, I don't,' Adam conceded. 'But I'm worried the drug use might be amplifying your fears, even distorting your perception of ordinary events and situations.'

Kassie shrugged, but turned away, clearly unhappy with that suggestion.

'Why do *you* think you experience these episodes?' Adam continued, keen to give Kassie a chance to lead the conversation.

'It's difficult to explain.'

'Try.'

Kassie toyed with the packet of cigarettes in her hand, while she considered how to respond.

'I don't know if I really understand it, but . . . it's like . . . it's like we all have a set time on earth and when it's up, it's up. I can just sense when that time will be.'

'And you can predict this accurately?'

'To the day.'

'How?'

'I've learned to gauge the strength of my reaction,' Kassie replied, shrugging. 'How to *read* what I feel. I never know the exact timings – to the hour, the minute – but I always know what your last day on earth will be.'

'Does that mean that the timing of our death is set in stone then? From birth, I mean?'

'Yes, probably . . .'

Adam noticed Kassie now looked unsettled, uncomfortable even, but he knew he had to keep probing.

'That would suggest that we have no free will, then? That we're all moving towards a prescribed end?'

Kassie nodded cautiously.

'It's like we're all connected . . .' she continued, slowly. 'That everything that happens, happens for a reason, pushing each of us towards a fixed point.'

Adam digested this. It couldn't be true, of course, but it was nevertheless an intriguing and unsettling notion.

'And have any of these . . . these premonitions *not* come true? Have they ever been wrong?'

There was a short pause, before Kassie shook her head.

'Have you ever been tempted to intervene before? Like you did with Jacob? You must have experienced hundreds of these episodes during your lifetime?'

'Once,' Kassie conceded, reluctantly. 'I mean there's not much I can do. I see guys who are going to be shot, stabbed, pretty much every day, but –'

'Tell me about that time,' Adam prompted.

Once more a frown gripped Kassie's face.

'There was this kid . . . a toddler who used to play in front of our house. I saw him all the time, playing with his sisters, his mom. I knew . . . I knew he was going to get hit by a car that day, so I tried to grab him, to stop him running out . . .'

She lapsed into silence, but Adam made no attempt to fill it.

'Afterwards, some people said I pushed him. That I *made* it happen. So after that I stopped trying.'

For the first time, Kassie now looked directly at him. Her expression was one of pure vulnerability, as if she were seeking support, even absolution, from him. Adam smiled sympathetically, made a note, then replied:

'Let's take a step back now. Can you remember when you *first* experienced something like this?'

Immediately, he saw her body tighten.

'Look, Kassie, we can take this as slow or as fast as you want. If you don't want to answer any of my questions, you don't have to. It's not my job to make you feel uncomfortable.'

He wasn't as disinterested as this, if he was honest. But they had to proceed on her terms.

'My dad.'

Two words, soft and quiet, which obviously cost her. Adam flicked back through his notes.

'Your father passed away when you were five?'

'Right.'

'And were you with him when you experienced these feelings for the first time?

Kassie suddenly looked very shaky, but managed to respond.

'I was too young to register what I was feeling at first . . . I was only a baby . . . but I knew something was wrong. I wouldn't let him hold me, would never let him look at me . . .'

Andrew nodded and scribbled 'Attachment issues? Abuse?' on his pad.

'And this caused problems? In the family?'

'Of course. He was a good man, a *loving* man. And it drove my mom nuts, I was always clinging to her skirts.'

Adam made another quick note, but his eyes never left Kassie.

'What did you feel? What did you see? When he looked at you . . .'

'Well, I couldn't breathe. That wasn't so strange – I often felt that. But with him . . . it was this horrible, overwhelming pressure. Like there was something pushing down on my chest, crushing the life out of me . . .'

Adam's eyes strayed to his typed notes. In the family context section, it stated: 'Father deceased, workplace accident.'

'As I got older, I saw it more clearly. A large metal structure falling down on me, just before that awful feeling. Then I *knew* something bad was going to happen – I tried to stop my dad from going to work, begged him to stay at home with us, but of course we needed the money and Mom just said I was looking for attention.'

Kassie paused now, anger mingling with her evident distress.

'It was only later, when I saw pictures of the stockyard, that I worked it out. There was this large metal ramp the hogs used to go up to get to the slaughterhouse. They called it the "Bridge of Sighs" – that was what fell on him . . .'

Kassie petered out, as if drained by sharing the experience. But Adam felt very alive and awake now, the admission of Kassie processing her experiences through the benefit of hindsight interesting him greatly.

'When your father died, did you understand what had happened? That he was gone?'

'No, I was only five.'

'Did you go to the funeral?'

'I wasn't allowed . . .'

'Did your mother try to explain his death to you?'

'Only much later.'

'You must have felt very confused, very sad. One minute your dad was there, and the next . . .'

Kassie nodded, the pain obviously still fresh ten years on.

'How do you think it affected you?'

'I don't know what I was like before it happened . . . but I guess it made me quiet, reserved maybe. It was just me and Mom in the house.'

'How did you fill your time, distract yourself?'

'I looked at books, I drew a lot, but they didn't like that.'

'Why not?'

'Because . . . my pictures were different from the other kids'.'

'Different how?'

Kassie paused, exhaled, then continued in a quieter voice:

'More adult . . .'

'Featuring death?'

'Sure . . . I drew what came into my head, it helped at first.'

'Do you think you were trying to make sense of the images in your head by reproducing them?'

'Maybe . . .'

Adam looked at her, debating whether to continue or not, then said:

'And do you think it's possible that the images of your father's death that you saw . . . were doing the same job?'

Kassie looked up sharply, confused, but also wary.

'What I mean is . . . you were clearly very confused by your father's death. You'd had a difficult relationship with him, but just before he was taken from you, you were getting closer. You hadn't wanted him to go to work, you'd wanted him to stay with you, but then suddenly he was gone. Of course, that didn't make sense to you. Why would he leave you like that?'

Kassie stared at him, saying nothing. But her eyes seemed to be hardening. It was too late to pull out now, however, so Adam continued.

'Perhaps as you came to understand the nature of his

death – his accident – you felt some guilt about it. You'd tried to stop him leaving for work but you couldn't and this was the result. Perhaps you might even have felt you *caused* his death?'

'No, I never felt that,' Kassie shot back.

'Not literally, of course. But if you had foreseen his death, but didn't manage to stop it, then his death would have made sense, wouldn't it? Something seemingly random, scary and distressing would suddenly have had a kind of logic.'

'You think I've made all this shit up? To make myself feel better?'

Her tone was withering, oozing disappointment and betrayal.

'Not consciously, but the brain often plays tricks on us –'

'So you *do* think I'm nuts.'

'Of course not, Kassie, but our brains are powerful organs. Their ability to process and reshape information into more palatable forms is well documented –'

'This is pointless.'

Kassie sprang to her feet, but Adam rose with her.

'Please, Kassie. I'm not belittling what you feel or questioning your honesty,' Adam continued, reaching out to her.

'Bullshit!' she hissed, batting his hand away. 'Do you think I haven't asked myself these questions? I've been talking to shrinks most of my life and every single one of them has their pet theory.'

'This isn't a game, Kassie. I'm trying to help you –'

'But not one of them has ever tried to just . . . *believe me.*'

Kassie was staring at him, breathing heavily, her disappointment evident.

'Not one.'

27

Kassie marched across the grass, fighting back tears. She had been a fool. For one fleeting moment, she'd thought she'd found someone who wouldn't judge her, who wouldn't label her, but Adam Brandt was just like all the rest. In his eyes, she was a whack job that needed to be deciphered and medicated.

'Kassie!'

Kassie turned to see Adam hurrying after her. She had been so caught up in her desire to flee – marching down North Lincoln Avenue and into Lincoln Park – that she hadn't registered that he was pursuing her. But there he was, cutting a ridiculous figure swathed in a baggy duffel coat, half walking, half running across the grass towards her.

'Kassie, please, wait.'

She turned and carried on. A softball game was taking place directly in front of her, but beyond that she could see Lake Shore Drive and after that the beach. She was suddenly overwhelmed with a desire to be lakeside, to be alone by the water.

She sped up, ignoring the outraged cries of the elementary school students, as she marched straight through the middle of their game.

'Hey, we're tryin' to play a game here.'

She carried on, quickening her pace further. She was trotting now, but feeling her pursuer bearing down on her, she broke into a jog.

'Kassie!'

He was closer now. She started to run. If she could just get across Lake Shore Drive, the natural eastern boundary of the park, then maybe he would get the message and give up. She was fifty feet from it, now forty . . .

But he didn't seem to be getting the message. She could hear his footfall behind her, getting closer and closer.

With a sudden burst of speed, Brandt darted in front of her, blocking her route, just as she was approaching the roadside.

'Kassie, please. Don't leave like this.'

He was breathless, but determined.

'The last thing I wanted to do was upset you. Come back to my office. I promise I won't say a word, I'll just listen.'

'What's the point? When you're not even going to *try* to understand?'

She sounded desperate, whiny, which only angered her further.

'I will. I do.'

'No, you don't. You *pretend* to understand, but that's not the same thing.'

'It's not like that at all –'

'Do you believe me?'

'It's not my job to believe you, only to *understand* you.'

'For God's sake,' Kassie replied, pushing past him.

'Kassie, what you've told me is incredibly unusual. And if you feel I haven't supported you properly, it's only because I haven't got the tools to process what you're telling me. It's my failing, not yours.'

Kassie hesitated. His tone was so contrite, so concerned, that she suddenly felt bad for stalking off without a backward look. She paused, turning to him once more, her arms folded across her chest. She was still furious, but she would give him one last chance.

'Teach me,' he continued. 'Help me to see what you see. But try to understand that I have spent my whole life studying brain function, psychological constructs, the rational and irrational processes of the mind. I'm a scientist – I decipher the world based on the evidence in front of me, so if I sometimes reveal . . . a lack of imagination, then don't judge me too harshly. I'm trying to get there, but maybe I need a little help.'

He sounded sincere, like he was genuinely keen to help, but Kassie had heard this speech many times before from a dozen different do-gooders.

'Give me your scarf.'

Adam looked bemused by the request, only now seeming to realize that the tail of his burgundy scarf was hanging from his coat pocket.

'Sure,' he replied stutteringly, pulling it from his pocket. 'Are you cold or . . .'

'Like I said, we all have our time.'

Kassie turned away from him, marching the last few feet to Lake Shore Drive with the scarf in her hands.

'Kassie . . . what the hell are you doing?'

The concrete barrier by the roadside was less than a foot high and Kassie cleared it easily. She took a brief look in front of her, at the eight lanes of traffic speeding up and down the coast, then placed the scarf over her eyes, tying the ends together tightly together at the back of her head.

'Kassie, for God's sake, you don't have to prove anything to me.'

Adam's voice was shrill, desperate, but Kassie didn't hesitate. Even though she couldn't see a thing through the itchy wool, she took a step towards the traffic. She could hear the roar of the trucks, could feel their side winds buffeting her as she approached the first lane, but she kept going.

From nowhere, a deafening horn blast. Kassie jumped, even as a truck roared past. Kassie felt a hand grab at her – Adam presumably – but pulling away, she pressed on. Her heart was beating, she could feel sweat seeping from her forehead, but there was no turning back now.

'Kassie, please don't do this.'

His voice was muffled by the noise of the vehicles. Suddenly, Kassie heard a shrieking squeal of brakes right next to her, followed by a volley of abuse.

'Crazy fucking bitch!'

On she went, faster and faster. Another deafening horn now, right under her nose. For a moment, she thought she'd been hit. But the car clipped the front of her toes, speeding on past her in a flash.

She pressed on remorselessly, but her shin now hit something hard, arresting her progress and sending pain searing up her leg. Groping, she felt the dividing barrier between the north and south carriageways and clambered over it.

'You wanna get yourself killed?'

The accusation faded, as another startled driver sped on his way. Gritting her teeth, Kassie kept going, but almost immediately she was stumbling forward – the jet stream of what must have been a sixteen-wheeler knocking her off balance. She tried to right herself, clawing at the air, but it was too late. She was already on her way down and hit the hot tarmac hard, her hands and knees jarring with the impact.

And then she heard it. An ominous, high-pitched whine, as brakes locked and protesting tyres skidded towards her across the dry, unforgiving surface. In that moment, she knew that she'd made a mistake, that the car would hit her.

She could see herself flying backwards, pirouetting across the lanes into the path of oncoming traffic . . .

But then the whining suddenly ceased, even as Kassie felt her right cheek kissed by the nose of the braking car. Grabbing hold of the grille, she hauled herself up, even as she heard the car door open.

'Mother of God, honey, are you ok?'

She lurched on, keen to be away from his concern, his questions. She could sense she was only yards from the other side now, so she moved faster, half stumbling, half running. She was almost there, almost there . . .

She felt her feet hit solid concrete and she stopped dead. Yanking her blindfold off, she took in the barrier next to her, then turned to look back across the eight-lane highway.

Adam Brandt was still there, staring at her from the other side of the highway, his face white with fear.

28

She was surrounded by death.

Looking around the carriage, Rochelle Stevens took in the wall of tabloid newspapers, all of which majored on the brutal death of a local state's attorney. She usually enjoyed her journey on the 'L' – it was a short twenty-minute hop from Loyola to Cermak – but today it was disquieting, even a little scary. The headlines in the local papers were gory and unpleasant, making great play of the fact that the mutilated body of a nice, middle-class attorney had been found in the trunk of a car, wrapped in a bloody plastic sheet. Several of them were already peddling a line of police incompetence – the paper claiming that the CPD had arrested and released a fifteen-year-old girl and were now scratching their heads for suspects. The coverage in the *Tribune* was scarcely better – most of the front page was given over to the grim discovery, while the inside featured a double-page spread about the life and death of the dedicated state servant. According to reports, the poor man was due to be married later this year.

Saddened, Rochelle flicked through the pages, hastening away from the news to the travel section. This was more like it. There were numerous adverts for breaks to the Caribbean – Puerto Rico, Cuba, Jamaica – but perhaps she should consider going further afield? Could she scrabble together enough money to go to Hawaii? The thought made her giddy and she suddenly realized she was smiling. She was the only one in the carriage who was.

Hang it, she thought to herself, she refused to be downcast today. She couldn't control what happened in the world, but she could steer her own destiny. It had taken her so long to get over her college experiences, to face up to what had happened, process it and then get to a better, more constructive place. She had rebuilt her confidence step by step, refusing to let her life be defined by the date rape inflicted on her by a trusted friend. Now that she finally felt she was on firmer ground, she was determined to enjoy herself. Hell, she'd earned the right to a little happiness.

It was time for her to stop worrying, to stop going over the same old ground and look forward. She would talk to some of her girlfriends, see if they fancied an impromptu spring getaway — but if they couldn't, her sister could be relied upon to row in. Suddenly, Rochelle felt exhilarated, excited by the possibilities, by the feeling of freedom. The days of self-reproach and recrimination were over.

It was time to live a little.

29

He ran a gloved finger over the chest of drawers, before letting it fall upon a set of framed photographs. He was tempted to wipe the dust from the glass – Rochelle really was so sluttish in her habits – but there was no question of betraying his presence in that way, so he contented himself with drinking in the family snapshots. They were obviously taken a few years ago: Rochelle's hair was much longer, badly dyed, and there was something awkward in her stance, as she stood flanked by mother, father and sister. She was so fragile, so uncertain. She was stronger now of course, but for all her self-proclaimed progress there was still an obvious vulnerability which he found appealing.

Replacing the frame carefully on the chest of drawers, he turned to survey the rest of the bedroom. Rochelle was not a tidy person, often leaving the bed unmade and odd items of clothing on the floor. He stepped over them carefully, as he made his way towards the bed and sat down on it. All was quiet, nothing was moving in the house, and he was suddenly intensely aware of his heart thundering in his chest. His excitement was growing, his anticipation of what was to come making him light-headed and sweaty. The first one had been good, but he felt sure the second would be better. Rochelle's fragility would make her reaction greater, her terror more extreme.

Even as he thought this, he was rocketed back in time. To the day his mom had woken up, drowsy and confused, to find him standing over her on the bed. He only had a bread knife on him and he had no intention of using it, but the shock . . . the fear in her cold grey eyes was indelibly stamped on his memory. He had been beaten for his misbehaviour – beaten half to death – but every one of those brutal blows was sweet. He cherished them, along with her bitter, addled curses. He had never felt more significant than on that day.

Outside a car horn honked. Rising quickly, he left the bedroom and returned to the living area. He still had to complete another circuit of the perimeter, wanted to double-check his plans, and it wouldn't do to become complacent. Not when there was so much at stake.

Rochelle lived alone on a quiet suburban road, she had no pets, so when she was out the whole place was filled with this reverential hush. He moved around it now, quickly and quietly, enjoying the freedom, commanding the silence. It made him feel like he owned the space, which in a way he did. Pretty soon, he would own Rochelle too. She was busy making plans of course – shopping, researching vacation options – unaware that it was all pointless.

She was living on borrowed time.

30

'Are you sure you're ok? You've not eaten anything . . .'

Adam snapped out of it, suddenly aware that his fork was hanging in mid-air. Faith watched him closely as he slid the fork into his mouth, chewing thoughtfully on his linguine. The change in his demeanour was striking. When he'd first arrived, he couldn't *stop* talking and, as he'd begun to explain what had happened with Kassie, Faith had understood why. But slowly Adam had receded into himself, and after a while conversation had ceased altogether.

'I'm sorry,' he replied eventually, placing his fork back in his nearly full bowl. 'I'm just preoccupied . . .'

'Look, if you're that worried about her, maybe you *should* have her sectioned? If you think she may harm herself, or others.'

Adam looked up. He seemed eager for her counsel, but was obviously torn as to what to do.

'I've spoken to her social worker and that should be enough for now,' he responded. 'Sectioning her will open a whole can of worms with her mother, her school, her outreach team, plus it will destroy any semblance of trust that we've managed to establish.'

'Are you going to see her again?'

'I don't think I have a choice. It's more a question of whether she'll see *me*. I nearly lost her today.'

'Do *you* think she's having a breakdown? Is she delusional?'

Adam considered his response, seemingly grasping for the right words.

'If you'd asked me that this morning, I would have said she was experiencing some form of psychotic break. Lord knows, she's been through enough to provoke that, plus she's very isolated and the drugs don't help . . .'

'But?'

'But she doesn't sound crazy, she doesn't act crazy.'

'Apart from running across eight-lane highways. And breaking into peoples' homes.'

'Apart from that,' Adam responded, managing a brief smile, which pleased Faith. 'She is lucid, calm, reasoned. Most people in the midst of a psychotic break struggle to be articulate, you can hear their brain misfiring in their odd patterns of speech, the lack of logic in their statements, their general disorientation. Also, they tend to let personal hygiene go, forget to change or wash their clothes, run out of cash . . . but she's neat, clean and self-possessed. And, actually, looked at from her point of view, her actions make sense.'

Faith could see Adam was struggling, so she reached out and took his hand, earning a warm, approving look from the middle-aged lady at the table next to them. They were in the brasserie at the Chicago Art Institute, Faith's favourite place in Chicago. She and Adam had spent many of their early dates here – they used to sit for hours in the Monet room, surrounded by those amazing canvases, exchanging confidences in hushed whispers. When Adam had called earlier asking to meet, sounding upset, she had immediately suggested lunching here, hoping it might have a calming effect.

'How close was she to . . . ?'

For some reason, Faith couldn't quite say it.

'She nearly got hit five, maybe six times. The cars must have missed her by inches.'

'And you're sure she couldn't see? It wasn't . . . I don't know . . . a trick?'

'No,' Adam protested, involuntarily shooting a look at his scarf, which was now stowed back in his coat pocket. 'She was blindfolded, and even if she could peek out it was still an incredible risk to take.'

'But if she's unwell, not thinking straight . . .'

'That's just it. She knew *exactly* what she was doing. She was proving a point. In her head it's not her time yet, which is why she didn't look scared *at all*.'

'Then maybe she's telling the truth.'

'Don't joke, Faith,' Adam reprimanded her, irritation creeping into his tone.

'I'm not. "There are more things in heaven and earth, Horatio, than are dreamt of in your philosophy,"' she replied reprovingly.

'Look, you know it's not my style to rain on anyone's spiritual beliefs . . .'

Faith could tell Adam was choosing his words carefully. She had always been more open to these things than her husband. She believed in Fate, in omens, even the power of mediums – insisting that a fairground fortune teller had once accurately predicted she would marry a doctor – and though Adam didn't share her views, he never mocked them.

'But this is off-the-scale weird and . . . it frightens me. She's only fifteen.'

Faith looked at him, worried by his fevered tone. She had been wanting to talk to him today, but it didn't seem the right time now to burden him with *her* concerns. They would have to wait for another day.

'Would it be worth referring her to someone else, then? A fresh pair of eyes?'

But already Adam was shaking his head.

'She's seen too many health officials already. What she needs now is consistency.'

'But why you? When you've got so much else on your plate.'

'Because I care. Because maybe I can help her.'

'You help people every day and you can only do so much.'

'I know, but still . . .'

'I'm just trying to understand what's so special about her. Why you feel you need to reach out to her specifically.'

'Because she's got no one else.'

The words hung in the air, simple but triumphant. Faith was an only child and had often been lonely growing up. Wittingly or unwittingly, Adam had pressed the one button that was guaranteed to sway Faith in Kassie's favour.

'Then you must do what you think is right. If you think you can help her.'

'I want to try . . .'

'That's my boy.'

It was said with humour, but also with love. She couldn't resist him when he was like this. Taking his hands in hers, she kissed them gently. He immediately leaned forward, resting his forehead on hers. And there they remained, Faith filled with love for her man, but also something else.

Pride.

31

Nancy Bright sat in the interview suite, her hands shaking slightly as she cradled a cup of coffee. She made no move to drink it, simply staring into its depths. Pale, drawn and restless, she was still a woman in deep shock.

'I know this is hard. There's so much for you to take in,' Gabrielle sympathized. 'But I do need to ask you these questions.'

Nancy nodded, but said nothing. So far, her answers had been monosyllabic.

'Had anyone threatened your fiancé recently?'

Nancy shook her head slowly, looking slightly mystified.

'Someone to do with his work? Someone he'd crossed or helped incarcerate?'

'Not that he mentioned to me.'

'Anyone in his personal life, then?' Detective Miller overlapped. 'Family member? Friend? Ex?'

'No, no . . .' Nancy insisted. 'He wasn't that kind of guy. Everyone liked him. Hell, most of his ex-girlfriends are *still* in love with him.'

It was said with rueful humour, but prompted tears to fill her eyes.

'Perhaps you noticed something out of the ordinary, then, in the last few weeks,' Miller persisted gently. 'Someone hanging around the house? Someone who didn't seem to fit in the neighbourhood?'

Nancy turned her gaze to the ceiling, as if racking her

brains. A single tear slid down her cheek, but she wiped it away.

'I don't think so. We've only just moved to West Town, but it's always seemed very safe.'

'And Jacob hadn't shared any concerns with you? Any worries, however insignificant, might have a bearing on this case,' Gabrielle suggested.

'Just the usual work politics. He . . . we were in a good place. We'd just bought the house, we were planning our wedding . . .'

Once more emotion mastered her. Dropping her eyes to the floor, she dug her nails into her hand, fighting to contain her distress. Gabrielle gave her a moment, then nodded to Miller, who opened the file in front of her.

'Nancy, I'd like to show you some photos. I won't burden you with the details, I just need to know if you recognize any of these faces.'

Miller had collated the mugshots while Gabrielle was on her way back from the morgue. They were faces of violent criminals that Jacob had successfully prosecuted in the last year.

'Do you recognize this man?'

A picture of a shaven-headed Colombian youth was offered to her. She studied it, then shook her head.

'And this guy?'

A young African American with braided hair and plenty of attitude.

'No, I'm sorry . . .'

'And this one?'

On it went. A brief look, then a small shake of the head. Until finally there was only one photo remaining.

'And what about this one?'

In spite of the studied neutrality of Miller's tone, Nancy realized that there was something special about this last photo. She studied the image of Kassandra Wojcek carefully, as Gabrielle watched her closely for any sign of a reaction. But when Nancy looked up, seemingly as mystified as ever, it was only to say:

'No. I've never seen that girl before in my life.'

32

Everywhere she went, their eyes followed her.

Kassie had never fitted in at school and on days like today she wondered why she'd ever tried. Was it the way she dressed that intrigued them? The way she spoke? Or was it just her flagrant, persistent infraction of the school rules that made her fellow students stare?

Kassie made her way down the long hallway. It was recess and the locker area was crowded – she had to push her way through the bodies to get to hers. As she did so, conversations ceased, gestures were made, words were mouthed. This wasn't uncommon – she was generally regarded as a freak – but Kassie sensed a raised level of interest – had her peers somehow got wind of her arrest? The police had had to inform the school, so it was perfectly possible.

'Hey, Mandy, look at that. Did you know the thrift store was having a sale?'

Kassie opened her locker and placed her books inside. Comments like this were commonplace and for a moment Kassie wondered if maybe they *hadn't* heard. But the next comment dispelled that fond notion.

'I heard she'd got a couple of new bracelets to go with her "look". Steel ones, joined together with a little chain . . .'

It was Amanda and Jessie – two classic high-school bitches. They usually started the round of insults, when they were bored or had no boys to flirt with.

'I know, so cute,' Mandy cooed in response to Jessie's jibe. 'Probably the most expensive jewellery she's ever worn.'

Slamming her locker shut, Kassie turned to face them. Normally she would ignore their taunts, but she was not in the mood today.

'Got something to say?' Kassie demanded, staring straight at Mandy.

'No, but I'm sure you do,' she responded, grinning.

'I should warn you though,' Jessie butted in, hanging on her girlfriend's shoulder, 'anything you say may be used against you in a court of law –'

'Oh, fuck off, Jessie.'

Kassie's words had the desired effect, a surprised Jessie shocked into silence.

'Now if you'll excuse me . . .'

Kassie barged past them, her shoulder catching Jessie sharply. There were howls of protest and angry responses, but Kassie didn't stop to trade insults, marching off down the hallway instead. It had felt good to tell them where to go, but she knew she would come to regret it. Mandy and Jessie were unpleasant and predictable, but quickly got bored if they weren't provoked. They could not ignore such a flagrant challenge, however, especially from someone with so few allies. And that was the bitter irony of school life for Kassie – however much excitement and amusement she generated, she was nevertheless always alone at Grantham High.

Their eyes followed her down the hallway. There was no question of returning to classes now – Jessie and Mandy would find an opportunity to take their revenge – so having navigated a couple of corridors, Kassie darted through the emergency exit and descended the fire escape.

Having checked that the recreation areas were deserted,

she hurried across the fading basketball courts, disappearing from view behind the garbage area. The municipal trash cans were huge, providing good cover – this space was often used by the more rebellious students, as the numerous cigarette butts on the ground revealed.

Pulling open her pencil case, Kassie fished out a freshly rolled joint and lit up. She inhaled greedily, wanting to lose herself amid the noxious-smelling garbage. But, as she inhaled a second time, an image of Adam Brandt shot into her mind. She'd been pushing thoughts of him away since their difficult encounter this morning, but now his pale, frightened face forced its way back into her consciousness. Why had she done that to him? Terrified him pretty much out of his wits? She had been angry at the time, not thinking straight, but now she felt bad about pushing him away. Maybe he didn't believe her, maybe he did think she was crazy, but he was still pretty much the only person in Chicago who was willing to extend the hand of friendship to her.

Should she seek him out? Apologize? Ask for his help? A strong part of her wanted to keep her distance, given what she knew, but another part of her sensed a greater design at work. Was it possible that they had been brought together for a reason? Was this the push she needed to fight her curse? To grasp the nettle?

It wasn't much of a choice. Willingly embrace danger to confront her birthright. Or stay here, alone and miserable among the foul-smelling dumpsters. Kassie drew deeply on her joint, hoping for some chemical inspiration, an image, a sign, something to help her choose.

But she had never felt as lost as she did today.

33

'You mustn't turn your back on her, Natalia. You must reach out to her.'

She didn't want to meet his eye, fearing he would see her weakness, but Natalia knew she had to. Avoiding his gaze would look shifty or, worse, imply a reluctance to heed his advice. And how she needed his advice. Not since her husband's sudden death had she felt so rudderless.

'I know it's hard. I know she says things that hurt you, that she has sinned and repented, then sinned again . . . but you are her mother. You were put on this earth to protect and nurture her.'

'Yes, Father . . .'

She murmured the words gratefully. Things always seemed so much clearer, so much simpler, after she'd spoken to Father Nowak – he was like your grandfather, father and older brother rolled into one. Smiling, he continued:

'Now let's think how we might help Kassie see things more clearly . . .'

They were huddled together in the empty pews of St Stanislaus Kostka church, talking in hushed, conspiratorial tones. St Stanislaus was still the most popular church for the Chicago Polonia, a place which reminded them of the old country, and it was usually besieged by those seeking comfort or guidance.

Even though Back of the Yards was a long way away, Natalia always made the effort to come here, sometimes three or four times a week. She was devoted to Father Nowak, loved the traditional services, but she was also partial to the regular social events and charity buffets, in which she could indulge her weakness for the food of her childhood – stuffed cabbage, spiced sausage and plums wrapped in bacon.

Father Nowak – 220 pounds of beard, belly and good humour – had been the heart and soul of the revered church for many years and still attended to his duties and parishioners with the energy and zeal of a young man. His words washed over Natalia now, banishing doubt, illuminating the way forward.

'Yes, Father, I think if I talk to her, she will come. She has always had a soft spot for this place, for you . . .'

If this was an exaggeration, it was not a lie. Kassandra had liked coming here as a child and had never said a bad word about Father Nowak. Natalia suddenly wanted the good priest to know this, to know that his efforts on their behalf were not unappreciated. He had always been a tower of strength for Natalia.

'Good, then that's agreed. Together, together, Natalia, we can help Kassie see more clearly. To cast off her weakness, her sinfulness, and get well again. Now I think it would be fitting if we were to pray to the Virgin. Will you join me, Natalia?'

Natalia clasped her hands together. The words tripped from her and with each passing moment she felt stronger and more determined. She had allowed herself to be laid low by her daughter's behaviour, to wallow in self-pity, but now she had a purpose. Now she saw what she must do.

By hook or by crook, she would bring Kassie back into the fold.

34

'So, are we definitely saying this is a two-man job?'

Detective Montgomery's question was a good one. She was relatively new to the team, but Gabrielle had a good feeling about her.

'We're saying it's a possibility,' Gabrielle responded, turning to face the phalanx of detectives crammed into the briefing room. 'This was a clean abduction and a brutal murder. Maybe it's a solo killer, maybe Wojcek has an accomplice, what we are looking for at the moment is *connections*.'

The sea of heads nodded gently. Gabrielle was pleased by their rapt attention and their resolve. She had already had Superintendent Hoskins on the phone – who himself had been called by the Mayor – demanding progress, so she'd called the entire investigative team together in the run-down, peeling briefing room. All their preliminary findings were in and when it came to assimilating it and assessing the possibilities, twelve heads were definitely better than one.

'You'll all have had updates from pathology and forensics. You should also have digested Kassie Wojcek's charge sheet and the witness statements. Detective Miller and I spoke to Jones's fiancée, Nancy Bright, earlier. She was unable to point the finger at anyone, so it's up to us to find the links. Suarez, how are you getting on with Jones's court history?'

'I'm still working the gang angle. Maybe the Cobras weren't involved specifically, but Jones has put a lot of guys away in his time. Maybe someone wanted revenge? Maybe he was actually compromising their operations? Andre Hill is a possibility, working out of Humboldt Park. Four of his runners were sent down last month – Jones was the prosecutor on every one. Grey has got form for aggravated assault, assault with a deadly weapon, likes to carry a big-ass hunting knife around with him.'

'Find him,' Gabrielle responded quickly. 'See who he's running with now, if he can offer up a decent alibi. Detective Miller?'

Her deputy stepped forward, as Gabrielle turned to her.

'My guys have been chasing down leads from the Joneses' personal life. Jacob's former partners were all on good terms with him, but Nancy Bright has an ex who didn't take kindly to her engagement to Jones. I don't think he's a fit for the attack itself, but he has motive and his best buddy has form. Dale McKenzie, former gym instructor turned bouncer. Numerous busts for drugs, verbal and physical abuse, *plus* he once took a tyre iron to a love rival, beat him half to death.'

'Might be a bit of a stretch,' Gabrielle replied straight away, to Miller's evident disappointment. 'Whoever did this was careful and precise – Aaron Holmes has confirmed that Jones was allergic to latex, so we know his attacker was wearing gloves. But talk to the ex, anyway. See if you can gauge the extent of his anger. And check out his digital footprint. Be good to know how *involved* he was in Nancy Bright's life. What else?'

'Jones has got a brother he doesn't speak to,' Detective Albright answered, keen to get in on the action. 'Seems to have vanished off the face of the earth though. Last sighted in Minneapolis four months ago.'

'Keep on it.'

'We're also running the rule over recent releases from

Cook County, guys who've done long stretches, who still have mental health issues, who enjoy this kind of thing,' Suarez interjected. 'It's possible that Jones was targeted at random.'

'Possible, but unlikely given the level of planning that must have gone into this. I'm guessing there was some reason he was targeted, however twisted. Anything else?'

'I think I might have a name . . .' Montgomery offered, a little diffidently.

'Go on,' Gabrielle replied encouragingly.

Montgomery cleared her throat.

'As you know, I've worked through Kassie Wojcek's charge sheet. They were all solo arrests, solo offences, and there's no obvious record of affiliations to gangs. This kid has few friends and seems to prefer her own company.'

'Agreed.'

'But she has had contact with some pretty bad boys and girls at the Juvenile Detention Center. She's been in and out of that place for years . . .'

'And . . .' Gabrielle prompted, intrigued.

'And I was wondering about this guy,' Montgomery went on, handing Gabrielle a sheet of paper. 'Kyle Redmond.'

Gabrielle looked down at the photocopied charge sheet and the full-colour image of a surly young man. He was shaven-headed, which only made the livid birthmark stand out more. Tattoos partially concealed it on his neck, but it drew your attention to the right side of his face, where the birthmark tugged at his lips and flirted with his nose and ear. He had a septum piercing and his ear was dotted with studs, making his appearance even more startling. Gabrielle drank in his features, especially his eyes – was that anger she saw there? Or something else?

'They overlapped when Redmond was fifteen and Kassie was eleven. We know this because of an incident report from the time. You can see a photocopy of it on page four.'

Gabrielle flicked to the relevant page, as Montgomery continued:

'One of the male inmates was bothering Kassie, hitting on her. Redmond took issue with this, put the guy in hospital. Now Redmond's a thug – maybe he just wanted a fight – but the warden felt that Redmond might have had feelings for Kassie, hence his desire to protect her.'

'And *she* would presumably have been grateful to her guardian angel, especially in a place like that,' Gabrielle added.

'Back in the day, we had people getting pregnant in there, knife fights, you name it,' Detective Albright agreed, cheerfully.

'So maybe they formed a friendship?' Montgomery continued. 'A relationship even? Anyhow, Redmond is nineteen now, but he's been busy.'

Gabrielle digested his arrest history – false imprisonment, torture, actual bodily harm and – intriguingly – alleged sexual assaults against men *and* women. His 'CV' smacked of a man who enjoyed power and had sadistic tendencies. She passed the sheet on to Miller, who whistled quietly at the extent of his misdemeanours.

'Sick puppy.'

'Where is he now?' Gabrielle demanded.

'No idea. He went off the radar five weeks ago. He's supposed to check into Central once a week as part of his bail conditions, but they haven't seen hide or hair of him.'

'Then we need to find him. Miller will coordinate, aided by Montgomery and Albright.'

The trio nodded, but didn't move.

'What are you waiting for?' Gabrielle barked, aiming her question at all the detectives. 'Get moving.'

The team obliged, scurrying away to their desks. Gabrielle watched them go, her spirits buoyed. For the first time since that awful discovery in the trunk she felt they were making progress. And not before time. The Chief Super was anxious, the media shrill and inflammatory, and the citizens of central Chicago edgy and unnerved. But the fightback started today.

35

Adam was alone in a sea of humanity. His next appointment wasn't until four o'clock, so on heading back to Lincoln Park, he'd visited the city zoo in an attempt to clear his head. He'd come here as a boy and in his mind's eye it was a huge, rambling place that you could lose yourself in.

Today, however, the zoo seemed smaller than he remembered. Furthermore, it was packed with family groups and school students enjoying the spring sunshine. Adam's first instinct was to abandon his visit. No entrance fee had been paid and there were other places in the park he could go, but after a moment's hesitation he decided to persevere. He didn't want solitude, he wanted distraction, and he wasn't prepared to give up on this trip down memory lane just yet.

And with each passing step his mood began to improve. There were some parts of the zoo he recognized and other exhibits, such as the lion enclosure, which were new to him. The lions had predictably drawn the biggest crowds, and as Adam stood by the barrier, taking in the scene before him, he found himself smiling. Dozens of rapt toddlers were virtually clambering over the safety rail in an attempt to get closer to the lions – they were fearless, transfixed, curious. He was just the same at their age.

Back then, it was one of his favourite places to come and he often nagged his parents to be allowed to visit. And though short on means and time, they always obliged. His father worked double shifts, six days a week, and was utterly spent by Sunday, but still he journeyed across town with his son on the bus, exchanging confidences, discussing baseball, weaving improbable stories, while sharing a bag of candy. And although it was slightly bittersweet for Adam to be back here, now that his father had passed away, the memory of their visits together filled him with love. Looking at the harassed parents today, juggling children, strollers, picnics and more, he realized how indulgent his father had been to him. But then perhaps that was the role of a parent, to subjugate one's own desires and interests in the hope of raising a balanced, happy child? It had certainly been the case with his folks.

Moving away from the lions, Adam made towards the wading birds. Still his thoughts lingered on his parents, whom he'd buried six months apart. That was over ten years ago now, but the memory still provoked a powerful emotional reaction in him, principally because of the sudden nature of his father's death. Happy, healthy, ebullient one minute, stone dead the next, the victim of a massive cardiac arrest. It had happened when his mother was alone in the house with her husband – in her panic, she'd called her son for advice, when she should have been dialling 911. Adam got there just after the paramedics, but by then it was already too late. His mother was not well and it was perhaps no great surprise that she succumbed soon after, but his father's sudden death had come as a terrible shock to them all. It was only later they found out that his father had been suffering from heart disease for years, just as his father had before him.

Adam walked quickly away from the birds, even as another, more disturbing notion forced its way into his mind. Kassie. Adam had successfully banished her from his thoughts momentarily, but now he found himself replaying their conversations again. 'I can see death before it happens.' 'I know how people die, *when* they will die . . .' In spite of himself, Adam found he was reflecting on his *own* fate. His blood pressure had been a little high of late and, as Faith's due date drew ever closer, he'd begun to wonder whether he should book himself in for a check-up. There was much more at stake now and given his family's history of heart disease . . .

Now Kassie presented herself in his mind's eye, talking animatedly about the awful curse of her knowledge. And just for a second Adam allowed himself to imagine what it would mean if there actually *was* something in what she was saying, as Faith had suggested. If Kassie genuinely *did* have 'second sight'.

It was a thrilling but terrifying thought. Not just the notion that he had no control over his destiny, but that Kassie could foresee his end. If she *could* accurately predict his future, would he want to know? If she could tell him whether he was going to die at fifty of a cardiac arrest or at ninety after years of good living, would he have the courage to ask? Normally no, a hundred times no, but given that so many of members of his family had been struck down by –

Adam stopped walking, surprised to find himself at the exit. He'd been too wrapped up in his morbid fantasies to notice where he was going, letting his mind run away with itself when he *should* have been thinking about how to help Kassie. Now he felt foolish to have been so absorbed in pointless speculation that he'd unwittingly brought his visit to a premature end. Still, perhaps it was telling him something – that idle distraction only leads to introspection and that work is the best antidote to anxiety. Experience should have taught him *that*. Casting a quick look at his watch, he pushed through the crowds and was soon away and out through the exit.

It was nearly time for his four o'clock.

36

Faith stared at the clock, watching the minute hand crawl round. Why was it taking so long? She had been lying on the bed, uncomfortable and exposed, for over twenty minutes now. It seemed wrong to leave her like this, when she was anxious and unnerved.

'Sorry, sorry, sorry . . .'

The midwife bustled in, making her apologies without even looking at Faith.

'Seems like everybody's decided to have their baby today,' she continued good-naturedly. 'Now let's see if we can set your mind at ease.'

Sliding the ultrasound machine over to the side of the bed, the midwife slipped on a pair of gloves. Faith watched her, calmed a little by her relaxed attitude, her smooth, practised efficiency. Perhaps she was over-reacting, perhaps it had been silly to come here. The baby was often quiet – she regularly joked with Adam that their offspring had inherited her laziness.

'If you could lift your gown for me . . .'

The midwife slid her hand into the jelly, then smeared it on to Faith's bump. As usual, it made Faith flinch – the silky substance cold against her taut, warm belly. Their early scans had been some of the happiest moments of her life, but Faith couldn't say that she'd ever actually enjoyed them. It always felt undignified and exposing and she hated the feeling of the midwife's probe digging into her flesh.

As she listened to the crackling of the scanner, Faith toyed with the amazonite crystal she always wore for good luck. The midwife was quiet now, diligently guiding the probe around her swollen belly, while keeping her eyes fixed on the small screen in front of her. Faith could picture her baby on the monitor, a small ghostly presence swathed in a sea of black, shifting and responding to the proddings of the midwife. Faith longed to hear the familiar 'boom, boom, boom' of her baby's heartbeat. To her it remained the most beautiful sound she'd ever heard.

Silence filled the room and Faith now turned to the midwife.

'How we doing?'

It was meant to sound casual, but Faith's anxiety betrayed her. The midwife smiled at her briefly, but did Faith detect a certain tightness in her expression?

'Is everything ok? Can you find a heartbeat?'

Concentrating hard, the midwife tried once more, then turned to Faith.

'Not yet, but to be honest this particular machine isn't the most reliable. I've been asking them to replace it for weeks now. I'm going to get one from next door and then we can have another go.'

She was about to depart, when she laid a hand on Faith's arm.

'Don't read too much into it, sweetheart. I'm sure there's nothing to worry about.'

But Faith was worried. As she watched the midwife scuttle from the room, she was gripped by a rising panic. Suddenly she was convinced that something was terribly, terribly wrong.

37

'I'm sorry if I scared you.'

It was offered so sincerely and with such feeling that Adam found himself replying:

'No harm done.'

It was a pathetic response and entirely untruthful, as Kassie had nearly got herself killed this morning, but he couldn't bring himself to reprimand her.

'I didn't mean to. I wasn't thinking straight –'

'It's ok. I understand.'

Once again, she shot a heart-breaking look of gratitude at Adam. He noticed for the first time in their brief relationship that she was happy to look him squarely in the eye. Guilt, it seemed, was helping her overcome her natural timidity and suspicion.

'Would you like to stay for a while? Have a soda? Watch some TV? I'm done for the day, so . . .'

'No, it's ok, I can't stay. I just wanted to apologize.'

Adam had been seeing his four o'clock out, when he'd noticed Kassie, standing across the road, her hands in her pockets. She looked ill at ease, hopping from one foot to the other, but wasted no time in hurrying across to him, once his client had departed. He'd immediately ushered her inside, away from prying eyes.

'You've nothing to apologize for. As I said before, it was my fault for not listening properly, for not responding appropriately.'

Kassie shrugged, but didn't contradict him. Once more

Adam felt a surge of sympathy for this awkward, isolated teenager. What a curse it was to be different.

'But I'd like to try again, if you'd agree to that. No charge, as I said before.'

'You want me to be your guinea pig?' Kassie responded, her tone hard to read.

'No, just another client.'

This seemed to please her.

'Then, ok. I just want . . .'

'Yes?'

'I just want someone to *try* to understand.'

'Of course.'

'And to help me maybe. I know it's difficult – that I'm not . . . normal – but it's so hard. I feel like I'm always alone . . . but never alone. Like there's a little bit of everybody else inside me . . .'

Adam looked at her, but said nothing.

'If I was a good person, a strong person . . .' she continued falteringly, 'I'd talk to all of them. Tell them that . . . that time wasn't on their side and they should kiss their kids. Or that it was and that they should buy that car, that house –'

'That's not your responsibility, Kassie. Whatever you feel, whatever you think you see, that's *not* your job.'

'Isn't it?'

'Of course not. Your only responsibility is to yourself, to making sure that you're ok.'

Kassie didn't look convinced, so Adam continued:

'Think about it, Kassie. Even if you could help all these people, how would you choose? There are millions of people in Chicago alone.'

'Don't say that.'

'It's true. And it's not fair for you to take the weight of their lives upon your shoulders.'

'But what if that's my fate? What if that's what I was *born* to do? Others have tried . . .'

'Such as?'

'Relatives,' Kassie replied evasively. 'People who've come before . . .'

There must have been something – surprise? Scepticism? – in Adam's expression, for a frown passed across Kassie's face.

'Do you believe me?' she suddenly said, quietly.

'I believe you believe it,' Adam said carefully. 'And I'd like to explore what that means.'

It was an artful reply, but was true nevertheless. On balance, he believed she probably was gripped by some form of magical thinking, the belief that she could alter the world around her through her own thoughts, but for her sake he was prepared to keep an open mind, to work with her to root out the cause of her affliction.

'Thank you,' she murmured.

Once more Adam was struck by how sad she looked. He was about to reassure her further when suddenly his cell phone started ringing on his desk. He darted a look at it – Faith. Instinctively, he moved to answer it – he monitored his phone constantly now that their due date was drawing near – then thinking better of it, he rejected the call, switching the phone to silent. He turned back to the teenager, only to find her staring directly at him.

'I don't want to be "cured",' she continued quickly. 'I don't want to be humoured.'

'You have my word on that,' Adam promised. 'And perhaps over time we'll understand what you're experiencing a little better. We can take as long as you like and, who knows, maybe we can straighten things out with your mom, the cops, even your principal, so you can go to the prom, get drunk, have a good summer . . .'

He had meant to raise a smile, but suddenly Kassie looked anguished. Dropping her gaze, she began to pick at her nails, refusing to look at him.

'What's up, Kassie? Did I say the wrong thing?'

Kassie didn't respond, shooting a quick look at the door instead.

'Is it school? Did I –'

'It's not that. It's not that at all.'

'What then?'

Even as he spoke, an awful suspicion crept over him. And as he looked at this lonely, sad child, he suddenly felt he knew exactly what she was thinking.

'You don't think you *have* time, do you? That's what's worry—'

Kassie nodded. Adam stared at her, suddenly very concerned. Instinctively, he took a step towards her.

'Kassie, have you seen your *own* death?'

'Of course.'

'And how . . . how do you die?'

It was a crazy question, but one he had to ask. If Kassie believed her own death was imminent, he needed to know.

'I'm murdered.'

Two simple words that took his breath his way. Not for the content – though that was shocking enough – but more for the conviction with which they were uttered. For a few seconds, silence gripped them both, then finally, falteringly, he found his voice once more:

'And do you know . . . do you know who kills you?'

An awful, elongated pause, then slowly Kassie raised her head and said:

'You do.'

Book Two

38

The two women stood opposite each other, defiant, unyielding. Topping six foot, Gabrielle Grey was a powerful, imposing presence, but her adversary was not easily intimidated.

'I don't want to talk about it. Not now. Not *ever*.'

'You don't have a choice, Dani. Obstructing the police in the execution of their duties is a criminal offence.'

'So arrest me.'

Gabrielle was tempted to accept the offer. Having failed to unearth anyone renting or lodging in the city under the name Kyle Redmond, she had focused their fire elsewhere. It had taken her team several days to track down Kyle's ex-girlfriend and the pay-off was proving to be disappointing – Dani Rocheford had been determinedly hostile since she first let Gabrielle in. The scrawny eighteen-year-old clearly didn't have much time for the police – a trait she shared with the other dropouts in this crumbling South Side squat.

'Look, Dani, I appreciate this is tough to talk about.'

'Do you?' the young woman spat back.

'I know what you went through, what you must *still* be suffering and, believe me, I'm genuinely sorry for that.'

Dani snorted, unconvinced.

'But I still need to ask you these questions. It's imperative we find Kyle as soon as we can.'

'If you'd done your job properly in the first place, he wouldn't be out there, would he?'

'No, he wouldn't, and I can only apologize for that. But I

don't want anyone else to have to suffer at his hands. I'm sure you feel the same way.'

The young woman shrugged a begrudging agreement, refusing to meet Gabrielle's eye. The police officer suspected part of her hostility stemmed from a misplaced sense of shame. Redmond had kept Dani hostage in the trailer they used to share for an entire weekend, torturing and degrading her. The memory of her trauma was still fresh.

'So, tell me, when *did* you last see him?'

'Three months ago, maybe a little more. He let himself in, was waiting for me when I came home.'

'Did he harm you?'

'A black eye.' She shrugged, nonchalantly, as if that was a good result.

'What did he want?'

'No idea – he tried to talk to me, but I screamed the place down.'

'Did he say where he'd been? Where he was staying?'

'No. He has an aunt who lives on West Garfield, he sometimes crashes there.'

'We've already visited her.'

'Then your guess is as good as mine. He's not a part of my life any more.'

Gabrielle sensed relief behind her bullishness.

'And when you were together, how would you describe your relationship?'

'*Really?*' she replied, disbelievingly.

'I know it's hard, Dani, I wouldn't be asking these questions unless I had to. It's important.'

The young woman looked a little mollified by Gabrielle's obvious sincerity. Pulling a packet of cigarettes from her pocket, she replied:

'Unpredictable . . . controlling . . . violent.'

'How often did he hurt you?'

'Whenever he had the energy.'

'What did he do?'

'He messed me up. Physically . . . sexually . . .'

'Did he cut you?'

'Sure.'

'With what?'

'Knives, cleavers . . . Once with a pair of bolt cutters . . .'

The last admission hurt. Gabrielle watched as Dani slid a cigarette from the packet with a shaking hand and placed it on her lips.

'How long was he living with you?'

'Six weeks, maybe seven.'

'And during that time was he working?'

Another shrug.

'He worked for a removals firm. A cleaning company. Construction firms. But he got fired from them all, for stealing, hitting on people . . .'

Gabrielle noted this down, making a mental note to call Miller.

'But you won't find him that way,' Dani continued grimly. 'That man changes his name more often than he changes his shorts.'

'While he was here,' Gabrielle replied, logging the warning, 'did he mention anywhere he went as a matter of course? A bar? A pal's house? A club?'

Dani hesitated, her mind turning, then answered:

'He had a trailer. Somewhere he used to keep stuff he was fencing. I think it was in the Lower West Side – I never knew the address.'

Dani continued to look at Gabrielle, the cigarette hanging

unlit from her mouth. Clearly she was hoping that the interview would soon be over. Gabrielle decided to take pity on her – being visited by the ghost of her tormentor had obviously left the young woman shaken and upset.

'Thank you, Dani. You've been very helpful. I really appreciate you taking the time to speak with me.'

Gabrielle held out her hand and reluctantly, embarrassed, Dani reached forward, submitting to a quick handshake, before once more dropping her hand to her side. It was the briefest of exchanges, but enough for Gabrielle to note that two of her fingers were missing. She must have been staring at the injured hand, because Dani now butted in, dismissing her.

'Shut the door on your way out.'

She turned away to light her cigarette and Gabrielle retreated. Moments later, she was on the street again, thoughts tumbling over one another as she walked back to her car. Pausing by her aged Pontiac, she chanced a look back at Dani's apartment. To her surprise, Redmond's ex was now at the window, wreathed in a cloud of cigarette smoke, looking directly at her. It was an image that would stay with Gabrielle for a long time.

The image of a woman haunted by life.

39

Faith sat on a stool, staring at herself. She had spent nearly two months working on this self-portrait, but now she didn't recognize it at all. The shape of her face, her expression, even her cheeky dimples were perfectly rendered, yet she felt as if she were looking at a stranger.

This was the first time she'd been out of bed since she returned from the hospital. She hadn't dared leave the sanctuary of the bedroom while Adam and her mother were at home, she couldn't bear their fussing and concern. But now that her mother had gone, now that she'd finally persuaded Adam to go to the office, she had the house to herself. Tentatively, she'd emerged from her bedroom – she was still sore and walking was painful – eventually making it to her studio.

As she'd stepped inside, she'd looked around her. All the fixtures and fittings were familiar, her trinkets, busts and souvenirs present and correct, yet she felt like an intruder, as if she were viewing the room for the first time. She wasn't surprised or unnerved by this disorientation – since that awful day at the hospital nothing had felt right. Everything was being played out at a distance, as if she were outside herself, watching events unfold from above. Adam would probably say it was some form of denial, an attempt to distance herself from events, and maybe that was true. But if it was, it didn't lessen the pain.

When the midwife had struggled to find a heartbeat, Faith had started to panic. When a second midwife had failed to find signs of life, this time with a new machine, Faith's heart had broken. What happened in the few hours after that remained a blur. She'd tried to get hold of Adam numerous times, but had finally given up – his absence just another part of the inexorable, unfolding nightmare. In the end, it was her mother who'd arrived first, who'd sat with her as she endured the tests which confirmed that the placenta had come away from the uterus, depriving her baby of oxygen and nutrients.

Adam eventually arrived – when, she couldn't say – and he was distraught of course, but she'd had no space for his anguish, not when she was being asked if she wanted to be induced. No, she didn't want to be induced. No, she didn't want a C-section. She just wanted her baby girl to be alive. But in the end, she had acquiesced to taking a cocktail of pills and twelve hideous hours later, baby Annabelle was born. Of course, she was perfect – a spitting image of her mother, right down to the dimples and the thick black hair – so much so that she looked like a resting angel, having a brief sleep before making her bow in the world. Those moments had been so precious, but even these were stained by the sounds of the other mothers in the labour ward, noisily giving birth to happy, healthy offspring.

A few hours later, Annabelle was gone. Taken away to the hospital morgue. Adam had stayed in Faith's room that night, but neither of them had slept a wink. Nor could they bear to walk the hallways for fear of encountering mothers, babies or nurses, none of whom knew quite where to look. Faith could have stayed longer in the hospital – the doctors wanted her to stay so that could monitor her, given her history of depression – but she had wanted to get home. Eventually, they had released her into Adam's care, with a prescription for Tramadol and a series of after-care follow-ups scheduled.

Returning home had not been easy, watching Adam discreetly sliding the bag of unused nappies and baby clothes into the utility room, walking past the closed door to the nursery, but it had been better than lingering in that awful place.

And here she'd remained, dreaming of Annabelle, then waking to the awful reality. She could scarcely distinguish between night and day, hadn't eaten much, but what was she supposed to do? How did you deal with something like this? Adam hadn't dared suggest that it would get better, that she would heal, but she knew he was planning to get her help. She wasn't ungrateful – it had worked before and she needed it badly – but it was still too soon. She wasn't ready yet to articulate her despair.

She'd hoped being in the studio might arouse some kernel of interest or energy, a desire perhaps to express her pain in abstract form. But in fact being here was having the opposite effect. Her self-portrait seemed to goad her, with its wistful, happy expression, seemingly ignorant of the fact that she had given birth to death. Rising, she placed a cloth over the portrait, hiding it from view. It didn't represent her or her life any more – it seemed wrong and untruthful. Everything had changed now. Her baby, her beloved baby girl, had died.

And a part of her had died too.

40

'My story's not very remarkable. It was dope and pills at first – usual stuff – but I had an experience last year which . . . which left me badly traumatized. After that I drank more . . . and eventually started doing H.'

She was right, Kassie thought to herself, as she investigated the frayed cuff of her sleeve, picking at a loose thread. This girl's story was just like all the rest – the nursery slopes of substance abuse, then personal trauma, then hard drugs, then burnout. Not that Kassie wasn't sympathetic – she pitied anyone who'd had a bad time and knew how drugs could take over your life – it's just that it was so predictable, so depressing.

This girl was the third speaker today. The counsellor – what was her name? Rachel? Rebecca? – was determined that everyone should get a chance. But the stories were starting to blur. Kassie knew she should be paying attention, emoting and nodding at the key bits, but the truth was that she didn't want to hear it. The girl was currently describing a family incident that had driven her to hard drugs, but right now Kassie didn't have the bandwidth to take on somebody else's pain. She didn't want to be here. She'd tried NA groups before and was only attending to honour her promise to Adam. Nor did she want to share the basis of *her* trauma. There was no way she could do so without provoking ridicule and, anyway, she had no intention of giving up drugs. Sometimes she felt they were the only things keeping her sane.

'And how long have you been clean now?'

The counsellor was gently moving the conversation on, shifting the girl's focus from past hurt to present successes and future goals. Kassie receded a little further into herself, slipping her hand into her pocket to ferret out the eighth of skunk she'd secreted there. She let her fingers play over the plastic baggie, reassured by its bulk and amused at her rebelliousness in bringing it here.

'I'm so grateful. I'm so grateful to all of you for your support and encouragement . . .'

The girl was crying now. If Kassie could have shoved her fingers in her ears, she would have. She knew she was being unfair, unkind, but her mood was fragile enough as it was.

'We'll take a break shortly,' the counsellor was saying, as the girl dabbed her eyes. 'But first it would be good to hear from our newest member.'

Kassie was jerked from her thoughts, alarmed by this sudden turn in the conversation.

'Welcome, Kassie.'

The group murmured a warm, collective greeting.

'What would you like to share with us today?' the counsellor continued beseechingly.

Kassie tugged at her cuff, the thread coming clean off. What she wanted was to be *away* from here. She could feel the others looking at her – suddenly she felt hot, uncomfortable, claustrophobic.

'Kassie?'

The counsellor – Rochelle, that was her name – was looking at her entreatingly, but still Kassie avoided her gaze. She was starting to feel dizzy, even a little nauseous – why did they never open the windows in these places? – and there was a dull stabbing pain in her head.

'There's no rush. But everyone here has to participate. So . . . in your own time, tell us about your experiences.'

Her words were becoming indistinct now. Kassie's heart was beating fast, she could feel the sweat sliding down her back. She wanted to flee, to burst out of the cramped room into the cool, fresh air, but something was stopping her. And now, though she'd tried to block out her scrutiny, Kassie felt compelled to look at her interrogator.

She fought it – fought it with everything she had – but she couldn't help herself. Slowly, she raised her head, looking Rochelle directly in the eye.

41

The incident room was buzzing. Over the past few days, the numbers of analysts, operators and detectives filling the cavernous room had steadily increased, as more manpower was brought to bear on this unsettling case. Normally requests for extra resources were met with Hoskins' blunt rebuttal, but not this time, such was the pressure from the top for a result. The *Tribune*'s continuing fascination with the case was not helping, and an emotive press conference from Jones's bereaved fiancée had only added fuel to the fire. The consensus in the media, and the general public, was that the CPD was dragging its feet on this one.

Gabrielle's gaze was glued to her phone – she'd just received a reminder from her husband about a school baseball match later – but she didn't need to have her eyes on her team to sense the energy in the room. If the naysayers could be here now, watching them hitting the phone lines, chasing down leads, arguing, analysing, then they would have a very different view of the department's efforts.

'Boss . . .'

Gabrielle turned to see Miller approaching.

'I think I may have something for you . . .'

Gabrielle slid her phone into her handbag.

'Go on . . .'

'Shall we?'

Miller gestured to Gabrielle's office, then stepped inside. Gabrielle followed her, catching a brief glimpse of Montgomery, who was hovering nearby, as she did so. She looked ill at ease, even a little downcast, leading Gabrielle to wonder whether it had in fact been *she* who'd unearthed this lead. Office politics would have to wait, however – hard intel was what they needed now.

'We've been ringing around local construction companies, cleaning outfits, removals firms,' Miller began, as Gabrielle walked past her, slinging her bag down on her desk, 'to see if anyone matching Redmond's description has worked for them in the last six months. And we found this . . .'

She handed Gabrielle a faxed copy of an employee form from a company called CleanEezy.

'Who are they?'

'Carpet cleaning, curtains, that sort of stuff. This guy's been working on and off for them as a freelancer for the past five months.'

Gabrielle looked at the name on the form – Conor Sumner – then at the attached photo. It was a small black-and-white photo, but unless Redmond had a doppelgänger, it was him. The birthmark was unmistakable.

'Have we checked out the address on the form?' Gabrielle asked, urgently. '1566 West Lamont Street. Is that Cicero? Forest View?'

'Doesn't exist,' Miller replied. 'The street stops at 1450. But that's not the interesting part.'

Gabrielle could see the ghost of a smile drift across Miller's lips, as she handed her superior a second piece of paper. Gabrielle took in the contents – it was a copy of a paid invoice from CleanEezy. Her eye was immediately drawn to the client name – Jacob Jones.

'When was this?' Gabrielle demanded.

'Two months ago. Jones gets his carpet cleaned twice a

year, likes to keep the house spick and span. On this occasion, the operative assigned the job –'

'Was Conor Sumner . . .'

Gabrielle's gaze was already fixed on Sumner's name, printed in bold on the company invoice.

'So, two months before Jones vanishes,' Gabrielle continued, thinking aloud, 'Kyle Redmond has the run of the place. Carpet cleaning takes . . . what? Three, four hours?'

Miller nodded.

'A busy guy like Jones isn't going to hang around for that. Presumably Redmond would have had free rein. To go where he liked, do what he pleased. Maybe there were spare keys . . .'

Gabrielle petered out, her mind turning on the possibilities.

'Ok, pull everyone off our other lines for the next few hours,' she continued suddenly. 'We need to find this guy *today*.'

Miller ran from the room to do Gabrielle's bidding. All thoughts of her sons' baseball match had already evaporated, as the familiar adrenaline kicked in. Five minutes ago, Redmond had been one of a number of suspects they'd been investigating. Now he had jumped straight to the top of the list.

42

Rochelle hurried down the street, tugging a packet of cigarettes from her bag. She paused to light one, but was soon on the move again. She had never liked this neighbourhood – there was a reason the rent for the community hall was so low – and she wanted to distance herself from the scene she'd just witnessed.

Inexplicably, she felt embarrassed. It wasn't she who'd freaked out, who'd been ranting and raving, so why did she feel so stupid? It wasn't *her* fault – though obviously something she'd said or done had set the girl off. Up until that point, things had been . . . ok. She had deliberately let some of the other girls share first, to avoid putting the newest member of the group on the spot. She'd hoped Kassie, who appeared closed and truculent, would relax into the session, realizing it was a show of strength, not weakness, to confide in the others about her addiction.

She had tried to be gentle with her, to give her all the time she needed. And, after some words of encouragement, Kassie *had* eventually looked up at her, as if about to speak. Rochelle had taken that as a positive sign . . . but actually that was the moment when everything went wrong. Kassie had stared at Rochelle for a moment, as if pole-axed, then had suddenly launched herself at her, screaming as she did so.

Rochelle had had to break up the group and send the other girls home. She'd called a cab for Kassie, but the teenager refused to leave, insisting she needed to talk to Rochelle, to *warn* her. Warn her about what, for God's sake? Rochelle should have stayed perhaps, but as soon as the cab arrived, she took her leave. Her expertise lay in addiction therapy, not mental health counselling, and, besides, if she was honest with herself, she was scared. The teenager appeared incoherent, yet persistent, clinging to Rochelle for dear life. The girl was actually hurting her, so Rochelle had extricated herself as best she could and got the hell out of there. Maybe it was cowardly, maybe it was an abrogation of her duty, but she had been attacked before during sessions and didn't want to go there again. As soon as she was home, she would call Kassie's outreach team – this was their domain, *not* hers.

A noise behind her made Rochelle turn. Somewhere in the middle distance, a can had been kicked and was now rolling into the gutter. Pulling her bag up on to her shoulder, she hurried on her way. The street was only intermittently lit and, like most of Chicago, had alleyways leading off it. Suddenly Rochelle felt scared and alone.

She picked up her pace, marching towards the 'L' station. She didn't want to run – she told herself that she was being paranoid and that it was unnecessary. In reality, it was because she feared that if she *did* break into a run, someone would suddenly burst out of the shadows in pursuit. She berated herself for her stupidity, but there was no denying how she felt. Her nerves really were shot today.

Another noise behind her. Without breaking stride, she craned her neck around. To her horror, she now spotted her pursuer. It was *Kassie*.

Rochelle stumbled on, dumbfounded, for a second, then turned and sprinted towards the 'L' station at the end of the road. The teenager had been looking directly at her, hurrying towards her – there could be no doubt that she was being pursued. Somewhere behind her, Rochelle heard a cry, but she didn't stop, tearing down the road, her heavy bag crashing into her side as she ran.

She was a hundred yards from the 'L', now fifty, now twenty. She could hear pounding footsteps behind, so she didn't hesitate, slamming her card down on the ticket barrier, before bursting into the station stairwell and climbing it three steps at a time. As she did so, she heard the familiar rattle, felt the vibrations beneath her feet – a train was coming.

'Rochelle, wait!'

Her pursuer had vaulted the barriers and was at the bottom of the stairs, breathless and crazed. Rochelle turned away and ran on to the platform just as the train ground to a halt. Turning left, she pushed through the small stream of commuters disembarking, diving into a carriage near the back of the train.

'Come on, come on,' she muttered, willing the doors to close.

Right on cue, the alarm sounded and the hydraulics sighed. Just as they did so, her pursuer made it on to the platform. A quick scan of the place, then the crazed girl lunged towards the train, even as the doors began to slide shut. Just as she did so, Rochelle made an instinctive decision, stepping purposefully off the train. The doors drew together and, to Rochelle's enormous relief, she saw that her pursuer was now trapped inside.

The train moved off, leaving Rochelle alone on the platform, caught in the gaze of the girl, whose face was now pressed to the window. Rochelle watched her go, breathless and relieved, but, even as she did so, her attention was drawn to the train on the other track, now rattling towards the station from the opposite direction. Without hesitating, Rochelle hurried back down the stairs, darting through the subway and up on to the adjacent platform. Catching the incoming train would take her in the wrong direction . . . but it would take her further away from *her*. Furthermore, there was a cab rank at the next station and today she was willing to swallow the cost of a cross-town journey.

Now more than ever, she just wanted to get home.

43

Adam stood in his office, suffocated by the silence. He had worked in this well-appointed suite for several years now and had had many interesting and surprising experiences. Family fist fights, crass attempts at seduction; he'd even had to chase one teenage patient down the street, after he'd vowed to kill the Mayor (who was an extraterrestrial masquerading as a human). There had been so much noise, so many tears, confessions, accusations and arguments, but now the place seemed lifeless.

Adam hadn't wanted to come here – Faith had virtually kicked him out of the house – but as he'd taken the short drive to his office, his spirits had risen very slightly, hoping that being in his office, dealing with work matters, might be a useful distraction from the agony of the last few days. But standing here, listening to his answering service, looking at his full to bursting inbox, he actually felt worse, his guilt at leaving Faith compounded by a feeling of having abandoned his patients too.

He could hardly have done otherwise, of course. Faith was struggling to process what had happened to them, and in all honesty so was he. He was medically trained, he knew how the human body worked . . . but even so, stillbirth just seemed so *wrong*. It was such a horrific, shocking dead end. All their hopes for the future, all the images they'd conjured of a bouncing, happy baby, seemed like cruel hoaxes now. The excitement had been building month on month only to deliver grief, shock and pain.

He felt like a man standing in the wreckage of life. Faith was at home, sharing his distress, but here were countless others, their files on his desk, their emails accumulating day by day, who were struggling too. People who were psychotic, depressed, suicidal or perhaps tentatively on the road to recovery. Today he felt he understood their pain a little more clearly, though that didn't make him feel any better.

A dog barked on the street outside, snapping Adam out of it. Taking a final swig of his cold coffee, he seated himself at his desk and began the task of messaging his patients. For a few days, they had got either the answering machine or an out-of-office email, neither of which explained the reason for his sudden disappearance. Now he had to articulate it, but as most of his clients knew nothing of his private life, he was able to get away with saying that it had been 'a family emergency'. He felt a fraud – it was much worse than that – but it saved him having to divulge more.

Working his way through the list, he soon came to Kassie. He skipped over her, to contact a couple of clients further down the list, but soon returned to her name. What should he do? He'd said he'd help her, but then had vanished from her life. A part of him still wanted to help her, despite what she'd said to him last time, despite a lingering resentment that she had kept him from Faith during her awful ordeal. But did he have the emotional resilience right now? He felt guilty enough being away from Faith for half an hour. Torn, he ran his finger down the list, searching for another, less complicated case.

The intercom buzzed furiously, making him jump. Crossing to the door, he picked up the receiver and looked at the flickering image on the little screen. Instantly he recognized her. Kassie was staring at her feet, swaying slightly back and forth, but now looked directly up at the camera. Adam's first instinct was to replace the receiver, to pretend there was no one at home. But that seemed childish and Kassie's expression was so earnest that instead he found himself buzzing her in.

He walked back to his desk and waited, listening to the creak of the floorboards as Kassie climbed the stairs. Moments later, she was standing in front of him, breathless and agitated.

'I've been trying to call you.'

'I'm sorry, Kassie, I had to take a few days off. Are you ok?'

'Yes. No . . .'

'What's the matter?' Adam replied carefully, marvelling at how quickly it was possible to slip back into the doctor/patient dynamic.

Kassie paused now, catching her breath, trying to calm herself. Adam had the distinct impression she didn't want to appear too 'crazy' in front of him.

'It's happened again . . .'

Adam could tell by the intensity of her gaze what 'it' meant.

'I went to the NA meeting, like I promised . . . and I saw it. Different person, same thing.'

'Tell me exactly what happened.'

'We don't have time. We need to *warn* her.'

'Kassie . . .'

'You know her. Rochelle . . . the group leader. I don't know her last name, or where she lives, but you have her address, right?'

'I might do,' Adam replied, evasively. 'But let's wind this back a bit. Tell me what happened.'

Kassie clearly wanted to push back, but Adam's tone was firm.

'I went there,' Kassie said impatiently. 'When it was my turn to speak, I looked up at Rochelle and . . . I saw it. It's the same thing, exactly the same as with Jacob Jones . . . Excruciating pain and that horrible, crushing fear.'

Adam stared at her, alarmed by the change in her demeanour.

'I don't remember exactly what happened after that – I lost it a bit, I think – then the next thing I know she's got me a cab and is running out the door. I went after her.'

'You *followed* her?' Adam asked, incredulous.

'Yeah,' Kassie replied, unnerved. 'I followed her to the "L", but she gave me the slip.'

'Kassie . . .'

'What else was I supposed to do?' she protested. 'She's going to die *tonight* and she has no idea.'

'We need to talk about this Kassie,' Adam pushed on, talking over Kassie's attempted interruption, 'but if it'll reassure you, I'll call Rochelle. I'll apologize for today, check that she's all right –'

'No, we need to go round there. She's got hours at the very most.'

'How can you be sure?'

'Because that's what I *see*,' Kassie insisted, visibly angry now. 'I know how people die, I know *when* they die. It's today, trust me, she is going to die *today*.'

'Kassie, we've talked about this. This is not your job. *Your* job is to kick the drugs and concentrate on getting better –'

'You think I'm nuts.'

'No. I don't like that word and I would never say it about you –'

'You look at my record, my . . . history and . . . and you write me off as –'

'No. A hundred times no.'

'Then try and understand that this is *real*. This is happening. You said that you would help me, that you would go with me.'

'And I will. But think about it for a moment, Kassie. You told me previously that everything you "see" is set in stone. What difference can your intervention possibly make?'

'I have to do *something*. I can't just abandon her to *that*.'

'But if it won't make any difference?'

'Maybe it *will*. Maybe I *can* save her.'

She was staring at him defiantly, her chest heaving, as she tried to contain her emotion.

'And if I can help her then . . . then maybe I can help myself.'

It was said hesitantly, even a little fearfully. And now Adam got it. Kassie's grim prediction of her murder had continued to occupy him, despite the weight of his recent loss. He saw now that Kassie's desire to 'save' Rochelle was driven as much by self-interest as by common humanity. If she could subvert one of her visions, if she could prove that her 'gift' was fallible, then maybe she could wriggle out of her own death sentence. It was scary to see how deeply she had been seduced by her alternative narrative of events.

'I know this feels very real to you, Kassie. And that it scares you. But, trust me, everything's going to be ok. First, we need to get you home, so you can get some rest, then maybe we should talk about other approaches. Consider some short-term medication perhaps –'

'For God's sake –'

'But I said I'll call Rochelle. We can do it right now –'

'We need to go *down* there.'

'*We?*'

'Yes! I'm fifteen, Adam.'

'But shouldn't you be running a mile from me,' Adam replied, irritation creeping into his tone now. 'If what you're saying is true . . .'

It was a base, disingenuous argument, but Adam didn't know how else to puncture her belief.

'Maybe,' she conceded calmly. 'But you're the only person who's ever been prepared to listen to me, to take me seriously, so . . . perhaps we've been brought together for a *reason*. If I fail, we both lose. But if we can save Rochelle, if we can stop this thing happening . . .'

Adam said nothing, silenced by her defiance.

'Please, Adam. I know you don't believe me. I know I sound crazy. But you have to trust me. You're the only person I can turn to.'

'I don't know that now is the best time.'

'I won't ask anything else of you. If I'm wrong, I'm wrong. I'll never mention it again. But I'm not. She's going to be killed now – tonight – unless we do something . . .'

Adam took in the shaking, determined teenager in front of him. He thought of her mother, the cops and teachers who belittled her, the strength of her illness, his promise to help her . . . and then he thought of Faith, her tears, her bitter anguish, and the silent baby girl he had held in his arms.

'I'm sorry, Kassie.

'Please –'

'I'd like to help you, but I can't right now.'

'Just do this one thing for m—'

'No.'

It had obviously come out harder than he'd intended, as Kassie flinched. Softening his tone, he took a small step towards her.

149

'I need to be with Faith right now.'

Kassie stared at him, scarcely believing what she was hearing.

'And you need to go home. I'll call you in a couple of days, or if you want to talk to someone today, I can refer you to a colleague who –'

'You promised me you'd help me.'

'Kassie, I'm doing what I can, but –'

'You're a liar.'

Kassie turned on her heel, furious.

'Kassie, please don't go. Let me drive y—'

The door slammed shut behind her, leaving Adam alone.

44

She killed the engine, extinguishing the lights. Moments earlier, they had illuminated the grim, urban vista of South Morgan Street, a horseshoe strip of warehouses and trailers on the banks of the South Branch Chicago River, but now the outbuildings were lost to the darkness.

'Ready?' Gabrielle asked, turning to Miller.

'Hundred per cent,' her deputy replied cheerily, patting the holster under her vest.

'Easy now. We just want to talk to this guy,' Gabrielle admonished her gently, picking up a flashlight and climbing out of the car.

It had taken some ringing round, but eventually they'd found a colleague from CleanEezy who thought he remembered the street where Redmond had his trailer. Further checks revealed a riverside unit that had been hired three months before, using one of the aliases Redmond favoured. Now it came into view, perched on the river bank, framed by the shimmering darkness of the Chicago River.

Gabrielle's eyes darted left and right, as she crept towards it, searching for signs of movement, for possible dangers. But the road, which was usually bustling and busy during the working day, was deathly quiet tonight. Her pace slowed as she reached the trailer and she raised her arm, signalling for Miller to hang back. Was it foolish to come here so light in numbers? Gabrielle had toyed with a show of force, descending on the remote trailer with a full team of officers, but had decided against it. Redmond was still only a suspect, she told herself, and, besides, a heavy-handed approach might alert him to their presence, which was the last thing Gabrielle wanted. There were plenty of possible escape routes – the river, the scrubland behind the trailers – and she couldn't risk him slipping through their fingers.

The trailer's heavy-duty door was securely locked with three industrial padlocks, so Gabrielle moved past it to the nearest window. She intended to dart a look inside, but as she peered through the metal grille, she saw only her faint reflection staring back. Moving closer, she saw that some kind of material, black and impenetrable, covered the window inside. There was another window further along, but this was similarly protected. This was not a place which welcomed visitors.

Gabrielle turned away, wondering what secrets it contained. As she did so, her eye fell once more on the river, which continued its steady, swirling flow, and the muddy banks that bordered it. Bending down, Gabrielle scooped up a finger's worth of mud and shined her flashlight on it. It was a deep black, just like the caked deposits on the tyres of Jones's Lincoln.

'Any sign of life?'

Gabrielle turned to find Miller approaching cautiously.

'Nothing so far,' Gabrielle replied, wiping the mud from her finger.

'What do you want to do?'

'There's not a lot we *can* do. We can set up eyes on the place, but other than that . . .'

Miller nodded as if agreeing, then said:

'Do you want to take a look inside?'

A frown settled on Gabrielle's brow.

'Not without a warrant.'

'Those windows are old and flimsy,' Miller continued, unabashed. 'And you get a lot of disreputable types down by the river at night . . .'

Her meaning was clear. And it was true it would take a day or more to get a warrant. But even though Gabrielle yearned to know what lay behind the blank exterior of the trailer, there was no question of risking any future prosecution by breaking protocol.

'When you're a little more experienced, Detective Miller, you'll understand why that's not a good idea. But I appreciate your enthusiasm.'

Miller looked disappointed, but took the admonishment in the spirit it was offered. Turning away, Gabrielle walked back to the car, deep in thought. She had come here hoping to find Redmond's hideout, but was leaving empty-handed. There were certain indicators linking this derelict place to their kill site, yet they had no concrete evidence that Redmond still used the trailer. All they could do for now was put out a general alert for him and hope an eagle-eyed officer or member of the public spotted him.

Irritated, Gabrielle climbed back in the car and fired up the engine. Despite their best efforts, they were no nearer finding their elusive prime suspect. Where *was* Redmond right now? And, more importantly, what was he up to?

45

Rochelle closed the door, securing the deadlock and sliding on the chain. She had checked and double-checked that she wasn't being followed but, after today's strange events, she wasn't taking any chances. She did a quick circuit of the house, making sure that the windows were locked and that the French windows were secured. Finding everything in order, she headed for the kitchen, slumping down on a chair, relieved but exhausted.

She needed a drink. A shot of bourbon, a glass of wine, something to calm her down. But even as she contemplated dragging her bones to the fridge, she remembered her resolution to call Kassie's outreach team. Sighing, she went back into the hall, dug her cell phone out of her bag and scrolled through her Contacts. Predictably, given the hour, Kassie's social worker did not pick up, but Rochelle left a brief, measured message, outlining her concerns, signing off with a suggestion that they speak in the morning.

Her duty done, Rochelle dumped her phone on the table. As she did so, it pinged loudly – flashing up an alert. The last few hours had been so unsettling, so confusing, that she'd forgotten that her favourite show was going to start soon. The drink would have to wait. She'd have a quick shower, then she'd call Kat, see if she wanted to come over. They could watch *Scandal*, eat Ben & Jerry's, empty a bottle of Pinot. Cheered by this thought, Rochelle afforded herself a brief smile, then skipped up the stairs to her bedroom.

46

His eyes followed her as she entered the room, wondering what she was going to do first. He had watched her on many occasions and discovered that she was a creature of habit. Normally, she would step out on to the balcony to grab a quick cigarette, before changing out of her work clothes. Other times, she would collapse on to the bed and lose herself in her phone, scrolling endlessly through Facebook. If things were bad, however, if she was tearful or agitated, she would shower straight away.

She was already undressing, unzipping her dress and stepping out of it. From his vantage point in her closet, he peered through the slats, watching intently as she slung the dress on the floor, then sat down on the bed to peel off her tights. He had no fear of discovery, she always tossed her clothes aside, leaving them on the floor until bedtime. A more fastidious person might have given him trouble, but not her.

She was down to her underwear now, a pretty matching set. Arching her back, she unclipped her bra, then slid off her pants. Then she stepped casually over her discarded underwear and walked into the en suite bathroom. Moments later, he heard the shower door shut, then the familiar groan of the pipes as the water started up. It was a sound which always made him smile, for reasons he couldn't fully explain.

He counted to fifty, tempering his desire to hurry to her, then quietly emerged from the closet. He darted a look towards the bathroom – the door was ajar, but he could see the shower screen was nicely steamed up – then padded quickly but quietly over the carpet. Placing a gloved hand on the handle, he eased the door fully open. Stepping inside, he checked his progress once more, waiting to see if his arrival had been detected. But Rochelle seemed oblivious, humming quietly to herself as she showered.

Now was the time to do it, now was the time to act, but he hesitated, unable to resist the sight in front of him. Blurred though his view was by the condensation, he could still make out the curve of her thighs, the swell of her breasts, her long, blonde hair hanging down behind her. Already he could feel his arousal growing, but this was no time for self-indulgence, so he took a decisive step towards her, pulling the bathroom door gently shut behind him.

47

Adam paused on the threshold, as he slid his key into the lock. He was trying to remain calm and composed, but he suddenly realized that he felt nervous. Crazy, really; this was his home – the pretty little row house he had always returned to with such enthusiasm – and now he was overcome with trepidation about what he might find on the other side of the door.

He knew he was being foolish. Faith had battled with depression as a young woman, but she was much more resilient now and wasn't the dramatic type, so he knew he wouldn't find anything *bad* bad. It was just that it hurt so much to see her in pain. For the past few days, she looked like she had been hollowed out by her experiences. Adam had spent his whole life dealing with other people's problems – the emotions and crises of total strangers – yet dealing with Faith's anguish was proving difficult. He found it so hard to keep his own feelings in check when the woman he worshipped crumpled in front of him.

Turning the key, he stepped inside. All seemed calm, all seemed quiet . . . except now he heard the kettle boiling. Unaccountably, this simple domestic act raised his spirits and he hastened into the kitchen, where he found Faith, dressed in jogging pants and top, leaning against the counter.

'Ta dah!' she joked grimly, highlighting the fact that she was dressed.

'I'm impressed.'

He was trying to sound jovial, but it sounded forced. He

could see Faith was making the effort, but her eyes revealed her pain.

'And that's not all,' she continued, her tone unreadable as she turned away to make herself a cup of tea. 'I went into the studio today.'

'Great. How did that g—'

'Too soon,' was the brief response.

'Of course, no need to rush. One step at a time.'

He had said the latter phrase so many times in the last few days that it already sounded like a cliché. Faith didn't respond, replacing the kettle on the stand and handing him a cup of tea.

'How did you get on?'

'Ok. I made most of the calls I needed to.'

'That's good.'

'Still a few more to do, but I've got their numbers. I can do them from here . . .'

Adam petered out, pointedly turning his attention to his tea. He'd decided not to tell Faith about his encounter with Kassie, but she was still looking at him, expecting more.

'Is everything ok? You look . . . tense.'

'Everything's fine,' he replied tightly.

'So . . . ?'

She was staring directly at him, allowing no room for evasion or obfuscation.

'Kassie came to see me. At the office.'

'Right,' Faith replied warily. 'What did she want?'

Adam wasn't quite sure how to respond.

'Adam?'

'She wanted help.'

'Because?'

'She had another episode.'

'Another vision?'

Adam nod-shrugged. He didn't like to call them that.

'And? Did she tell you who it involved?'

'Yes.'

'So . . . ?'

'So nothing.'

'What do you mean?'

'I . . . I sent her away.'

Even as he said it, he felt a little ashamed.

'What?' Faith responded, sounding genuinely shocked.

'I didn't want to . . . but I can't get involved with her right now. We've got too much on our plates –'

'This is work –'

'So?'

'So it's got nothing to do with us and if you can help her –'

'I've told her I can't, so there's no point discuss—'

'I think you should reconsider.'

'Why?'

'Because I'm not a fucking china doll.'

The words shot out, hard and angry. Adam looked up at his wife, could see the emotion bubbling just beneath the surface.

'I know you're trying to help me,' Faith continued, struggling to master herself. 'But I'm a big girl. I'll get through it.'

'I just want to make sure –'

'And being treated like a child is *not* going to help. Shitty as it is . . . life goes on.'

Adam couldn't deny that. Much as he'd wanted to blot out the world during the past few days, life kept on intruding.

'So, if Kassie is in trouble, if she needs you enough to seek you out at your office . . .' She fixed him directly in the eye as she concluded: '. . . then you must help her.'

48

'Have a seat, *kochanie*, and something to eat.'

Kassie was struggling to take in the scene in front of her. Her mother was sitting at the table, smartly dressed in a pretty, floral-print dress with a smile stretched across her face. In front of her was a small feast – lots of Polish delicacies of course, but a few American treats too that generally were not allowed.

'Please . . .'

Kassie seated herself cautiously and began to nibble an Oreo. The whole situation was so staged, so forced, that Kassie half expected her mother to produce a nice Polish boy for her to marry, like a magician pulling a rabbit from a hat. She had been expecting the usual interrogation, or at least a bout of recrimination, but not *this*.

'How was your day? How was your . . . NA meeting?'

Her mother had so far avoided any mention of her latest round of addiction counselling, so this was another alarming note.

'It was good, thanks,' she lied clumsily.

Kassie had returned home in despondent mood, racking her brains as to how she might get Rochelle's address or cell number. She had no idea of her last name, no friends within the group, and, after today's performance, it was highly unlikely that any of them would take Kassie into their confidence. Not that her mother knew – or cared – about that.

'How was *your* day?' Kassie continued, fumbling an attempt at conversation.

'It was fine, thank you. I went to church after work, so I visited the deli there, picked up a few of your favourite treats . . .'

'Thank you,' Kassie murmured, picking up her fork and leaning over to spear a dumpling.

Kassie slid it into her mouth, before helping herself to a slice of stuffed cabbage and disposing of that too. Her mother let her eat for a few minutes, before resuming their conversation.

'I was speaking to Father Nowak the other day . . .'

Kassie's fork stopped in mid-air, as she turned to look at her mother. Now they were getting to the meat of this particular feast.

'You remember Father Nowak?'

'Of course.'

Kassie was tempted to add, 'How could I forget?' but resisted.

'He certainly remembers you and is very keen to see you back at church.'

'Sure, whatever,' Kassie replied inconclusively.

'I was thinking we might go today, after you've eaten of course . . .'

'Today?'

'There's a service starting in one hour. We could easily make it.'

She had already done the math, probably knew exactly what time the No. 22 bus would turn up, so though a trip to St Stanislaus Kostka was the very last thing Kassie wanted, there was no point fighting it. She suspected her mother would spontaneously combust if she refused, and, besides, she could use the service as thinking time – somehow she *had* to find Rochelle.

The journey across town was uneventful and before long they were in the cavernous church that Kassie remembered so well from her early years. The service was just beginning, so they took their seats quickly, three rows from the front. Even as they sat down, Kassie saw a look pass between her mother and the portly priest. Clearly this whole thing was a set-up, hatched by a concerned mother and her benevolent confessor.

Kassie tried to push her growing anger aside and concentrate on what was being said – she owed her mother that at least. There were Father Nowak's usual introduction, then the Invocation, then the Liturgy, and before long Kassie found herself dropping down on to her prayer cushion, as the Eucharistic prayers commenced.

'The Lord be with you . . .'

She closed her eyes and clasped her hands together, muttering the words that came automatically to her.

'And with your spirit.'

She wanted to focus on their meaning, to see if they held any residual power for her, but her mind kept straying to Rochelle and she found it hard to concentrate. An elbow in the ribs suggested her mother had noticed her distraction – was she making noises again? – so she redoubled her efforts.

'Blessed is he who comes in the name of the Lord . . .'

But now she became aware of something else, another distraction. Someone's cell phone was ringing. No, *her* cell was ringing.

She plucked it out and looked at the screen. A few people had turned to look at them and her mother gripped her by the wrist.

'Turn it off,' her mother hissed.

But Kassie was already pulling away from her. The caller was Adam Brandt.

At last, someone had answered her prayers.

49

'When we get there, I'll do the talking. You stay in the car.'

Kassie didn't look happy with this suggestion, but she shrugged her acquiescence. Whether Adam could rely on her to honour this deal when it came to it was another matter entirely.

'What are you going to say to her?'

'I'm going to say that I heard about the incident at today's session and that I wanted to check that she was ok, to apologize.'

Adam knew Rochelle Stevens, having met her at several industry seminars. Not well enough to call on her at home really, but he thought he could get away with it, and if it helped to calm Kassie, it would be worth it.

'And then what?' Kassie interrupted, intruding on his thoughts.

'Then nothing. We are doing this to reassure you, not to freak her out.'

'Just because she's ok now doesn't mean she will be later –'

'Look, I'm not sure what else we can do,' Adam replied impatiently. 'Unless you want me to lock her up.'

Kassie was about to respond, but Adam saw it coming and talked over her.

'So, we'll stick to the plan. We'll check she's ok and then we'll be on our way. Your mother's probably already freaking out as it is.'

'I'll deal with her.'

Adam wasn't sure exactly how Kassie was planning to do this and in an unchivalrous moment hoped she wouldn't drag his name into it. What he was doing was unprofessional and unethical – not to mention foolhardy.

'Here we go,' he said steadily, as they turned into Washington Close.

The road was quiet and dimly lit, but the house numbers were clearly marked and Adam counted them down as they crawled along the tarmac.

'Twenty . . . eighteen . . . sixteen . . .'

No. 14 came into view and Adam guided the car gently to the kerb.

'Stay,' he said warningly, as he opened the driver's door.

'All right, all right, I'm not a dog,' she responded, irritably.

Adam didn't linger to hear the rest, shutting the car door and marching away. The house seemed lifeless, dark inside save for a single light burning on the first floor. Swallowing his misgivings, he walked quickly up to the front door and pressed the doorbell.

It sounded, long and loud, echoing through the house. Adam's anxiety was mounting – what would he say to her? – but there was no sign of movement within. So he rang again, keeping his finger pressed down this time.

'Well?'

Adam withdrew his finger and turned to find Kassie standing next to him.

'I told you to stay in the –'

'Any sign of her?'

'Not that I can see.'

Abandoning the front door, Kassie pressed her face up against a window. Squinting, she tried to penetrate the darkness within.

'I can see her bag. She had it with her this afternoon. And her cell is on the hall table, so she definitely came home.'

'Perhaps she's gone to bed.'

'She's not answering the door. And it's hardly late.'

'Maybe she's gone out?' Adam replied.

'Without her phone and bag?'

Kassie was already on the move, marching up to the garage door and trying the handle. But it remained locked and unyielding. Adam cast a nervous look across the street.

'Kassie. Come away from there.'

But his hissed warning had no effect. Instead, Kassie moved off again, rounding the front of the house and disappearing down a passageway to the side. Wary of drawing attention to himself, Adam decided against calling out again and hurried after her instead.

He found her in the backyard, peering intently through the French windows.

'Locked.'

She banged on the window. But it elicited no response inside. Adam turned to her once more.

'Ok, we've done all we can do for now. I'll text her, asking her to call me in the morn—'

But Kassie was already climbing up on to the windowsill.

'Kassie, what are you doing?'

'The French windows are only bolted at the top, so if I can get a hand in . . .'

'And how do you intend to –'

Kassie rammed her elbow through a tiny feature window. Brushing the glass away, she covered her hand with her sleeve and reached inside to slide the bolt open, before jumping down once more. Teasing open the French windows, she turned to Adam and whispered:

'Coming?'

50

'Hello?'

Kassie's voice echoed round the interior of the house, but there was no reply. Adam joined her, stepping carefully over the broken glass. She half expected him to grab her and drag her out again but, shooting an irritated look at her, he strode past her and shouted:

'Rochelle?'

Silence filled the house.

'Rochelle, it's me, Adam Brandt. There's no reason to be afraid, but if you are here, perhaps you could come down?'

There was no response, but a slight creak upstairs made their ears prick up.

'Rochelle?'

Still nothing. Kassie stepped cautiously into the living area. It was gloomy, empty, so she moved forward into the hall. Immediately her eyes fell on Rochelle's shoulder bag and the cell phone and keys on the table. She reached out to pick them up, but Adam put his hand on hers to stop her.

'Don't get yourself in any deeper than you already have.'

For once Kassie did as she was asked. Adam passed her now, poking his nose into the small kitchen. But there was nothing of any interest there, so, turning, they mounted the stairs to the second floor. The third step creaked loudly and, wincing, Adam changed his route, keeping close to the edge of the boards. Kassie followed suit and they soon found themselves on the upstairs landing.

Only two doors led off it, both to small bedrooms. Kassie stepped cautiously into the first one, but, flicking on the light, she found an ordinary guest bedroom. The bed was neatly made, freshly laundered clothes were hanging on a rack nearby and as Kassie ran her finger along the chest of drawers next to her, she discovered that a thin film of dust coated the surface.

Turning, she joined Adam in the master bedroom. There were framed photos here, a full linen bin and one of the closet doors was ajar, but otherwise the room was neat and tidy. Adam teased open the closet and again Kassie held her breath – foolishly, she knew, as she didn't really expect any-one to be in there – before turning away to investigate the linen bin. She wasn't surprised to find the dress that Rochelle had been wearing earlier stuffed in it at the top, alongside a bra, panties and a pair of tights.

The sight of these made Kassie feel inexplicably tense. Had she changed and gone somewhere? Or had she been attacked while naked and vulnerable? Marching forward, she pushed open the bathroom door. It was warmer than the bedroom, a little humid too, but, as with the other rooms, everything seemed to be in order. There was no sign of dis-ruption, or a struggle . . . or Rochelle.

'So?'

Adam had joined her. Kassie studied the bathroom, say-ing nothing.

'She's not here, Kassie. And nothing's out of place.'

'She obviously came home, went for a shower . . .'

'Like normal people do.'

'Something's not right. Why would she go out without her purse, her phone?'

'Perhaps she forgot them. Or popped out to visit a neighbour.'

'I don't buy it.'

'Look around you, Kassie. There's no sign of the bogeyman.'

Kassie gave Adam a dirty look – didn't like his tone – and moved away. She knew he was here on sufferance, but she wasn't prepared to be mocked.

She scanned the sink, the mirror, the shower. The screen was still wet and kneeling down she ran her fingers over the surface of the shower mat. It was wet – no, it was saturated.

Immediately Kassie's mind began to turn. Why was it so wet? Was it possible that Rochelle had been attacked while showering? That her attacker had used the mat to mop up the spilled water? Or was it possible she had got it all wrong? That the scene in front of her was entirely innocent? Whatever the reason, she wouldn't get the chance to speculate further, because she now felt Adam's hand on her arm.

'That's enough now, Kassie. It's time to go.'

51

Her lips moved silently, but relentlessly. Head down, her hands clasped together, she was pleading for mercy.

St Stanislaus was all but deserted and Natalia cut a lonely figure among the empty pews. The worshippers had departed and Father Nowak had retired to attend to some administrative matters, much to Natalia's relief given Kassandra's sudden, unforgivable departure. She had promised to bring her to heel, to help her connect with the church again, but Natalia's lack of control, her lack of authority, had been cruelly exposed by her daughter's disobedience. Nobody had said anything of course, but Natalia was sure they were all talking about her – another black mark against the family. This she could handle, she was used to the elderly housewives gossiping, but it was the look of disappointment on Father Nowak's face which had cut deep.

Embarrassment had turned to fury, then eventually to despair. She had tried to put her foot down, she had tried to be nice, but nothing was working. She felt helpless, alone, and not for the first time cursed her husband for departing this life so early, leaving her to soldier on by herself. As ever when these dark thoughts assailed her, she turned to God. She had always been a dutiful Christian, raising money for the church, going on peace marches, praying for the Holy Father every day, and she felt sure that she would not be deserted in her hour of need. So she prayed fiercely, relentlessly, mouthing the words that would bring her – and Kassie – salvation.

But somehow they weren't landing tonight. The wind had picked up steadily throughout the service, as it often did in Chicago, whistling through the huge church. Wood creaked, doors banged, shutters turned on their hinges – during the service Father Nowak had had to turn the volume up on his microphone to be heard above the racket. Since then, the ferocity of the wind had only increased. Natalia wasn't one to be paranoid, but it seemed tonight as though the more she prayed, the more violent the wind became. Was it possible God was angry with her? For her failures? For her weakness?

Bang! A shutter slapped the fabric of the church once more, making Natalia jump. She raised her voice, saying the words out loud now, fighting nature's interruption. Bang! Bang! The response was swift and violent, the volume rising another notch. Now the wind was shrieking through the church, seeking out the tiny gaps and cracks, ruffling hymnals, blowing newsletters up into the air. Clamping her eyes shut, Natalia persevered, calling out now for God's mercy, for his guidance. Bang! Bang! Bang!

Suddenly Natalia found herself on her feet, her nerve failing her. Looking around at the creaking doors, the flapping shutters, she suddenly felt unaccountably scared, as if she was in danger, as if the church might suddenly collapse in on itself. For a moment, she thought about calling for Father Nowak, then suddenly she turned and fled for the exit.

Bursting out on to the street, she was immediately knocked backwards, the wind roaring directly over her. It was starting to rain, big drops landing with a splat on the stone steps in front of her. Pulling her scarf around her face, Natalia hurried away down the road.

She had come here seeking salvation, but had found only anger and violence.

52

'We should call 911.'

Adam and Kassie were back in his car, having left Rochelle's house.

'And tell them what?' Adam countered.

'That Rochelle is missing.'

'We don't know that.'

'Her keys and phone are there, you saw that. Why would she leave them behind?'

She turned, her eyes boring into him. It was a direct challenge – and one he had to face down, for both their sakes.

'Look, Kassie, in the police's eyes, you are still a person of interest in the Jacob Jones murder . . .'

Kassie paused, looking confused, even a little troubled by this information.

'And I'm an indulgent shrink, who shouldn't be humouring you. They will say that there is no evidence that a crime has been committed.'

Kassie tried to interject, but Adam talked over her.

'And they would be *right*. I admit Rochelle's behaviour –'

'Her disappearance, you mean.'

'– is a little odd. But that's all it is. Unless we have concrete proof that she's been abducted or hurt, then the cops won't do a thing.'

'So we're just going to abandon her?'

'We can try again in the morning. She may have resurfaced by then.'

'She'll be dead by then . . .'

'You don't know that.'

'. . . and it will be on *your* conscience.'

The words exploded out of her, stunning Adam into silence. Kassie was flustered, red in the face, and he was surprised to see tears pricking her eyes.

'This was a mistake,' she continued accusingly, wrenching the door open.

'Don't run off, Kassie. It's late – you shouldn't be out alone.'

She paid him no heed, however, clambering out of the car.

'At least, let me give you a lift home . . .'

But his words drifted away into the night. She was already halfway down the street, hurrying away as fast as she could.

Adam drove home, drumming his fingers on the steering wheel. He was angry and distracted – worrying about Kassie, about Rochelle and – if he was being honest – himself too. What was he doing? Why had he volunteered to help Kassie at all, if he didn't believe what she was saying? What was he hoping to achieve? If he was really concerned for her welfare, as he'd intimated to Faith, then he should have talked her down, persuaded her not to pursue Rochelle. But he had singularly failed in this – Kassie's conviction that Rochelle was in danger was rock solid and she'd been determined to act upon it. She, at least, had no doubts about the significance or accuracy of her 'gift', about her ability to read the future.

Privately, Adam had resisted her reading of events from the start. Not simply because it ran counter to his education, his training, but also because of its implications. If Kassie was right about Jacob Jones, about Rochelle, if she *could* accurately predict people's fates, then it meant . . . what? That he was a murderer? That he would *kill* her?

The idea was ridiculous. He had spent his whole life helping people, healing them. He was *not* a violent man. More than that, he liked Kassie, so in what world was it possible that he would harm her? He pushed the thought away, irritated by himself for thinking it. He must help Kassie, not encourage her wild fantasies. He should revert back to his original approach, using the skills he'd fostered over many years to counter the source of her psychosis. That was the way to help her – not by playing detectives in the middle of the night.

He was cheered slightly by this thought, as he pulled up outside his house. It had been a disturbing evening, but things would be different from now on. He would concentrate his efforts on trying to get back some sense of normality – at work, at home, in his heart.

Easing open the front door, he stepped inside. He expected to find Faith still up – she had been watching a lot of late-night TV since returning from hospital. But the lights were out and the house was shrouded in darkness.

Dropping his keys on the hall table, he padded through the living room, past the deserted kitchen and on towards the bedroom. The lights were out here too and, stepping inside, Adam spotted the horizontal form of Faith, swathed in the duvet. She had obviously opted for an early night, though whether this was a good sign or not, he couldn't tell. Either she couldn't face the world and had retreated to bed, or she finally felt genuinely tired and was trying to refresh herself with a decent night's sleep. God knows it had been a while since either of them had experienced one of those.

He shed his clothes in the darkness and slid into bed

beside her. She didn't stir and as he settled himself down carefully on his side of the bed, he listened intently, hoping to pick up the sound of her breath, rising and falling gently. But he could hear nothing. Pulling the duvet up around his chin, he closed his eyes and tried to blot out the thoughts buzzing round his head.

'Everything ok?'

Her voice made him jump. He'd been convinced that she was asleep.

'With Kassie, I mean.'

'False alarm,' he replied, turning to her.

'Good.'

'She's gone home. To be with her mom.'

It was a lie – he had no idea where she'd actually gone – and he regretted telling it. The image it conjured up of mother and daughter in the family home could only be hurtful to Faith.

'I'm glad she's ok,' Faith muttered, her voice catching slightly.

She turned away from him and said no more. But Adam could tell by the slight movement of her shoulders, by the sharp, silent intakes of breath that she was crying. For a moment, he felt utterly stricken, hollowed out by the sound of his wife in pain, then, remembering himself, he rolled over and put his arm around her. Normally, he would have slipped it round her belly, but this time he laid it gently on her thigh. He held her, hoping this might be enough to stem her distress.

'Do you think . . . do you think we'll ever be ready to try again?'

For a moment, Adam was speechless. Where had this thought come from? It was far too early to be thinking about that. They were still trying to process the awfulness of Anna-belle's death and, besides, after everything they'd been through to get pregnant in the first place, it seemed a huge mountain to climb. Something they could only consider once they had lived through their present grief.

'I . . . don't know, Faith,' he said falteringly, aware he had to say something. 'But maybe . . . we need to give ourselves a little time first?'

Time was not on their side. Faith was already in her late thirties and, given their history, the odds were stacked against them. But it was also true that neither of them was in the right frame of mind to take on something that could be so damaging, so hurtful. Even so, he knew it wasn't what Faith wanted to hear, his weasel words sounding unconvincing and evasive.

Adam waited, expecting – fearing – a follow-up. But to his surprise Faith didn't respond. Instead she turned away from him, pulling the sheet up to her chin. Reluctantly, he disengaged, returning to his side of the bed. He had said the wrong thing. And he desperately wanted to make amends. But there was nothing he could say to ease her pain. So instead he lay there, next to his motionless wife. Husband and wife united in grief and silence.

'Look what the cat dragged in . . .'

Gabrielle was used to her husband's good-natured barbs and was never riled by them. Principally because, on the whole, his censure was deserved.

'I know and I'm sorry . . . Tell me the ball game was a non-event.'

'Your elder son hit two home runs, your younger son *three*.'

'Man . . .' Gabrielle moaned, tossing her bag and coat on to a chair and collapsing next to Dwayne on the sofa. 'I am in so much trouble.'

'I think we're talking one video game at least. Possibly two.'

He eased himself up off the sofa, kissing her gently on the forehead.

'Still it wasn't all bad. I got to spend some time with the moms, some of whom are *hot*.'

Gabrielle threw a cushion at him, but he was already half-way to the kitchen.

'I'll get beer and chips, you hit Netflix. You eaten something?'

'Chips are fine,' Gabrielle responded, picking up the remote.

Lying back, she scrolled through the menu, until she found *When We First Met*. Moments later, Dwayne was back by her side, clinking bottles with her as the show began. Gabrielle treasured these moments – small oases of normality in a life that was riddled with stress, anguish and danger. She knew her job took its toll on her husband, her boys and herself too, if she was honest, which is why the opportunity to play at being a normal, happy couple was so important.

The episode began and Gabrielle worked hard to immerse herself in it. The romantic shenanigans of Noah Ashby and his cohorts usually provided much needed escapism, but tonight she couldn't settle – thoughts of their fruitless search for Kyle Redmond returning to nag at her. Despite a city-wide alert, there was still no sign of him. Chicago was a big place, nearly three million souls pounding its busy streets every day, but was it really possible to just *disappear* like that?

'Ow.'

Dwayne's elbow had jabbed her in her ribs.

'Focus. You're not at work now.'

Jabbing him back, she obliged, concentrating hard on the unfolding drama. But the reality was that with cases like these you were *never* off the job. Every mistake, every delay, was significant because of what it might mean. Despite their best efforts, they were still no closer to an arrest, no closer to bringing this distressing case to a satisfactory conclusion.

Somewhere out there a killer was stalking Chicago.

54

'Please, talk to me . . .'

Her voice sounded weak and cracked.

'Why won't you *speak* to me?'

The man in the mask ignored her, pulling a duffelbag across the floor towards him. Desolate, Rochelle started to cry, salty tears and mucus stinging her battered throat. She had never felt this bad in her life – it was like she'd been in a serious car accident. She felt dizzy and disoriented and was unable to turn her head without vicious pains flaring up her neck, yet she knew this was the least of her worries. Her abductor had not said a word since she'd come to in this awful place and with each passing second her terror increased.

She had been at home, washing away the cares of an upsetting day, when suddenly the shower screen had flown open. Rough hands had grabbed her and before she could register what was happening, she was on the bathroom floor, her naked legs sliding hopelessly over the wet tiles. Then that awful choking feeling.

The next thing she knew, she was here, swathed in darkness, naked and exposed, her arms and legs bound behind her, feeling the crinkle of that awful plastic beneath her toes. Disoriented, terrified, she had screamed and screamed, but her abductor hadn't responded, calmly going about his business unperturbed. He was dressed in a boiler suit and would have looked like an ordinary, everyday workman, were it not for the ski mask which concealed his features and his persistent, pitiless silence.

'Please . . .' she croaked once more. 'Tell me what you want? I've got money . . . my dad's got money . . . What do you *want*?'

The man said nothing, but ceased searching now. Straightening up, he turned towards Rochelle. The room was dark and close, a single paraffin lamp offering a weak light, but still the sight of him chilled her blood. Clamped in his right hand was a butcher's cleaver. The flickering light of the lamp danced wickedly off its glistening blade.

'Please don't hurt me . . .'

Tears were streaming down Rochelle's face now. Her captor didn't react, merely cocking his head to appraise her distress, before moving towards her.

'I'm begging you . . .'

She was sobbing freely.

'Don't kill me . . .'

He came to a halt right in front of her. Calmly, he ran the blunt edge of the cleaver down her cheek. The steel felt cold and cruel on her skin.

'Do you know who I am?' he breathed.

'No, no, not at all . . .'

'Do you know what I *do*?'

'No, I know nothing about you . . .'

'Good.'

He raised the cleaver high in the air, preparing to slam it into her skull. Jerking back, Rochelle howled in fear. But to her surprise, her attacker now lowered his arm, chuckling quietly to himself. Rochelle stared at him in blank astonishment, her heart thundering out the rhythm of her terror. In that moment, she'd expected to die. Now she feared something much worse lay in store for her.

Sensing this, the man lowered himself to her level. His

nose was almost touching hers. She could smell tobacco on his breath, the sharp tang of sweat.

'We're not going to rush this, Rochelle,' he whispered.

Rochelle couldn't speak. The malevolence in his voice, the sparkle in his eyes, was too much. She wanted to pass out, for this all to be over, but cruelly her body wouldn't oblige. She was locked in this nightmare.

'We're going to do this nice and slow . . .'

'Please, no,' she moaned.

'Piece by piece . . .'

He stroked her arm with the cleaver. Rochelle wanted to vomit – suddenly she knew exactly what was coming.

'Starting with that pretty little tongue of yours.'

55

Morning sunlight crept through the gap in the curtains, illuminating a sombre scene. Natalia sat alone on her daughter's neatly made bed, feverishly fingering her rosary beads, as she stared at the floor. She was angry with her daughter, embarrassed, aggrieved, but, above all else, she was worried. Kassie hadn't come home last night.

What on earth was she up to? Where was she? She had no friends to speak of, no family that she was close to, so who had summoned her? She certainly hadn't needed asking twice, tearing from the church without a backward look. Did she have a boyfriend? Or a new girlfriend from one of the numerous help groups she'd attended over the years? Or was it possible that it was that psychologist, who had done nothing so far but encourage Kassie in her delusions, who'd called her last night? She suspected the latter, though for now of course she had no way of knowing.

Rising, Natalia crossed to the windows, drawing back the curtains and scanning the street for the fifth time that morning. Having waited up until 2 a.m., Natalia had eventually gone to bed, reasoning that Kassie had stayed out late before. But as the clock crept round to 4 a.m., 5 a.m., then 6, Natalia had given up on sleep, calling Kassie's cell phone once more, before dressing and hurrying out to check the street for any sign of her errant daughter.

Disappointed, she had retreated to Kassie's bedroom, hoping to find some clue as to her whereabouts, but there was nothing. Just the usual dirty clothes on the floor, the school textbooks carelessly scattered on the makeshift desk. And there she'd remained, waiting . . . hoping that Kassie would reappear. But there was no sign of her. Was she alive? Dead? In trouble? Natalia felt sure she would know if something bad had happened to her, she would feel it in her bones, and the fact that she didn't provided her with some small crumb of comfort. But, beyond that, she couldn't say what might have happened to her. Should she call the police? Surely not, after all the recent problems with the authorities. At the very least, she would have to contact Kassie's school to account for her absence – but this was not a phone call she was looking forward to. They were already skating on very thin ice with Principal Harrison as it was.

Natalia slumped down on the bed, suddenly robbed of energy and hope. And as she lowered herself on to the sagging mattress, something caught her eye. A framed photo on the side of the bed. It was of a young Kassie with her parents, beaming happily as Wrigley Park stretched out behind her. A maelstrom of emotions stirred in Natalia's breast – joy, pride, regret, all wrapped up in a deep sadness. She had tried so hard with Kassie. Knowing full well that she was not the most demonstrative person, she had gone out of her way to offer her precious baby affection. Dressing her nicely, feeding her well, taking her on trips when they could afford it. After Mikolaj's death, it had been much harder of course – she'd had to work several jobs just to survive and was often too tired to engage with her difficult, unknowable child – but still she'd tried, determined not to repeat the mistakes of the past.

Natalia's own childhood had been troubled and lonely – her mother was a troubled woman who'd eventually lost her wits, but not before having reared six children. Right from the off, she'd had her favourites, and Natalia was *not* one of them. Aleksy, the blond, blue-eyed boy and Emilka, her wilful, beguiling eldest daughter, were the apples of her eye. Both had died before reaching adolescence, but while they were alive, everyone else had had to wait in line. This neglect had left its mark on Natalia and she'd determined to do things differently. She had only one child, so it was easier of course, but she had tried to make Kassie feel wanted and cared for, while also teaching her the correct way to live. How to be polite, useful, obedient, respectful of the church and her forebears.

And what had been her reward? Disobedience, rejection, isolation. She had tried to give her daughter the love she'd never had, but had received nothing in return. Which is why she now found herself sitting alone on her daughter's bed — sad, confused and scared.

56

In his worst nightmares, Adam had never imagined himself having to do this. It all seemed so unreal – *horrifically* unreal – and he now regretted volunteering to take on this burden alone.

It had seemed the right thing to do at the time, the logical thing, but medical training only takes you so far. The cold logic of illness and death is easy to grasp in principle, but harder to experience for yourself. It can be tough dealing with strangers who are in pain – Adam had often found himself in that situation – but it was nothing compared to dealing with someone you care for, someone you love. Adam could still picture Faith's ashen, tear-stained face, as he'd raced into the labour ward that night, blustering his apologies and excuses. She had looked stunned, blank, as if she'd just been in an accident. In reality, she was in shock, still in denial that life could be so merciless, brutal and cruel.

Since then she had pushed through the shock to copious, unrestrained despair, then bitterness and anger and now . . . well, where was she now? She had been solicitous this morning, perhaps regretting their awkward exchange last night, and though they had not spoken much, they had at least held each other, wordlessly clinging together as the sun came up. To him, it seemed as if she was now deep in full-blown grief which, in the long term, might be no bad thing. He, he had to admit, was nowhere near this. He was still in shock, barely processing the events that had rocked his world during the last few days.

'Take your time. Whenever you're ready.'

He looked up to see the hospital administrator smiling sympathetically at him.

'Sorry, I . . .'

'There's no rush, Dr Brandt. No rush at all.'

Smiling tightly back at her, Adam looked down at the form in front of him, the pen in his hand. It was the simplest of tasks – just a signature on the dotted line – but suddenly it seemed the hardest thing in the world. The hospital needed his permission to release Annabelle's body, and of course he would provide it, but he hesitated now. Oddly, he had drawn some comfort from the fact that she had been safe and secure in Rush University Medical Center, a hospital he knew well. By signing the form, he would release her little body to the undertakers and the grim process would begin – the funeral preparations, the ceremony, the wake. And suddenly he didn't want any part of it – it all seemed so final. A giant full stop to their hopes and dreams.

Tears threatened now, as an image of Annabelle came to him. She was nestled in his arms, looking up at him with that glassy, benign expression, as if she had just zoned out for a minute. It was a memory he clung to, even though it caused him the deepest pain. Standing here in the relatives' room, flanked by a well-meaning stranger, Adam realized that he had taken none of their misfortune on board, that his despair was still waiting to erupt. But he would not do it here, not in front of a woman he barely knew. So, scrawling his signature on the form, he handed it back.

He had to remain strong. For himself. For Faith. And for Annabelle too.

57

She was nothing like Kassie had imagined.

Ever since Adam Brandt had first mentioned Faith, Kassie had had a picture of the eminent psychologist's wife in mind. She was groomed, sophisticated, operating in a world that was entirely alien to Kassie. Kassie imagined her gliding around an imposing brown-brick mansion, entertaining, achieving, nurturing. The reality was somewhat different. Adam's home was impressive, but still cute, and Faith was not polished in the slightest. She was floaty, bohemian, even a little dishevelled, with a manner that was both nervy and distracted. She stood in the doorway, her dressing gown hanging off one shoulder, eyeing Kassie with something that looked very much like irritation.

'I'm sorry to disturb you,' Kassie blustered, dropping her eyes to the ground as her prepared speech evaporated.

'Look, if you're selling something —'

'I'm looking for Adam . . . Dr Brandt. I'm Kassie Wojcek.'

Silence. Kassie darted a look in Faith's direction and spotted a subtle change in her expression. Recognition certainly, but also something else. Surprise? Curiosity?

'I shouldn't come here, I know, but he's not at his office and he's not answering his phone.'

'No, he's had to . . .' Faith replied, faltering. 'He's had to go out.'

'I see.'

Suddenly, Kassie didn't know what to do. She was aware

that there had been some kind of family emergency – she guessed at bereavement given Adam's sombre tone, one of Faith's parents maybe – and had convinced herself that he would be at home, comforting his wife. She hadn't really made an alternative plan in the event that she was wrong. She rocked back and forward on the spot, biting her nails.

'Shall I get him to call you?'

Faith's voice cut through her introspection.

'Yes. Please,' she mumbled. 'And can you tell him it's urgent.'

'Of course.'

The conversation petered out – Kassie lacking the requisite polish to know what to say next, she hovered on the doorstep, uncertain whether to stay or go. For the last hour or so, local news feeds on Twitter had been abuzz with rumours that a second body had been discovered and Kassie had felt compelled to seek Adam out. But now she was lost as to what to do next. Disappointed and frustrated, she turned to leave, feeling angry at herself for having achieved nothing but disturbing someone who was clearly in pain.

'Look, you can stay if you want.'

Surprised, Kassie paused, turned.

'He'll be back in half an hour or so. He's not planning on going into the office today, so if it's important . . .'

Kassie wanted to accept the offer, but found herself saying:

'It's fine. I don't want to distur—'

'It's ok. Really.'

It was said gently, but firmly. Kassie arrowed another look at her and was surprised to see kindness, even sympathy in Faith's expression. A sense of one soul in pain reaching out to another. Smiling her thanks, she stepped inside.

*

187

Five minutes later, Kassie found herself in a spacious studio at the back of the house. They had bypassed the living room, which was decorated with numerous family photos and holiday souvenirs, heading straight for the kitchen instead. Coffee had been swiftly produced and they'd then made the way to the rear of the property, to Faith's Aladdin's cave.

Kassie had never seen anything like it. The room was full of sculptures, tapestries and trinkets – corpulent Buddhas rubbing up against Irish faeries and Chinese 'lucky charm' cats. But it was the paintings that really took her breath away. They came in many different sizes – some small and intimate, others huge and imposing – and in many different styles. They were all portraits – some in electric, almost luminous colours, others in austere charcoals – but each one drew you in, challenging you to explore the personality of the subject.

'Are these all yours?' Kassie found herself saying.

Faith looked around her, as if surprised to find the paintings there, then replied casually:

'Uh-huh.'

'They're amazing.'

Kassie was aware she sounded like a gushing fan, but couldn't help herself.

'How long did it take you to paint all these?'

'Years,' Faith replied uninterestedly.

'They should be in a gallery. Or a shop,' Kassie continued, gabbling.

'Sure . . .'

Faith sounded disconnected, as if the paintings weren't hers, as if they weren't worthy of anyone's interest, least of all hers, and as Kassie turned to look at her, she realized how pale Adam's wife looked. She seemed bereft, hollow even, and as Kassie allowed her eyes to wander over her, she noticed for the first time the small bulge around her belly. And suddenly she thought she knew what had unbalanced this lucky couple's world.

'Look, maybe I should go,' Kassie said, putting her coffee cup down.

'Don't. I'd rather you were here. It's very quiet when I'm on my own.'

Kassie hesitated, uncertain whether to follow her instinct to depart or stay and keep her wounded hostess company.

'We lost a baby,' Faith continued quickly.

'I'm sorry.'

'Sometimes I like to be alone . . . it's easier . . . but other times . . .'

She petered out, emotion mastering her. Kassie suddenly had a painfully clear image of a grief-stricken woman rattling around this empty house, her unfulfilled hopes for the future goading her in the quiet, child-free rooms. Instinctively, she took a step forward, and laid a hand on Faith's arm. To her surprise, Faith grasped it, as if hanging on for dear life.

'It must be hell,' Kassie found herself saying, stroking Faith's arm with her free hand, trying to bring some comfort to the distraught mother.

Faith nodded forcefully, as a couple of tears slid down her face.

'It's worse than that.'

Kassie murmured her agreement, unsure how to respond. Faith was more than twice her age and the teenager felt seriously out of her depth. Once again, she wondered if it would be better if she left – Adam would hardly thank her for upsetting his wife – when Faith looked up. She scrutinized

Kassie for a moment, as if weighing up whether to speak or not, then said:

'Do you think . . . ?'

Still she hesitated, searching Kassie's face for answers.

'Do you think she suffered?'

Kassie was wrong-footed by the question, but Faith was staring at her intently now, as if yearning for her counsel. Flustered, uncomfortable, Kassie dropped her gaze.

'When Annabelle died, did she suffer at all?'

Kassie tried to keep calm, but she felt unnerved, unsettled, out of her depth.

'Please, Kassie . . . I need to know.'

What was she expected to say? What exactly had Adam told Faith about her? She had no idea what the unborn baby had experienced, she had no image of her, no concept of her existence. Yet such was Faith's clear need for solace, for succour, that Kassie surprised herself by replying:

'No. No, she didn't suffer at all.'

And, to Kassie's immense shame, Faith smiled back at her through her tears.

58

Gabrielle felt sick to her stomach.

She had received the call first thing this morning, as she was dropping her boys off at school. Such was the absurdity of her life – chatting amiably with the Principal about Zack's college plans one minute, digesting Suarez's garbled bulletin the next. She'd raced over to the crime scene – a sailing club on the edge of the lake – hoping she might contain the incident – but as she'd pulled into the crowded parking lot she'd realized this was a fond hope. CSI officers were already on site, as were uniformed CPD officers, and beyond them a handful of bystanders and a growing number of journalists.

The abandoned Ford Ranger stood alone in the empty parking lot. Emily Bartlett, the CPD's Chief Forensics Officer, had recently arrived at the scene and joined Gabrielle as she took in the contents of the trunk. She had known what to expect but still the sight was profoundly shocking. A plastic sheet, wet with gore, containing a mutilated body. The ashen face of the female victim looked horrified, her long, blood-caked tresses hanging down over a hideously deep neck wound. Disgusted, Gabrielle turned away, gesturing to Bartlett to proceed with her investigation. As she did so, Miller appeared by her side.

'Who found her?' Gabrielle asked, still reeling.

'Manager of the sailing club. Car was here when he arrived. He noticed the trunk wasn't shut properly, so . . .'

'And do we have any idea who she is?'

'No ID yet . . . obviously,' Miller replied, cautiously. 'But the car is registered to a Rochelle Stevens.'

An hour later, Gabrielle and her team had conducted a preliminary search of Rochelle Stevens' smart suburban house. The owner worked in addiction therapy, so Gabrielle assumed her property was parent-funded, as there was no evidence in the numerous framed photos of a boyfriend or husband. There was little out of place in the well-maintained property, but a window at the rear had been smashed and the French windows were unlocked. If an intruder had gained access, this was presumably how he or she had done so. The crime scene team had already set up a common approach path to avoid contaminating the entry route and they were hard at work scouring the surfaces for fibres, skin cells and more.

Gabrielle was fervently hoping they would come up with something because, other than the broken window, there were no obvious signs of disturbance. The furniture was in place, the beds were made, the towels were hanging neatly in the bathroom. The owner's purse, keys and cell phone were lying on the hall table, next to yesterday's post, and a grey shoulder bag lay on the floor beneath it, the latter containing a ticket that had been used on the 'L' yesterday afternoon. Her car was gone – obviously – but the garage door was secured, so, overall, were it not for the fact that Rochelle had failed to turn up for work this morning, there was nothing obvious linking the owner of this house to the devastated body found in the trunk.

With little concrete evidence to go on, Gabrielle set about investigating the missing woman's cell phone. There was nothing interesting in her recent emails or texts, so Gabrielle proceeded straight to her diary. This was more illuminating. Rochelle was clearly a woman who liked to organize her life. Everything was scheduled and pre-planned, right down to her favourite TV programme – *Scandal* – which she seemed to watch religiously every Tuesday night. Yesterday afternoon, she had led an NA meeting in the Lower West Side. The time stamp on her 'L' ticket corresponded more or less with the conclusion of the NA meeting and her bag and keys were here, so presumably Rochelle had returned straight home from her session . . . then vanished off the face of the earth. In all likelihood then, the last confirmed sighting of Rochelle was at her rehab group in the Lower West Side.

Which was precisely where Gabrielle was heading now.

59

Adam wrenched the steering wheel sharply to the left, sliding across two lanes of traffic and into a vacant parking bay. He took it too fast and at a crazy angle, his tyres buffeting the kerb and throwing him forward in his seat. All around he could hear car horns blaring, angry motorists signalling their displeasure, but he didn't care. His attention was riveted to the voice on the radio.

'. . . just before seven a.m. this morning. According to a source close to the investigation . . .'

Adam turned the volume up, his hand shaking slightly as he did so.

'. . . the body had been extensively mutilated and the victim's throat cut. Jacob Jones, an Illinois state's attorney, was murdered in similar fashion less than a week ago and questions are now being asked of the investigation run by the CPD's Bureau of Detectives . . .'

The words washed over him, but Adam struggled to process them. When he had parted with Kassie last night, nothing had been amiss, there had been no sign that a crime had taken place. It was just possible, of course, that the two crimes were *not* connected, but even that faint hope was now extinguished by the sombre newscaster.

'We've had no official identification as yet, but we're hearing that the victim is female, in her late twenties and from the West Town area. We believe that she was known to the authorities because of her work in addiction therapy and has been a resident of Chicago for some time . . .'

The bulletin continued, the newscaster going as far as she dared without actually *naming* the victim. But Adam knew exactly who she was talking about. Rochelle Stevens was dead, just as Kassie had predicted. How was that possible? Adam realized now that he had been clinging to the hope that Kassie would be proved wrong, that Rochelle would eventually surface, alive and well, forcing the teenager to confront the deeper reasons for her 'visions'. But what now? What game was Kassie playing here? What did she *know*?

For the first time in his adult life, Adam felt adrift. Leaning forward, he turned the radio off, unable to listen to any more. A difficult, distressing day had just got a whole lot darker.

60

'Isn't it terrible? Such a young woman. Her whole life ahead of her . . .'

Madelaine Baines had a very full schedule this morning – dropping off the dry cleaning, picking up the groceries, a trip to Phone Shack *and* the Nail Bar – but some things were too important to let pass without comment. She wasn't sure her designated server, who was busy sorting out her handset upgrade, shared her feelings, but this did not deter her from making her emotions plain.

'They said on the news that she was only twenty-six. To end up like that, in the trunk of a car. They're saying that she's the second victim . . . You know, after that poor man . . .'

'Right . . .' her server grunted, as he laboured to insert her new SIM card.

'What was his name? Jacob something?'

As she spoke, Madelaine cast around for someone else to engage with. Men were so useless sometimes . . . but the store was busy this morning and there were no other servers to share her shock with. They probably weren't from round here anyway and wouldn't understand why it was so alarming. God knows, Chicago was no stranger to homicide, but this was something else.

Two innocents, abducted from their homes, then brutally murdered. From West Town of all places, the neighbourhood she'd made her home since she moved to Chicago twenty years ago. Jacob Jones – *that* was his name – had lived a few blocks from here. Was it possible this young woman lived close by too?

Madelaine continued to let her mind turn on this, as she hurried back to her car. She had plenty of other things to distract her – the kids, Paul, her charity work – but already a plan was beginning to form. Madelaine knew she was a strong flavour – that occasionally people found her bossy, even a touch domineering – but say what you like about her, she was never found wanting in a crisis. She was always ready to step up to the plate.

And that's what she would do now. They would not be intimidated. They would not be cowed. It was time for the people of West Town to fight back.

61

'You can't come here, Kassie. That's not how it works.'

Adam stared at the teenager in blank astonishment. The day had taken on a surreal quality, as if he were imagining it all. His heart-rending ordeal at the hospital, the news that Rochelle Stevens' body had been found, then finally his discovery of Faith and Kassie chatting earnestly in her studio, as if they knew each other, as if they were *friends*. Was it possible he was dreaming it all? Would he wake in a minute and find that all was well? That a happy, pregnant Faith was slumbering next to him?

'I know that and I'm sorry,' Kassie replied sheepishly.

'You know I want to help you, but I have a life – a private life – and when I'm not working –'

'I understand that, I really do. I never meant to intrude on you, on Faith . . .'

Adam followed Kassie's brief glance towards the studio, to which Faith had discreetly retreated.

'But surely you see why I had to come? You've heard the news?'

'Of course.'

Adam had thought of nothing else on his drive home. The fact that Rochelle was dead – a woman he had spoken to, had a drink with – was horrific. The fact that he and Kassie had broken into her house made things much worse.

'Kassie . . .'

He hesitated, struggling to find the right words to frame his question.

'Kassie, if you know anything about these murders, you must tell me now. If you're in trouble, I can help you, but I need to know the truth.'

He was trying to keep his voice steady. Kassie stared back at him, almost as if she didn't understand the question.

'What are you *talking* about?'

'You followed Rochelle last night, after your therapy.'

'She gave me the slip. I told you that . . .'

'Did something happen at the therapy session that upset you?' he persisted. 'Something between you and Rochelle?'

'I've told you *everything*,' she insisted. 'I was scared by what I saw. So I screamed, that was it . . .'

'Where did you go last night, after we separated. Did you go home?'

For the first time, Kassie looked sheepish. Dropping her gaze, she replied:

'No. I couldn't face it.'

'So . . .'

'So . . . I spent the night on the "L". I got on the Loop and just did circuits until the morning. Loads of people do it, hobos, winos, runaways . . .'

She looked up at him as she spoke, trying to gauge if he believed her. Adam found it hard to read her expression. Was that guilt he could see? Or embarrassment?

'You must see why I have to ask,' Adam continued, avoiding her eye. 'You knew Jacob Jones, he'd prosecuted you in juvenile court. You knew Rochelle too.'

'I'd met her *once*. And I couldn't even remember Jones. I was in court for half an hour, I didn't take in names, faces . . .'

Adam said nothing, staring at the distressed teenager.

'And, no, I didn't have anything to do with their deaths,'

Kassie concluded testily. 'I wanted to help them, I want to *stop* this guy . . .'

'Kassie, you're a fifteen-year-old girl.'

'I don't have a choice. You *know* that.'

She was staring directly at him. Adam exhaled, long and hard, rubbing his hand over his face. In truth, he didn't know anything any more.

'That's why I came here . . . to ask for your help.'

'I don't see what I can do.'

'I want you to take me back there.'

'To Rochelle's house?' Adam replied, incredulous.

'No, to my vision. To the things I saw.'

Another shock on a day that continued to surprise him.

'You obviously doubt what I feel, what I *see*, but I think my experiences might be . . . helpful. I've tried to remember what was happening, I've tried to cast my mind back, but I can only remember fragments . . .'

'I don't even know how we'd begin,' Adam replied, on the back foot suddenly. 'They are not your memories, they are not . . .'

He just stopped himself saying 'real', but Kassie was clearly filling in the blanks herself.

'Even so,' she continued, unabashed. 'I *experienced* them. I felt like I was there with her and some of the things I felt about Jason were *true* – the cold stuff under his feet, that could have been the plastic sheeting –'

'You're putting two and two together and making five, Kassie. You're allowing what you want to believe to lead you –'

'For God's sake,' Kassie blurted out. 'Two people are *dead*. The police have got nothing, so if there is a chance that I can help, don't you think we should try?'

'What if it affects you negatively?' Adam countered.

'If it unbalances you, exacerbates the trauma you've already suffered –'

'That's a chance I'm willing to take.'

Her response was decisive, definitive: leaving Adam with a choice to make. Engage with her on her terms. Or turn her away.

'Look, there are distancing techniques we might use,' he said eventually. 'To allow you to access those . . . experiences without fully being *there* . . .'

To Adam's surprise, Kassie now smiled, laying a hand on his arm.

'That's all I ask,' she said quietly, tears suddenly filling her eyes. 'I just want us to *try*.'

62

'I've never seen anything like it. One minute everything was normal and then . . .'

Gabrielle Grey took in the tearful girl in front of her. Simone Fischer was one of a dozen people gathered outside the down-at-heel community hall in the Lower West Side. Some carried flowers, some clung to each other for support, all were visibly shocked by the breaking news of Rochelle Stevens' murder.

'Go on,' Gabrielle prompted.

'Well, it was so strange . . . Rochelle was encouraging the group to share, which we did, then she turned her attention to the new girl,' Simone continued. 'Rochelle asked her if she wanted to tell us about her experiences . . . then it all went sort of crazy.'

'In what way?'

'The girl . . . she didn't say anything. She just started making these odd noises.'

'What sort of noises?'

'Grunting and gasping, as if she couldn't breathe. Then she screamed, screamed the place down. I thought she was having a fit at first, but then she looked up with these . . . wild eyes and started moving towards Rochelle, clawing at her . . .'

'I see,' Gabrielle responded, suddenly very interested.

'Obviously, the group broke up after that. We were all sent home – we were glad to get out of there, to be honest – while Rochelle stayed with the girl.'

Simone came to a sudden halt, wondering perhaps if their hasty departure had cost Rochelle her life.

'And does this girl have a name?' Gabrielle responded, keen to keep the conversation on track.

'Sure,' Simone blustered. 'Her name is Kassandra, I think. But Rochelle said we should call her Kassie.'

Ten minutes later, Gabrielle was striding down the road, dodging the upended trash cans and garbage that littered the ground. She was aiming for the 'L' station that Rochelle had used after her abortive NA meeting, scanning the desolate street for potential witnesses. Her initial impressions were not favourable. The buildings in this part of Chicago were largely derelict – few people wanted to live here, let alone set up businesses, meaning the streets were always sparsely populated. On and on she went, but Gabrielle was the only person on the streets this morning and she would have felt distinctly vulnerable, were it not for the Colt .45 nestling next to her ribs.

Before long, she had made it to the 'L'. Frustrated, she now had an idea and hurried inside the station. And there it was – a lone security camera covering the ticketing area. Walking up to the ticket booth, Gabrielle banged on the glass, then flashed her ID at the surprised CTA employee, who was halfway through a jelly donut.

'That thing recording?' Gabrielle barked, gesturing towards the camera.

'Sure. I guess,' was the mumbled response.

'Then I wanna see what you've got.'

Five minutes later, Gabrielle found herself sitting in front of a grimy monitor, staring at the familiar staccato images. Luck was on her side for once – the recordings were usually deleted after twenty-four hours, but less than a day had passed since Rochelle's disappearance and, after a little patient scrolling, Gabrielle found what she was looking for.

The slight figure of Rochelle Stevens hurried into the ticketing area, shooting a brief look behind her as she did so. She delved into her purse, slammed her travel pass down and passed through the barriers, then suddenly looked up. Had she heard a train approaching? Without hesitating, she then ran through the parting barriers and sprinted up the stairs. She soon disappeared from view, but Gabrielle kept her eyes glued to the screen and moments later her patience was rewarded.

A tall girl ran into the ticketing area, climbing up and over the ticket barriers, before hurrying up the stairs. Winding the footage back again, Gabrielle waited until the pursuing female entered the ticketing area, then paused the feed. She studied the image closely, then, exhaling, sat back in her chair.

It was clear as day. Even from a side angle, there was no doubt that Rochelle's pursuer was Kassandra Wojcek.

63

Faith stood stock still, staring at the canvas in front of her.

She hadn't wanted to come into the studio, but it was the brightest, most welcoming room in the house. Bathed in the warm glow of the morning sunshine, it had seemed the obvious place to bring Kassie, as they waited for Adam's return. When he did eventually stumble through the door, looking pale and distracted, he had immediately ushered Kassie into his office, engaging her in what was clearly a fairly heated conversation. Standing outside in the hallway, a forgotten figure, Faith had felt self-conscious and awkward. Adam had never had a client in the house before and she didn't want to be accused of eavesdropping or interfering, so she had retreated to her studio once more, pulling the door shut behind her.

Now the large room, which had seemed bright and airy earlier, felt uncomfortably warm, even a little suffocating. The numerous canvases, which Kassie had taken such delight in, now seemed to crowd in on her, goading her by flaunting her past productivity, the ease with which she had previously set down her latest bout of inspiration. Turning away, she found herself confronted by her self-portrait once more.

Faith stared at Faith, flesh and blood facing her painted self, as if in a stand-off. The portrait was nearly complete. It was a morning's work – a day at the most – to finish it off. A tube of black oil paint was sitting on the easel, where she had left it that morning, and now, carefully, cautiously, she picked it up and squeezed it, depositing its oozy contents on to her palette. Dropping it without replacing the lid, she did the same with a tube of white paint, before picking up the nearest brush to mix the two colours. Soon an appealing, rich grey coated the hairs of her brush and slowly she raised it to paint.

The tip of the brush touched the canvas, which felt odd, yet familiar, and slowly Faith completed a stroke. Then another. This, however, was faltering, less certain, and Faith saw that she'd blurred the line. She was about to wipe it off, start over, when suddenly she paused. She was close to the painting, was looking directly at her own face, her eyes glued to the features in front of her. But suddenly she wasn't seeing her features any more, she was seeing Annabelle's. Her tiny upturned nose, her dimpled chin, those achingly beautiful blue eyes. Those glassy, *lifeless* eyes . . .

Shaking, Faith dropped the brush. It clattered to the floor, but she didn't notice. She swayed a little, as if she might be about to faint, then leaned forward, resting her head on the taut canvas. She could feel tears running down her face now, falling on to the paint, but she didn't care. She hadn't the strength to move even if she had wanted to.

It was a mistake to have tried. She wasn't ready yet and something made her wonder if she ever would be. She wanted to paint – she needed to paint – but for now it was impossible. She could not see, could not feel, anything but Annabelle. She was haunted by the ghost of a child she had loved and lost.

64

They had driven to his office in silence. Adam hadn't wanted to leave Faith, but she had angrily shooed him away when he put his head round the studio door. There was no question of conducting the session at home, with Faith in earshot, so Adam had tipped Kassie into his Lexus and set off for Lincoln Park.

Climbing the stairwell to the top floor, Adam had been struck by the silence in the building. He had no clients scheduled for today of course, but where were all the other people, the office workers and couriers who he regularly passed as he climbed the stairs? Nothing seemed normal today. Everything seemed slightly *off*.

Five minutes later, they were seated opposite each other in his client space, Kassie sitting bolt upright on one of the comfy chairs. She had refused the offer of a drink, with something akin to impatience. There was a clear sense that, now the decision had been made to do this, she just wanted to get on with it. Adam, for his part, was more circumspect, but had concluded that there was nothing to be gained by rejecting Kassie. If he really wanted to get to the bottom of this, if he really wanted to help, then he had to engage.

'Distancing techniques work in a number of ways,' Adam found himself saying. 'But they all have the same purpose. They allow the subject to relive a trauma from a safe space, so they know they can't be hurt or affected by the experience.

Like an outsider looking in. So we need to find something that will work for you as an individual. Some people like to imagine they are in a comfy living room, watching their experiences on a TV. You are in control, you can turn it on or off at any time. Other people like to put themselves back in the experience directly, but this time they are in a bubble. They cannot be touched or hurt and nobody in the original experience can see the –'

'The bubble,' Kassie interrupted quickly. 'We'll do the bubble.'

Adam paused, unsure whether he should unpack this decision or let it slide. Seeming to sense his doubt, Kassie said:

'It'll be the best fit for me. There's no point discussing other options.'

She seemed confident, assured, so Adam continued:

'Now I'm going to put you under hypnosis, but remember you will be in your bubble *at all times*, totally safe and secure.'

Kassie nodded, so Adam got her to count to fifty as he slowly began to hypnotize her. Once he was confident she was properly under, he began to guide her back in time.

'I want you to empty your mind, Kassie. Imagine you're floating through a blank space. It has no colour, no markings, nothing. It is empty, clean, pure. You're soaring gently through it, happy, relaxed, weightless.'

Adam paused to let his words register. Kassie appeared to be responding to his words, so he continued:

'Now in the distance you see something. It looks like a light, something real, something tangible. Now you're moving towards it at a steady speed, slowly it's getting bigger and bigger, clearer and clearer. Now you can see what it is. It's your therapy group and you're there with Rochelle, Simone and the others. Can you see it, Kassie?'

The teenager nodded.

'You're in the room with them, but you're safe. You're secure. Watching them from inside your bubble. Now, Kassie, slowly, I want you to look up. I want you to look into Rochelle's eyes. Can you do that for me?'

The effect on her was immediate. Kassie gasped, then spit flew from the teenager's mouth, as she screamed:

'Oh, God, no. Please don't hurt me. I don't want to . . . PLEASE . . .'

The final word erupted from her, as she fell forward off her chair, landing in a heap on the floor. Adam was on his feet at once, hurrying to her, lifting her up off the carpet. She was conscious, out of hypnosis now, but still Adam was amazed by the transformation in her. She was sweating profusely and her face was deathly pale.

'It's ok, Kassie,' he said gently, guiding her back to a chair. 'You're quite safe. You're here with me, Dr Brandt, in my office and –'

'It's ok. I'm ok . . .'

She whispered the words, breathless but coherent. Even as she spoke a tiny bit of colour came back to her cheeks.

'I'm sorry. I shouldn't have done that,' she said quietly.

'You've nothing to apologize for, Kassie.'

'I was just so scared . . .'

'I understand. You just sit there. I'm going to get you a glass of water, then we'll think about getting you a cab home.'

'I want to try again.'

'Absolutely not.'

'We *need* to try again.'

'No. I wouldn't be doing my duty if I –'

'Please,' she countered. 'Just one more time. I know what to expect this time, I can handle it.'

After further discussion, Adam eventually conceded, insisting, however, that they take a fifteen-minute break to get some fresh air and a glass of water. The quarter-hour on the balcony passed quickly and before long they were facing each other once more. Despite some fairly serious misgivings, Adam put Kassie under hypnosis once more.

As before, he guided her towards the therapy room and as previously he asked her to look directly at Rochelle. Kassie, who had been slouching slightly, sat up sharply and began to make quiet, keening noises. Her body was rigid, her face contorted, the muscles twitching around the side of her mouth. She didn't fall this time; instead she seemed to be fighting something, perhaps fighting to keep herself in the experience.

'He wants to hurt me,' she suddenly blurted, her voice tight, rising in pitch with each word. 'He's going to *kill* me. I can feel his hand on my neck –'

She broke off, screaming long and loud, before stopping abruptly. Her breathing was feverish, her chest rising and falling rapidly.

Adam's instinct was to break off the session, but suddenly Kassie spoke again:

'He's right on top of me, I can smell him. And –'

She suddenly went quiet again and the colour drained from her cheeks.

'What is it, Kassie?'

'He's going to cut my throat.'

She half gasped, half groaned. Despite himself, Adam actually shivered, as if he could feel Rochelle's throat being cut.

'Is it just him there?'

'Yes . . . no . . . I can hear laughter . . . It sounds like female laughter . . .'

'Can you see this woman? Is she there?'

'No . . . I can't see . . . anyone any more,' she breathed, still seeming to struggle for breath. 'I'm staring up at the ceiling. I can see the moon. A big, pink moon . . .'

Kassie started to choke now, greedily gasping for oxygen, while clawing at the air, so Adam intervened, bringing her swiftly out of her hypnosis. She looked extremely shaken and Adam had an inkling of how she felt – he had never had a distancing session where the patient had been able to feel trauma so keenly.

'Am I as pale as you?'

Kassie's question punctured his introspection – Adam was surprised to see the trace of a rueful smile in Kassie's expression.

'Worse,' Adam replied, as lightly as he could.

'So, what now?'

'Now . . . if you're up to it . . . tell me everything you saw.'

He sat opposite her, pen poised to write down her account. He had done this many times before, but never had his hand shaken so.

'I was in a hut or an outbuilding.'

'Was this the same place as last time?'

'Yes.'

'But you said Jacob was in a basement.'

'I was wrong, it's definitely above ground. When I looked up . . . I could see through the broken rafters. I could see the moon, a big pink moon . . .'

Adam noted down 'pink moon'. These celestial rarities happened in spring, so Kassie's timing was right. But whether this was by accident or design, he couldn't say.

'Could you see who was with you? This man?'

'Not really, it was dark. But I could smell cigarettes on his breath. I could hear his voice. He was close by, taunting her, enjoying himself.'

'Did he have an accent?'

'He's from the Midwest, I think, but it's hard to say.'

'And the woman?'

Kassie shook her head.

'I just heard her laughter. It was high-pitched and cruel . . . so cruel . . . like she couldn't stop.'

Kassie shuddered, wrapping her arms around herself.

'And she was in there with you?'

'Yes . . . no . . . I don't know. It sounded more distant, but it was very clear.'

'And did you recognize her? Her voice, I mean?'

'No,' Kassie replied firmly, as if irritated by the suggestion.

'Were you clothed?'

'No . . . definitely not. I was so cold . . .'

'And did you see the blade?'

'No, I just felt it on my skin. It was long and thin – I could feel it digging into my throat, cutting me . . .'

Now Kassie started to weep, low scared sobs. Adam called time on the session, taking time to comfort her, before settling her down to watch TV, so he could write up his notes. Though she appeared to contradict some of her earlier testimony, Kassie's thoughts today had been clear, concise and detailed. But the question remained – was any of it even remotely real?

65

'I've told you I've no idea where she is.'

Natalia's tone was agonized, fervent. She sat at the kitchen table, casting horrified glances at the police officers turning her house upside down. What were they searching for? What did they expect to find?

'The last time I saw her was yesterday afternoon in church. We were at St Stanislaus Kostka –'

'When was this?' Detective Grey interrupted.

'The service began at nine p.m. She left about twenty minutes later. Took a phone call and ran off.'

The police officer noted this down. Natalia watched her closely. Was she getting Kassie into more trouble by mentioning this?

'She didn't come home last night?'

'No, I waited up for her, but . . .'

'Does she often stay out all night?'

'No, never. Well, hardly ever.'

'Your daughter is missing then?'

Natalia shrugged an affirmative. She didn't like to admit it, but it was true.

'And yet you've not reported it?'

Natalia hesitated, embarrassed, before responding quietly:

'I thought we were in enough trouble already.'

'At least we can agree on that,' the police officer responded curtly. 'A woman was murdered last night – brutally murdered. Your daughter was seen following her.'

Detective Grey spoke calmly and carefully, terrifying Natalia even more. What had Kassie got herself involved in now?

'It's very important we find Kassie,' Grey continued briskly. 'For her own safety, as much as anything else. So, if you know anything – anyone she might be staying with, anywhere she might have gone – now would be a very good time to tell us.'

As she spoke, she fixed Natalia with a penetrating stare. Natalia's whole world seemed to be collapsing in on itself, but she knew she had to do something to protect herself, to protect Kassie.

'I wish I could help,' Natalia stuttered, desperate to appear helpful. 'But there's no one – it's just me and her. Honestly, I have no idea where she goes any more, but . . .'

A flicker of interest in Grey's expression now.

'. . . I have an inkling of who might have called her last night. Where she might have gone . . .'

Grey was staring directly at her. For the first time in this distressing interview, Natalia felt she had the upper hand.

'In fact,' she concluded, enjoying this brief moment of respite, 'it's someone you know . . . Someone you introduced to her.'

Natalia was primed to deliver the punchline, but the detective's face told her she didn't need to. Gabrielle Grey knew exactly who she was talking about.

66

Kassie slunk back into the shadows, as Grey emerged from the squat bungalow. From her vantage point across the street, Kassie could see all that was going on, but she wondered now if her meagre cover would save her from detection. The trash cans weren't particularly tall or wide and the CPD detective was looking purposeful and energized.

On leaving Adam's office, Kassie had turned on her phone, to find a series of messages from Grey, urging her to get in touch. Wary, Kassie had turned off her phone and hurried home. But as soon as she'd entered the street, Kassie had spotted them. Her neighbourhood was so listless, so dull, that the three CPD cars and the battered Pontiac stood out like sore thumbs. Natalia and Kassie *never* had visitors – to have so many people descend on them at once was almost comical. But nobody was laughing – not Grey, not Kassie and certainly not her mother. Kassie had caught glimpses of Natalia as she paced back and forth in the kitchen. Even from this distance, Kassie could see she looked very upset.

Grey was marching to her car now, her cell phone clamped to her ear. The other officers remained inside, continuing their humiliating search of the small suburban house, but Gabrielle Grey was on the move. What had she discovered? What had her mom told her? Her mother might naturally want to protect Kassie, but she was not a good, nor a practised, liar. She would presumably have told Grey that she didn't come home last night, that she had appeared restless and agitated during her enforced visit to St Stanislaus, but what else had she said to prompt such a sudden, purposeful departure? Suddenly Kassie was filled with foreboding.

Grey was pulling away from the kerb now, darting looks left and right to check for oncoming traffic. Kassie took a step further back, fearful of detection even now. On leaving Adam's office, she'd decided to return home, to seek refuge from the world for a few hours, but there was no sanctuary here, not while the CPD were turning her family home upside down.

For the first time in her short life, Kassie felt hunted.

67

Madelaine Baines finished tweeting, then immediately opened WhatsApp. Since her earlier discussion at the Phone Shack, she had been full of energy, remorselessly hitting social media to make her views known. News of a second murder in this part of town had already filtered through now, even to those who didn't regularly follow the radio or TV bulletins. But reaction and gossip were not enough. Something had to be *done*.

Madelaine had always been someone who liked to give back. Since giving up work to look after the kids, she had had time on her hands. More time than she was comfortable with, if she was honest. So she was happy to help out at charity drives, cake sales and other community events. She knew she had been lucky in life – loving parents, devoted husband, lovely kids – and that pushed her to help others less fortunate than herself. Whenever there was a local disaster or a sick kid whose health insurance didn't cover a vital operation, she would be first in line to do her bit. It made her feel useful, made her feel like she still had *value*. And she felt that familiar drive now, that energy and excitement building inside her. Her husband often said she took on too much – that she couldn't shoulder *everyone's* troubles – but to her, helping was as natural as breathing. Which is why she had to get involved now.

Obviously local people would want to pay their respects to those who'd lost their lives – a public servant and a young counsellor needlessly slain. She had thought of a church service, but then backed away from that, as she had no idea what religious beliefs the victims held. Instead she had set-tled for a candlelit vigil in Granary Square. That would be a fitting venue and a perfect rallying point. Because, as well as remembering the victims, it was vital they ensured that it didn't happen again, that the local community was *protected*.

In reality, this was her principal driver. She had lived in this neighbourhood for twenty years – her husband worked here, her kids went to high school here. The idea that any-thing would happen to them . . . Rochelle Stevens was only eight years older than her eldest and to think what that poor girl went through . . . No, it was vital that local people came together to protect each other, to root out this evil. No one, not even the most skilled or determined criminal, was a match for the eyes and ears of a whole community.

Having tapped out a rallying cry on her local WhatsApp groups, she moved on to Facebook. Already responses were flooding in – appalled, but determined and resolved – and Madelaine felt her optimism rising. They could do this, they could fight back. One of the first people to respond had been Amy, her younger daughter, who shared many of Madelaine's characteristics and was clearly already recruiting fellow stu-dents for the vigil. In spite of herself, Madelaine felt a flush of pride – for Amy, Joanne, her husband, Paul. On this, she knew they would be four square behind her when the time came. That was the thing about tragedies like these. However awful they were, they always reminded you how fortunate you were to be part of a happy, loving family.

68

'Let me get this straight . . . You went around to Rochelle Stevens' house last night and you *broke in*?'

Gabrielle Grey's tone was a mixture of bewilderment and shock.

'Yes,' Adam conceded awkwardly.

Gabrielle continued to stare at him, trying to process this unexpected development. It was profoundly odd for Adam to see her standing in his office – their interaction had always been on *her* turf – but she had turned up unannounced twenty minutes ago. She had come hoping to track down Kassie, but had already got far more than she bargained for.

'What time was this?'

'Just after ten p.m.'

'Do you *know* Rochelle?'

'Professionally. We've met a few times and I often refer teenagers to her for addiction therapy.'

'Is Kassie Wojcek one of her patients?'

'Yes, I put them in contact a week ago. I told you that I felt it was important Kassie received treatment.'

Gabrielle was still looking directly at him, as if trying to read him. Though Adam had nothing to hide, he nevertheless felt tense.

'Why did you go there last night?'

'Kassie was determined to track her down, so I accompanied her. She was very worried about Rochelle and wanted to make sure she was ok.'

'So you broke in to ask her?' Gabrielle persisted, incredulous.

'That was Kassie, not me. I would have waited until the morning, but –'

'Is this something you regularly do with your clients? Breaking and entering –'

'Rochelle wasn't answering the door,' Adam interrupted, irritated. 'But she'd clearly made it home –'

'How could you know that?'

'We could see her bag and phone in the hallway.'

Adam knew it sounded bad – the pair of them peering through Rochelle's windows before breaking in – but carried on, determined to guts this out.

'Look, Kassie was convinced that something was wrong an—'

'On what basis?'

This was the question he'd been dreading. Choosing his words carefully, Adam continued:

'Kassie had the strong sense that Rochelle was about to be attacked . . . by the same person or persons who murdered Jacob Jones, so –'

'She wanted to *warn* her?'

'Yes,' Adam replied, ignoring her sarcasm. 'That's why she followed her from the NA meeting.'

'And did you ask her *why* she was so convinced that Rochelle was in danger?'

The question hung in the air for a moment, then:

'She had . . . a kind of vision. During the therapy session.'

'*Another one?* Does she have these visions daily or just when someone's about to be cut into small pieces?'

'Gabrielle, I'm trying to answer your questions honestly,' Adam growled. 'I'd appreciate it if you did me the courtesy of taking me seriously.'

'And I'd appreciate it if you'd answer my question.'

'Yes,' Adam continued, testily. 'She claims to have them every day. But we've only discussed the two concerning Jacob and Rochelle.'

Gabrielle digested this.

'So, what happened when you were in the house?'

'Nothing. Nothing at all,' Adam insisted, aware he was sounding increasingly defensive. 'We looked for Rochelle. She wasn't there. We left.'

'What time was this?'

'Ten fifteen p.m. . . . ten twenty . . . we didn't stay long.'

'And you left together?'

'No . . .' Adam conceded. 'I drove home. Kassie . . . I think Kassie spent the night on the "L".'

'The whole night?'

'That's what she told me.'

'And where were you? After, say, ten thirty p.m.?'

'I was at home, with my wife.'

'All night?'

'*All night*,' Adam replied, riled.

'Is there anyone else that can verify that?'

'Not really. Unless a neighbour saw me coming back.'

Gabrielle said nothing, removing a small pad from her jacket pocket and making a few notes.

'I'm not seriously a suspect, am I?' Adam demanded.

'I'm keeping an open mind.'

'Oh, for God's sake.'

'You broke into Rochelle Stevens' house last night. This morning we found her body.'

'We were trying to *help* her.'

But he knew it sounded weak.

'Where's Kassie now?' Gabrielle asked, ignoring his protest.

'I don't know. If she's not at home, she might be at school.'

'She's not. The Principal told me she hasn't been in for several days.'

'Then your guess is as good as mine.'

Adam met her eye this time, determined not to look cowed. But Gabrielle seemed unaffected by his defiance, staring right back at him.

'Tell me something,' she said eventually. 'Why were you at Rochelle's last night?'

'I've already explained that.'

'You told me Kassie was worried about her. Why were *you* there?'

'I wanted to prove to her that Rochelle was ok, that there was no reason to be concerned.'

'So you revealed the address of a fellow professional to a client . . .'

'It wasn't like that –'

'And not content with that, you accompanied your client to her house, where you promptly broke in and –'

'Look, I shouldn't have done it, I know that. But Kassie was convinced that Rochelle was in danger and as it turns out she was *right*.'

The words escaped before he could stop them. Immediately Adam wished he could take them back, but it was too late.

'Oh. My. God.'

Gabrielle's hand rose to her mouth, genuine surprise replacing suspicion.

'You believe her, don't you? You *actually* believe this girl is some kind . . . some kind of psychic?'

'Of course not,' Adam spat back.

'What then?'

'I'm trying to *help* her.'

'By encouraging her in her delusions?'

'By *listening* to her. That's the difference between you and me, Gabrielle. You instantly disbelieve *everything* you're told. I don't have that luxury. I have to work with what people tell me.'

'You mean you have to swallow their lies.'

'I have to listen to them, interpret what they say, then try to help them.'

'If you could only hear yourself –'

'Why would Kassie lie about this?' Adam interrupted, his volume rising with his temper. 'If she's involved, why would she draw attention to herself by talking to me in the first place?'

'That's what I intend to find out.'

'It doesn't make any sense. She has no motive.'

'That's not true.'

'Plus there's no way she could have carried out the killings herself.'

'Just how close *are* you to Kassie, Dr Brandt?'

'What's that supposed to mean?'

'You seem very protective of her. And as I recall you've got *form*. Your wife was a patient of yours first, wasn't she?'

'Go to hell!' Adam barked. 'Kassie's fifteen years old. What do you take me for?'

Gabrielle said nothing. All pretence at politeness was now gone. Adam and Gabrielle had rubbed along well in the past, but their working relationship now lay in ruins.

'Thank you for your time,' Gabrielle said suddenly, picking up her bag. 'One of my team will be in touch to take a full, written statement. In the meantime, don't go anywhere, ok?'

Adam nodded, not trusting himself to speak. Gabrielle turned as if to leave, then paused to deliver a parting shot.

'I don't know what's going on here, Adam, but let me give you a piece of advice. Cut your ties with Kassie Wojcek *today*, go back to your day job and then . . .' She locked her gaze on his. '. . . Take a long, hard look in the mirror.'

69

Stepping inside the house quietly, she turned to survey the scene. She had expected her mother to fall upon her with an avalanche of recrimination, but actually the house was deathly quiet. The CPD officers had departed ten minutes ago, having made little attempt to tidy up after themselves. It cut Kassie to the quick to think that they had been in here, trampling all over their perfectly ordered, pristine little home.

Upset, nervous, Kassie headed quickly towards the rear of the house. As she padded along the narrow hallway, she heard movement ahead and pushed inside the master bedroom. Her mother was there, but to Kassie's surprise Natalia said nothing to her, angling only a quick look at her before resuming her packing. One nearly full suitcase lay on the bed, another sat on the bedroom floor.

'What's going on?'

'We're leaving.'

Kassie said nothing, lost for words.

'I just got off the phone to Aunt Marija. She's prepared to put us up for a while, though God knows it's not ideal.'

'We're going to *Minneapolis*?'

'As soon as we're ready. I've packed your clothes. If there's anything else you want from your room, get it now.'

'We can't just leave.'

'You expect me to stay?' her mother spat back viciously. 'So the police can come back again? Turn this house — *my house* — upside down. So, the neighbours can gossip and . . . bitch.'

She crossed herself, even as she said it.

'Mama, I'm sorry.'

'Don't you dare . . . don't you . . .'

She held a finger up to silence her daughter, as she suddenly petered out, emotion mastering her. She continued to pack, tears pricking her angry eyes.

'I have tried, Kassie. I have tried to bring you up the right way. To respect the church, to respect the law, to respect *me*. But I have to be grown up enough now to admit that I've failed.'

'Don't say that,' Kassie urged her, suddenly tearful herself.

'I don't know what you've got yourself mixed up in, what you think you're doing, but I'll tell you this. I am not staying here to be . . . *humiliated*. The Lord knows I've had enough of *that* over the years.'

Kassie stared at her mother, stunned.

'Maybe we'll come back, maybe we won't. But I need help. And you need to get away from here. Maybe your Uncle Max can sort you out, he's not as *soft* as I am.'

Kassie shuddered at the mention of her uncle. Her mother called him a disciplinarian. She called him a bully.

'Anyway, I want to be on the road before rush hour, so don't stand there like a stuffed fish —'

'I can't go, Mama.'

'Why? Why can't you go and visit your aunt, who's always loved you?'

'You know why.'

'No, I don't. And I don't want to.'

'People are dying . . .'

'So the police told me.'

'What did they say?' Kassie replied, suddenly concerned.

'Never mind what they said. They're wrong. And if you're

226

not here, they can't go poking their noses in, insinuating things. We're going and that's that.'

'But what if I can help?'

'You never helped anyone but yourself.'

Kassie blinked, shaken by the vitriol of her mother's reply, but gathering herself responded:

'Then this may be my chance to make amends. To do some good.'

Natalia looked horrified, staring at her daughter as if she had lost her mind.

'I am *leaving*, Kassie. I am leaving this house. If you want to remain part of this family, you'll come with me now.'

'But what . . .' Kassie hesitated to say it. 'What if there's a reason I see these things?'

Her mother stared directly at her, bitter resignation etched on her face.

'Then you've made your choice.'

Without another word, Natalia zipped up her suitcase and marched out, brushing past her daughter. Kassie was left alone in the room, shaken and upset. Despite everything, she loved her mother – loved her deeply.

But she knew now that she would never see her again.

70

She pounced on her as soon as she entered the room. Jane Miller had been trying to get hold of her boss for hours, but had been repeatedly diverted to voicemail. When Gabrielle Grey finally entered the packed incident room, looking distracted and uneasy, Miller hurried over to her.

'Detective Miller,' Gabrielle greeted her, as she approached. 'Please say you've got good news for me . . .'

Miller was surprised by the forced cheeriness in her voice. Her boss was usually such a vital, dynamic presence, but she seemed jaded this morning. In truth, the pressure had steadily been mounting on *all* of them, as they tried to grapple with this unsettling case. Superintendent Hoskins had put in a personal appearance earlier to remind them of the importance of a swift arrest. He came armed with a copy of the *Chicago Sun*, whose lurid front page revelled in the deeds of the killer they had dubbed 'The Chicago Butcher'.

'Suarez and I have been looking at Rochelle Stevens' financial footprint. And on last month's bank statement we found this . . .'

She handed Gabrielle a printout with one entry highlighted.

'Eighty dollars paid to CleanEezy. I rang them and they confirmed the job — carpet cleaning at her home address. And guess what? The operative was —'

'Conor Sumner.'

'Aka Kyle Redmond.'

Miller watched as Gabrielle digested this.

'So, both victims let this guy into their house,' Gabrielle continued, thinking aloud. 'He would have had plenty of time to plan their abductions . . .'

'Sure.'

'. . . and if we're right about the connection to Kassie Wojcek, then he's a good fit to be her accomplice. Has *anyone* got a lead on where she might be?'

'Not so far.'

'What about Redmond?' Gabrielle continued, clearly frustrated.

'No sightings as yet, but we spoke to a couple of CleanEezy's clients, who'd dealt with him in the last couple of months. According to them, he's driving a brown Ford pickup truck with Louisiana plates. We don't have the full registration, but –'

'Let the Traffic Unit know anyway. We need their eyes and ears on this. And make sure the whole team is up to speed. We should get our own people on the streets ourselves, see what we can turn up.'

'Absolutely.'

'In the meantime, I'll chase down the warrant. We need to get back to that trailer –'

'Came through an hour ago,' Miller replied happily, handing it to her.

'What would I do without you?' Gabrielle replied lightly, finally breaking into a smile. 'Ready to go in five?'

Gabrielle turned and marched away to her office. Miller felt a small flush of pride, but swallowing it down, she hurried back to her desk to gather her things. Finally, they were making progress. They had a prime suspect.

All they had to do now was bring him in.

71

He put the cigarette to his lips and drew on it, filling his mouth with its bitter fumes. As he did so, the lit end flared violently, its glowing tip becoming intensely bright, sending a shiver down his spine. He found meaning in even the small things these days – the tiny, crackling embers seemed to him a fitting testament to his power.

The TV was playing in front of him, the sober newscasters concealing their excitement as they jabbered on about the body in the parking lot. They had talked about nothing else for the past few hours. Another nice, middle-class do-gooder had been abducted from her home, ending up in pieces in the trunk of her own car. For the overly made-up woman mouthing the news and her knuckle-headed viewers, it was a terrifying thought. Violence could come to *them*. Could find them in their own homes, as they slept, took a shower, said their prayers . . . It thrilled him beyond measure to think of the thousands of middle managers, school moms, newlyweds and singletons who would be tossing and turning tonight. The nightmare was no longer in their heads, it was standing right in front of them.

'The Chicago Butcher'. It was predictable, given the media's prurient interest in the state of Jones and Stevens, but it angered him nevertheless. It sound boneheaded and brutal, as if these folk were selected at random and sliced up. Yes, the pain, the fear excited him – the horror in their eyes as life spurted out of their flapping throats – but that was not what this was about. The media, the police, had no idea *why* these deserving folk had been chosen, nor how much planning had gone into their destruction. None of this was accidental. None of this was *luck*.

He took another long drag on his cigarette. Maybe he was stupid to get over-excited — none of it mattered anyway. They could call him what they liked, but it didn't change the fact that the city was running scared. Chicago, his hometown, this bitter, messed-up, careless metropolis, was quaking with fear, terrorized by its own. How little they had cared. How much they would be made to suffer.

Jones had got what he was due. Rochelle Stevens too. And they would not be the last. Out there somewhere, amid the millions of doomed souls in the city, was another whose hour had come. She did not know it yet. She could not know it. But that unsuspecting bitch had a date with the butcher's knife.

72

Madelaine Baines looked out at the sight in front of her, moved and inspired. She knew that her rallying cry to the community had gained a lot of traction on Facebook and Twitter – and subsequently a mention on the local news bulletins – but still she hadn't expected such an impressive turnout. People were heading into Granary Park from all quarters, carrying flashlights, lanterns, candles, as well as pictures of Jacob Jones and Rochelle Stevens. It was at once intensely sad and also incredibly moving, deep grief mixed with defiance and determination.

The vigil was due to begin shortly, so Madelaine took a moment to cast another eye over her speech. She had had to write it quickly and hoped that she would acquit herself as well as the other community leaders on the hastily erected stage. They had the local priest, a prominent politician, a friend of Rochelle's, but it would fall to Madelaine to conclude proceedings. She hoped she'd prove worthy of the task – she had not asked to be the de facto leader of this vigil, but as she had set the ball rolling, it had kind of just happened. Now she suddenly felt nervous, as well as excited – she was used to community work, but public speaking was not her thing.

She had been so invigorated this morning, contacting local dignitaries and opinion shapers, mobilizing those whom she knew would care, that she had never stopped to think what she might have started. Now, as she looked down at the local citizens gathering in the small community park, she started to get an inkling of it. The square was filling up quickly; soon not an inch of grass would be visible. It was heartening to see that there were still so many people out there who cared. A couple of TV crews circled, talking to local residents, taking shots of the growing crowd. Madelaine had wanted the media to be present of course, but still the sight of them set butterflies dancing in her stomach.

Madelaine ran through her lines once more, reminding herself to speak slowly, to make the words count. After all, this wasn't about her feelings, it was about keeping people safe. If she could alert people to the dangers, if she could focus minds on rooting out this evil, then she would have done her job. And who could doubt this crowd's determination or their reach? They were packed into the park, linking arms, lighting candles, occasionally even breaking into song. It was awesome to behold, an expression of stoic solidarity as young, old, black, white, gay and straight stood shoulder to shoulder, their candles and lanterns flickering in the breeze. It was more than just a statement of an intent.

It was a thing of beauty.

73

The pretty teenager was clutching a photo of Rochelle in one hand, a flickering candle in the other. She was singing, as were many others at the vigil, but the camera remained glued to the young girl's face, as tears crept down her cheeks. She was defiant, she was vocal, but the teenager was also distraught that one of their own had been taken from them in such brutal fashion.

Adam turned away, unable to watch. The bar's TV had been tuned to WGN for some time and most of the regulars were glued to it. Adam just wanted to blot it out, however, so returned his attention to his drink, only to find that his pint glass was already empty.

'Another, please.'

The barman refilled it without even looking at him, far more interested in the rolling news than his strung-out customer. Adam took it from him and drained half of it in one go, but didn't feel any better. Perhaps he needed something stronger? He diverted his eyes to the long line of bottles on the back shelf, which stood proud in front of the grubby mirrored wall, and caught his own reflection staring back at him. Was this the mirror that Gabrielle Grey had been referring to, he thought to himself bitterly.

Ever since he'd taken refuge in the bar, he'd been replaying their conversation. It seemed impossible that their relationship had soured so quickly. But then nothing about the last few days seemed normal. A week ago, he was a respected psychologist, a friend to the police and confessor to many, with a happy wife, a baby on the way. And now what was he? A man drowning his sorrows, wishing, like so many others in this seedy bar, that he could turn back the clock . . .

Was he going mad? Having some kind of breakdown? When he was with Kassie, he was borne along by her passion, entertaining thoughts he knew were preposterous, doing things he knew were risky and unprofessional. But as soon as he was away from her, back in the real world, he came down to earth with a bump. Gabrielle's words had been so cutting, her tone so full of scorn, that he couldn't help but reflect on his recent actions with embarrassment. She was right, he had been foolish, reckless, indulgent.

Yet could he hand on heart say that Kassie was lying? Playing him? Her description of the murders had been detailed and affecting and her performance under hypnosis appeared genuine. Normally he would have marked her down as suffering from some form of delusional psychosis, but she *had* accurately predicted Rochelle's death. Which meant that she was either involved in the killings or knew something about the perpetrator and was involving Adam as . . . what exactly? A diversion? A fig leaf? During their session today, he had wondered for one crazy moment whether the woman whose laughter Kassie had heard was actually Kassie *herself*, that she was somehow mentally repackaging her involvement in these murders, leading Adam towards the heart of this riddle in her own twisted, roundabout way? This explanation of events was not fully satisfactory either, however – he had never encountered a fugue state *this deep* before and he was pretty sure she wasn't acting. Then again, the only other possibility was that Kassie's gift was real, which was impossible.

Looking down, Adam noticed that his glass was empty again, even though he had no recollection of finishing it. Even the most mundane actions seemed to have taken on a surreal quality these days, leaving him barely able to function. What should he do for the best? Carry on drinking or head home to Faith? Call Kassie to alert her to the police's suspicions or cut her off for good? For the first time ever, Adam Brandt genuinely had no idea what to do.

It was at times like this that he missed his father. Throughout Adam's life, his father had been a source of guidance. He was a man with rigid views, a strong sense of personal morality and a strong, decisive nature. Tonight, hunched over an empty beer glass in a down-at-heel bar, Adam felt a pale imitation of him.

74

The smell was overpowering. As they levered open the reinforced, metal door, the acrid aroma hit her. It was sharp, industrial, nauseating. Slipping a mask over her mouth and nose, Gabrielle turned to check that Miller was ready. The pair of them looked faintly ridiculous, dressed up in forensic suits and shoe coverings, while clutching flashlights and firearms, but there was no alternative. If this was the kill site, they needed to preserve it, but they also needed to protect themselves. Gabrielle didn't expect anyone to be inside – the place looked cold and lifeless – but it wouldn't do to take any chances, especially with a junior officer in tow.

'On the count of three. One, two, three –'

Gabrielle pushed inside, flashlight on full, gun raised. Movement to her left made her turn, but it was just a shadow dancing on the wall. They pressed on, Gabrielle scoping the left-hand corner, while Miller covered their right flank. They prowled forward, eyes searching the darkened trailer for signs of life. But there was nobody here – the place was echoing and empty, save for a pile of cleaning aids and machinery in the far corner.

Turning towards it, Gabrielle brought her flashlight to bear on the discarded gear. There was an industrial carpet cleaner that had seen better days, a torn hose hanging off it, but there were other items that appeared to be newer. Shoe coverings and protective suits. Plastic sheeting and latex gloves. Gabrielle crouched down to examine them, her mind darting back to the marks on Jacob Jones's neck, caused by his allergy to latex. Had Rochelle's body also revealed evidence of being handled by latex gloves? Gabrielle knew they had found no fingerprints or fibres on the body, but she had not asked Aaron Holmes this specific question and made a mental note to do so as soon as they were finished here.

Next to the pile of plastic sheets was a large drum. Firing her flashlight on it, Gabrielle saw a plethora of warning symbols, denoting the contents' toxicity, but also the name of the substance. Sodium hypochlorite.

'Sodium hypo—...what is that stuff?' Miller questioned, reading the label from over her shoulder.

'Industrial bleach. Though why you need it for carpet cleaning beats me.'

Gabrielle moved away from the drum, sweeping her flashlight beam over the empty floor.

'And why so much of it?'

Pausing, she bent down to examine the surface of the trailer. For such a tired, forgotten place, the floor was scrupulously clean, not a trace of dirt visible anywhere. Was Redmond meticulously hygienic or did the smooth, clean surfaces conceal something more sinister? Gabrielle's beam fell on a drain outlet, in the right-hand corner of the room.

'Give me a hand with this, will you?' she said, hurrying over to it.

The drain was topped by a heavy, metal grille. Between the two of them, they lifted it easily and Gabrielle pointed her flashlight down. The beam illuminated a deep, wide pipe that descended for roughly five feet before hitting a body of water. It was dirty, dark, and even with the powerful flashlight it was hard to make anything out, the light dancing back up off the reflection of the water. What was clear was that vast amounts of bleach had been poured down it – the toxic aroma was as strong in the drain as it was in the room above.

'We need to get CSI down here,' Gabrielle said, as they replaced the drain cover. 'Take this place apart.'

'I'll call her now,' Miller replied promptly, pulling her phone from her suit pocket and scuttling off towards the door.

Gabrielle stayed where she was, drinking in the lonely trailer. The place gave her the shivers – there was something ugly and sinister about it – and she yearned to know what had happened within these four walls. That, however, would have to wait until Bartlett and her CSI team descended upon it first thing tomorrow. Whatever secrets this lonely trailer possessed would remain concealed . . . for now.

75

Stepping into the hallway, Adam took a moment to gather himself, noting that once again his emotions felt oddly heightened. He was tempted to blame this on the beer swilling around inside him, but the truth was that every time he came home these days he felt something different – tense, angry, relieved, nervous. It was all such a far cry from the days – so recent really – when he would walk up the front steps with a light heart and a smile on his face.

Now his emotions tumbled over each other. There was guilt at leaving Faith alone, irritation that she had pushed him away, anger that life could be so shitty and occasionally a burning desire to shout and scream, to tear down the walls. Above all, there was nervousness, a sense of not knowing what he might be walking into.

Tonight, he had expected things to be quiet. He assumed that Faith would have either retreated to her studio or retired to bed, but now, as he gently closed the front door behind him, he heard voices coming from the living room. Stepping inside, he was shocked to see Kassie and Faith chatting on the sofa.

They turned as he entered, Kassie blushing slightly, as Faith turned to him.

'Hi, there.'

'Hi,' Adam replied, smiling in a way that he knew didn't look unconvincing.

'Kassie's had a bit of trouble with her mom,' Faith continued.

'She's left town suddenly, so I said Kassie could stay here for a couple of nights, until she sorts herself out.'

It was said lightly as if it was no big deal and Adam found himself mutely nodding his acceptance. In reality of course, this was a massive red light. There were no circumstances under which it was a good idea for a client to stay with her psychologist. Much better to engage her social worker to find a hostel or hotel for her and normally this is exactly what he would have suggested. But Faith seemed keen to help her and in that moment Adam couldn't face slapping her down in front of Kassie. There was no doubting that Faith knew her request was a big ask, hence the forced lightness of her question, but it nevertheless seemed important to her.

'Well, we're glad to help,' Adam said, which was half true.

'It'll only be for a day or so,' Kassie added quickly, shooting a self-conscious look at her bag, which stood next to the sofa.

'It's no trouble,' Adam reassured her. 'Though the police are still keen to talk to you, so first thing in the morning we should give them a call. See if we can sort this thing out.'

Kassie looked uneasy at this prospect, but nodded her agreement. Faith glanced at Adam, her face betraying a suspicion that he was trying to make Kassie feel unwelcome.

'Would you like something to eat, Kassie?' Faith said, turning to the girl.

'No, it's ok, I don't want to get under your feet –'

'It's really no problem,' Faith interjected. 'We're getting takeout.'

'That's kind, but I've already eaten and besides . . .' Kassie replied, hesitating slightly before continuing, '. . . I'd like to go down to Granary Park, to the vigil . . .'

'Of course.'

Faith's easy acceptance of this suggested she had almost

241

been expecting Kassie to say this. To his shame, Adam now realized that the community meeting tonight had gone clean out of his head.

'I don't know if it'll achieve anything, but I feel so helpless doing nothing,' Kassie continued with a self-conscious shrug.

'Then let me get you a key,' Faith now said. 'In case we're not up when you get back . . .'

She bustled out the room, leaving Adam and Kassie alone.

'Are you ok?' Adam ventured.

'I'm fine.'

'And your mom? What's happened?'

But Kassie just shook her head and seconds later Faith returned, pressing a key into Kassie's hand.

'I'll make up the bed for you in the guest room.'

Their spare room had been her mother's home from home in recent weeks, but had been unused in the past few days.

'That's very kind. And thank you,' Kassie replied. 'I didn't know where else to go . . .'

'And we're glad you came. Aren't we, Adam?'

'Absolutely.'

Kassie squinted at him, perhaps trying to gauge the sincerity of his response, then took her leave. For a moment, silence filled the house, the sound of Kassie's footsteps receding slowly, as Faith and Adam continued to stare at each other. Then, abruptly, Faith turned and walked to the table, picking up the takeout menu.

'So, do you want Indian or Chinese?'

'Faith . . .'

She stopped reading and turned to him.

'Are you sure this is wise?'

'"Wise"?'

'She's a patient of mine.'

'I'm aware of that.'

'And a person of interest in an ongoing homicide investigation . . .'

'That's bullshit. They're clutching at straws.'

Adam stared at his wife for a moment, envious of her uncomplicated certainty. She stared back, refusing to apologize for her hospitality.

'What I mean is . . . if it should get out that I had a patient stay over, well, that could have some pretty serious professional ramifications.'

'I understand that, but it'll only be for a couple of days. And we don't need to advertise the fact that she's here.'

Adam wanted to relent with good grace, but somehow he couldn't. He knew that Kassie being here meant trouble. Faith seemed to sense this and went on the offensive.

'I mean what's the alternative? A hotel? One of those grim hostels they send runaways to?'

'They're not that bad.'

'She's *a girl*, Adam. A vulnerable girl –'

'I know that. But there are other ways to help her, it doesn't have to be us.'

'In case it's escaped your notice,' Faith shot back, her colour rising, 'she hasn't *got* anyone else. Her own mother, the one person who is supposed to protect her, to . . . nurture her, has left town – possibly for good. The rest of her family don't want to know, she has no friends –'

'There are safe places she could go. If I talk to her social worker –'

'Kassie needs to be *protected*,' Faith insisted, talking over him. 'She needs love, she needs guidance. You must be able to see that?'

'Of course, I do.'

'And yet still you want to throw her out on the streets?'

She was glaring at him now. Adam felt bad – he was right, but so was she, trusting her maternal instincts and doing what any decent human being would. He loved Faith's strength, her simple morality, her honest fellow feeling, and suddenly he wanted very much to make amends, to be reconciled. But he didn't get the chance, as Faith was already on her way from the room, but not before she had delivered her final, crushing verdict.

'I thought you were better than this.'

76

Kassie marched along the street, her feet slapping the sidewalk. Even though the vigil had begun, there were still stragglers heading towards Granary Park and she fell into step with them. A joint was concealed in her hand and she toked on it discreetly, keen not to miss out on the last few precious puffs.

She'd hoped a smoke would raise her spirits, but nagging questions continued to swirl around in her mind. Why was she such a fuck-up? Why did she spread misery and division wherever she went? Her own mother had despaired of her, cutting her off completely. And what of her new 'carers'? Faith had been welcoming, but Kassie could tell her presence in the Brandt household troubled Adam, however much he tried to conceal it. She couldn't face returning home – though home was an odd word for somewhere that now reeked of rejection and sadness – yet she wasn't unaware of the atmosphere she had created between the Brandts. Were they arguing even now, Adam labouring to persuade Faith to retract their offer of hospitality? The thought of this made Kassie glummer still and she tossed her spent joint into the gutter. Nothing seemed to be going her way today.

But now she heard voices up ahead – loud amplified voices – and also applause. Looking up she realized that she had reached the entrance to the park. She was obviously picking up the PA system within – she could hear a man's voice urging those present to remain resolute, to stand shoulder to shoulder with their fellow citizens.

It was a message that struck a deep chord with Kassie, tonight of all nights. She had felt lonely most of her life, had never felt truly wanted or accepted, and she now found herself hurrying towards the sound, keen to experience the community solidarity for herself. Passing a couple of dawdlers, she rounded the curve of the path and entered the main body of the park.

Immediately she came to a halt. Not just because her route was blocked – the small park teemed with people – but more because she'd never seen such a heart-warming sight. There was not an inch of free space anywhere, the place was overflowing with locals, almost all of whom were carrying candles or lanterns. There were pensioners linked arm in arm, little kids riding on their parents' shoulders to get a view, young couples supporting each other through their distress. Kassie felt tears prick her eyes – it was almost too magical.

The man continued to talk. Kassie couldn't be sure from this distance but he looked like a priest. Normally she would have taken anything he said with a pinch of salt – her experience making it hard to believe in the benevolent God that her mother prayed to – but tonight his words were comforting.

'Shoulder to shoulder we stand, hand in hand with our fellow man. And believe me, there is no evil that cannot be overcome if ordinary, decent citizens refuse to be cowed, refuse to be intimidated. Believe in each other, look out for each other, and this awful period will pass. Deliverance *is* at hand, but it is up to you to make good on it . . .'

His listeners were responding positively and so was Kassie. She found herself smiling and suddenly wanted to laugh – to expel all her anguish and misery and embrace optimism and hope instead. She felt her cares slipping off her as she lost herself in the priest's rhetoric and the crowd's fervour. For the first time in ages, Kassie felt happy, excited even, and she pushed a little deeper into the crowd, keen to get closer to the heart of the action. Something – adrenaline? A desire to belong? – was urging her forward and she happily gave in to it, revelling in the warmth of the people around her. Smiling to herself, she lowered her head and wriggled her way towards the stage, slowly disappearing from view amid the sea of bodies.

77

The car purred along the tarmac, moving slowly but with intent. The occupants were silent – their eyes glued to the street, taking in every parked car, every passing face. They had been searching for nearly two hours now and privately both yearned for a break, but there was no question of letting up yet.

Gabrielle and her deputy had been trawling the Lower West Side since leaving Redmond's trailer. Though he might be hiding out anywhere in the city – or perhaps even outside it – it nevertheless made sense to commence their search in the areas closest to the trailer site. They were not alone in the hunt: two dozen traffic officers and a handful of detectives from Gabrielle's own team had been doing the same thing, completing circuits of Pilsen, Chinatown, the Medical District, the Near West Side and beyond. But so far no one had had so much as a sniff of Redmond's pickup truck or the man himself.

It was perhaps a mark of desperation that Gabrielle and Miller had joined the hunt, rather than directing operations from back at base. But there was no new strategy to plot and no new intelligence to sift, until Bartlett had completed her investigations at least. For now, all roads led to Redmond and until they found him their investigation would continue to stutter.

Miller stifled a yawn, raising a hand to conceal her fatigue. But Gabrielle wasn't fooled, nor was she insensitive to her plight. Her deputy had barely slept this week, spending every waking hour chasing leads or pounding the streets.

'You know, if you want to go home, I'm happy to do this alone. I've only got a couple of hours left anyway.'

'I'm fine, really.'

'It's not a problem. You've worked your tail off these last few days.'

'"We serve and protect",' Miller responded cheerfully.

'And I'm grateful that you do, but you mustn't burn yourself out. Everyone's got a right to a life.'

'Not me,' her deputy replied cheerily. 'I love my job, it gives me everything I need.'

'What about family?' Gabrielle queried, aware how little she knew about her deputy.

'All in Detroit.'

'A partner then?'

'No time for that.'

'Really? I thought young people spent all their free time swiping right, swiping left . . .'

'Not my scene,' Miller replied, turning away to check out a pickup truck rolling past in the opposite direction.

The female driver smiled at them as she sped past. They drove on, abandoning the Medical District to head north. The giant Chicago–Kansas City expressway loomed overhead, as they passed through to the Lower West Side. Gabrielle doubted they would have any better luck here, but they had to try.

'Mom and Dad in Detroit?' Gabrielle asked, as they turned the corner on to South Laflin Street.

'Uh-huh.'

'Get back there often?'

'Once a year maybe. We're not close.'

Gabrielle glanced discreetly at her colleague, who continued to survey the road, seemingly unperturbed by her confession.

'You know, Jane, we all appreciate your dedication, but it is important to have someone to fall back on. This job is demanding and sometimes you'll need –'

'I have the team, that's enough.'

'And that's great, but teams change. You'll get promoted one day and then you'll have a whole new set of faces . . .'

But Miller was shaking her head gently.

'I'm happy where I am. This team is the closest thing to a family I've ever had.'

It was said simply, like a matter of fact, but still took Gabrielle by surprise.

'I've never really fitted in anywhere before,' Miller went on, sensing Gabrielle's reaction. 'At school, at work, at home even. But you took a chance on me . . . and I'll never forget that.'

'You've more than repaid my faith in you.'

'I mean it,' Miller continued urgently. 'I had no focus, no direction at all until I joined your team.'

Gabrielle was taken aback by emotion in Miller's voice. She had never heard her deputy talk like this before. Pulling up at a red light, Gabrielle took the opportunity to turn to her deputy, curious to know what had brought on this uncharacteristic openness. Miller returned her gaze briefly, then quickly averted her eyes.

'I probably shouldn't be talking to you like this,' Miller continued, staring at a point somewhere above Gabrielle's shoulder. 'It's just that . . . I guess nobody's ever *believed* in me before. That's why it means so much. Why I wouldn't even consider promotion if it was offered to me. I just want to be in the Bureau doing good work, with you, the team . . .'

There was a zeal in her voice, in her expression, but something else too. Something that troubled Gabrielle.

'And does this goodwill extend to Detective Montgomery too?' Gabrielle replied.

'She's young,' Miller said quickly. 'She's still learning, but she'll get there.'

'With the right guidance.'

'Of course,' Miller responded. 'I've got no problem with her at all. She will be . . . she *is* a good detective. And I'll help her in any way I can. It's my duty, given what you've done for *me* –'

Gabrielle braced herself for more – a stumbling, awkward protestation of solidarity and intent – but to her surprise Miller suddenly ground to a halt. Gabrielle turned to her, unsure what to expect next, but was wrong-footed once more. Miller was not looking at her, but at something directly behind her.

'Look,' Miller breathed, gesturing over Gabrielle's shoulder.

Gabrielle swivelled in her seat, scarcely daring to hope. But this time she was not to be disappointed. Hidden in a shadowy alleyway off the main street was a brown Ford pickup truck with Louisiana plates.

78

'Do you want to wait for backup? Or should we go in?'

The two women stood in the shadows of the crumbling apartment block. All trace of her earlier emotion had vanished – Detective Miller was back in the zone. She was itching with excitement, pacing round the parked pickup truck, even as she checked and rechecked her firearm.

Gabrielle stepped back to take another look at the derelict building which rose above them. The battered greystone was forlorn, but not forgotten, covered in signs revealing that it was scheduled for demolition. The work was not going to start for another three months, however, making the empty shell a perfect hiding place. The whole place appeared lifeless and abandoned, but screwing up her eyes Gabrielle could just make out a faint light coming from within.

'I say we go in.'

'Fine by me,' Miller responded eagerly.

'Backup will be another twenty minutes. And there's every chance the cavalry will alert him to our presence.'

It was a tough call. Going in without backup was dangerous, but with the element of surprise they might take Redmond without a fight. Slipping her firearm from her holster, Gabrielle eased off the safety catch.

'Ok, let's do this. But we take it *slow* . . .'

Nodding, Miller stepped forward. The main door had planks nailed across it in a forbidding 'X' shape, but arching her body through the gap, Miller was able to grasp the handle.

Neither woman was surprised when it opened easily and Miller now wriggled through the gap in the boards. Gabrielle followed suit, disappearing into the darkness.

They crept forward, barely daring to breathe. The building had been derelict for a considerable period of time – floorboards creaked ominously, plaster came away in their hands and exposed wires hung from the ceiling. Gabrielle assumed they weren't live, but she wasn't going to test her theory and worked her way carefully forward, testing each foothold before advancing. The place was rotten – it looked like it might swallow you up if you took a wrong step – and each move was fraught with danger.

Someone was in the building – she could hear movement – the question was *where?* The noises seemed to be coming from ahead of them, but the darkness was disorienting. Gabrielle was sorely tempted to fire up her flashlight, but to do so would risk alerting Redmond to their presence. So, she pressed on through the dark, her weapon raised.

She could just make out a doorway on their left. Gabrielle paused to make sure Miller was with her, then whispered:

'On three. One, two, three –'

They moved swiftly into the room, their eyes searching the gloom, their guns seeking a target. Something scurried away quickly into the shadows and Miller reacted sharply to it, but Gabrielle laid a restraining hand on her arm.

'Rats,' she whispered.

Turning, they examined the rest of the room. It was empty, so retreating quickly, they moved on. There was another door off to the right and they hurried there now, but this too was deserted. The final room on the ground floor was too dangerous even to enter, several floorboards having completely given way. No one had set foot down here for some time.

They were about to turn back into the hallway, when a sudden noise made them stop. A loud creak, emanating from almost directly above their heads. Followed by dull, muffled voices. Was someone up there with Redmond? She nodded to Miller, and the pair retraced their steps, moving swiftly but silently along the hallway until they reached the main staircase. Once again, Gabrielle flashed a look at her watch, its face glowing up at her in the gloom. Backup was still ten minutes away – too long to wait when there was a chance of catching the killer – or killers – unawares.

Gabrielle took the stairs steadily, but swiftly. This was partly because she was nervous, but mostly because the sound of voices was getting clearer now. They could definitely make out a female voice now. Gabrielle gripped her firearm tightly, hoping she wouldn't have to use it, praying that luck would be on her side if she did.

Cresting the staircase, she found herself in a long, gloomy hallway. The noises were coming from a room close by on the left. Inching along the wall, Gabrielle kept her steps light and wide – even the tiniest noise now might betray their presence. Butting up against the door frame, she gestured silently to Miller, then stepped confidently but quietly across the open doorway, taking refuge on the other side. The women were well positioned now to cover the interior of the room from different angles. Gabrielle pushed away thoughts of family, of the danger she was putting herself in, then nodded to her deputy. Spinning around the door frame, they trained their guns on the room beyond.

To Gabrielle's surprise, it was empty. There were a chair and a table. On the latter sat a number of takeout boxes and a smouldering cigarette, balanced delicately on the lip of an ashtray. There were a couple of cardboard boxes on the floor, some old newspapers and beyond that a flickering TV screen, which appeared to be playing the evening news bulletin from WGN. The female newscaster's delivery of the latest developments of the hunt for 'The Chicago Butcher' were crisp and clear, making Gabrielle pause. Was this the female voice she had heard downstairs? The still-lit cigarette suggested someone was in here. The question was *who*?

Unsettled, Gabrielle retreated to the hallway, her Colt .45 leading the way. She pressed on purposefully, thinking only of bringing their suspect in, so much so that her foot almost went through a rotten board – the seasoned officer managing to extract it just in time. Righting herself, she gestured at Miller to follow, then took a step forward.

As she did so, a figure darted across the far end of the hallway, his gun roaring as he went. Gabrielle lurched to the right – the bullet slamming into the wall where she'd been standing. Immediately she returned fire – once, twice, three times – the bullets tearing down the long hallway, just missing their target, who darted into the room opposite. Gabrielle turned swiftly to check that Miller was ok, firing an order at her startled deputy.

'Stay behind me.'

Miller obliged. Keeping close to the wall, Gabrielle slid along the hallway, her gun fixed on the open doorway of the room. Her finger was tensed against the trigger, ready to fire again. She hadn't wanted it to play out this way, but now it was do or die. She moved quickly down the corridor and, on reaching the open doorway, swung round it, keeping low to the ground. She was ready to fire, but the room was empty, a bitterly cold wind roaring in through the open window.

Hastening over to it, Gabrielle peered out cautiously – just in time to see a tall, shaven-headed man pulling himself to his feet amid the garbage bags below. For a moment, their eyes met – it was Redmond. Gabrielle raised her gun to fire, but he was already on the move and she was a second too slow. Cursing, Gabrielle turned and fled the room almost knocking Miller over as she did so.

She reached the stairs in seconds and threw herself down them. Now she was advancing across the hall. Wrenching the door open, she kicked once, twice, smashing the wooden planks from their holdings. She could hear Miller close behind her, but didn't hesitate. Darting out into the cold air, she sprinted to her right, angling sharply down a narrow alleyway, which led to the back of the building. Rounding this, she raced along the rear, hurdling broken furniture and abandoned toys until she found the window Redmond had jumped from. Orienting herself, she now spotted his escape route, a wider alleyway leading north, and sped down it. To her enormous relief, Redmond could be seen ahead, scrambling towards the end of the alleyway.

'Police. Freeze!'

A bullet flew several feet above her head, but Gabrielle didn't flinch, hurrying down the alleyway after him. Redmond's eyes met hers briefly – then, deciding against chancing another shot at such long range, he turned and fled.

The chase was on.

79

Kassie kept her head low, weaving her narrow frame through the crowds. She was only forty feet or so from the stage now, but the wall of humanity in front of her was making progress difficult. People had been tolerant of her so far, but now she was starting to excite comment and the odd expletive as she eased past people, connecting with elbows and shoulders. It was stupid really – she could hear perfectly well and if she bothered to look could have taken in the stage perfectly, but something was propelling her on.

Was it hope that was driving her? A need to believe that everything would be ok? Or something else? Her heart was beating fast and she felt a little dizzy. One minute she felt overcome, like she might suddenly faint amid the crush of the crowds, the next she felt light-headed and euphoric. It was bewildering, a little scary and yet somehow compelling, hence her stuttering but persistent progress.

On and on she drove, treading on someone's foot, but moving forward too swiftly to hear the full extent of their displeasure. And then suddenly there she was, pressing against the crash barriers that bordered the stage. Turning around to look back, she took in the multitude of faces and wondered for a moment how she had made it through such a forbidding mass of flesh and blood, but another loud cheer from the crowd jolted her out of her thoughts and she turned back to the main event.

A middle-aged woman was talking, urging the citizens of Chicago to police their city, to root out the evil within their community. She seemed to be the main draw, the organizer of the vigil perhaps, and the volume of the crowd's responses seemed to be growing with her every utterance. It felt like the gathering was reaching its climax – turning into something different and more raucous – a clarion call to concerned citizens everywhere.

The West Towners present were borne along by it, as was Kassie. The speaker was not unaffected either, raising her voice as she pointed to people in the crowd, urging them individually to act, to fight back. It was like she was anointing people, giving them special licence to lead the fight, and Kassie sought her approbation, craving her favour and the reassurance it would bring.

The woman seemed not to see her, gazing to the left of her, above her, to the right of her . . . and then suddenly she found her. She paused for a moment, then launched back into her speech, even as she lowered her eyes to meet Kassie's. Immediately, Kassie stumbled, knocking into the person behind her.

'Hey. What'ya doing?'

The words sounded muted and distant. Kassie wanted to cling on to them, to drag herself back into the present, but it was too late. Her eyes had locked on to the woman's and there was no going back. There was a moment's breathless silence, then without warning Kassie screamed long and loud, before crumpling to the ground.

80

He was in agony, but still he pressed on.

He had plunged fifteen feet or more from the window, landing heavily below. His fall had been partially broken by the garbage bags that littered the alleyway, but he had smashed his elbow into the hard ground. His whole arm was numb – had he broken it? – but there was no question of tending to it now, not when his pursuer was so close behind.

How the hell had they found him? It didn't make sense. He had been so careful, holing up in one of the few derelict apartment buildings that hadn't been turned into crash pads for hipsters. It was the perfect bolthole for someone who needed to remain below the radar.

Another shouted warning from behind. The cop was gaining on him and he half expected a bullet to slam into his back at any moment . . . but he wasn't beaten yet. He knew these alleyways like the back of his hand and he put his knowledge to good use now, cutting left, then right, before doubling back on himself to confuse his pursuer. Chicago is a city of alleyways and he had always used them to his advantage.

Still she dogged his footsteps. She was clearly no fool. Nor was she a coward, running towards danger rather than from it. CPD officers were supposed to be tough and she was the evidence to back up this claim, but he still had one thing in his favour. She wouldn't shoot if there were civilians in the line of fire and the streets were *busy* tonight. He could hear noise in the distance – there was obviously some event going on – and as he'd dodged and weaved his way down the alleyways that linked the city's main thoroughfares, he'd caught glimpses of people, all heading in the same direction. He wasn't sure what it was all about – there wasn't a game on tonight – but it offered him a chance of salvation. There was no chance of outrunning his pursuer, but he could outthink her.

He had kept out of sight so far, fearing that he would be spotted by patrolling uniformed officers, but caution was no longer an option. She was only fifty feet behind him, in range if she could get a decent shot away and he didn't want to die in a fetid Chicago alleyway – not when he still had so much more to do.

Reaching the end of the cut-through, he stumbled out on to the street.

A startled woman looked up at him, taking in his red, sweaty face, before walking away. He followed her progress, noting that she was heading to a nearby park that appeared to be overflowing with people. He didn't hesitate, overtaking the woman and pushing as fast as he could towards the far side of the road, hoping to lose his pursuer in the crowded park.

But the cop – a middle-aged black woman – was already on the street, her eyes seeking her prey. A moment's indecision, then she cut left, in the same direction as him. He cursed quietly – he had gained a few feet on her, but she would soon catch up, if he couldn't find somewhere to hide. Redoubling his efforts, he limped hard towards the busy park ahead.

As he did so, he began to pick up sounds again. A woman's voice – amplified by a PA system – but also applause and occasional shouts of defiance. And now it dawned on him what it was. He had seen it on the TV but hadn't paid attention at the time – and now here it was right in front of him. The candlelit vigil for Jacob Jones and Rochelle Stevens. It was almost too good to be true. It was *perfect*. And now, in his hour of need, it would be his salvation.

Busting a gut, he darted towards the entrance. But suddenly he found himself flying sideways. He hit the sidewalk hard, his throbbing head striking the ground. The wind had been knocked clean out of him, but even so he scrambled to his feet – only to find his assailant doing likewise. The young female officer was already reaching inside her jacket, pulling her weapon from its holster.

'CPD. Drop your weapon and . . .'

Redmond didn't hesitate – smashing his forehead into her face. She reeled away, stumbling drunkenly backwards on to the ground. He snatched up his weapon – he could waste her now, easy as shooting fish in a barrel – but he had to keep going. The park was within reach.

He took a step forward, but, even as he did so, the cold barrel of a gun jabbed into the back of his head. In the confusion, he hadn't registered his original pursuer approaching. What now? Could he shrug her off and turn and fire in time? He thought it was possible, but even as he weighed the odds, a cool voice behind him said:

'Go for it, Kyle. Give me a reason to pull the trigger.'

81

Kassie sat on the cracked plastic chair, holding an ice pack to her throbbing head. Her eyes were closed – the hospital's strip lighting only serving to aggravate her headache – but now she heard footsteps approaching. Even without looking up she knew who it was.

'I'm so sorry,' Kassie said quietly. 'They insisted I call *someone . . .*'

'It's ok,' Adam said wearily, seating himself next to her. 'While you're staying with us, you're our responsibility.'

This made Kassie feel even worse.

'What happened?' Adam said softly.

Suddenly Kassie felt a rush of gratitude towards Adam. Despite everything, he was still *trying* to be kind. Few people had been so patient with her.

'I fainted at the vigil, hit my head . . . Next thing I know I'm in the back of an ambulance. I told them to let me go, but they insisted on bringing me here.'

'How are you feeling now?'

'I'm fine . . . and the doctors say there's no harm done. To be honest, I just want to get out of here.'

'Had you been smoking? Before you fainted?'

Kassie hesitated, so Adam persisted:

'The doctor said he could smell the skunk on your breath.'

'One joint, that was all.'

'You're supposed to be giving up . . .'

'I know and I will, but that's not what this was about.'

'So, what happened?'

Kassie knew this moment was coming, but wasn't ready for it.

'Was it the crush of people? Did someone *harm* you in some way?'

Kassie picked at her fingernails.

'Look, I'm not angry with you, whatever you might thin—'

'I had another vision.'

Adam pulled up short. From the look on his face, this was what he'd suspected, feared perhaps.

'I was at the vigil and it was great,' Kassie continued quickly. 'It was exciting, uplifting . . . but then I saw her . . .'

'Saw who?'

'The woman who was speaking . . . Madelaine something.'

'Madelaine Baines.'

'Right . . . I didn't mean to, but I met her eye and I saw it. Her pain, her terror, then fire all around her, *consuming* her . . .'

She turned to Adam, her voice quivering:

'Madelaine Baines is going to be his next victim.'

82

Kyle Redmond glared at Gabrielle, tugging at the straps that anchored him to the restraint chair. He had been calm while he had a gun to his head, but as soon as he was in custody, he'd gone berserk – kicking, punching, even biting the officers who laboured to process his arrest. In the end, they'd had to restrain him, before moving him to the interview suite. Restraint chairs were more often associated with Guantanamo Bay, but Gabrielle was within her rights to use one and wasn't taking any chances. Detective Miller was still getting checked out, but Gabrielle suspected her deputy had a broken nose.

'Jacob Jones. And Rochelle Stevens.'

Gabrielle slid photos of the two victims across the table, until they sat under Redmond's nose. He made no attempt to look at them, however, instead staring directly at her. His eyes seemed to be crawling over her features, as if trying to commit them to memory.

'Both brutally murdered. Can you tell me when you first met them?'

Redmond turned his attentions to Detective Suarez, who was sitting in for the injured Miller, staring directly at him. It was an obvious play for a thug like Redmond – divide and rule – but she knew Suarez wouldn't be intimidated. He was a seasoned officer who'd faced down plenty of bad folk in his time.

'Let me help you. You cleaned Mr Jones's house on West

Erie Street. And Rochelle Stevens' property on Washington Close. Did you talk to them while you were there, Kyle? Get to know them?'

Lazily, Redmond returned his gaze to Gabrielle. He seemed almost amused by proceedings. There was no sense at all that he was cowed by his capture.

'No? Maybe they were in a hurry to get to work,' Gabrielle continued easily. 'They're both busy people. I guess you had the place to yourself after that? Pick up anything, did you? Spare set of keys, perhaps?'

Redmond's eyes narrowed fractionally, but he maintained his stony silence.

'Because here's the thing. Whoever abducted these guys had access to their homes and all the householders' keys have been accounted for, so . . .'

Gabrielle let this hang in the air, but Redmond wasn't biting.

'No? ok, let's do the basics, then,' she pressed on. 'Where you were on the night of April 10th?'

Redmond took in the question, but said nothing.

'No? How about April 17th then? The night Rochelle Stevens was murdered.'

Redmond shifted in his chair, pulling angrily at his restraints once more.

'I asked you a question, Kyle.'

Reluctantly, Redmond stopped tugging.

'I was out. I don't remember where.'

'Out doing what? Partying? Drinking?'

'Driving, I guess.'

'Go anywhere near West Town?'

Redmond shrugged.

'That's where the victims lived. But, of course, you'd know

that, wouldn't you? Having visited them before,' Gabrielle continued, conversationally.

'I've a bad memory for faces,' he replied defiantly.

'Really? Two handsome creatures like them? Look at the photos, Kyle. These two are hotties. You couldn't see those faces and not remember them, surely? But, then again, maybe they wouldn't give you the time of day.'

Redmond looked up sharply, to see if Gabrielle was mocking him. His own face was dominated by a large birthmark – this, added to the heavy tattooing, piercings and angry, shaven head, meant Redmond was the type of character you would cross the road to avoid.

'You enjoy having power over people, don't you?'

'What?'

'Sexual assault, false imprisonment, torture. It's all here in black and white. You enjoy terrorizing people, degrading them . . .'

Redmond snorted and yanked at his restraints once more. He was getting visibly frustrated at his helplessness now, sweat forming on his creased brow.

'You're not going anywhere until you start talking to me, Kyle. So, tell me about Dani. What had she done to you?'

Redmond ceased his struggling, surprised by the mention of his ex-girlfriend.

'She liked you. She took you in. And, in return, you kept her hostage for forty-eight hours. Tortured her, cut off two of her fingers.'

'Bitch had no loyalty, no class –'

'Also, I see from your juvenile reports that you attacked your mother.'

'No one deserved it more than her,' he said, a smile spreading across his features for the first time.

'Also, your siblings, fellow students . . .'

Redmond shrugged, but Gabrielle could see his pride at the memories.

'And now Jacob Jones and Rochelle Stevens. Tell me, what did it feel like when you had *them* at your mercy?'

Redmond was watching her closely now.

'Did you want to destroy them? To make them unrecognizable to their families, their loved ones? Did they say – or do – something that belittled you? That made you feel small?'

Redmond lowered his eyes to the photos on the table, drinking in the images in front of him.

'No? Maybe I've got this all wrong then? Maybe you *are* innocent?'

'Now you're getting it . . .'

He smiled mirthlessly, revealing several gold teeth. Gabrielle got a blast of stale tobacco breath, but concealed her distaste, determined not to react to his provocation.

'So why did you run from us?' Gabrielle countered. 'If you're innocent, why did you shoot at a police officer? Assault my colleague?'

'I've broken parole. If I get taken in, I'm back in jail.'

'Bullshit. You don't attempt to murder a CPD officer over a parole violation.'

'You ever served time in Cook County?' he replied scornfully.

'Of course not.'

'Then how would *you* know? All sorts of freaks in there. I'd rather take a bullet – shit, I'd rather meet my mother in *hell* – than go back in there.'

'Is that right?'

'You know it,' Redmond replied confidently, as if he'd just landed a three-pointer.

'Well, that's a shame,' Suarez added, 'because that's exactly where you're going.'

Anger flared in his eyes now. Redmond was about to launch a volley of abuse at Suarez, but Gabrielle stepped in.

'Where did you do it, Kyle?'

'Jesus Chrrrisssttt . . .'

'We know it was by a body of water,' Gabrielle countered. 'A river or lake. I'm wondering if you did it in your trailer on South Morgan Street?'

Now Redmond tensed, visibly wrong-footed by Gabrielle's assertion.

'A couple of people knew about it, sure, but no one significant, right? It was private, out of the way and very quiet at night.'

'Plus, you had everything on hand to wash away the evidence,' Suarez overlapped. 'Nice and easy . . .'

'What you talking about? I ain't got a trailer on South Morgan Street.'

'Yes, you do, Kyle. It was rented in one of your favourite aliases.'

Another reaction. Finally, Gabrielle sensed she had Redmond on the run.

'Our CSI teams are heading down there right now. If we find a single hair belonging to Rochelle Stevens or Jacob Jones . . .'

'You won't find jack,' he countered.

'So why *had* you cleaned so thoroughly? The whole place stunk of bleach and I'm talking the heavy-duty stuff, not your everyday household product.'

'This is bullshit.'

'You knew the victims, you've got form –'

'No, no, no, no.'

'Plus, you have no alibi *and* the perfect kill site.'

Redmond said nothing in response, staring at his feet. Gabrielle let the silence hold for a few moments, before continuing.

'Now, you've been lying to me since you sat down, but . . . I'm going to give you another chance. I know you're not acting alone. I think that maybe you weren't even the one that started all this, so I'm going to ask you one more question. And this time I'd like the truth.'

Redmond continued to stare at the floor. He looked like he'd lost his bearings now, like he didn't know what was coming next.

'Do you know this girl?'

She slid a photo of Kassie Wojcek across the table. Reluctantly, Redmond looked up, his brow creasing once more, as he took in the photo.

'What you say next will have a big bearing on how this plays for you, Kyle. So, think very carefully and tell me – do you know this girl?'

Redmond stared at the photo for a long time, as if debating how best to react, then muttered:

'No . . .' He shook his head slowly, but wouldn't meet Gabrielle's eye. 'Never seen that bitch.'

83

The radio burbled quietly, as they drove through the darkened streets. Kassie's head was beginning to clear, the pain was less intense, and once more she felt embarrassed and ill at ease. Adam had said little in response to her latest vision, concentrating instead on signing the necessary paperwork to get her discharged and into his care. Kassie had the distinct impression he wanted to get her away from the hospital before she said anything else.

The Lexus rolled smoothly along the road, exacerbating the silence within. They were on their way home . . . to do what? Go to bed and forget all about it? Discuss her latest episode and act on it? Call social services? It all seemed so complicated, so confusing, and suddenly Kassie longed for some kind of clarity. Adam had agreed to help her confront her gift, hadn't he? Or had he been humouring her all along?

Kassie watched as Adam leaned forward to turn the radio up. Clearly the silence was getting to him too. It was WKSC, a classic dad's station full of eighties rock and nineties grunge. Kassie surprised herself by having to suppress a smile – she kind of liked the cheesy hits this local station played, but surely it was a bit old for Adam, who prided himself on being a trendy, youthful fortysomething. Swallowing down her amusement, Kassie tried to lose herself in the music – a rock anthem being swiftly succeeded by an eighties power ballad. It was fun to switch off, to sink into the clichéd lyrics and overfamiliar melodies. But too soon it was over, the latest news bulletin shattering the spell.

'Before we bring you the weather, we have some breaking news,' the newscaster announced. 'At roughly nine p.m. this evening, CPD officers arrested and detained a suspect in connection with the murders of Jacob Jones and Rochelle Stevens, the so-called 'Chicago Butcher' murders. According to CPD sources, the suspect is now at their headquarters in Bronzeville, being questioned by CPD detectives . . .'

Kassie sat perfectly still, stunned by what she'd heard. The presenter's voice burbled on, but if anything the silence in the car was now even more pronounced. Kassie's head was spinning – what did it all mean? It wasn't possible that she'd got it wrong, was it? That had never happened before . . .

Turning to Adam, she noted his pale complexion, the way he was gripping the steering wheel tightly. Anguished, nervous, full of doubt, she found herself saying:

'Do you believe me?'

But Adam said nothing, staring straight ahead into the night.

'I asked you a question, Adam. Do you believe me?'

There was a long pause, before Adam replied:

'To be honest, I don't know what to believe . . .'

'Don't say that,' Kassie responded, stricken.

'You tell me there's going to be another murder, but the police have arrested a suspect. You tell me a woman is helping the killer, but the only female on the CPD's radar is you. You tell me that I'm going to . . . to harm you, yet the thought has never entered my head, never would enter my head.'

It was all coming out in a rush – too fast and too devastating for Kassie to counter.

'So, tell me, Kassie, what am I supposed to think? Just . . . what?'

Kassie stared at him for a moment, shocked by his words and his aggressive, desperate tone. Then she swiftly turned away.

'Look, I don't mean to vent,' he continued, shooting an anxious look at her. 'But, honestly, I don't know which way is up any more.'

Guilt hit Kassie like a sledgehammer. The enthusiastic, committed doctor who'd offered to help her now looked beaten and drained. She sank back into her seat, feeling utterly forlorn. She could tell Adam regretted his outburst and wanted to engage with her, but she wasn't capable of that right now. So, instead, she stared out of the window, hiding her tears from him as they drove on through the quiet Chicago streets.

84

Madelaine Baines closed the front door and rested her head against it. She was utterly spent – drained of energy, her throat dry – but she was happy. It had gone better than she could ever have expected.

Sliding the deadlock into place, Madelaine gathered herself and dragged her bones to the kitchen. There she was heartened to see a brightly coloured note lying on the breakfast bar. Written in felt tip, it read: 'Well done, SuperMom. You're the greatest!!!' Bordered with pretty flowers, and written in her daughters' spidery handwriting, it made Madelaine's heart sing.

She had toyed with allowing them to come to the vigil, but in the end had decided against it. They had school tomorrow and she didn't want to upset them unnecessarily, so Paul had stayed home with them, with strict orders to let them watch the minute's silence, then take them up to bed. Clearly this had been enough, however – the sight of the hordes of well-wishers clutching candles impressing them sufficiently to put pen to paper.

Picking up the note, Madelaine located the magnet they had bought at the Grand Canyon and attached the drawing to the refrigerator. The sentiment made her blush, but actually the girls were right – she had achieved something. Where there was panic and fear, now there was determination and resolve. It gave her a warm feeling, almost taking the edge off her crushing fatigue.

Grabbing a glass of water, Madelaine padded up the stairs. The house was totally quiet – the twins were almost certainly fast asleep and, by the sound of the gentle snoring emanating from the master bedroom, Paul was too. Madelaine felt a little pang of disappointment, as she joined him in the spacious room – part of her wanted to sleep of course, but another part wanted to share her triumph with someone, to process the many and varied emotions she felt.

There had been a little disruption towards the end – a teenager fainting in the front row – but other than that everything had passed off exactly as Madelaine had hoped. There had been many tears of course, but also applause for the contributions the two Chicagoans had made to city life before their untimely deaths. The minute's silence had been impeccably observed, the speeches rousing, and though she wouldn't say it out loud, Madelaine felt her own efforts had been on the money. The crowd seemed to appreciate her words, and as they drifted away, consoled and encouraged afresh, Madelaine had had a moment to reflect on a job well done. Shortly afterwards, the phone calls had begun – from radio and TV stations, the press. She was now due to appear on WGN news tomorrow morning, followed by an interview with the *Tribune*. It was dizzying and, if she was honest, a little exciting too.

She was tempted to turn the TV on, keen to see how the local news channels were reporting the vigil, but that would have to wait until tomorrow. She was too tired even to pick up the remote, so, crossing the bedroom to her side of the bed, she lowered herself gently down on to the mattress and carefully, quietly, switched on the bedside light.

She turned to Paul, to see if she'd disturbed him, but he hadn't stirred. Satisfied, she began to undress, unbuttoning her blouse and tossing it into the laundry basket, before removing her earrings. She placed them on her bedside table, next to her glass of water and as she did so she spotted something. Her favourite family photo – of the four of them rafting in Montana – was out of place. Normally it was perfectly positioned so she could lie in bed and drink in the heart-warming image of happy days gone by. But now it was marginally off kilter, facing slightly away from the bed, so she could only make out the girls.

Madelaine paused. The cleaner hadn't been in today and Paul never ventured over to this side of the bed – her face creams and health serums scaring him off. It must have been the girls then, but why would they be messing around her bedside table? There was little of any interest for them here – iPads not being allowed in bedrooms.

It was a small mystery, but that is what it would have to remain, because Madelaine was far too tired to work it out now. She would ask the girls in the morning, and was already looking forward to hearing what awkward excuses they would make up to cover for their intrusion.

Smiling to herself, Madelaine shed the rest of her clothes, then slid into bed. With one last, happy look at the photo, now correctly positioned, Madelaine leaned over and switched out her light, plunging the room into darkness.

85

Faith kept her eyes closed, her breathing steady.

'Faith?' Adam repeated softly.

She had heard them return ten minutes ago. Shortly afterwards, Adam had entered the bedroom, slipped off his clothes in the dark and climbed into bed. Now he was craning over her.

'Are you asleep?'

She kept perfectly still, not moving a muscle. Moments later, Adam turned away and settled down to rest. She could tell he was disappointed, she had heard a small, almost inaudible sigh of frustration, but she couldn't face further discussion. She knew she'd been too hard on him earlier, but she wasn't ready to apologize yet. She had been angered by his apparent willingness to push Kassie away, yet she knew he didn't deserve the character assassination she'd meted out to him. Perhaps it was her grief that made her overprotective of Kassie, perhaps it was the hormones pouring fuel on her anger – either way she'd felt bad about her harsh words, especially as Adam hadn't hesitated to go to the teenager's aid when the hospital rang. His silent departure from the house, his selfless mercy mission in the middle of the night, was the most eloquent riposte to her accusations.

And yet . . . Faith *did* feel protective of Kassie and bridled at any attempt to reject her. Not just because the troubled teenager was alone in the world, not even because Faith sensed some kinship with Kassie – she too had suffered from mental health problems during her teens and twenties. It was also because Kassie was such a good listener. Adam was too, of course, but their conversations about Annabelle were so loaded, framed in her mind by her failure to carry their baby to term and the unanswered question of when — *if* — they would ever try again. Kassie had no investment in their situation, was new to their lives and was content to share Faith's grief, to share her pain. Which is why she valued her company.

Adam had rolled away and appeared to be asleep now, his chest rising and falling rhythmically, so Faith slipped out of bed and trod softly towards the kitchen. She felt hot and clammy tonight — her mouth was dry and she longed for a cool glass of water. Entering the kitchen, she was about to reach for the tap when she suddenly became aware of a figure sitting alone in the darkness. Swallowing a squawk of alarm, Faith switched on the main light to reveal Kassie at the kitchen table. A glass of milk sat in front of her, as well as the remnants of some cookies.

'Sorry, couldn't sleep,' Kassie said quickly, worried that she had scared Faith.

'Me neither,' Faith replied, filling a glass of water.

'I hope you don't mind me —'

'Not at all. Take whatever you like. Honestly, I've been living off crackers and cheese these last few days. Can't face anything else . . .'

Kassie nodded, but didn't respond. This was one of her best attributes, the sense that sometimes it was ok not to talk. Tonight, however, something was different. Something was troubling her.

'Are you ok?' Faith said, seating herself next to Kassie.

'Sure.'

'What did the hospital say?'

'It's nothing. Bump on the head . . .'

'Did they give you anything? For the pain, I mean? We've got Xanax –'

'I'm fine, honestly.'

Kassie flashed a brief, tight smile at Faith, then took another drink of milk. She looked so melancholy, so deflated, fidgeting restlessly in her seat. The oddness of the situation was suddenly brought home to Faith – the difference in their ages, their lack of knowledge of each other – and she now found herself unsure what to say. So instead she just watched. She had never taken the time to examine Kassie's face properly but now Faith found real beauty there – the scattering of freckles over her pale skin, the neat frame provided by her rich, auburn hair – but a weariness too, a sense that she had been marked by life. It was a beguiling mixture.

Kassie was now playing with her glass, turning it round and round in her hands. The motion seemed to soothe her a little, but looking up she now caught Faith looking at her and suddenly stopped.

'Sorry,' she mumbled, looking embarrassed.

'It's fine,' Faith replied. 'Carry on if you like . . .'

But Kassie didn't and once more silence descended. Faith couldn't think of anything to say, yet neither of them was going to be able to sleep any time soon and the absurdity of this irritated her. What were they going to do? She was about to suggest switching on the TV – even at this late hour there might be something on that Kassie would like – when another idea struck her. She hadn't been planning this, but suddenly it seemed precisely the right thing to do. In fact, she might even enjoy it, the novelty of a new subject. Which is why she now found herself saying:

'Could I sketch you, Kassie?'

86

'Drop your chin a little and look towards the door.'

Kassie complied, but still the angle wasn't quite right, so Faith crossed to her, laying a hand on her chin and moving it fractionally. Returning to her position a few feet in front of Kassie, Faith was pleased to see that the teenager's look was perfect. There was beauty there of course, a certain bearing, but there was vulnerability and complexity too.

Whenever Faith began a portrait, this is exactly what she looked for. The aesthetics were important, but it was the depiction of a basic truth that was crucial – this was supposed to be a picture of someone's *character*. Feeling that she had found this, Faith took up her pencil and began to sketch.

To her surprise, she worked swiftly. A day, two days ago, the pencil would have felt thick and alien in her hand. The subject would not have interested her, moreover, caught up as she was in her own tragedy. But now it seemed easy – the strokes were natural and she actually felt as if she were enjoying herself. Before long, she had a workable outline of the face and a decent first pass at the girl's petite features. The latter would need finessing of course, as it was in the eyes, the crease of the brow, the attitude of the mouth, that one found character. It would take several attempts, and a deeper understanding of the subject, to get it right, but she had made a good start.

'I wish I had your colouring,' Faith said suddenly.

She had always thought redheads looked more exotic and beguiling than other women.

'I wish I had your style,' Kassie replied simply.

'Come on, you look great.'

'Are you kidding?'

Kassie ran her fingers down one of her tresses, looking self-conscious and dissatisfied.

'I always cut my own hair and Mom was never very keen on me wearing make-up.'

'Well, we can fix that,' Faith responded. 'Where do you get your colouring from? Is your mom like you –'

'No, she's dark. I get it from my grandma. My mom's mom . . .'

'Tell me about her.' Faith put her pencil down and perched on the edge of her stool.

Often it was a forced, stilted affair to get subjects to open up, to reveal something of their character, their family. But suddenly Faith felt as though she really wanted to know more about this mysterious, melancholic teenager. Kassie, however, hesitated and for a moment Faith thought she was going to refuse, but eventually the teenager responded, weighing her words carefully.

'My grandma is in a home now – she has dementia – but when she was younger she was very spontaneous. She was heart, not head. She could be tough, harsh even at times, but to me she was always very loving and generous.'

'What's her name?'

'Wieslawa. Wieslawa Zuzanna,' Kassie intoned, a smile tugging at the corner of her lips.

'And you're close to her?'

'Very close.'

It was said firmly, almost defiantly.

'She didn't get on with everyone – well, in fact, with quite a few people – but me and her . . .'

'Why was that do you think?'

Kassie paused, seemingly unsure how to respond, so Faith continued:

'Would you say you're like her?'

'Yes and no. She's a strong woman, much stronger than me. She has been through several tragedies in her life, but she's toughed it out. Came to the States with nothing, built a home for herself and her children . . . but she had been touched by her experiences, by her childhood. So she's often short-tempered, she can be hard on people. And she had her favourites . . .'

'Your mother?'

Kassie laughed, but it was not a happy sound.

'No, not her. Me, yes, but not my mother.'

Faith leaned forward, intrigued now.

'Why don't they get on?'

'Because . . . they're opposites. My mother is dutiful, pragmatic, responsible. My grandmother is none of those things . . .'

'That happens in families. Different characters, different temperaments . . .'

'No, it was more than that,' Kassie insisted. 'My grandma . . . had seen things that made her doubt the wisdom of playing safe, of banking on the future.'

'The war, you mean?'

'Of course,' Kassie replied, nodding. 'Poland suffered terribly during the World War II. My family was lucky, they got out. They saw what was coming, well, my grandma did at least. Fortunately her parents *listened* to her, they weren't as suspicious as my –'

'How could she have known?' Faith interrupted.

'Sorry?'

'She could only have been a child at the time.'

'She was nine,' Kassie confirmed.

'She was so young. I mean, how could she have possibly foreseen what was about to happen?'

But even as she spoke the answer presented itself to Faith, as if it had been obvious all along. Suddenly all of her conversations with Adam – his agonized, confused responses to Kassie – swirled around her brain. She hesitated to ask the question, but now found she couldn't resist.

'Was your . . . was your grandmother like you? I mean, could she see things? Sense when people would . . .'

Faith couldn't complete the sentence, but she didn't need to. Kassie nodded briefly.

'I didn't realize until quite late in her life. I went to visit her in the home and she told me things, things that scared me, but which also made perfect sense. It was only later, when I'd turned them over and over in my mind, that I understood why she'd had her favourites, why she'd given more of her love to those children who would die young, why my mother felt . . . left out.'

Faith said nothing, her mind struggling to process what she was being told. It was impossible, bewildering, but Kassie spoke as if it were the simplest, most straightforward thing in the world.

'I remember once she told me about her childhood in Poland . . .'

Kassie was no longer looking at Faith. It was almost as if she was talking to herself.

'She often cut school . . . She hated it, was never very popular. But on this particular day the headmaster caught her, marched her to class, and as she entered the room all the other pupils turned around to look at her. And that's when she saw . . .'

Kassie was shivering slightly now, as if suddenly ambushed by emotion. Faith was tempted to reach out and touch her, but held back.

'She saw that . . . in less than a year's time two-thirds of her classmates would be dead. Murdered by the Nazis.'

Kassie wiped a tear away. Faith noticed that her face was even paler than usual.

'I think that image haunted her . . .' Kassie continued quietly, her voice quavering slightly, '. . . for the rest of her life.'

And suddenly Faith understood. The gift that Kassie shared with her grandmother – if it was real, if what Kassie was saying was true – was extraordinary, God-like even. It was as if she had a map of everybody's life, as if she could shine light into the darkest corners, answer the most fundamental questions. But this knowledge came at a terrible price. It thrilled Faith to think that her instinctive belief in the spiritual world might have some basis in truth, but Kassie's confessions unnerved her too. The curse of foresight was obviously profound – both Kassie and her grandmother had been drowning in death ever since they were born.

Looking at her sketch once more, Faith seemed to see it clearly for the first time. At last she understood *why* her subject wore such a haunted expression.

87

The dawn was cold and lifeless, a suffocating blanket of cloud blocking out the sun. Climbing out of her car, Gabrielle Grey took in the dirty grey water as it swirled and eddied its way downstream. The Chicago River had been the making of the city, but today it looked tainted and tired, like blood starved of oxygen. Whether it was this or the chill of the spring dawn which made Gabrielle shiver, she couldn't say.

Pulling her coat around her, she hurried over to the trailer. Previously the site had felt forlorn, but today it was a hive of activity. Police divers mingled with CSI operatives, while uniformed officers kept intrigued bystanders at bay. In the middle of it all, her nose heavily strapped, stood Detective Jane Miller.

'I told you to take a couple of days off,' Gabrielle said accusingly.

'Doc says it's just badly bruised and, besides . . . there was no way I was going to miss this.'

She gestured to the activity behind her.

'Bartlett inside?'

'Waiting for you,' Miller replied, standing aside to let Gabrielle pass.

Smiling briefly at her, Gabrielle entered the trailer. The contrast to her last visit couldn't have been more striking. Previously empty, the trailer was now well populated, powerful arc lights illuminating every corner. Emily Bartlett, swathed in her forensic suit, was standing by the corner drain, which had now been removed. As Gabrielle approached, she spotted one of Bartlett's officers in the drain well and suddenly remembered why she had opted to join the Detective Bureau, rather than the forensic team.

'Sorry to call you so early,' Bartlett said brightly, spotting Gabrielle's approach.

'Two hours of sleep is plenty . . .'

'But I thought you'd want to see this.'

She was clutching an evidence bag, which at first sight appeared to be empty.

'We've been in the drain for almost four hours,' Bartlett reported, handing Gabrielle the bag. 'To be frank, it's the cleanest drain I've ever seen, plus it empties straight into the river, so you couldn't really get a better disposal site, especially as the bleach has had time to do its work.'

Gabrielle was taking in every word, but her eyes were now drawn to something tucked in the corner of the evidence bag. Something small and golden.

'But there is a natural lip in the drain well, where the two halves of the pipe come together. They've warped slightly, creating an edge that things can get snagged on and that's where we found this.'

Gabrielle held the bag a little closer and now she glimpsed what appeared to be one half of a gold cufflink. The chain linking the two ends seemed to have snapped, explaining the missing half.

'Obviously, we haven't run forensic tests yet, but look at the underside.'

Already Gabrielle had an inkling of what she might find there, but still her heart skipped a beat as she looked at the bottom of the fractured link and saw two monogrammed initials: 'J.J.'

Gabrielle looked up at Bartlett, relief etched across her face. Finally, they had found their kill site. The place where Rochelle Stevens and Jacob Jones had spent their last, agonizing hours on earth.

88

He stared at the empty room, confused and alarmed. The bed was unmade, her possessions were scattered on the floor, but there was no sign of Kassie. Turning, Adam headed quickly into the kitchen.

'Have you seen Kassie this morning?'

Faith shook her head. She was sitting at the kitchen table, hunched over a cup of coffee.

'I can't find her anywhere. She's not answering her cell phone.'

'She left before I got up,' Faith said dully.

'Any idea where she might have gone? Did she say anything to you yesterday?'

Faith shrugged, but didn't reply. She seemed far more interested in the contents of her cup than her husband.

'Try her cell again if you're worried,' she eventually offered, rising and crossing to the sink.

Adam was tempted to do just that. He'd hoped to talk to Kassie this morning, to discourage her from attempting to contact Madelaine Baines, to persuade her to engage with the police, but the sight of Faith shuffling around the kitchen made him pause. She still hadn't looked at him yet and seemed more distant than ever this morning.

'Look, Faith, I'm sorry about yesterday . . .'

Adam wasn't sure it was his job to apologize, but he desperately wanted to restore peace between them. Faith had been doing better the last couple of days, but suddenly looked very fragile again.

'. . . if you felt I was unfeeling or unwelcoming to Kassie. Her safety obviously comes first, so she can stay here until we find a better alternative.'

But the words seemed to drift over Faith's head — almost as if she hadn't heard them.

'Faith?'

'Do we have to talk about this now?'

She was still hovering by the sink, leaning on the side as if supporting herself.

'Are you ok?'

'Just a little tired.'

'Look at me, Faith.'

Slowly, reluctantly, she turned to face him. Adam was saddened to see how pale her skin was, how dark the rings were under her eyes.

'Did you manage to sleep?'

'Off and on.'

'Were you up in the night?'

'I'm finding it hard to switch off.'

'Are you still taking your meds? It's really important that —'

'Yes, *Doctor*. I'm doing everything you told me to do.'

'Faith, I'm trying to help you,' Adam replied, stung by her gentle sarcasm.

'By interrogating me?'

'By caring for you.'

'I've said I'm fine,' she said quickly, making to leave.

'Stay a minute, talk to me . . .'

'And say what? What is there that we could possibly say to each other that would make . . . *this* any better?'

She sounded beaten, rather than hostile. Adam suddenly

felt overcome with emotion – all the sadness of the last few days rushing up on him. Why had this had to happen to *them*?

'There's nothing I can say to make it better,' Adam replied, sincerely. 'Of course there isn't. But if you're feeling unhappy, I want to know about it. Because I love you . . .'

To his surprise, his words seemed to cut straight through her anger and she crumpled slightly, tears pricking her eyes.

'I know,' she murmured, toying with the cord of her dressing gown. 'I know and I'm sorry. I just . . . don't like being watched.'

'No one's watching you.'

'Like I'm a weak link, a child.'

'Come on, love, I'm not saying that.'

Adam took a step towards her, but Faith held up a hand to stop him.

'Please, Adam. I mean it.'

Adam checked his advance.

'Go and find Kassie. Go to the office. Do *something*. Just . . . give me a bit of space.'

It was the last thing he wanted to do, but her tone brooked no argument. She walked to the doorway, pausing briefly on the threshold to whisper:

'I love you too.'

Then she was gone.

89

Kassie sat alone at the bar, ignoring the curious looks of the grill chef who was distractedly flipping breakfast pancakes. She spun her cell phone on the brushed steel surface, watching it turn round and round. If it ended up pointing at her she would call, if it didn't, she wouldn't. Its movement was mesmerizing, hypnotic, and she kept her eyes glued to the phone as it slowed and slowed, before finally coming to a halt aiming directly at her.

'Best of three,' she muttered and spun it again.

The phone slowly completed its revolutions, before repeating the same result. Angrily, Kassie snatched it up and shoved it into her pocket. Who was she kidding? She knew she should call Adam to apologize for her sudden departure, to explain why she had to go, but could she really find the words? Besides, wouldn't that just draw Adam back in, when she'd already made the decision to proceed alone?

She didn't blame Adam for his doubts, his scepticism, but it was clear that he was not prepared to back her any more. He would protect her, guide her, even try to 'heal' her, but there was no question of him taking her concerns, her fears, at face value, so there was no point outstaying her welcome. Better to leave Adam and Faith alone – she had caused them enough trouble already.

'You buying anything or just keeping the seat warm?'

The grill chef was still staring at her. Snapping out of it,

Kassie rummaged in her pocket, eventually locating a crumpled ten-dollar bill.

'Two breakfast pancakes, please.'

She had no appetite, and no intention of eating them, but the diner was warm and welcoming, a temporary sanctuary. She slid the money across the counter towards him, but, as she did so, she suddenly became aware of sounds – words – that sounded ominously familiar: '. . . Jacob Jones . . . Rochelle Stevens . . .' Rotating in her seat, she could see the radio perched next to the chef's station.

'Can you turn that up a bit?' she asked.

Reluctantly, the surly chef obliged. Kassie listened intently, her body rigid with tension.

'. . . that Kyle Redmond, a former resident of Bedford Park, has been charged with the brutal double murder. We understand that Redmond will shortly be transferred from CPD headquarters to Cook County Jail and that a bail hearing is set for tomorrow. The funeral of Jones, his first victim, is due to take place in two days' time, and you can expect great media interest . . .'

Kassie turned away, scarcely believing what she was hearing. Madelaine Baines was going to die today, so why were the police convinced of Redmond's guilt? Was it possible that someone else was going to target her? An accomplice? The obvious alternative was that Kassie was mistaken, had somehow misread the experience, but she felt certain she wasn't. Her vision of Madelaine's death had been so powerful, so clear – she could still hear that cackling, inhuman laughter.

No, something didn't fit. The police might have charged Redmond, might have convinced themselves that he was 'The 'Chicago Butcher', but Kassie knew that something was very wrong here. The only question now was what she was prepared to do about it.

There was no way she could stand by and do nothing. Her fate, as well as Madelaine's, depended upon it. So, sliding off her stool, Kassie snatched up her jacket and ran to the door, even as the bemused chef slid her steaming hot pancakes on to the counter.

90

The garage doors rose and moments later the black Cadillac Escalade slid out. Madelaine Baines paused briefly on the drive – he saw her hand emerge from the car window, zapping the garage doors with her key fob, once, twice – then drove off. Moments later, the garage doors descended stutteringly to the ground and all was quiet once more.

He watched the Cadillac disappear around the corner, then eased his cellphone from his pocket. Having cast a quick look around to ensure he wasn't about to be surprised by nosey neighbours, he returned his attention to the phone, swiftly pulling up Madelaine's calendar. He was relieved to see that nothing had changed. She was due at WGN this morning and then the *Tribune* at noon. Relieved, he tucked the phone back into his pocket. He had plenty of time.

Once more, he swept the street for potential witnesses, but the suburban road was deserted, so climbing out of his car, he hurried across the street to the Baines residence. There was a large shrub to the side of the drive and, not for the first time, he took cover behind it. Another quick check, then he pressed the button on his RollJam and immediately the garage doors started to rise. Once they were five feet up, he entered quickly, ducking low to avoid contact. The doors were still rising, but he pressed the button again and they juddered to a halt, then began to descend.

Smiling, he turned away, slipping the small gadget into his pocket. It had only cost him thirty-two dollars and was worth every cent. It effortlessly hacked and recorded a key fob's wireless command, meaning that he could subsequently open garage doors or unlock a car unhindered. The owner of the key fob might notice that their fob didn't work first time round, but they were seldom suspicious. They just tried the fob again and, once it worked, carried on with their busy lives, little realizing that they had just been hacked.

The door connecting the garage to the house was unlocked. He had used it a couple of times before and the Baines family never bothered to secure it. Why would they, when they lived in such a prosperous, crime-free suburb? Recent events had not made them alter these arrangements – strange really given the brutality of the crimes – but they hardly expected this thing to have a direct impact on *them*.

Closing the door quietly, he paused. If by chance there was someone at home, it wouldn't be hard to retreat unnoticed. But, of course, the house was empty – he had watched them all leave – so he had the place to himself.

He stood there, allowing himself to savour the moment. He had done this many times before, in many different houses, but it still gave him a thrill – he was an intruder, an invader, but this was *his* space now. The Baines family were going about their day, full of their own busy-ness and self-importance, little realizing that a stranger was standing in their front room. He could do whatever he wanted, without fear of discovery or detection. There was much to achieve in a limited time, but he was determined to enjoy this moment to the full. He was still learning, sucking more pleasure from his actions each time, but one thing had become abundantly clear.

For him, the hunt was as satisfying as the kill.

91

'Please call me as soon as you get this.'

The disembodied voice filled the office, as Adam stood by his desk.

'I had a rather worrying chat with Gabrielle Grey yesterday and . . . well, I'd like to hear your side of the story.'

The voice disappeared, replaced by a harsh bleep. Adam hit the red button, killing his voicemail, but made no move to pick up his phone. He knew full well what Gabrielle had told Dr Gould, Chairman of the Illinois Board of Professional Regulation, and he had no idea what to say in response, nor how to defend himself. His actions over the past few days were indefensible – to the outside world at least.

Ignoring his phone, Adam sat down at his desk and turned his laptop on. Following replies to the emails he'd sent earlier in the week, he now had a few regular clients booked in for appointments over the next couple of days. He still wasn't sure he was up to it, but there seemed no alternative to getting on with things. Perhaps slipping back into the normal routine would do him good.

But as he opened his schedule he was surprised to see that it was virtually clear. He had had five appointments scheduled in his diary when he checked yesterday. Now he had only two – three clients having cancelled in the last twenty-four hours. It could be a coincidence, of course, but the timing was curious. As well as being a highly skilled psychologist, Dr Geoff Gould was also a notorious gossip. If he'd spoken to colleagues, friends in the industry, about Grey's concerns, then it was perfectly possible that people already knew about him revealing Rochelle's address to a client, breaking into her house, as well as his close association with one of the suspects in an ongoing homicide inquiry.

Picking up the phone, he speed-dialled Vestra Healthcare, the agency from which he got most of his third-party referrals.

'They just rang up and cancelled this morning,' his contact explained in a bored voice, totally missing the anxiety in Adam's inquiry.

'Did you give them a chance to rebook?'

'Yes, I offered all of them alternative times. But they said they'd call back . . .'

Adam ended the call, slumping back into his chair. Rochelle was a popular member of the healthcare community in Chicago – rumours implicating him in any wrongdoing concerning her death could be terminal to his career. Chicago was a big city, but his professional world was small, and it wouldn't take long for his practice to be choked off at source. First things first: he would have to call Gould and see what he knew. But it was a prospect that filled Adam with dread. How honest should he be? How honest could he be?

His day had started badly and was getting worse. Kassie had vanished – he still had no idea where she was or what she was doing – and Faith had pushed him away. Even at his workplace, a space which had for so long been his sanctuary, things were turning against him. Adam suddenly had the strong feeling that forces beyond his control were at work, tilting his world on its axis, threatening to pitch him into the abyss. It was stupid to think like this, he was being crazy, paranoid even, but try as he might to dismiss his feelings, he couldn't deny that, for the first time in his life, he felt genuinely scared.

92

Gabrielle Grey stared out the window, looking down on the courtyard below. She had chosen this out-of-the-way hallway on the fourth floor because it had the best vantage point, giving unrestricted views of the prisoner transfer area without revealing the watcher. She had used this perch many times before and wasn't going to pass up this opportunity.

Redmond cut a slight figure in the courtyard below, flanked by burly prison officers. When she'd brought him back up for questioning this morning, he'd refused to play ball. She'd confronted him with the new evidence, to be met first with dull, stony silence and then later with violent recriminations and threats. He had actually spat in her face – a small assault that she had taken great pleasure in adding to his charge sheet. It would never be acted upon of course, given the magnitude of the other charges, but Gabrielle was not the kind of person to let it go.

Redmond would now be taken to Cook County Jail, where he would exchange his tatty garments for an orange jumpsuit – the first stage in his transition from suspected killer to convicted felon. Sometimes Gabrielle felt sympathy for those she charged – many of them came from desperate, impoverished backgrounds – but not Redmond. His crimes were too brutal, too sadistic, to be excused. She would enjoy watching the cell door swing shut on him.

Redmond was by the van now, looking on grimly as the back doors swung open to receive him. Gabrielle settled in to enjoy the last few seconds of his discomfort, when she heard footsteps hastening down the hallway. Turning, she was surprised to see Detective Montgomery approaching.

'Now, how would a new officer know about this hidey-hole?' Gabrielle greeted her.

'Detective Suarez,' Montgomery replied blankly. 'He says you're often up here.'

'Does he now?' Gabrielle countered happily. 'Come to enjoy the show?'

She gestured to the courtyard below.

'Not really,' Montgomery responded tightly.

Now Gabrielle paused. There was something in Montgomery's tense expression that concerned her.

'What is it, Detective? What's on your mind?'

'I need to talk to you.'

'Shall we go to my office then?'

'No, I think it's best we do it here.'

Gabrielle's anxiety rose another notch, though she couldn't say why.

'Go on.'

'Well, the evidence that was found this morning,' Montgomery said, keeping her voice low. 'I've got some concerns about it.'

'Meaning?' Gabrielle replied, taken aback.

'Well, the cufflinks are pretty distinctive. Gold-plated, engraved –'

'And given to Jones by his fiancée. We know this –'

'What I mean is . . .' Montgomery continued, faltering slightly, '. . . they are quite recognizable. Which is why I realized that . . . that I'd seen them before.'

'What do you mean?' Gabrielle responded, alarm bells ringing now.

'I spotted them at Jones's house, when we were doing our initial search of the property on April eleventh. They weren't of any interest, so I made a brief note of them and moved on. But I'm sure they were on Jones's bedside table.'

Her words hung in the air for a moment, before Gabrielle responded:

'It could have been another set of cufflinks. How can you be so sure?'

'Because I remember seeing the engraving. It made me feel a little sad, given that the guy was dead.'

'How certain are you?'

'Well, I've got my original notes and here . . .'

Montgomery handed Gabrielle a see-through file.

'Crime scene photos from Jones's house,' she continued, as Gabrielle opened the file. 'We've only got a medium shot of the bed and bedside table, but look . . .'

Montgomery pointed at the photo, but Gabrielle had already observed what looked like a pair of gold cufflinks, almost hidden on the table, beside a dark-brown paperback.

'You can't see the engravings obviously, but I promise you, these are the exact cufflinks – or cufflink – that Bartlett found this morning.'

'So, first thing we do is go back to the Jones house,' Gabrielle said purposefully.

'Already done it,' Montgomery said, a little awkwardly.

'And?'

'They're not there any more.'

Gabrielle felt her stomach lurch. She wasn't convinced yet – she would need to see it with her own eyes first. But if Montgomery was right, if the evidence had been planted, then they had just made a terrible mistake – one which could have catastrophic consequences.

93

Madelaine shut the door and breathed a sigh of relief. She was home.

It had been a gratifying day, but an exhausting one. She had been a bag of nerves before her TV interview, but actually she had performed well under the hot studio lights – the stream of positive Twitter comments attesting to that. She had felt drained afterwards, but there was no time to rest – she had been contacted by two more radio stations wanting interviews and only just managed to fit those in before she was due at the *Tribune*. This had almost been the most satisfying part of the day – walking into that famous building and being treated like royalty, as she was interviewed and photographed. From nowhere, in a matter of a couple of days, she had somehow become the voice of Chicago.

The thought made her giddy, but she was almost too tired to enjoy it. Even if she had had the inclination to wallow in self-congratulation, there would be scant opportunity anyway. It was nearly two o'clock and before long she would need to leave the house again to watch the girls' softball match. She could have asked Paul to do it of course, but actually she didn't want to. She wanted a bit of normality to balance out the craziness of the last forty-eight hours.

Shooting a look at the clock, Madelaine hurried up the stairs, pulling off her suit jacket and beginning to unbutton her blouse. If she hurried, she would just have enough time to change and touch up her make-up, before she had to go.

Already she was looking forward to the relaxing afternoon and evening, a chance to spend time with the family and have a quiet, unremarkable night together.

But as she crossed the landing to the master bedroom, she paused. The loft hatch was just above her and looking up she noticed light stealing around the edges. She suppressed a desire to curse – Paul often went up there, fiddling around for tools he'd squirrelled away for a rainy day, frequently forgetting to turn the light off when he descended. She hesitated: she ought to push on as the clock was ticking, but already she knew she wouldn't – she couldn't bear to waste electricity. So, removing the stepladder from the nearby closet, she reached up, opened the hatch and clambered into the dusty loft.

She scanned the scene quickly, with something close to annoyance – the whole space was so cluttered, it really was time Paul did something about it. Shaking off her irritation, she took a few short steps to the light switch, flicking it off with a satisfying click. Gloom descended, the only light now coming from the landing downstairs. But as Madelaine started to turn, this too was suddenly extinguished, the loft hatch closing with a bang.

What the hell?

Her heart was racing, but she tried to calm herself. Perhaps she had not opened it fully? Was it even possible that the wind had blown it shut? It seemed unlikely, but still . . . She turned to switch the light back on, but as she did so, she heard a small creak, as if someone had taken a step towards her.

'Hello?'

Her voice sounded weak and strangulated.

'Hello?' she said louder, but still without eliciting a response.

Now Madelaine was panicking. She had never liked the

dark and was starting to imagine all sorts of horrible things. Retreating, she fumbled for the light switch, but even as she did so, she finally got a response – one that chilled her blood. A soft voice whispered two words, so close to her that she could feel his breath on her neck.

'Hello, Madelaine.'

94

She stood stock still, taking in the sight in front of her.

The Baines residence was an impressive family home. There was money here for sure. You could see that both in the immaculately painted exterior and in the opulent interior. Madelaine and her husband, Paul, were clearly very proud of it – the house featured in numerous Facebook posts, ostensibly publicizing yard sales and charity bakes, while actually underscoring both the exclusivity of their neighbourhood and the splendour of their home. It hadn't taken long for Kassie to divine the neighbourhood, then the street, and the silver mailbox, sitting proudly on top of a crisply painted post with the family name embossed on it, was the final giveaway.

Checking that she wasn't being watched, Kassie hurried across the road to the house. Pressing her face up against the window, she took in the huge plasma TV, the leather sofas, the artwork in the well-appointed living room. All was quiet inside and the blinds were not drawn, which suddenly gave Kassie hope. Perhaps she wasn't too late after all.

Abandoning the window, she pressed the doorbell down, then waited. There was no sign of movement within, so she rang again, but there was still no answer. Frustrated, she resorted to hammering on the door.

Still nothing. Kassie took a few steps back, raising her eyes to the upper floors, searching for something, anything. Finding little of interest, she looked up and down the street, but there were no neighbours visible and the road was quiet. Kassie suddenly wondered whether the killer – or killers – deliberately targeted these quiet suburban homes. It would be much harder to pull off these crimes in the raucous chaos of South Shore.

This thought brought what lay in store for Madelaine crashing back into focus. Stepping away from the house, Kassie cupped her hands round her mouth and hollered:

'Madelaine, are you in there?'

No response, just Kassie's voice dying away in the street. So, raising the volume, she tried one more time:

'Madelaine . . . can you hear me?'

95

Madelaine Baines turned her head, looking groggily in the direction of the cries, but her captor remained stock still. He peered through a tiny chink in the curtains at the figure below, struggling to take in what he was seeing. Who *was* this girl? And what did she want?

He chanced another look outside. Was she a friend of Madelaine? He knew her far less well than he knew Rochelle and Jacob, so it was hard to say, but he didn't think this girl belonged in her world. She looked like a charity case with her badly cut hair and Motörhead hoodie. So what was her connection to Madelaine? And why did she want to get hold of her so urgently?

Sweating, he looked at his watch. There was no way he could leave the house while she was there – even if he could get Madelaine into the garage and into the car without being spotted, he would surely be intercepted as he departed. Even if the girl couldn't stop the vehicle, she would see him. He could wear the ski mask of course, but that would only arouse her suspicions, prompting her to call the cops. Meanwhile, Madelaine was due at the softball shortly. When she didn't turn up, questions would be asked, the alarm raised. Her husband would then race home, perhaps the twins would get a lift home too. What would he do in that scenario? Slit her throat and escape out the back? No, no, no, that was not how it was supposed to be at all.

The girl had stopped calling and was hammering on the

door. Now she was stepping back, scrutinizing the upper floors. Such was her level of interest that for a moment he thought he'd been spotted, but eventually her gaze moved on, sweeping the other side of the house.

Breathing heavily, he turned to look at his victim, wondering if she could enlighten him? He would love to ask her, but removing her gag was not an option.

No, the best thing to do for now was to wait. Wait and see what the girl's next move was. Would she eventually tire and depart? Or would she try to gain access to the property? Suddenly he was desperate to know.

His fate, and Madelaine's, depended upon it.

96

'This is bullshit. Total bullshit . . .'

Miller was pacing back and forth in Gabrielle's office. She was angry, aggrieved, protesting her innocence. But Gabrielle noted that her deputy had not looked at her once.

'I'm just asking the question, as I'm *duty-bound* to do.'

'Sure, but if someone's pointing the finger, then it's because they've got an agenda. A score to settle. God knows, maybe they want my job . . .'

'It's not about that.'

'Really?'

Her scepticism was strongly expressed, but felt forced to Gabrielle.

'What else could it be?' Miller continued. 'I have been *very* loyal to you, to this team, working night and day –'

'I know your work means a lot to you –'

'Damn right it does.'

'But I also know that at times you can be impetuous, that you are tempted to take short cuts. We've talked about it before.'

Miller said nothing, but finally ceased her pacing.

'We've all been under a lot of pressure. This is an extremely challenging, high-profile investigation. And I can see why, if we had the prime suspect in custody, but not enough evidence to make things stick, it might be tempting for an officer to help things along . . .'

'No, no, no,' Miller retorted, shaking her head vigorously.

'Jane, when we were at Redmond's trailer that first night, you offered to break in, to scope the place. What's the betting if you and I went down there right now, we'd find one of those windows had been forced?'

Suddenly Miller ceased her protestations. Her gaze ranged across the floor, as if seeking a missing penny. Still she wouldn't look at her boss.

'Now, I've been to the Jones residence this morning. The cufflinks that were clearly in situ in the crime scene photos aren't there any more. Someone's moved them.'

Miller continued to stare at the floor.

'So I'm going to ask you again, Jane. Did you plant Jones's cufflinks in the trailer?'

Miller hesitated a second too long before opening her mouth, and in that moment Gabrielle *knew*. For a second, it looked as if her deputy might continue to protest her innocence, but the words wouldn't form and suddenly she broke down in tears, her body shaking with distress.

Gabrielle stared at her. She wanted to berate her, to scream in her face, to vent all her anger on her, but when she finally opened her mouth to speak, it was with sadness that she gasped:

'What the hell have you done, Jane?'

97

'Are you going to tell me what this is all about?'

Paul Baines was surprised that the nervy teenage girl in front of him had made it past security. He was even more surprised that she was asking him questions about his wife.

'I just want to know if you've been in contact with your wife recently.'

'Right . . . Are you a friend of hers?'

'I met her at the vigil,' Kassie lied. 'I was supposed to meet her today, but there was no reply when I went to your house.'

Baines scrutinized her, clearly sceptical of her story.

'When was this?'

'Just after two p.m.'

Paul digested this, confused, even a little suspicious now.

'She really arranged to meet you then? She was due at a school softball match shortly after that –'

'It was only going to be a quick meet . . .'

The girl looked shifty, avoiding eye contact as she spoke.

'Could you call her?' she said suddenly. 'To check that she's ok.'

'She should be on her way home with the girls now. Why don't I get her to call you –'

'Please . . .'

'What is this? What's going on?'

'It's nothing to worry about. Please . . . Just call her. If she's ok, I swear I'll get out of your hair. It's really important.'

And something in her simple, concerned manner cut

through. Snatching up his cell phone, he speed-dialled his wife.

'Hi, this is Madelaine. Leave a message . . .'

'It's me,' Paul said, when the automated voice had completed its greeting. 'Call me when you get this.'

He rang off and tried again, but getting voicemail once more cut the call.

'She might have made it home already,' he said, as much to himself as to his visitor.

He called their home number, but the phone rang and rang, before clicking on to the answering service, a recording of his wife's friendly voice greeting him. He tried her cell again, but it was still going to voicemail, so he rang off, turning to face the curious girl once more.

'No sign of her, I'm afraid.'

From her reaction, he could tell that she was worried by this news. And, suddenly, so was he.

98

A thousand questions raced through Madelaine's mind, each more alarming than the last. Where was she? Who was the man that had attacked her? And what did he intend to do with her?

He had fallen upon her in the loft – she'd been too stunned to react and came to a little while later on the floor of her bedroom. Her memory of what had happened then was confused and hazy – there seemed to have been some kind of commotion outside the house – and not long after she was being bundled into the trunk of her own car. She was bound, gagged and blindfolded and the hour or so that followed, as she rolled backwards and forwards in rhythm with the car's stop-start progress, was the most terrifying of her life.

The darkness was all-consuming, the heat rising every minute, the air stale and unpleasant. Initially, she was convinced that she would die in there and that that was what her attacker had intended all along. But as the minutes passed, as the traffic noise outside lessened, another possibility presented itself to her. Was she being taken somewhere remote? If so, to what end? To be held hostage? Attacked? Killed?

Madelaine tried to keep her thoughts positive, to play out the best possible scenarios that might come from this horrific situation, but before she could settle on one which was palatable, the car juddered to a halt. Moments later, the trunk popped and she was hauled out into the open air. She was then dragged over rough ground, her ankles jarring nastily on what felt like small rocks, then suddenly she was inside again. Seconds later, she was forced down on to something hard – a seat of some kind – which her arms were secured to.

And then . . . she'd been left alone. She could hear the man moving about, but he wasn't touching her, so she tried to gather her thoughts, to get a sense of her surroundings. She could smell paraffin, but also something else. Wood. Damp, rotting wood. She could hear things too. The man ranging around, the creak of the boards, but also the faint sound of laughter.

She sat helpless on the chair, her heart beating out the rhythm of her terror. She longed to know why she was here, what she had done to provoke this attack. She moved her head, desperate to free herself from her bonds, desperate to see or hear something that would give her a clue as to her likely fate. And as she shook and wriggled, she noticed something. Her blindfold had shifted slightly as she'd been manhandled into the shed and the material over her left eye was thinner and more gauze-like than the fabric which covered her right. Perhaps it was the border of the material, perhaps it had been torn – either way, if she closed her right eye, but kept her left open, she could just about make out the scene in front of her through the thin material.

She was in an outbuilding of some kind. The walls were a dark, brownish colour, but the floor was much lighter, almost white. Confused, Madelaine ran her feet over the area just in front of her to discover that it moved and crinkled. It was cold to the touch and felt like . . . plastic. Confused, terrified, Madelaine turned her attention to her attacker, who was busying himself nearby. He was average height and slightly overweight, the stomach area of his blue boiler suit bulging slightly. He still wore a ski mask, which terrified her, as she could only imagine what kind of monster lurked beneath it.

She had tried to remain positive in the midst of her ordeal, but now she instinctively knew that her abduction was linked to her recent actions on behalf of the community. She'd pushed this thought away, but now it returned, nagging and insistent. Suddenly she knew exactly why she'd been taken and what fate awaited her, a suspicion confirmed now as the man turned towards her, a large cleaver in his hand.

Her first instinct was to scream, but somehow she kept a rein on her terror. She was in grave peril now, but she had one tiny lifeline. Unless she was mistaken, her attacker didn't know that she could see him. So, in spite of her hammering heart, Madelaine kept still. He was standing right in front of her – and Madelaine braced herself for the kiss of his blade – but instead he lowered himself to her level. They were almost nose to nose now, her captor taking great delight in studying her, hoping perhaps to see her quivering with fear.

Without warning, Madelaine launched herself forward. She was not thinking now, she was acting on instinct, crunching her forehead into her captor's face. Howling in pain, the man fell backwards, hitting the floor hard. Madelaine didn't hesitate, tipping herself forward, until her feet hit the floor and she could stand. Immediately, she overbalanced, the chair that she was now secured to almost dragging her back down. But wobbling, tottering, she regained her balance and scuttled forward as best she could.

Her attacker was still on the ground, moaning, so Madelaine made for the door. It didn't appear to be locked and if she could open it, perhaps she could get away, call for help.

Her progress was stumbling, but miracle of miracles she had made it to the door. It was ajar, so, turning sideways, she wriggled the toes of her right foot into the crack and pushed with all her might. The door opened and she saw the muddy shoreline outside, the water beyond it. She scuttled forward . . . but suddenly found herself falling backwards. For a moment, she was bewildered, confused, but, craning round, she saw that her captor had hold of her chair and was dragging her back.

It was a fight to the death now and Madelaine struggled violently, screaming out her anger and fear all the while. But the momentum had shifted and she was pulled inexorably back into her prison. Moments later, she was back on the plastic sheet, exhausted and despairing. A savage blow rocked her back in her seat and when she'd managed to gather her senses again, she saw her captor standing in front of her, breathless, with flashing, angry eyes and that awful blade clutched in his hands.

She wanted to sob, to beg, but was suddenly unable to produce a sound, terror robbing her of her voice. And as her captor approached her, his blade raised to strike, all she could hear was that hideous, ringing laughter.

99

She felt their eyes upon her. All around the incident room, officers of every rank had paused in their work to take in the spectacle. With each passing second her shame increased, as indignity piled upon indignity.

She had had to wait for thirty minutes in Gabrielle's office, while a team from Internal Affairs was summoned. They were the longest thirty minutes of her life. In the past, she and Gabrielle had often been closeted away in that office together, bitching about the station coffee, while dissecting new leads in an investigation. To her, it had always felt like a special, even slightly magical place which they shared. Their little oasis away from the chaos and darkness. But today it seemed like a prison, as if Gabrielle – the woman she admired too much – was holding her hostage. Her boss had said nothing throughout, perhaps, Jane suspected, because she could not trust herself to speak.

Eventually, the I A officers arrived – a sour-faced, pinched woman and a malodorous bear of a man – and now here she was, standing by her desk, as the contents of her drawers and files were picked over, labelled and bagged. Her phone had been taken, her laptop too, but they saved the best for last.

'Your purse, please,' the male officer said, without looking up.

She obliged, handing over her battered bag to him. Slowly, deliberately he began to remove the contents – a scrunched-up Kleenex, her CTA pass, her tampons, even the cigarettes

315

which she'd told everyone she'd given up. None of this was about the investigation of her misconduct – its sole purpose was to humiliate her and chasten those watching.

Jane kept her eyes glued to the floor. She would make bail, of course, but what then? Her pay would be suspended pending an inquiry and she had no savings to speak of. What was she going to do? She had a couple of friends locally, but no one whom she could possibly take into her confidence. Would she have to return to her parents in Detroit? Upstanding Mary and Eric Miller who loved their handsome, successful, eldest son to the exclusion of all others? How disappointed they would be, though not surprised. The thought of seeing their sullen faces made her want to cry, but she swallowed down her distress. She was not going to give them *that*.

'Ready to go?'

The weariness in the officer's voice was crushing. This was regular, workaday stuff to him, whereas for her it was a personal catastrophe. She nodded curtly.

'Let's get moving then,' he continued, gesturing her towards the exit.

For the length of her ordeal, she had wanted to be out of this place, but now she hesitated. The room had gone quiet, there was not even the pretence that her colleagues were working any more. They were all glued to the drama, shocked and horrified in equal measure. She wanted them all to . . . just disappear, for this whole, awful nightmare to be over, but there was no easy way out for this sinner.

So, turning away from her desk, away from the woman she had cherished, she began her long, slow walk of shame.

100

Kassie dragged her feet across the tired linoleum. Eyes flicked up at her as she passed, but she barely noticed them, keeping her gaze firmly fixed on the frail form silhouetted on the terrace ahead. Why she'd come here she couldn't say – what could it possibly achieve? – yet there was no question of her going anywhere else. When life reduced her hopes to ashes, she always retreated to the only person who had ever shown her real love.

Wieslawa was looking out over the lake, her eyes fixed on the birds. She was wearing a warm housecoat and had a woollen blanket wrapped round her legs, which Kassie adjusted now to ensure there were no cold draughts. Kissing her on the forehead, Kassie sat down next to her grandmother, taking her liver-spotted hand in hers.

Wieslawa barely reacted, raising her eyes momentarily to her granddaughter, before returning her gaze to the view. But at least she did not pull her hand away, as she occasionally did when she was flustered or upset. Over the years, Kassie had come to learn that you could never predict what mood her grandmother would be in. Some days she would be passive and inert, others bright and engaging. On those days, Kassie almost believed Wieslawa *did* recognize her, her grandmother muttering phrases, even mentioning places or events, from the past. On other days, however, she was tearful and restless, casting suspicious looks all around her. As time passed, the doctors had come up with a number of ways to describe her condition – dementia, delusional psychosis, others which Kassie had forgotten or blanked out – but Kassie held a different view. Wieslawa had always been surrounded by death, but never more so than here, where elderly relatives were placed to die by their children, out of sight and out of mind. She shuddered to think what Wieslawa must see, imminent death for so many she met in the hallways, the recreation room, at the lakeside tables. She prayed that her grandmother was too far gone to see it, but a good part of her feared that she wasn't.

'*Babcia*,' the old woman murmured.

Kassie looked up hopefully, but Wieslawa continued to keep her eyes fixed on the horizon. Kassie hung her head once more, suddenly feeling utterly crushed. She had come here seeking sanctuary, to gather her thoughts even as she faced up to the fact that she had failed Madelaine, failed herself. The loving mom of two was about to be brutally murdered and Kassie herself had less than two weeks to live. Her failure would be fatal for both of them. The fact that this might save her from her grandmother's fate was no comfort today – Kassie felt utterly hollow and beaten.

'*Babcia*,' her grandmother whispered, a little louder this time.

But Kassie didn't look up, couldn't bear to believe that the old woman understood or cared about her distress. Instead, she kissed her hand and, laying it gently on the woollen blanket once more, took her leave. She couldn't bear the claustrophobia of the visitors' lounge, so, instead of retracing her steps, Kassie walked down to the water's edge. She would find another way out – one where she wasn't spied on – but as she reached the lake, she paused, struck by the sight in front of her.

Lake Michigan looked magnificent tonight, the setting sun

streaking over its vast surface, the golden light dancing hither and thither as the water ebbed and flowed. In the distance was central Chicago, full of energy and activity, but the lake itself was serene, devoid of all human presence, confident in its scale and majesty. Nothing molested it, nothing broke the calm, apart from the waders and egrets, eagles and plovers, who swooped overhead, calling to each other. Kassie stood on the bank, craning up to watch their elegant circles, hoping to find solace in their unhurried industry. Year in, year out they came, regardless of what dramas and darkness played out in the city. And year in, year out, they would *continue* to come. This thought cheered Kassie slightly – her own life, her own narrative, were perhaps insignificant in the wider scheme of things – and she remained where she was, wanting to lose herself in this distraction, to find a moment's peace.

But, even as she stood there, something started to intrude on her consciousness. A thought . . . no, not a thought. A sound. A sound she had heard before. For the tiniest second, Kassie's mind spiralled back into that awful shack, to *him*, to the horror and the fear, then suddenly she was back in the present once more, staring at the skies in wonder.

And suddenly she *knew*.

101

She took the stairs three at time, racing up, up, up. She'd been burning with frustration all the way to Lincoln Park and, arriving at Adam's office block, she hadn't hesitated. A young woman was coming out of the main door and Kassie barged past her, sprinting across the lobby and charging up the stairs.

Bursting into the reception area on the eighth floor, Kassie sprinted towards the office door, throwing it open. Adam was on the phone, and looked up sharply as Kassie crossed the room towards him. Cupping his hand over the receiver, he was about to remonstrate with her, but didn't get the chance. Kassie snatched the phone off him, ending his call.

'What the hell are you doing?' he blurted.

'I need to talk to you.'

'That was an *important* call . . .' Adam protested, looking angry and distressed.

'I know what it is,' she replied, ignoring him.

'What do you mea—'

'I know what it is. The laughter.'

Still Adam looked lost, so Kassie elaborated.

'The woman's laughter, in the shack . . . I said it sounded inhuman. And that's because it is. It's the birds . . .'

She gestured to the floor to ceiling windows, which framed the lake. In the distance, the birds could still be glimpsed, completing their endless rotations.

'It's the birds,' she repeated, half smiling, half laughing now.

Adam was looking at her as if she was deranged, so Kassie crossed to the windows, throwing them open. Numerous birds visited the lake – bitterns, eagles, herons – and their constant, high-pitched cackling could be heard even at this distance.

Kassie turned back to look at Adam. Moments earlier, he'd looked as though he was about to explode, but now he paused, taking in the nasty, malevolent noise.

'Madelaine . . . she's by the water,' Kassie intoned. 'She's being held somewhere on the lake or by a river, I'm sure of it.'

Even as she spoke, she saw a cloud pass across Adam's face, as if something she'd said had chimed with him.

'We just need to find out where.'

'Kassie . . .'

'She's got hours left to live. But now we've got a *chance* . . .'

'Be sensible, Kassie. The lake is huge and there are numerous rivers.'

'We need to find out where the birds are grouping. It'll be somewhere remote, where there's no chance of this guy being disturbed, then we can go there –'

'It'll be like looking for a needle in a haystack.'

'We can save her, I know we can,' Kassie insisted, refusing to be beaten back. 'But I don't know where to start, who I should talk to about this.'

In spite of himself, Adam reacted. Suddenly Kassie was flooded with hope that Adam *could* help her – if she only she could persuade him to.

'Do you know someone?'

'No. Well, yes. But I can't just turn up and –'

'Then we need to go to them now.'

'Not until you tell me where you've been and why you think that this –'

'We don't have time!'

The words erupted from her, shocking Adam into silence.

'Twice I've been right about this and we did *nothing*. Please don't make me responsible for another death. I couldn't stand it.'

Still Adam hesitated.

'Do this for me and I *swear* I will never bother you again.'

'I don't know, Kassie . . .'

'If we save her, then maybe everything will be ok. For you *and* for me. Please, Adam, do this one last thing for me. I'm *begging* you.'

Kassie's tone was beseeching, imploring. But had she done enough? Adam was staring at her, visibly torn between indulging her and telling her to go to hell. Then, to her enormous relief, Adam snatched up his phone and coat and ushered her towards the door.

102

Tears poured down her ravaged face, but it made no difference. There was no mercy here.

Her captor had beaten her savagely, to the point of uncon-
sciousness, before suddenly relenting. Madelaine remained
tied to her chair, naked, bruised and shivering, but her captor had loosened the bonds to one of her wrists, bringing her
free hand up to rest on a small table he'd pushed next to her.
Her eyes were glued to the hideous cleaver that lay on the
battered surface close by, but he seemed momentarily to have
forgotten about it. He seemed much more interested in *her*.

He held her hand in his, seemingly delighted to see that it
was shaking.

'Are you scared, Madelaine?'

Madelaine made a strange noise – half sob, half affirmation.

'You should be.'

She could see his stained teeth break into a smile, even as
another sob crept from her.

'Let's play a game,' he continued brightly.

'I don't want to . . .'

'Normally I start with the tongue, but today I'll make an
exception.'

'*Please* don't hurt me.'

But he ignored her, continuing to cradle her hand, running his finger over her thumb.

'This little piggy went to market . . .'

He slid on to her index finger.

'This little piggy stayed at home . . .'

'No . . .'

'This little piggy had roast beef . . .'

'Please . . . no . . .' she gasped, louder this time.

'And this little piggy had none . . .'

He passed from her fourth to her pinkie finger.

'And *this* little piggy went wee, wee, wee, all the way home.'

Still clutching her pinkie, he reached for the cleaver. Madelaine screamed – long, loud, terrified – but he seemed not to hear her. Placing the blade on the base of her finger, he took aim, lifted the cleaver, then brought it back down sharply. Madelaine erupted – her keening howls masking the soft 'plump' as her severed finger hit the plastic sheeting beneath.

A moment's dull shock, then a savage flame of agony. The pain was unbearable and for a moment Madelaine lost consciousness, blacking out briefly before sliding hideously back into the present. Now she started to babble, pleading with her captor for mercy, invoking everything she held dear, but that only seemed to excite him further. To her utter horror, she saw the makings of an erection in the taut groin of his boiler suit.

Madelaine screamed once more, screamed till her lungs burned. She felt dizzy, numb – she was assailed by the deepest despair and prayed that her heart would give out, that she would escape this awful nightmare. But her captor wouldn't allow it, slapping her hard to stop her shrieking. This silenced her momentarily, but before long she was spluttering and growling out her anguish and fury. Such was the agony that it was impossible to keep quiet, she desperately needed some kind of release. But none was forthcoming.

'Now then, Madelaine . . .' Her captor was purring now, taking her bloody hand firmly in his grip once more. 'Are you ready to play again?'

103

'This is really important, Brock. Think . . .'

Brock Williams had been in the middle of a meeting, talking his finance partners through the drawings for the condo development on Lakeshore, but when his secretary mentioned Adam's name, he'd dropped everything and hurried out. He had left a message of sympathy following Faith's stillbirth, but hadn't actually seen Adam since it happened and, as he ushered his old friend and his strange, teenage companion into his private office, he'd apologized profusely for being such a bad, absent friend.

To his surprise, Adam had batted his apologies away. He had come to him for one reason alone – Brock's knowledge of birds. Brock assumed Adam was joking, teasing him even, but when it became apparent that he was deadly earnest, he wondered if Adam had been drinking. But, actually, Adam appeared his usual self – a little agitated perhaps, but otherwise lucid, intelligent and precise.

'It sounds like you might be describing an eagle of some kind,' Brock said hesitantly. 'Could you give me the sound again?'

The teenager – whom he now learned was called Kassie – mimicked the bird's cry as best she could, cackling long and loud. Brock immediately crossed to his laptop and opened YouTube.

'Is this what you mean?' he offered, hitting the play symbol on a clip.

The room filled with raucous cackling, as a host of birds called to each other.

'Yes, that's it. That's definitely it,' the girl cried, looking oddly moved.

'Then it's a bald eagle you heard.'

'Where's that from?' Adam followed up quickly, pointing at the clip.

'It's just a generic clip. It's not from around here,' Brock replied, surprised by the urgency of his friend's tone.

'But you do find them in Chicago, right?'

'Sure, they come here every spring.'

'And where do they nest?' the girl interrupted.

'All over. They come to feed, stay for maybe six weeks –'

'Where *specifically*?'

'On any large body of water,' Brock blustered, sensing the pair were dissatisfied with his answers. 'Lake Michigan is a big draw –'

'That's too large an area,' Adam interjected. 'Is there anywhere else you might find them? We're looking for somewhere remote.'

'Well, Lake Winnebago has a large population, but that's north of Milwaukee.'

'Closer than that,' the girl urged.

'Well . . . if you really want somewhere *local*, there is one body of water that might fit the bill. I haven't been down there because it's hard to access, but they say there's a huge population of bald eagles there this year.'

'Where?' Adam demanded.

Brock paused, before concluding:

'Lake Calumet.'

104

They drove in silence, each absorbed in their own thoughts. Lake Calumet lay to the south of the city and had once been a busy shipping station and industrial centre. When business declined, it became a landfill site, but even that had proved unsustainable. Now it was just an abandoned industrial wasteland in the shadow of the Bishop Ford Freeway, popular only with migratory birds and the occasional intrepid birdwatcher.

It was a place Kassie had heard of, but never visited. And as they rolled up the rough track to the chain link perimeter, ignoring the 'Danger! Keep out!' signs, Kassie could see why. A huge, derelict grain elevator, skeletal and sad, stood guard over a plethora of abandoned industrial buildings. A relic of former prosperity, the whole place was now forlorn, decaying and probably dangerous, numerous signs on the fence warning of toxic chemicals buried within the landfill site.

It was impossible not to feel sad when taking in the decrepit spot, but the sight of a bald eagle circling overhead reminded Kassie of why they were here. Playing nervously with the hem of her sleeve, she stole a look across at Adam. She could tell he was feeling the same as her — he looked very tense, repeatedly drumming his fingers on the steering wheel.

The car rolled to a stop and Adam killed the engine. Pocketing the keys, he peered out at the ominous sight beyond.

'We'll take a quick look and if we see anything suspicious, we'll call it in,' he said quickly, making to open his door.

'Adam, wait.'

He turned to her, as she laid a hand on his arm.

'You've done what I asked. You should go home now.'

Adam was about to protest, but she talked over him:

'Whatever's out there, I can face it alone.'

'Give me some credit, Kassie,' he replied, dismissively.

'I know you never wanted any of this, that I've caused you nothing but trouble.'

'I'm not letting you do this alone.'

'Please, Adam,' Kassie insisted. 'You have a wife, responsibilities. Go home to Faith, let me finish what *I* started.'

'I said I would do this last thing for you and I will. There's no question of me leaving you here alone . . .'

He gestured to the desolate wasteland.

'But if this proves fruitless, if you're *wrong*, I want you to promise that you will let me help you. We can get you some residential care perhaps.'

'Agreed, but –'

'Then let's get on with it. We're wasting time.'

Adam's words pricked her conscience – every second could cost Madelaine dear – but still she hesitated. Was this *fair*? Could she really do this? But Adam had already climbed out, circling round to the trunk of his car, and reluctantly Kassie followed suit. He rejoined her swiftly, having found a flashlight. The sun was nearly below the horizon now and soon they would be lost to the darkness.

'Let's do this.'

He marched off and Kassie hurried after him. They followed the tall, imposing fence until they found the main gates. They were solid, well-made structures, designed to keep out metal thieves, and were secured with a large padlock. They walked towards the forbidding barrier, wondering

how they might gain access, but as Adam's flashlight beam
fell on the padlock, they immediately saw that it was broken.
Adam flipped it out of its holding to examine it more closely,
then showed it to Kassie – one arm of the padlock had been
cut clean through, presumably with bolt cutters.

'Doesn't mean anything,' Kassie mumbled. 'Could be
thieves . . .'

Adam didn't look like he believed this any more than she
did, but to his credit he held his nerve, yanking the gates
open. They walked slowly on, passing an old warehouse. The
dying sun cast weird shadows over the ground, and on more
than one occasion Kassie felt she saw the outline of a man.
But it was just her mind playing tricks on her, or so she told
herself. On they went, past stacks of abandoned packing
cases, deserted grain stores and empty offices, walking in
silence, their eyes raking the site for wooden outbuildings.

'Do you think we should kill the flashlight?' Kassie said
suddenly. 'I mean, if there is someone here and they see our
beam . . .'

Adam was looking at Kassie as if she had finally gone
mad, but, reluctantly conceding the point, switched it off.

'There's probably enough light from the freeway for us to
make our way.'

'Ok,' Adam replied, sounding a little less than convinced.
'But stay close.'

They pressed on, pushing deeper into the site. The buildings were closer together here and they were forced down a
narrow alleyway. Kassie kept tight to Adam, her eyes roving
the darkness. Surely they would be at the water's edge soon
and then –

Suddenly someone lunged at her. A dark shadow coming
straight for her. With a half-scream, she stumbled back into

Adam's arms, a hand up to protect herself . . . but it was just a startled pigeon, flapping its shabby wings as it fled up and away into the night, fodder perhaps for the circling eagles.

'Sorry,' Kassie whispered, as she righted herself.

Why she was whispering she couldn't say. But she had a knot of tension in her stomach and something was telling her to be watchful. Stealing her way to the end of the alleyway, she peered around the corner and finally she saw the lake. It looked like a large, black spot on the landscape, framed by the towering freeway, a dystopian image of decline and decay. It sent a chill down her spine, but screwing up her courage she emerged from the alleyway and took a couple of faltering steps forward.

Even as she did so, she felt a firm hand restraining her. Adam pulled her back into the shadows and directed her attention to a small building that stood a little further along on the edge of the lake. It was a shack of some kind, old and weatherbeaten, and wouldn't have looked any different to the other abandoned structures on site, except for the fact that a dancing light emanated from within. More intriguing still was the SUV that was parked in the shadows beside the shack.

'Do you think that's Madelaine's?' Kassie gasped, pointing at the vehicle.

Adam shrugged, but Kassie thought she knew the answer. She turned back to the shack, which stood in glorious isolation by the lake, utterly alone save for the dozens of birds nesting on the surrounding wetlands. This was it then. They had found Madelaine. And if they wanted to save her, it was now or never.

105

She had reached the end. She had fought him, fought with every fibre of her being, but she had reached the limits of her resistance. The torture had been unremitting, his cruelty endless. Her tongue had been cut out, her fingers and toes amputated. With each abomination, she had passed out, the pain assailing her, but each time he had revived her – throwing water in her face, slapping her, whatever was necessary to keep her conscious.

On a couple of occasions, she had thought her heart would burst. At those times, she'd prayed for a cardiac arrest, for some relief from this purgatory. But her attacker was well practised, bringing her back from the brink repeatedly. Now, however, the end was near and as if sensing this, her captor spoke to her again.

'Look, Madelaine, look what you've become . . .'

Obediently, Madelaine raised her head – to find that he was holding a small mirror up for her. The sight made her retch – she was a battered, bloody mess, an abomination.

'Pretty, aren't you?'

She retched again, bringing up pure bile.

'There is just one thing missing. You like necklaces, don't you?'

Madelaine wasn't sure she'd heard him properly, but half nodded her head.

'Good,' he cooed, reaching for his cleaver and placing the blade on her throat. 'Because it's time for the final cut.'

106

The trunk of the Escalade lay open, like the gaping mouth of a predator expecting prey. Kassie crept past it – she didn't want to look at it – her eyes trained on the shack instead. The door was ajar and as they moved closer to it, they could hear voices. A man's voice, low and sinister, and a woman's voice – weak, fractured, plaintive.

Alarmed, Kassie stepped forward, reaching out a hand towards the door, but Adam pulled her back.

'Me first,' he whispered.

He held the flashlight tight in his hand, then teased the door open. Kassie was on his shoulder and what she now saw took her breath away. The interior was dimly illuminated by a paraffin lamp, but its flickering light was enough to reveal a man in a blue boiler suit standing over Madelaine Baines – or what remained of her. Her hands and feet were bloody stumps, she was caked in gore and the blade of a cleaver was pressed to her throat.

The masked man appeared to be taunting her, revelling in her fear. He was poised to slit her throat, but when his victim saw movement by the door, she groaned long and loud. Immediately, the man turned, cursing in surprise.

Kassie was frozen to the spot, but Adam sprinted forward, even as the masked man prepared to defend himself, sweeping the cleaver away from Madelaine towards the intruder. But Adam didn't hesitate, swinging his flashlight violently, batting the cleaver from his hand. Realizing the danger he was in,

Madelaine's captor responded immediately, throwing his head forward, attempting to butt his attacker. But Adam dodged him, driving his knee into the man's groin. Groaning, the man staggered back, knocking his devastated victim over, allowing Adam to pounce.

He landed a heavy punch and the masked man stumbled. Adam moved in for the kill, grasping the man's head and attempting to pull him around. But suddenly it was Adam who was falling backwards, the ski mask having come clean off in his hand. Kassie glimpsed the man's face – white, pasty, goateed – but suddenly he spun round, landing a fierce blow on Adam's chin. The latter had not been expecting it and collapsed backwards, landing with a heavy thud on the floor. And now Madelaine's captor leaped upon him, knocking his flailing arms aside, clamping his hands around his throat.

Adam was squirming on the floor, his legs kicking violently, as he tried to break his attacker's grip. And now Kassie came alive, sensing the danger and rushing forward. Adam's attacker clearly hadn't registered her presence, for he made no attempt to defend himself. Kassie took full advantage of this, wrapping her arm around his sturdy neck and tugging backwards with all her might.

The man groaned – in surprise and pain – and briefly released his grip. Kassie tugged harder, but now he launched himself backwards at her, ripping her arm from his neck and ramming an elbow into the side of her head. Suddenly she was sliding sideways, the room spinning and moments later she felt her cheek collide harshly with the rough floor.

She lay there, groaning, unable to move. She felt dizzy, the room seeming to spin around her. Still, she knew she had to get up, so falteringly she stumbled up on to her knees. She wanted to help, to save Adam and Madelaine from this pitiless killer, but even as she looked she realized it was hopeless. The man had resumed his attack on Adam, his hands locked around his victim's neck, squeezing, squeezing, squeezing . . .

She had to intervene. She crawled towards them, but lost her balance, stumbling sideways. She had only seconds now – Adam's eyes were bulging, his face purple – yet still she couldn't will her body forward. Cursing, she began to cry. Was this *really* how it was going to end?

But now, to her surprise, the man was scrambling to his feet. Adam was still conscious – just – retching and coughing on the floor, so why had his attacker risen? And now Kassie became aware of the awful, insidious smell that was beginning to fill the room. Darting a look over to her right, she saw what had happened. The paraffin lamp had been knocked over in the melee, spilling its deadly fuel on to the small table, which had in turn ignited the fabric of the building. One wall was already on fire and in seconds the whole building would be ablaze.

Stunned, Kassie watched as the man snatched up his cleaver and fled, abandoning his victim and his attackers without a second glance. Moments later, she heard the SUV start up and roar away. The sound seemed to bring her to her senses and without thinking she scuttled over to Adam.

'Are you ok?' she cried, clawing at him.

'I'm fine,' he croaked, struggling to right himself.

Turning away, Kassie spotted Madelaine, lying prone on the floor, even as the flames threatened to encircle her. She raced over to her and, slipping her arms under Madelaine's, tried to right her. Kassie could feel the heat of the blaze, could hear the wood crackling overhead, but try as she might, she couldn't get any purchase. So instead, she turned her attention to Madelaine's bonds, yanking at the ropes that secured her to the chair.

But even as she did so, an awful keening sound made her look up – just in time to see a flaming timber crash to the ground right next to her, rebounding off the plastic sheet and sending sparks flying up into the air. Kassie darted a look at the blazing roof, which was creaking ominously, and re-doubled her efforts.

She tugged and tugged, digging her fingers between the ropes and trying to loosen the knots, but it was no use. Acrid fumes now filled the shack, as the plastic sheeting they were standing on began to melt. The smoke was stinging her eyes, filling her lungs, but she knew she couldn't stop. She had to get Madelaine *out*.

The sweat was running down the side of her face, it was getting increasingly hard to breathe, but now she grabbed hold of Madelaine's mutilated hands and started to pull. If all else failed, she could drag her from the shack. One of her nails cracked, then another, but she ignored them. She moved Madelaine a few inches, then a few more.

Another timber crashed to the ground, clipping Kassie on the shoulder, knocking her off balance. For a moment, she lost her bearings, the smoke swirling all around her, but then she glimpsed Madelaine's prone form again and started to tug once more. She managed to shift her a couple of inches, but then her progress was suddenly halted. Had the chair caught on something?

'Madelaine?'

Her cry was cracked and reedy. And there was no response. Kassie yanked again but even as she did so, two more timbers fell, showering her with sparks. She heaved again, but now she felt someone grab her from behind. She spun around and through the gloom was surprised to make out Adam's face. He was trying to say something, she could see his mouth moving, but what he was saying was lost as another roof timber crashed to the floor beside them.

Still he pulled at her. Kassie tried to fend him off, but his grip was vice-like. Now he was dragging *her* towards the door. Furious, she turned, trying to grab hold of Madelaine once more. But she had lost her now in the smoke.

'—ssie, we've got to get out of here.'

Now Adam's voice cut through and seconds later she felt a rush of cold air, as he pushed her from the blazing shed. For a moment, she struggled in his arms, but she knew it was hopeless. The whole structure was ablaze and anyone inside would be lost for sure.

'There's nothing more we can do, Kassie,' Adam gasped, holding her to him.

She continued to struggle, but it was half-hearted now, her body buckling as the tears came. Moments later, the entire roof collapsed in on itself.

'We were too late . . .'

Now she went limp in his arms, despair and exhaustion mastering her. Adam made no move to release her, hanging on to her. They had tried their best, but they had failed. There was no longer anything they could do, so the pair stood there, swaying, their eyes glued to the burning shack, as huge flames leaped from it, framed by the inky black waters of the lake.

107

'Tell me again what he looked like.'

Kassie looked up, disbelieving. She was exhausted, reeked of smoke, and had only just been cleared by the paramedics, but still Gabrielle Grey seemed determined to torment her.

'What more do you want me to say?' Kassie croaked.

'The "man" you've described could be anyone. Did he have any distinguishing features at all?'

'It was dark, the place was full of smoke. I only glimpsed him –'

'So, "white, middle-aged, goatee". That could describe half the men in Chicago.'

Kassie glared at her, her deep dislike for this cynical cop growing. They had hurried away from the blazing shack, immediately calling 911. To their dismay, Gabrielle Grey had arrived five minutes after the uniformed officers, waiting patiently for the paramedics to give Adam and her the all-clear, before separating them and spiriting them away to CPD headquarters for questioning. Kassie just wanted to be left alone, to lie down and cry herself to sleep, but she knew she had no power here.

'His beard was greying,' she continued unenthusiastically. 'And he was a little overweight. I grabbed his fat neck when I was trying to pull him off Adam –'

'We didn't find any skin under your fingernails when we swabbed you.'

'It must have come off when I was trying to free Madelaine. I lost two nails ripping at those ropes . . .'

Kassie's voice caught, tears pricking her eyes. The thought of Madelaine's fate was too awful to contemplate.

'Eye colour?' Grey continued, remorselessly.

Kassie shook her head.

'Any tattoos?'

'Not on his face or neck. I couldn't see the rest of him.'

'Scars? Birthmarks?'

'No.'

'But you'd recognize him if you saw him again?'

'Yes. Yes, I would.'

'Well, thank heaven for small mercies . . .'

This final comment was aimed at her colleague, but Grey's attempt at gallows humour fell oddly flat. The experienced detective seemed to have changed since Kassie last saw her – she looked washed out, beleaguered even.

'And you say this guy drove off?' her colleague pitched in mechanically. 'While you were still inside.'

'Yes, in a black Escalade. You must have seen the tyre tracks.'

'We saw some tyre tracks,' he responded coolly.

'Jesus Christ!' Kassie exploded, her voice cracking with emotion. 'Why won't you believe what I'm telling you? Dr Brandt will confirm everything I say.'

A look passed between the two police officers. Kassie wasn't sure what it meant. Adam had backed her up, hadn't he?

'There *was* a man there. You should be circulating an image of him, getting his face on the news.'

'Is that right?'

'He's probably injured, bruised. Someone will notice something, someone will know who he is.'

'Tell me again about your connection to Madelaine Baines,' Gabrielle interjected, dismissing Kassie's suggestion.

'I've told you, I've never met her. I saw her at the vigil, but that was it.'

'And you were at Lake Calumet because . . . ?'

'I've explained why we went to the lake –'

'Sure,' Grey interrupted. 'But here's the thing. I don't believe in fortune tellers or mediums . . . or Santa Claus or the Tooth Fairy. I believe in evidence, facts, concrete connections, so I'm curious as to why you and Dr Brandt keep turning up in this case. So far you are the only thing that links all three victims. You accosted Jacob Jones, you broke into Rochelle Stevens' house. A teenage girl matching your description was seen hammering on the Baineses' front door earlier today.'

'This is nuts.'

'Is it?'

Gabrielle's tone was hard, her gaze unflinching. But Kassie wasn't finished yet.

'If I was involved, why would I set fire to the shack? Risk my own life? Why would I call 911?'

'Maybe there was an accident. Maybe the fire got out of control. Maybe you're telling me a pack of lies.'

Kassie shook her head, lost for words.

'You've admitted you knew Rochelle from your NA meet. And Jacob Jones was responsible for a prior conviction of yours. What I'd like to know is how you knew Madelaine Baines.'

'I don't.'

But the look on their faces suggested they knew otherwise.

'I swear I don't,' she repeated, less firmly.

'We've had a look at Mrs Baines's schedule over the last few months,' Gabrielle continued. 'Turns out she helps out with a charity that runs reading schemes in failing schools, trying to get rough, tough kids to read "proper" literature. You were one of the kids registered to the scheme –'

'What . . . ?'

'But your membership was suspended because of disruptive behaviour –'

'I never met her,' Kassie insisted.

'Kassie –'

'Lots of people came into our school and, besides, I was hardly ever there.'

'Madelaine Baines was in and out of your school for months. You seriously telling me you never met her? That she didn't have some hand in your exclusion from the programme?'

'If she did, I don't remember.'

'Not good enough, Kassie. Three authority figures have been brutally murdered, three authority figures who *you* came into contact with.'

'No . . .'

But Kassie's protestations were weak now and Gabrielle went in for the kill.

'You are the link, Kassie. You and you alone.'

108

He stared at himself, angry and unhappy.

Having fled the lake, he'd driven hard and fast through the night, eventually abandoning the Baineses' SUV in a desolate parking lot in South Shore. This had been the planned dump-site all along, but still he felt unsettled and agitated as he disposed of the vehicle. As he wiped down the interior, the smell of the disinfectant making him nauseous, he kept firing anxious looks across the empty lot. He knew that the gangs were active at night and the last thing he needed was to be jumped while carrying out his clean-up operation.

He'd had enough surprises for one night.

He'd been so caught up in Baines's death throes, that he hadn't heard her would-be rescuers' approach. He had been stunned at first, unable to process what was happening. Then, as he'd fought back, eventually regaining the initiative, he'd been shocked to realize that he *recognized* one of them. It was the same girl who'd disturbed him at the Baines residence.

Who the hell *was* she? And how had she found her way to Lake Calumet?

These questions haunted him as he'd scurried through South Shore, sticking to the shadows, keeping an eagle eye out for the night bus. Had she tailed him? No, he would have seen her. Did she have some kind of tracking device on Baines's vehicle? No, that was absurd. Just as pressing was the question of *how* she knew. How did she know that Madelaine Baines was in danger, when he alone had decided her fate? It was impossible and yet somehow she was on to him, somehow she *knew* what he was planning.

Now, safely back in his down-at-heel, rented home, the thought still made him shiver. How? How was she doing this? But the mirror held no answers, just warnings of discovery. One of his front teeth was damaged, but he could ride that out – it was just chipped and he seldom smiled anyway. There were scratches and marks on his right cheek too, but those could also be explained away – a domestic accident, the house cat, whatever. It was the large, livid bruise on his cheek – a legacy of that bitch Baines's head butt – that would be harder to find an excuse for. He had already stolen some foundation from one of his housemates and though this had dulled the deep purple circle, it couldn't hide it completely. Would people comment? Or would they avoid drawing attention to it? He had never been very popular – at home or at work – and this might play to his advantage now.

The bruise, however, was not his only problem. The girl had seen him – she was probably giving chapter and verse to the cops right now. Were they drawing up an e-fit to circulate? A likeness of him? There was nothing for it, he would have to lose the goatee straight away. This would probably help, but was hardly a foolproof solution. He would just have to hope against hope that no one recognized him. The thought made him distinctly uneasy. This girl – whoever she was – had inserted herself into his story from day one. Initially she had been a suspect – he felt sure she was the fifteen-year-old arrestee whom the papers had mentioned in the aftermath of Jones's death – but now what was she? Some kind of vigilante? Why had she turned up at the shack, attempting to save Baines? How *could* she predict his every move?

For the first time since he'd started, he could feel the net tightening.

109

'What is the nature of your relationship with Kassie Wojcek?'

Adam stared at Gabrielle, stunned by her persistence and hostility. He had been made to wait for over an hour in the freezing interview suite, not allowed to make phone calls, or even get a glass of water. And now he was being subjected to a lengthy, and hostile, interrogation.

'We've been through this. She's my *patient*.'

'And tonight was what? Therapy in action?'

'Look, you know that we thought Madelaine Baines was in danger –'

'Because of Wojcek's visions?'

'I don't call them that –'

'But you were there because of her, right? Because she'd convinced you that Baines would be targeted?'

'Yes.'

There was no point denying it – everything that had happened recently had been because of Kassie. Gabrielle digested this, then asked:

'Were you involved in the murders of Jacob Jones, Rochelle Stevens –'

'No!'

'– and Madelaine Baines?'

'Of course not.'

'Yet you're always around, aren't you? You help get Kassie out of the Juvenile Detention Center and hours later Jacob Jones is abducted, murdered.'

'I was doing my *job* –'

'You break into Rochelle Stevens' home together and hours later *she* is dead. Madelaine Baines is brutally murdered in a remote shack and there you are again . . .'

'I've explained my involvement, given you an alibi for the nights Jacob Jones and Rochelle Stevens were targeted.'

'At home with your wife, we know,' Suarez said, shaking his head.

'Look I've tried to play straight with you guys,' Adam countered angrily, 'but if you *seriously* want to go there, then I need a lawyer.'

Gabrielle waved his objections aside, as if his indignation was of no importance.

'Is Kassie Wojcek directing these murders? Did she plan them?'

'No. I was there with her tonight. Fighting off the guy, trying to save Madelaine. I had to drag her out of the shack.'

Gabrielle nodded, but seemed unimpressed.

'Kassie's got injuries,' Adam continued hotly. 'So have I for that matter. Look at these bruises, for God's sake.' He gestured to the deep purple marking around his neck. 'You think I did this to myself?'

'I've no idea, but the fact remains that she *knew* all the victims.'

'No, she didn't.'

'Jacob Jones prosecuted her. Rochelle Stevens counselled her. Madelaine Baines did outreach at her school – with kids like Kassie.'

Adam didn't respond, silenced by this new information.

'Three people who intervened in her life – tried to discipline her, tried to help her – are now dead.' Gabrielle continued. 'You want to watch yourself, Dr Brandt. You might be next.'

344

'Don't be absurd.'

'Last time we met, you intimated that you believed in Kassie's "gift".'

'I did no such thing,' Adam protested.

'At the time, I thought you were cracked, but now I think she's using you, involving you in her game. Maybe as cover, perhaps to shield her from us, perhaps just for the hell of it. I think you're part of the puzzle.'

'My only aim has been to help her.'

'And what have you achieved? Three people are dead. And, in each case, Kassie Wojcek knew they were going to die. With Madelaine, she even took you to the kill site, because . . . what was it, Suarez?'

'Because she'd heard some birds in a premonition,' he offered dutifully.

'Because she heard birds in a premonition,' Gabrielle parroted. 'A vision she had in your office, allegedly under hypnosis. Can't you see what's happening here?'

'I don't know what you mean.'

'Do you believe she's psychic?'

'No. No . . .'

'Then what other explanation is there?' Gabrielle leaned in. 'Face it, Adam. She's been playing you since day one.'

110

Kassie sat on the cold bench, taking in the obscene graffiti on the walls, the unpleasant stains beneath her feet. She had been in a police van before, after brawls and busts, but never on her own. Suddenly she felt vulnerable and scared.

Nothing would happen to her here of course – it was just a short ride from CPD headquarters to the Juvenile Detention Center – it was what lay ahead that worried her. Her questioning had been unrelenting, Grey and Suarez taking it in turns to batter her with accusations. Grey in particular seemed determined to make her sweat, picking away at Kassie's past misdemeanours, relentlessly going over dates and times, establishing a concrete connection to all three murder victims.

Was it possible that they would charge her? Did they have enough? The thought made Kassie shiver. She was a fifteen-year-old girl, uneducated and naïve – what chance would she have against Grey and the law enforcement machine? They had promised her a lawyer, someone to make sure due process was followed, but Kassie needed to talk to someone who knew her, someone who cared. She had tried to call her mom, during a brief break in questioning. She promised herself that if her mother came to her aid now, she would spend the rest of her life working hard to be a model daughter. But Natalia's cell phone had rung and rung and, as there were other people waiting to call their loved ones, Kassie had eventually been forced to give up.

Kassie had never needed a word of sympathy, of support, as much as she did now. But her mother was gone and Adam . . . well, who knows what had happened to him? Suddenly Kassie felt utterly overwhelmed. All the misery, anger and sickness that had filled this wretched van over the years now assailed her, coating her in despair, robbing her of her resolve. She felt trapped, cornered, a prisoner in the system, at the mercy of the storm winds that continued to batter her. She would end her days surrounded by suspicion and reviled by all who knew her.

As the van moved off, rumbling through the gates and out on to the darkened street, Kassie dropped her head into her hands and began to cry.

III

Adam hurried down the steps, scanning the street for a cab. His car was still in the police pound, but the city's taxi drivers haunted this stretch of road, picking up the lawyers who went in and out of CPD headquarters in a never-ending carousel. He felt uneasy – Gabrielle's assertions spinning round his brain, even as a residual loyalty to Kassie, even a sliver of *belief*, fought back. Troubled, distressed and exhausted, now Adam just wanted to be home.

A cab sped by and he waved at it frantically, but it sailed serenely past. Cursing, he pulled his cell phone out and turned it on. The least he could do was tell Faith what had happened, reassure her, then call a cab. But as the phone came to life, it started buzzing feverishly. Looking down, he saw he had five voicemail messages.

Alarmed, he hit playback. The first message was from Faith, but it was hard to hear her over the traffic. She appeared to be crying and was almost whispering her words. So he skipped to the next, then the next. All of them were garbled – now Adam's heart was pounding – so he jumped straight to the final message. This was short, but more alarming still.

'I'm so sorry, Adam. So, sorry for everything. I love you . . .'

Dropping the phone, Adam started to run.

'Faith?'

His cry echoed round the empty hallway. He had made it home in under ten minutes, hailing a cab on South Giles

Avenue, throwing money at the startled cabbie as they pulled up outside their row house.

'Faith, are you home?'

His voice sounded strained and desperate. There was no response, so he marched into the kitchen. The radio was playing, as it had been this morning, but there was no sign of his wife.

'Faith?'

He ran down the hallway to the studio. But it too was deserted, swathed in darkness. The sight made him shiver – this place which had been so special to Faith now seemed lonely and lifeless. Turning on his heel, he hurried into their bedroom, but this too was empty.

Swiftly, he crossed the landing towards the home phone, intending to call Christine. Perhaps Faith had taken refuge with her mom? But, as he did so, he noticed something. The door to the nursery was closed, a thin strip of light creeping out from underneath it. Suddenly Adam felt short of breath. Faith had not set foot in there since . . .

'Faith?'

He grasped the handle. It turned easily and the door swung open. To his surprise, the floor was covered in baby clothes – the baby clothes he'd hidden in the loft – all neatly laid out as if ready to wear.

Confused, terrified, Adam took another step forward, then suddenly stopped in his tracks. He remained frozen for a second, unable to process the sight in front of him, even as he let out an ear-splitting cry. Faith *had* entered the nursery and her limp body now hung from the high beam, twisting slowly back and forth.

Book Three

112

The street was busy, bodies constantly buffeting her. Her right foot had been stamped on, a stray elbow had connected with her ribs, but Kassie barely noticed. She had to keep going. She had to find him.

A week ago, she would not have been able to keep up this pace. Her experience at Lake Calumet had taken its toll – her throat and lungs had been damaged by the smoke and she'd suffered mild concussion as a result of the blow to her head. She'd felt utterly washed out as she slotted back into the routine at the Juvenile Detention Center. Guilt over her failure to save Madelaine and deep sadness at Faith's needless death mingled with a sickening certainty that she would become the scapegoat for the brutal murders. But a day passed without her being charged, and on the eve of her second full day of custody, she had suddenly been released.

This unexpected development had revived her, and though she'd returned to an empty house, she nevertheless sensed a change in the tide. Her possessions were still at Adam's, so she'd had to use the spare key, hidden beneath a plant pot for emergencies, but having entered and dug out the few remaining dollars she had to her name, she'd made a dash to the grocery store. She blew forty dollars there and then and having eaten too much and drunk a six-pack of beers, she'd crashed out, enjoying her first decent night's sleep in weeks. When she awoke the next morning, she felt refreshed. The question was what, if anything, should she do next?

Initially, she'd wondered if it would be safer to do *nothing*, to concentrate on her own predicament and yet . . . *he* was still out there. This simple fact haunted her. Briefly, she'd had a hold on him, but he'd shrugged her off and escaped. Thanks to her, Chicago was still at his mercy. So, despite her reservations, despite the gnawing fear growing inside her, she'd decided to act.

Sidestepping a young businessman who was heading directly for her, Kassie came to a halt outside a large laundromat. She had already visited a diner, a hardware store and a nail salon on this street and was beginning to feel dispirited, but she pushed inside nevertheless. Immediately, eight pairs of eyes swivelled towards her, the bored customers wresting their attention away from the hypnotic cycle of the washing machines. Kassie met their gaze, flitting swiftly from one to the next, barely pausing to take in the details. A heart attack, a brain haemorrhage, a drowning, a workplace accident, another heart attack . . . Kassie stumbled slightly as these visceral images punched into her, but she managed to maintain her composure, until the last person present had been checked. They were looking at her strangely – why was this girl hanging around in the doorway, staring at them? – so, turning, she retreated. There was no point drawing attention to herself – there was nothing for her here.

On she went, pounding the street, her eyes examining the shoppers and workers who hurried past. There seemed to be no rhyme or reason to the killer's choice of victim, *except* the neighbourhood they all lived in. So Kassie had decided to start her search here, haunting West Town's coffee shops, sandwich bars, restaurants, parks and cinemas, hoping to winkle out the killer by seeking out his next victim. She knew it was a hopeless task – thousands of people passed through this neighbourhood every day – but she had to try.

She'd trekked down West Grand Avenue, up West Chicago Avenue, through the Ukrainian Village, as far east as Noble Square, as far west as North Sacramento Boulevard. She had investigated most of the popular community spaces, scrutinizing the visitors at the Talcott Museum and the Met West Community Garden, even causing a stir among the suspicious parishioners at St Columbkille's church, who'd taken exception to her invasive presence. The irony was not lost on Kassie. She had run from her visions most of her life, but now she actively sought them out, drowning daily in a hideous kaleidoscope of death. And all to no avail. The identity of the killer's next victim remained as opaque as ever.

Dodging a gaggle of chattering women, Kassie paused to catch her breath, leaning her head against the window of a dog-grooming store. As she did so, she caught sight of a young female jogger in the reflection, bending down to tie up her laces on the opposite side of the road. No doubt the other undercover officer – whom she'd labelled 'skater boy' because of his failed attempt at youth wear – was also close by. They, and others like them, had been on her tail ever since she'd been released from the Detention Center. Clearly she was not out of the woods yet.

Their presence did not disturb Kassie, however. In fact, she was glad of it. Time was running out and if she was to stumble on to the killer's trail, unmask him even in the short time she had left, then she would need their help.

Today of all days, she welcomed their dogged presence.

113

'How sure are you?'

Hoskins' question was blunt and to the point.

'Ninety-nine per cent,' Gabrielle replied tightly. 'We just need the evidence . . .'

'You just need the evidence.'

His response dripped with sarcasm. Superintendent Hoskins didn't often put in an appearance on the eighth floor, but when he did, he made his presence felt.

'Kassie Wojcek is linked to *all* the victims,' Gabrielle continued unabashed. 'She was seen stalking them just before their deaths.'

'So you keep saying.'

'And now she's spending her days in West Town, scoping the shops, diners, community centres. Which fits, because all the victims –'

'Lived in West Town. I've read your reports, Gabrielle. I also read the newspapers. In fact, I brought a few of them with me, in case you haven't had a chance to look at them . . .'

He tossed a tabloid on to the desk, reading the headline aloud:

'"Reign of terror. Chicago Butcher continues to elude authorities . . ."'

Another tabloid landed on top of the first:

'"Inferno at Lake Calumet. The TRUE story . . ."'

Then the *Tribune*:

'"CPD clutching at straws in triple homicide . . ."'

Beneath the banner headline was a snatched photo of Gabrielle looking stressed. Reporters and photographers continued to lurk outside CPD headquarters, hoping to discover snippets of information or, at the very least, evidence of police incompetence. An intrepid snapper had even stationed himself outside Gabrielle's house – leading to a furious row between her and Dwayne this morning. He was increasingly worried about the toll the case was taking on her and the family in general. Gabrielle agreed with him completely – this was affecting *everyone* – yet there was no question of her walking away now.

'Twenty-four hours and we'll have this thing wrapped up,' she replied, as confidently as she could.

Hoskins raised an eyebrow.

'You think so?'

'Absolutely. We have an eight-man undercover unit shadowing her every move. She *will* lead us to her next victim. And when she does . . .'

Hoskins was still looking sceptical.

'Trust me, the day after tomorrow, the headlines are going to look a lot better.'

'When you have no idea who her accomplice is? If she even *has* an accomplice,' Hoskins countered.

'*Wojcek* is the key. And she's going to make a mistake. We are *so* close.'

'I wish I could believe you, Gabrielle,' Hoskins replied heavily. 'But this investigation has been compromised from the start.'

He looked out into the incident room, his gaze settling on Miller's vacant chair. Hoskins had nearly removed Gabrielle from the investigation *then* – she could remember every word of his expletive-laden reaction to Miller's confession and suspension – and had only been dissuaded from doing so because of the negative headlines Gabrielle's dismissal would inevitably generate. Still, her position was hanging by a thread, and Gabrielle knew it.

'Sir, you gave me this job because you had faith in me, because you trusted me to lead this department,' she continued, forcing down her anxiety. 'Keep that faith for one more day. If, after that, I've failed to deliver, then bring the Feds in, do whatever you have to do. But don't rob us of the chance to end this thing on *our* terms, to show that the CPD is up to the task it's been entrusted with.'

It was a naked appeal to his pride, to his sense of legacy and reputation. Hoskins deliberated for an age, sizing up the possible risks and rewards, before nodding his head curtly and taking his leave. Gabrielle watched him go, relieved to have survived their latest skirmish, but aware that her reprieve was temporary.

Her head was on the block now.

114

'What the hell are you looking at?'

Kassie jumped, startled by the angry voice. Coming to, she realized that she had been caught staring. Already heads were turning towards her, the man's aggressive complaint echoing round the silent library.

'I asked you a question.'

He was rising now, irritated and unsettled by Kassie's scrutiny of him. Backing away, Kassie racked her brains for a suitable response, something to diffuse the situation, but all she could think of, all she could *see*, was this poor man choking to death on his vomit, even as he continued to grip the dirty syringe.

'I'm sorry . . . I didn't mean to disturb you.'

'Too late,' he countered, heading directly towards her.

Kassie's eyes were drawn to his arms – his sleeves riding up to reveal track marks. Why had she been so stupid? He wasn't relevant to her main purpose, so why had she stared at him? Alarmed, Kassie speeded up her retreat from the tatty community library. The guy looked unhinged and clearly meant business.

Immediately, Kassie hit something hard, knocking the breath from her. Disoriented, she froze, bracing herself for the young addict to launch himself at her. But to her surprise, he now backed away, returning swiftly to his seat. Confused, Kassie turned, to discover that she had collided with the sizeable frame of the library's security guard. He was looking down at her unkindly, distaste writ large on his face.

'I think it's time you got your bony ass outta here, don't you?'

Stumbling out into the light, Kassie sank down on to the library's cold, stone steps. The burly guard had marched her to the exit, outlining what punishment awaited her *should* she attempt to return. He clearly didn't like the look of her — Kassie could tell from his expression that he thought she was suffering from mental health problems, something that scared and disgusted him in equal measure. Adding a few pointed insults, he had launched her from the premises.

Chastened, Kassie had wanted to run, to put as much distance as possible between herself and the scene of her latest embarrassment, but instead she crumpled to the ground, careless of the reactions of passers-by or the undercover cops who no doubt loitered nearby. Resting her throbbing head on her knees, she closed her eyes and let the darkness engulf her.

Each morning she rose with renewed hope, somehow shrugging off the disappointment of the previous day. But almost a week had passed now, and she was finding it harder to maintain her optimism. She knew she stood on the edge of destruction, that there was not a second to waste, but her body was revolting against her, paralysed by fear and despair. And, as ever, there was no one to raise her up.

Her mother was hundreds of miles away. She had no friends to turn to. And she had been expelled from school for persistently cutting class — the formal, typed letter had been waiting for her on her return from the Detention Center. With nowhere else to go, she now spent her waking hours on the streets, conducting her fruitless search, retreating home only when she was too exhausted to continue. The few hours she spent in the family home were filled with fear and regret, a forlorn figure rattling around in an empty box. A week ago, she would have called Adam, sought out his company, but, of course, there was no question of doing that now.

Kassie rubbed her forehead roughly against her knee, willing herself not to cry. But her loneliness was total, her misery complete. She'd liked Adam, Faith too, yet she had destroyed them both. One had left this world, the other remained, suffering in ways that Kassie couldn't bring herself to imagine. This was the wreckage of the lives she touched. In truth, it had always been this way. Wherever she went, disaster followed. The fact that her time was drawing to a close provided no solace – she had done more damage in fifteen years than most managed in an entire lifetime. This would be her legacy.

How strange life was. Two weeks ago, after she'd collided with Jacob Jones on North Michigan Avenue, she'd been full of purpose, determined to challenge her gift, to stare Fate down, to save the lives of those whose death she had foreseen. But now? She would raise her bones and continue her quest no doubt – what else could she do? – but it was more in hope than expectation. She'd clung to the idea that her involvement in these murders *meant* something, that she had a role to play. But perhaps, after all, she was just a chance witness to a killer's pitiless cruelty? Maybe all this frenzied activity was the pointless thrashing around before the inevitable end?

Reluctantly, Kassie picked herself up off the cold steps. There was nothing she could do but carry on. She knew now, however, that she was doomed to fail.

Her time was up and she was staring down the barrel.

115

She had haunted the house ever since Faith's death.

Adam was used to having Christine around – she had her own key and let herself in fairly often during Faith's pregnancy – but this had been during happier times, when they were expectant, excited, full of hope. Now things were very different. Adam was still in shock, stumbling from day to day, but he at least had things to do. Many of these duties were unpleasant – informing stunned friends, family and colleagues of her death, arranging a joint funeral for Faith and Annabelle, preparing for the obligatory inquest – but they gave Adam purpose and point, in the short term at least.

Christine appeared to have no such comfort, vacillating between vocal, anguished despair and stunned apathy. Christine had invested all her hopes in her daughter, and the prospect of a grandchild, but had been left with ashes. She lived alone, her husband was long gone, so Adam understood why she felt the need to be in the house, to be with someone else who shared her pain. But it didn't make it any easier to stomach. Christine ghosted around the house, crying, making endless cups of undrunk tea, only pausing to sit in front of the TV, staring hopelessly into space as the presenters talked to themselves. Adam found the latter particularly troubling, his mother-in-law acting like a zombie, providing no comfort by her presence, instead underlining the needless, pointless cruelty of Faith's death.

She was there now – staring morosely at the Weather

Channel. Christine seemed unaware of his presence, so Adam slipped past the living room door into the hallway. He was heading for the front door, but paused now to look at himself in the floor-to-ceiling mirror. He was wearing the Ermenegildo Zegna suit Faith had bought him for his fortieth birthday, the one she had taken such pains to select, ensuring the colour, the fabric, the cut, were perfect. It moved him to tears now to think of the love she had poured into this gift and he fervently hoped that some of her goodwill, her affection, would rub off on him today. He needed it.

His appearance before the Illinois Board of Professional Regulation was due to start in under an hour. Part of him was still angry that he had been summoned, but another part of him knew that it was inevitable, given his recent behaviour. He had initially concealed the summons from Christine, convincing himself that it wasn't relevant, that his involvement with Kassie hadn't contributed to Faith's death. But this wasn't true and eventually he'd overcome his embarrassment and told her. She had reacted calmly, but Adam could sense her silent judgement, her belief that this 'reckoning' was fit and proper. She, of course, was not interested in the main thrust of the Board's grievances – the numerous lines Adam had crossed during his treatment of Kassie. Her accusations were more pointed and more personal. Why, as her husband, as a trained psychologist, had Adam not spotted the signs? Why had he not foreseen what was coming? Why had he abandoned Faith on that fateful day?

He had posed himself these questions many times since Faith's death, torturing himself during the long nights, when the minutes seemed to crawl by. Still he had no answers. Yes, Faith had been suffering. Yes, her moods had been variable – cogent and defiant one moment, inconsolable and despairing the next. But he had never, never in his worst nightmares, thought that she would take her own life. Despite her early mental health problems, she had been stable and level-headed of late. It was true that her desire to be a mother had on occasion overwhelmed her, during their many failed attempts at IVF, and that at times she had been depressed, but she had never relinquished her desire to live. She loved her mother, she loved *him* – that had never been in doubt. And yet . . . she had chosen to leave them.

She had left a scrawled note on the floor, but it simply read: 'there is no hope', which defied reason. Was it possible that her depression had morphed into a form of psychosis, a mental state in which she was unable to fully consider the consequences of her actions? Perhaps her desire, her need, to be a mother had simply crushed her? Her choice of the nursery as the site of her suicide strongly suggested that this was the case, but still, if this was the case, how had he not seen it coming? Faith had been hostile, upset, that last morning, pushing Adam away, but still it was so unexpected . . . The only mercy was that she had not suffered – her neck had broken cleanly – but this did nothing to lessen Adam's profound shock and grief at her passing.

Sometimes he was angered by Christine's unspoken desire to blame him, other times he welcomed her censure, feeling he deserved it. Sometimes, his thoughts turned to Kassie. He had barely had time to process Gabrielle Grey's insinuations before he discovered Faith, and since then those concerns had gone clean out of his mind. Over the last couple of days, however, they had started to return. Grey had poured scorn on Kassie's alleged abilities as a psychic and Adam's indulgence of that idea, and though he had resisted her attack at the time, now he felt instinctively that she was right. Yes, Kassie's ability to predict the identity of the victims was uncanny, but she did know them all personally. Yes, she seemed to have been trying to help, but who had she saved? No one. They had all died in the most awful of circumstances. What, then, had Kassie got out of it? The attention of numerous people – her mother, the authorities, but most crucially him and Faith. She had won them over, come to live in their house, inserted herself into their lives.

One telling fact kept gnawing away at Adam. Despite stepping inside their bereavement, despite living at close quarters with both of them, literally looking them in the eye day after day, Kassie had not foreseen Faith's death. The two had spent a good deal of time together, Faith seeming to find Kassie's presence comforting – she had even started drawing her. And yet Kassie hadn't foreseen her fate, hadn't realized that her death was imminent.

What, then, did that mean? That her gift was intermittent, sometimes on, sometimes off? Or that there was no gift at all.

Adam was floundering, tortured by unanswered questions. But on one point there was little doubt. The one thing – the most important thing – that Kassie *should* have seen coming, she had not. Which made Adam wonder if he should ever have believed a word she said.

116

He cradled his coffee, stroking his chin. The smooth skin felt strange to his touch – he had shaved his goatee off a week ago, but was still getting used to it. Its sudden disappearance had caused a few comments at work, but he'd rehearsed the reasons for the change and no one seemed suspicious – the consensus was that it took years off him. Some even speculated that he might have a new lady friend, which had made him chuckle. The bruising on his face had aroused more interest, but this too had been explained away, his colleagues having no trouble believing him foolish enough to collide with a branch while jogging after dark. Their low opinion of him was finally paying dividends.

After the disaster at Lake Calumet, he had initially pan-icked, terrified his carelessness would result in his capture. But an e-fit had not appeared in the press the following morning – indeed, a whole day passed before an image of a middle-aged man with a goatee started appearing in media outlets. It was a passable likeness, but no more – the eyes, the shape of face both wrong – and, besides, the police appeal was caged in muted terms. This man was a 'person of inter-est' that the police needed to talk to. He was not officially the prime suspect, or even *a* suspect, they just wanted to speak with him. This had cheered him – but also puzzled him. What kind of game were they playing?

Confused, unnerved, he had pored over the newspapers and online news sites, hoovering up the coverage of the

investigation. And on Blacklisted.com he had got a break —
the notorious news website publishing an inmate's snatched
cell phone photo of a fifteen-year-old being led to a police
van. The girl was in handcuffs, on her way to the Juvenile
Detention Center — the website alleging that she was the
CPD's prime suspect, the *same* girl that had been arrested
after Jacob Jones's murder.

He had recognized his youthful nemesis immediately —
the sullen-looking teenager who seemed able to predict his
every move. Claiming family illness, he had immediately
taken a couple of days off work, bending his steps towards
the Juvenile Detention Center on South Hamilton Avenue.
A few bored journalists haunted the main entrance, but he
had taken up a position across the street from the rear exit.
He knew from his own experience that inmates were usually
released via this discreet route, either first thing in the morning or last thing at night. And before long he had been
rewarded for his foresight — the awkward teenager shuffling
out to freedom through the back doors, into the gloom of a
cold Chicago night, a couple of days after her initial arrest.

He had been tempted to approach her — to abduct her,
demand answers from her — but the sight of undercover officers
tailing her stopped him in his tracks. Instead he had followed
them at a discreet distance, all the way to Back of the Yards,
where the girl entered a small, neatly kept bungalow. The tailing
officers immediately took up positions on the other side of road,
their eyes glued to the house. He had driven away fast, his
thoughts in tumult. It seemed impossible, ridiculous even, but
the website was *right*. Clearly the slight girl *was* the prime suspect
for the murders. There could be no other explanation for it.
Obviously, the police had no idea what they were dealing with.

It was a trait they shared with his co-workers, who had

shown no interest in his brief absence from work and even now seemed more interested in tech mags than the monster in their midst. Shaking his head at their boneheaded ignorance, he tugged his phone from his pocket and pulled up Jan's profile, heading straight for his calendar. This confirmed that the young Slovakian was working the early shift and would be clocking off at 3 p.m. Had he expected any different? Of course not, he had checked Jan's schedule three times already today. He was being overcautious, but he also knew this ritual was part of the build-up, the constant monitoring of his victim's schedule an enjoyable prelude to what lay ahead. Poor Jan had such big plans, for himself, his girlfriend, his sister, little realizing that he had only hours to live.

Sliding the phone back into his pocket, he went through the plan once more. It was risky to strike again, so soon after Calumet, but there was no way he could stop. The terror of his victims – their begging, their distress, their agony – was one thing, but it was the wider reaction of the city that excited him now. His murders had engendered a gnawing anxiety that rippled through the well-to-do suburbs of Chicago. The city's movers and shakers were used to reading about violence in the *Tribune* – pictures of the latest drive-bys – but the thought that death could stalk *them*, could walk right into their house and tap them on the shoulder, had them running scared. If *they* weren't safe, then no one was.

You saw it in the television interviews, heard it on the radio phone-ins, read it on the online community bulletin boards – fear. Danger had never felt so close before and they wanted it to stop. They were holding community vigils, organizing protests, demanding extra police on the streets, desperately wanting this reign of terror to end.

All because of him.

117

Gabrielle Grey sat in her office, the blinds down, the door locked. This was not her usual style – she liked to encourage an informal, sharing dynamic within the department. But, right now, she needed to be alone.

Her meeting with Hoskins was still fresh in her memory. Following his departure, she had immediately checked in with Suarez in the incident room, then with Detective Richards, who was her point man on their surveillance team. The news was not encouraging – Kassie Wojcek continued to stalk West Town, but seemingly to no purpose. Her behaviour was becoming ever more unpredictable – she had just been thrown out of the local library for disturbing the readers – and Gabrielle could tell that her team were beginning to doubt that their surveillance would prove fruitful.

Feeling beleaguered, frustrated, Gabrielle had retreated to her office. The expected breakthrough with Kassie Wojcek continued to elude them. The teenager maintained her lonely hunt, but hadn't actually done anything interesting or incriminating. Nor had she contacted anyone. This latter detail was particularly unnerving, their working theory being that Kassie had an accomplice, selecting and stalking her prey before handing them over to a more experienced killer. Yet over five days of surveillance, her officers had not seen her contact anyone. She hadn't used her phone, nor had she attempted to meet with anyone, so how exactly was this partnership working?

Gabrielle racked her brains, turning over the possibilities, but she could make no headway. It was maddening: Kassie had to be involved somehow – she knew the identities of the victims before anyone else and had inserted herself into the narrative at every opportunity. Also, she had reason to dislike them. And yet . . . there were aspects of her behaviour, aspects Adam Brandt had been keen to point out, that ran counter to the idea of Kassie being a threat to these people. She had insisted she was trying to warn Jacob Jones, something he had confirmed in his brief statement to the uniformed officers who dragged her away from him on North Michigan Avenue. Furthermore, her actions at Rochelle Stevens' house and Lake Calumet could be read as suggesting she was trying to help the victims. The latter was particularly confusing – it was Kassie who had started the chain of events that led to their presence at Lake Calumet. If she was in league with their killer, why would she lead Adam Brandt to the kill site, disturb the attack on Baines, injure herself in the process?

Still Gabrielle pushed these doubts away. If Kassie wasn't involved in these killings, if she *was* trying to help them, then she had to be telling the truth. But that was impossible. Gabrielle had never believed in the supernatural and she wasn't about to start now.

However, she wasn't stupid, nor had she spent years working cases to ignore the possibility that there was more than one potential explanation, that there was something she had not yet alighted on that would illuminate everything. Say the girl was mad, that somehow she knew or thought she knew who these victims would be, and *was* trying to help them, then that suggested that she had no connection to the killer and would never lead them to him . . .

Unnerved by this thought, Gabrielle pulled open her files

once more. She knew it was pointless – staring at the photos of the victims was hardly going to inspire a flash of inspiration – but riven with doubt, she felt there was nothing to do but go back to basics, in the hope – the fear – that they had missed something.

She placed the photos of Jones, Stevens and Baines next to each other in a row. These were not the grim post-mortem images, but rather the photos provided by the families for use in their appeals for witnesses. They were happy, smiling photos and Gabrielle shuddered as she looked at them now. All these people had loved ones – partners, mothers, fathers, husbands, children – and yet they had been abducted and murdered without hindrance.

Their attacker had timed his actions to perfection. Jacob Jones's fiancée had been away at a conference, Madelaine Baines's family had been at work and school, and Rochelle Stevens had been targeted when she was home alone, watching her favourite TV programme. Unless their killer was extremely lucky, he had done his homework. This suggested that he was a stalker first and a killer second, yet there was little actual evidence to support this theory. Security footage feeds had not revealed any of the victims being tailed in the lead-up to their disappearance, nor had their neighbours spotted any suspicious figures or unusual activity in the run-up to their deaths. This killer was obviously scrupulously careful, but still you would expect something to show up, some evidence of his craft. How else would he know that Madelaine's twins always played a softball match on a Thursday, that Rochelle was regularly home alone on Tuesday nights, watching her favourite show?

And now a thought landed. A thought so simple, but so insistent, that Gabrielle found herself rising to her feet.

There *was* one way he would know all their movements without ever going near them. Rounding her desk, she hurried out into the incident room.

'Montgomery . . .'

The young officer looked up, as Gabrielle approached.

'Rochelle Stevens' phone. Where is it?'

'Right here,' she replied, crossing to the evidence store and removing a plastic bag in which the young woman's phone lay.

Slipping on latex gloves, Gabrielle took the bag from her. Turning the phone on, she opened the dead woman's calendar. All her appointments, right down to casual coffee meets, grocery deliveries and television viewing, were scheduled there. This was a woman who liked to *plan*.

'And Baines's phone?'

Montgomery handed her a battered Samsung.

'Recovered from her house, just like the others. We're assuming the killer left them there so his movements couldn't be tracked.'

Nodding, Gabrielle opened up Madelaine's calendar. It too was rammed full of appointments, charity events, school pickups and softball matches. Gabrielle stared at the long list of engagements, her mind turning.

'Was Baines's phone synced to anyone else's?'

'Sure,' Montgomery replied, looking momentarily wrong-footed. 'To her husband's, I think. They shared a diary.'

'And do we know where Baines bought the phone?'

Montgomery stared at her for a moment, then started leafing through a mound of paperwork.

'I think she got it from Phone Shack. She went there quite regularly, I think.'

'Which one?'

'West Town,' Montgomery replied a little hesitantly, as if fearing she had overlooked something important.

Gabrielle digested this, before continuing.

'What about Rochelle Stevens?'

Montgomery was already rifling through her files. Gabrielle watched her, hungry for answers.

'I know she was with Verizon, had been for a while . . . She set her contract up over two years ago at a Talk Warehouse in the Loop. It's near where she works, I think.'

Gabrielle stared at her. Was she barking up the wrong tree after all?

'But I'm sure there was a payment from her account to a Phone Shack,' Detective Suarez interrupted, crossing to join them. 'A couple of months ago. It stood out to me, because she hadn't used them before and it was only a one-off payment.'

'Yeah, there it is,' Montgomery confirmed, pointing to a line on Rochelle's bank statement. 'A one-off payment to the Phone Shack in West Town . . .'

She petered out even as she said it.

'You're thinking the Phone Shack is the connection?' Suarez asked, handing the statement to Gabrielle.

Gabrielle paused before answering, trying to gather her thoughts.

'All three victims were targeted when they were home alone. Now, Rochelle Stevens was out *a lot*. She had therapy sessions or social events most nights, *except* Tuesday, when she religiously watched *Scandal*. Baines was also very busy, but her girls always played a softball match on Thursdays, so stayed late at school. Neither woman was a regular tweeter or poster – you couldn't monitor their movements that way – but they were both scrupulous users of their calendars, so if you had access to them, it would be easy to work out when they'd be alone. Jones was more of a home body than the others, but his fiancée was away at a conference on the night he was abducted –'

'Which had been in his diary for weeks,' Suarez added pointedly.

'So we're saying Jones visited Phone Shack too?'

'Possibly,' Gabrielle replied carefully. 'Maybe someone there encountered them all, took the opportunity to clone their accounts or sync phones . . .'

'If he did . . . then he could see all of their apps, their diaries . . . everything,' Montgomery overlapped. 'He could even pinpoint their whereabouts in real time, by switching on location services.'

'Exactly. He'd know where they were, where they were going to be, when they were likely to be alone . . .' Gabrielle's voice dropped to a whisper as she concluded: '. . . he'd know everything about them.'

Kassie pushed the door open and stepped inside. There were numerous Starbucks in West Town, but this was by far the busiest, and though she had passed through it several times already over the last few days, she returned to it now, anxious to warm her bones after a deeply dispiriting morning. Making her way to a vacated table, she took ownership of an abandoned cup of coffee, hoping that the staff would think she'd bought it and leave her alone.

It was a good vantage point – centrally located in the store, with a clear view of the entrance, the counter, the staff area. She examined the faces that passed by, trying to look uninterested as she read their fate, while quietly dying inside. Minutes dragged by and, as her mood plummeted, her desire for actual refreshment started to grow. The smell of the coffee was intoxicating and the sight of other patrons wolfing down almond croissants and granola bars was too much to bear. She'd forgotten to eat anything this morning and now, in spite of her dizziness and unease, her stomach was growling.

She delved into her pocket, eventually finding a twenty-dollar bill, the meagre remnants of her savings. Rising, she crossed quickly to the counter. A middle-aged Korean man was stationed at the register, awaiting new orders.

'Latte, please,' Kassie mumbled. 'And a chocolate croissant.'

'Sure,' the man replied, in a flat tone of voice, taking the proffered bill and gesturing her to wait at the pass. Kassie moved along the counter and lingered, shifting from one foot to the other, as she did so. Moments later, a hassled young barista approached with her coffee.

'There you go, ma'am,' he said, his strong European accent mangling the words.

Kassie snatched it up eagerly, but as she did so, her eyes rose to meet his. Immediately, she felt a jolt of naked fear, an electrical surge of terror that seemed to rip right through her. Her mug tumbled to the floor, shattering as it sprayed her legs with hot coffee, but Kassie didn't move. She could no longer see her server, was no longer in Starbucks. She was in a room she didn't recognize, writhing in a pool of blood, gasping for air, as the life drained from her . . .

Screaming, she lashed out, trying to find purchase, some way to drag herself from that awful, gore-spattered room. Her hand connected with something and she grasped it eagerly – and now suddenly she was back in Starbucks again, gripping the startled barista's shirt. The young man looked confused, even a little scared and was desperately trying to loosen her grip.

'You need to leave.'

The young man hadn't spoken, which confused Kassie. But then she became aware of the store manager standing right next to her.

'You're scaring the other customers. You need to go.'

He plucked Kassie's hand away from the man's shirt. Kassie glimpsed the barista's name – Jan Varga – on his badge, but had no time to communicate with him, as she now found herself being marched towards the exit. Too late, she tried to recover the initiative, twisting in the manager's vice-like grip, but her feet skidded on the floor, as he dragged her away from the counter.

'You don't understand. I have to speak to him –'

Her voice was high and hysterical. She knew she sounded crazy, but she had to try.

'He's in danger. Serious danger. I have –'

'The only one who's in danger is you,' the manager replied angrily. 'Now beat it, before I call the cops.'

Heaving the glass doors open, he shoved her outside. Regaining her balance quickly, Kassie charged back towards the entrance, but the burly manager stepped in front of her, blocking her path. She screamed and shouted at him – what the hell was this moron thinking? – but he remained unmoved. Beyond him, Kassie could see Jan being comforted by other baristas, but there was no way to reach him. Only she knew what lay in store for him – what agonies he would have to endure – but for now she remained a frantic but hopeless presence, on the wrong side of the thick glass doors.

119

'No, no, no!'

Adam slammed his hand on the table, beating out the rhythm of his defiance.

'It was *never* my intention to put my clients in danger.'

'And yet that's exactly what you did,' Dr Gould countered forcefully. 'You endangered the life of a vulnerable teenage girl, endangered your *own* life . . .'

'And that was wrong. I've admitted as much. But I felt that, in the circumstances, we had no choice. A woman's life was in danger and the police weren't doing anything –'

'So you chose to follow your client to Lake Calumet –'

'I felt I had to, to protect her.'

'Chose to believe the testimony of a troubled young woman,' Dr Bown added.

'If she was deluded, if she was making it up, then there would be no danger,' Adam retorted quickly. 'But if she *wasn't*, if there was some truth in what she was saying, then I couldn't let her go there alone.'

'The proper course of action would have been to have sectioned her, for her own safety, and then to have removed yourself from responsibility for her care,' Gould continued. 'You have obviously become far too close to her.'

'I have already passed responsibility for her on to a colleague, but as to sectioning her, I had no grounds to do so. She was cogent, she was lucid, she wasn't in the midst of a mental health breakdown –'

'So, you're saying you believed her? You took her visions at face value?' Dr Barkley asked, one eyebrow raised.

'No, of course not.'

'Then why were you there? If you didn't believe her story, why *did* you go to the lake?'

There was no answer to this, of course. Not one which made sense anyway. Adam had been twisting on the wire ever since he met Kassie and was still no closer to defining the root or substance of her affliction.

'Well?'

The question hung in the air. The massed faces of the board were expecting an answer, but what was the point? They would only follow it up with more unanswerable accusations. Why hadn't he intervened more forcefully when Kassie first exhibited these self-destructive tendencies? Why had he revealed Rochelle Stevens' private address to a client? Broken into her home? Why had he disregarded his training, every rule and protocol he'd ever been taught?

Rising to his feet, he stared at his accusers for a moment, surprising even himself by saying:

'Do what you want.'

Then, turning, he marched towards the door.

120

Going into the back room, he pushed the door quietly shut behind him. The shop was busy now, a full roster of staff in action, and he couldn't risk being disturbed. Crossing to the battered bank of lockers, he slid his rucksack off his shoulder and punched in the access code. Wearily the lock slid across and he pulled the locker open.

It was empty, save for a crumpled plastic bag. Snatching it up, he removed a couple of items from it. A spare ski mask. A crowbar. The cleaver. Stowing the objects in his rucksack, he shut the locker door and secured it once more.

Funny how useful this place had become. Billed as a staff recreation area, it was nothing of the sort – just a locker bank and a couple of chairs to complement the rising damp and rusty pipes. He used to avoid this place like the plague, but now he was a fairly regular visitor. His colleagues continued to steer clear of it, however, which suited him just fine.

It had become his sanctuary, musty and unpleasant though it was. Initially, he had stored his equipment at home, though 'home' was an overly affectionate term for the bedraggled house he shared with four other tenants. The rooms were small and cold, the bathroom dirty and the less said about the kitchen the better. Even so, he had liked it initially. Most of the tenants spoke little English, so weren't likely to ask him why he occasionally disappeared for the night. They weren't much interested in what he did during the day either, so *were* anyone ever to come there asking questions, they would prove to be of little help. Even the landlord, a huge Romanian guy who accepted the rent in cash without ever bothering to challenge him on his patently fake ID, would be unable to provide the authorities with any cogent information.

Over time, however, his enthusiasm for his rented home had waned. He didn't trust the other tenants – he was sure that one or two of them had taken advantage of his absences to enter his room. The padlock on his door was designed to keep them out, but he was sure someone had gained access, rummaging through his cashbox. They wouldn't have found anything incriminating there, but the intrusion had alarmed him and he'd decided to stow his gear at work, away from prying eyes.

It was strange how history repeated itself. His childhood home had been no less chaotic or unfriendly than the ramshackle house he now lived in. His mother had seven children, but two great loves – one of which she took from the bottle, the other from a glass pipe. Her kids had largely been neglected and would have starved were it not for the best efforts of his eldest sister, Jacqueline, who begged and borrowed to buy bread and milk. He had loved her at first, until she too became crabbed and bitter, eventually doling out more violence than even his mother. Generally, it was best to keep a low profile, which of course most of them did.

But that was never in his make-up. While others took neglect and misery as their due, he had not been prepared to go quietly. Now he shunned the attention of his fellow house dwellers; back then he went out of his way to announce his presence to his siblings. He would smash treasured keepsakes, urinate on their beds and expose himself to his younger sisters. They beat him for his troubles, labelling him a jerk, a freak, the runt of the litter. The memory made him smile. They'd thought they were better than him, destined to achieve more, to be the ones that got away and made something of their lives. How wrong they had been. They were all small-town addicts, drunks and fuck-ups now, a litany of bad decisions and failed marriages behind them, whereas his deeds would go down in history. He only wished he could be there to see their reaction – on the day they opened the newspapers and saw that *he* was the big dog now.

Suddenly the door rattled, snapping him out of his reminiscences. For a horrible moment, he thought his sanctuary was about to be violated . . . but it was just a co-worker lumbering past the forgotten room, shouting to a colleague as he went. Relieved, he snatched up his rucksack and marched towards the back door. He remained invisible to those dullards, but nevertheless it wouldn't do to linger. Legends weren't dreamed up, they were *made*.

And he had work to do.

Jan hung his apron on the hook and hurried away down the hallway towards the back of the building. It had been a gruelling shift and now he just wanted to be away.

The early rise was a killer and, once he reached the Starbucks, the grind was never-ending. They were short-staffed because of a stomach bug, so they'd all had to chip in, cutting short their breaks to help out at peak times. In this part of town, it was pretty much *always* peak time – thanks to the suits and nannies, the students and gym bunnies, who frequented it – so the pace was relentless. Still, this would have been fine, he was used to it, were it not for the knot of tension in his stomach, the nagging, debilitating sense of unease he'd had since he'd noticed *her*.

He'd hardly registered her at first – she was like so many gawky teenagers, staring at her shoes, swaying nervously from side to side, as she awaited her caffeine fix. But when he'd handed her the latte, something had happened. She'd seemed . . . *repelled* by him. So much so that she'd dropped the hot coffee and screamed the place down. She had had a fistful of his shirt, seemed intent on shouting at him or talking to him or something . . . but then Max had come to his rescue, ejecting her from the shop.

Though shaken, Jan had relaxed a little afterwards, assuming she would move on or turn her attention to someone else who crossed her path. A wandering nut job in search of trouble. But to his surprise she had remained outside, banging on the glass and staring directly at *him*. Eventually a patrol car had pulled up and she'd been forced to depart, haring off before the attending officers could talk to her. But the memory of her intense, horrified reaction lingered.

Which is why he wasn't taking any chances now. It was quite possible she was lurking outside, so instead of using the main doors he aimed for the fire exit instead. It was strictly forbidden to use it of course, but he was sure he wouldn't get caught and it would deposit him safe and sound in the back alley behind the store. Pausing by the emergency exit, he peered along the hallway behind him, then eased the door open, slipping out on to the iron stairwell.

The cold immediately bit him – a nice spring day had cooled quickly and it was now spitting with rain, so he didn't hesitate, quickly descending the stairs. Less than a minute later, he was by the bins in the stinking alley. Pulling his hoodie up, he hurried away. Already his anxiety was starting to dissipate, the knot in his stomach unravelling. He had made it away – now, finally, he could relax.

Only as he reached the far end of the alleyway, head down against the wind and rain, did a figure emerge from her hiding place at the other end of the cut-through. She was a slight young woman in tired, second-hand clothes. Silently, she watched as he disappeared around the corner, before setting off after him, quietly dogging his footsteps.

122

He didn't know whether to stay or turn and run.

Adam had entered Faith's studio determinedly, shutting the door firmly in Christine's face. She hadn't seen him leave, hadn't noticed his smart suit and anxious manner earlier, so had been alarmed by his sudden reappearance, as if dressed for a funeral. Unnerved, confused, she had interrogated him. But Adam had no desire to rehash the details of his morning's disgrace with her – she would learn soon enough that he would never practise psychology in Chicago again.

Fleeing to the studio, Adam had hoped to find some peace, a moment of calm to gather his thoughts. But as he looked around the large, lifeless room, he was suddenly assailed by an overpowering wave of grief. The studio was Faith's space, this room more than any other had her imprint on it, and being in here underlined just how much he had lost. Her spirit seemed to fill the room – her artwork on the wall, her painting smock hanging on the peg, even a half-drunk coffee, nestling in a cheesy tourist mug she had bought on their trip to Niagara Falls. For some reason that mug had always made her smile.

Choking with love, Adam suddenly wanted to turn and flee, but that would mean he'd have to face his mother-in-law's questioning once more, so he remained where he was. And, as each second passed, the pain, though still intense, lessened slightly. There *was* a great sense of loss in this room, but there was also an element of familiarity that was oddly comforting. Faith was gone, but she had lit up his life for many years and the evidence of this was all around him. In the friends and colleagues she'd painted, in her distinctive, deep-brushstroke style, in the squiggly signature that always adorned the bottom right-hand corner of her paintings.

Summoning his courage, he made his way across the room and sat down on her stool. He had seldom done so when she was alive – it was very much *her* stool, and he felt ill-equipped to sit on it, given his complete lack of artistic talent. He'd often thought during their time together that this was why they were so compatible – both of them sincerely respected the other's calling, but could not hope to understand or practise it. Love had always been fused with admiration.

This thought had often warmed him in the past, but it had the opposite effect today. Evidence of Faith's talent was right in front of him – an almost finished sketch of Kassie – but what evidence was there of his? He had not spotted the warning signs, had not provided the necessary support to his wife, even though he knew she was depressed and struggling. Perhaps the Board was right. Perhaps Christine was right. What kind of doctor, of professional, was he, if he couldn't even tend to his nearest and dearest?

'There is no hope.' The words sprang into his mind once more. Four wretched words, scrawled on a scrap of paper and left in the nursery beneath her feet. Faith had been in complete despair, unable to see a way forward, and he had not been there to comfort her. This certainty ripped him in two, but also troubled him, convincing him that she must have become delusional. Why was there no hope? They were grieving, suffering terribly, but they still had each other. Communication was fractured for sure, but they had still held each other silently in the half-light of morning, an intimate and tender moment that Adam clung to in his darkest hours.

Faith had shown moments of strength – when she had kicked him out of the house to go in search of Kassie. 'I'm not a fucking china doll.' And there had been odd moments of forward thinking, a will to repair the damage, when she'd asked him if he ever thought they'd be ready to try again.

Unforgivably, he had missed that opportunity to bolster her sense of optimism, but it was she who had ventured it, which was interesting. Faith had found their numerous failed rounds of IVF emotionally crippling, and had struggled to be around friends who had children, but her determination, her strength of character, had never wavered. Obviously, the stillbirth would have rocked her confidence, but none the less why should she despair? She had conceived once and could do so again. Surely all hope was not lost, unless she knew for certain that she wouldn't have a baby, which was hardly likely, given that the hospital staff had been at pains to point out that one stillbirth did not mean the next pregnancy would go the same way. So where had this desolation, this despair, suddenly come from?

Adam rose from the stool – there was no point sitting here, torturing himself – but, as he did so, his gaze fell on the sketch in front of him. Kassie stared back at him, her head and neck expertly rendered in pencil. Or rather she didn't – her eyes were in fact dropped towards the floor. It was a brilliant evocation of the troubled but beguiling teenager and yet something about it worried him, as he took it in properly for the first time. He had at first assumed Kassie was being bashful, the classic down-turned expression of a teenage girl uncomfortable at being the centre of attention. But now, as he stared at the picture, he was taken back to their early sessions, when Kassie had talked about her self-isolation, about how she deliberately avoided company and kept her gaze permanently lowered so as not to have to look anyone in the eye . . .

And now, as he continued to peer at her face, he began to see it differently. Her averted eyes appeared not innocent or bashful, but guilty and haunted, as if she couldn't bear to look at Faith, as if she *knew* something.

Adam sat heavily back down on the stool, suddenly overwhelmed by the thought. Was it possible that Kassie *had* foreseen Faith's fate? Had even *communicate*d it to her? It seemed a ridiculous, preposterous notion, and yet what other explanation could there be for Faith's sudden certainty that all was lost, that she would never be a mother?

Despite all the love he had given Faith, despite all their hopes and plans for the future, was this how it was always destined to end?

123

'Yeah, she was in here last week. Mrs Baines is a regular visitor . . . was a regular visitor . . .'

Jason Schiffer petered out. The manager of West Town's Phone Shack was not used to being questioned by a police officer, nor to his customers meeting untimely and unpleasant ends.

'When did she visit the store?' Gabrielle replied calmly.

Schiffer screwed up his eyes in concentration, raking his memory, then:

'Wednesday. It was definitely Wednesday. She was due a handset upgrade and came in to collect it.'

'And what about this woman?' she asked, proffering another photo. 'Her name's Rochelle Stevens. We think she may have visited the store here on February 19th . . .'

Schiffer appraised the photo, intrigued, then rounded the counter to access a computer terminal. As he typed, Gabrielle surveyed the store – it scored low on design, but high on gadgetry – every phone, tablet and device currently available was on display and had drawn a good crowd. The store was obviously popular.

'Here she is. Looks like she'd lost some photos off her phone, wanted to see if we could recover them.'

Gabrielle's mind was turning now.

'And what about Jacob Jones?'

She handed him the final photo. He studied it for a moment.

'Don't recognize the face. But that doesn't mean anything. I'm often out back.'

He typed again, Gabrielle watching him closely.

'No, nothing. No record of him having come here.'

Not what Gabrielle had been expecting. Or hoping.

'Could you ask some of your staff? I know they're busy, but it's —'

'No problem. No problem at all.'

He scurried off with the photo, clearly enthusiastic about the idea of helping police, but also keen to get to the bottom of the matter. If his store *was* somehow involved in these murders, he needed to know. Gabrielle watched him interrupt his servers, pulling them aside to ask them discreetly about Jacob Jones. The young blonde shook her head, so he moved on to another server nearby. But he too shook his head, after careful consideration.

Gabrielle turned away, unable to watch. Suarez stood nearby, looking as tense as her. He was about to say something – make some ill-advised joke to break the tension no doubt – when Gabrielle's phone started buzzing.

It was Hoskins. This was not the first time he'd tried to call her since their tête-à-tête. Nor would it be his last. She could imagine him getting more and more irate with each failed attempt to reach her – but she had a sense of what he wanted to say to her. And she didn't have time for it right now.

'Got someone here who might be able to help you . . .'

Snapping out of it, Gabrielle turned to see a young woman being shepherded towards her.

'Tell Detective Grey what you just told me, Jodi,' he encouraged.

The woman – who was no more than nineteen – cleared her throat, then said:

'I remember him. He . . . he came to the store because he had a cracked screen, on his iPhone, you know . . .'

Gabrielle Grey nodded, hanging on to the young woman's words.

'So we fixed it, then he came to the register and I rang it through.'

'It was a drop-in, "while you wait" job,' Schiffer added, 'and he paid in cash, so his name wouldn't show up on our records.'

'When was this?' Gabrielle asked.

'About six weeks ago. He wasn't here very long,' the young woman confirmed.

'But you're sure it's him?'

'Yes,' she replied firmly. 'I recognized his face on the news, I told my mom all about it. She was as upset as I was.'

The young woman was becoming distressed, so Gabrielle quickly concluded their conversation. She thought for a while, then turned to Schiffer.

'Would you have a record of who served these three customers?'

To her immense disappointment, Schiffer shook his head.

'We can tell who rang through the transaction, but not who served them. We operate a hot-desk system here, so . . .'

'Ok, we'll need details of everyone who works here. Management, servers, tech guys, anybody who might have come into contact with these three customers.'

Jason Schiffer looked a little taken aback by the scale of the request and, Gabrielle sensed, the implications of it. But it was clear from her tone that she was not going to leave until she'd got what she needed, so he hurried off to the back room to complete the task. She watched him go with a growing sense of excitement. The adrenaline was beginning to flow – perhaps they had finally turned a corner in this troubling case. She was convinced that someone working at the Phone Shack had synced his phone to those of the victims, allowing him full access to their movements, their lives. This guy was good – a twenty-first-century stalker.

But his time was running out.

124

It had to be today. It had to be now.

Jan Varga lived in a dilapidated two-bedroom apartment with his girlfriend, Marsha. This had immediately presented him with two problems – first, that there was no garage door to hack for silent, risk-free access, and second, that his girlfriend didn't have a job. Getting unfettered access to Jan was therefore problematic. Faced with these obstacles, he had at first considered giving up and moving on to someone else, but his pride had stopped him. He refused to be beaten and, besides, the way Jan had treated him demanded *payback*.

The guy's accent was horrible, his English even worse, and he was a barista, for God's sake, but that didn't stop him looking down his nose at the overweight, middle-aged man helping him with his phone upgrade. It was a look he'd seen before – from Jones, Stevens, Baines and others before them – a look which suggested that he was not even human, but rather an automaton helping them service their needs. People often made that mistake – assuming that he was a nobody, nothing more than a backdrop to their important lives. The Stevens girl had been particularly bad – not looking at him once during the entire transaction.

These people – these successful, handsome, *arrogant* people – had been made to suffer. He had enjoyed their terror, their helplessness, their agony. Jan would suffer too. He might even add a little *extra* pain this time – he'd never liked foreigners. Marsha was in hospital overnight, thank God. From

Jan's texts, it sounded like a routine procedure, but it would keep her away until tomorrow afternoon, making this the perfect opportunity to strike.

Access was still going to be problematic, but he'd recce'd the building twice and actually things had gone like clockwork. He got to the second floor of the fire escape without being seen then, donning his mask, used his crowbar to lever up the back window, whose lock was worse than useless and pinged happily from its moorings.

Climbing inside, he had briefly been unnerved by a dog barking outside, but, pulling the window down quickly and dropping the blind, he hurried away into the interior of the flat. There he stowed himself, in the closet of the guest bedroom, to bide his time.

He felt confident Jan would be here on his own tonight. Which is the way he wanted it. Each attack became more hazardous, more complicated, but the stars were in alignment tonight.

It was time to kill again.

125

Jan was thirty feet ahead of her, head down as he walked the busy streets, intent on getting home. Occasionally he would cast a quick look over his shoulder, but Kassie kept low, ensuring there was a sufficient knot of shoppers in front of her to mask her pursuit. On the odd occasion when the crowds dispersed and she suddenly became more visible, she kept a beady eye open for doorways that she could dive into if necessary. She wondered if the police officers following *her* were doing the same thing? Probably, though there was little point – their tailing of her was as clumsy as it was obvious.

Jan turned the corner, arrowing right down West Huron Street. Kassie kept her pace steady, telling herself not to run, casually sauntering around the corner in pursuit of him. This street was also packed, but to Kassie's alarm Jan was nowhere to be seen. She scanned the sidewalk in front of her, but she could see no sign of his distinctive green hoodie. Where had he gone?

Searching the streetscape frantically, she suddenly spotted him. He had crossed to the other side of the street and was making good progress down the block. Hopping off the sidewalk, Kassie hurried across the road towards him.

A horn screamed, as a car came to an abrupt halt beside her. But she didn't linger, nervously shooting a glance at Jan, fearing the horn may have attracted his attention. Thankfully he appeared not to have noticed, so Kassie kept on going, ignoring the volley of abuse from the startled driver.

She was now in serious danger of losing him. He was fifty, maybe even sixty yards ahead and there was a host of bodies between them. He kept dropping in and out of sight, so Kassie increased her pace, drawing the ire of shoppers as she barged past them. As she did so, she became aware of something else. The car horn – or a car horn, at least – was still blaring. Putting it out of her mind, she carried on – but the sound seemed to be getting louder. Kassie's eyes were set dead ahead, but now she became aware that a car was keeping pace with her.

'Kassie!'

She was astonished to hear her name. She was even more surprised to see that it was Adam Brandt driving the car.

'I can't talk now, Adam.'

'Get in the car, Kassie.'

'I'm sorry, I can't.'

She could still glimpse Jan up ahead, but he was nearly at the next intersection. It was vital that she didn't lose sight of him.

'I need to talk to you, Kassie. And it has to be now.'

Still the car kept pace with her. Adam had one eye on the street and one eye fixed on her. He looked wired, even a little unstable.

'How did you even find me?' she replied, keeping her pace steady.

'Found your laptop. Used "Find my iPhone",' he replied, utterly unrepentant about rifling through her possessions.

'Well, I'm sorry, but I can't help you,' she mumbled, then broke into a run, dodging shoppers in her desperation to keep up with Jan.

Adam now sped up, roaring away from the kerb and for a brief, wonderful moment, Kassie thought she had got rid of him. But to her horror his Lexus now pulled over twenty yards ahead of her. Ignoring the fact that his car was in a tow zone, Adam leaped out and hurried towards her. Kassie tried to dodge him, but he reacted quickly, blocking her way.

'Please, Adam,' she begged, suddenly tearful. 'I can't stop –'

'I don't care.'

'It's a matter of life and death.'

'You'll stay and you'll talk to me.'

His tone was so fierce, his gaze so intense, that Kassie suddenly felt a little scared. She tried to brush past him, but he gripped her right shoulder, pushing her hard against the wall. Passing shoppers looked intrigued, even a little concerned, but they gave the pair a wide berth, leaving Kassie trapped.

'What did you say to Faith?'

'What do you mean?'

'During your conversations together, what did you talk about?'

'Please, Adam,' Kassie whimpered. 'Why is this relevant?'

'Tell me.'

Kassie slumped against the wall, angry and upset.

'We talked . . . about Annabelle. About what happened at the hospital. About everything that has happened since . . .'

'What else?' Adam barked.

'I don't know . . . we talked about the murders. About you. About my mom . . .'

'Did Faith talk about herself?'

'Of course.'

'What did you say to her?'

'I tried to comfort her.'

'Did you talk to her the night before she died?'

Kassie hesitated. Now she knew exactly why Adam was

asking these questions. This was a conversation she hoped she'd never have to have.

'Yes, I did,' she replied, quietly. 'We couldn't sleep, so she asked if she could sketch me.'

'And?'

'She drew, we talked.'

'What about?'

'About babies, families, how she was dreading Annabelle's funeral –'

'Did you talk about the future?'

'Yeah, I guess –'

'*Her* future?'

'Yes . . .'

Her words were barely audible. She knew where this was leading and she wanted it to stop.

'What did she ask you?'

Kassie dropped her eyes to the floor.

'What did she ask you?' he demanded, louder.

'She asked me . . . if she was going to have kids one day, a baby . . .'

'And what did you tell her?'

'Please don't do this, Adam.'

'What did you tell her?' Adam repeated grimly, tightening his grip on her jacket.

'I didn't want to answer her, but she kept on and on at me. She told me she *had* to know.'

'And?'

'And . . . I told her she wouldn't.'

'Fuck!'

The word erupted from him, flecks of spittle landing on Kassie's face. He released his grip and turned away in anguish, clawing at the air in his exasperation and fury. A woman passing close by paused, as if debating whether to intervene, but her husband hurried her on, casting wary looks at them. As he did so, Adam rounded on Kassie once more.

'Why? Why would you say something like that?'

'I didn't want to, but she begged me.'

'But how could you know that? How could you possibly *know*?'

Adam's eyes were boring into hers, challenging her to respond.

'You know how I know,' Kassie responded, bleakly.

Adam stared at her, as if his worst fears had been confirmed.

'Did Faith understand what you meant?'

'Not at first. But she could see I was getting upset, which unnerved her. She wanted to know *why* I was so sure, so certain.'

'Did she . . . did she ask you directly if you knew when *she* would die?'

A sob seemed to escape Kassie, then:

'Yes.'

'And?'

'And I refused to answer her . . . but it was too late by then. She saw it on my face.'

'Saw what?'

'She realized *why* I never looked her in the eye, why I avoided talking about the future, why I didn't want to answer her questions.'

'What happened?' Adam demanded angrily.

'I tried to leave the studio, told her I didn't want to talk any more, but she grabbed me, told me she *had* to know if her death was imminent.'

'And?' Adam asked, desperately.

'And . . .' Kassie could barely say the words, but she knew she had to. '. . . I told her the truth . . . that her time was nearly up.'

Adam slammed his hand against the wall behind her head, making Kassie jump. She backed away, but he was no longer looking at her. She could see his mind was elsewhere, turning frantically, as certain pieces of the puzzle finally slotted into place.

'We argued,' he breathed, angrily. 'That last morning we argued. She was upset, hostile, because of what *you'd* just told her . . .'

Kassie could barely look at him.

'Jesus Christ, is that . . . is that why you were so keen that I should go home? When we were out playing detectives at Lake Calumet, you were trying to get me to go home. Because you *knew* what she was going to do.'

'It wasn't going to happen until the next day. I thought that we . . . you would be back in time, that maybe you could do something to help her. I didn't know we would get arrested, questioned. If they had let you out even an hour earlier . . .'

Adam let out a sound, a nasty inhuman sound that was half scream, half roar.

'I should have turned you away,' Kassie continued quickly, 'made you go home. I had the opportunity to do so and I didn't. Because I'm selfish. Because I wanted to save Madelaine, save myself . . .'

'You looked her in the eye,' Adam insisted, seeming not to hear her. 'You looked a vulnerable, grieving woman in the eye and you told her . . .'

For a moment, he seemed as though he wouldn't have the strength to finish the sentence, but then:

'. . . that she was going to die.'

'I didn't know what else to do,' Kassie pleaded. 'She would have known if I'd lied to her.'

'*You* made her do it. By telling her that, *you* made her kill herself –'

'No, Adam, that's not how it works.'

'You pushed her over the edge.'

'No, no. I don't have any power, any influence over events. Things happen for a reason –'

Adam raised his hand and for a moment Kassie thought he was going to strike her. But instead he jabbed a finger at her.

'Don't you say that. Don't you dare say that . . .'

But even as he gestured at her, the violence was ebbing from him. He looked washed out, hollow.

'Why could you not . . .' His voice was reedy and broken now. 'Why could you not just have *lied*?'

Kassie hesitated, before responding. She didn't want to say it, but she had to.

'Because . . . the result would have been the same.'

A handful of simple words, which had a devastating effect. Adam's gaze was still fixed to hers, but his expression was changing fast, as if a terrible realization was taking hold.

'Please believe me, Adam, I never wanted for any of this to happen.'

But he was backing away from her now, looking horrified and bewildered. He crashed against passers-by as he stumbled back to his car and instinctively Kassie wanted to reach out and help him. But there was no chance of that. She had lost him.

Just as she had now lost Jan.

126

'Look again. We must have missed something.'

Gabrielle's voice was harsh, insistent.

'I've run it three times,' Albright protested. 'Nobody at the Phone Shack has a criminal record.'

She and Suarez had returned to CPD headquarters, clutching armfuls of personnel files. Immediately the team had set about investigating the male members of staff. They prioritized those who matched the description given by Kassie Wojcek after the Calumet inferno, but that placed over a dozen people in the frame, including Jason Schiffer himself. The cavernous Phone Shack seemed to be a haven for middle-aged white men with bad facial hair who couldn't find jobs elsewhere. When they had drawn a blank running criminal-record checks on those names, they ran them for the rest of the male members of staff, but had no more success. In desperation, they had run the female names, but the result was the same.

'What about freelancers or short-contract guys?' Gabrielle replied, more in hope than expectation.

'They don't do that,' Suarez piped up. 'They contract staff up, do everything in house. It's cheaper that way, more reliable.'

'So, do we think we're wrong, then? That we've got this all sideways?'

'Well, on paper it looks a good fit,' Suarez answered. 'Someone who's tech savvy stalking these people, targeting them . . . but if we're not getting any hits . . .'

'Let's stay with it,' Gabrielle said defiantly. 'Odds on, this guy was a stalker or a housebreaker first. He's too good to be an amateur. So he's probably got form for that and possibly violence or indecent exposure. He's gonna have a rap sheet, we just need to find it.'

'What do you suggest?' Montgomery asked.

'Well, he obviously gained employment at the Phone Shack under a false name. So, we're going to have to do detailed background and ID checks on every Caucasian male who works there, checking for aliases, known –'

'Talk about a needle in a haystack. That'll take days,' Albright moaned.

'So, let's stop talking and get on with it, shall we?'

Shrugging, Albright hurried off to do her bidding, gathering the team around him. Despite her frustration, Gabrielle felt a small spike of satisfaction as her officers snapped into action. Her back was against the wall and she was running out of time.

But she wasn't beaten yet.

127

Leaning against the door, Jan breathed a long sigh of relief. His journey home had been uneventful, which was a blessing after his distressing day. Pulling off his hoodie, he shook it out, then hung it up on the peg next to the front door. He would get into trouble with Marsha, for not leaving it outside, but what the hell . . .

Crossing the hall into the kitchen, he pulled a beer from the fridge and cracked it open. Taking a deep swig, he let the cool lager wash over his tongue, before swallowing it down. Instantly, he felt refreshed and revitalized. He loved this beer, which he bought at the Slovakian shop around the corner for a dollar fifty. Tipping up the bottle, he emptied it in one go, before casually tossing it in the trash.

He was very tempted to have another. Laying a hand on the fridge door, he was about to pull it open, when suddenly he paused. A small movement on the periphery of his vision had caught his attention. The blind over the kitchen window, which was fully lowered, was flapping slightly.

Puzzled, Jan crossed the room. Raising the blind, he noticed that the window was fractionally open, a tiny gap visible just above the sill. Immediately he felt his body tense up. Marsha had been the last one out and there was no way she would have left it open. She was paranoid about security, about living in a big American city, always checking and rechecking windows and doors before going out. And he knew he had not opened the window this morning, so . . .

He examined the lock. This had always been flimsy — another source of concern for Marsha, who'd urged him to buy a new one — but now it came off in his hand altogether. Seriously alarmed, he opened the window to examine the sill and found a telltale scuff mark where some of the wood had splintered. Someone had used a crowbar or a chisel to gain access. Someone had been in the flat.

Crossing to the kitchen unit, he pulled open the bottom drawer. He kept all his tools in here and now removed a hammer, before sliding it shut once more.

His heart was beating fast, but slowly, cautiously, he crept from the kitchen, before darting his head into the living room. The sight of the TV and DVD player relaxed him, as did the pristine state of the furniture. Had someone gained access and then been scared off? Leaving the small room, he edged along the hallway towards the back of the flat. Their home was tiny and he felt sure he would know if there was someone in here with him, but still he had to check.

Teasing the bedroom door open with his foot, he looked inside. Everything seemed in order, so he entered carefully. The room was quiet and seemed deserted, but he checked behind the door, in the closet, even under the bed. Relieved, he crossed the landing to the guest bedroom. Already he felt better about things, there was nothing of value in here.

This too seemed unmolested — there was nobody under the bed, behind the door — so lowering his hammer and breathing a long sigh of relief, he opened the closet door.

To find a man in a ski mask looking directly at him.

128

Her lungs were burning, but still she kept running. Her progress was clumsy but swift, shocked shoppers leaped out of her way, as she hollered at them to move. The crowds were parting for her, save for a couple of bystanders who looked angry and affronted, but even they stood aside when they saw the wild teenager tearing towards them. Was it her flailing, auburn hair, her crimson, sweaty face or the desperation in her voice that made them retreat? It didn't matter, just as long as they got out of her way.

She had been deeply shaken by her encounter with Adam and had remained rooted to the spot for several minutes afterwards, leaning against the wall for support. But in spite of her crushing guilt and her very real concern for Adam, her thoughts had slowly returned to Jan. To an innocent man who was living on borrowed time.

She had little to go on, but tugging her phone from her pocket, she had typed his name into Searchbug. To her relief, she discovered that there was a 'Jan Varga' living in a block in the Ukrainian Village, not ten minutes from where she was. Peeling herself off the wall, she looked intently to her right, at the female jogger who had spent an awfully long time examining the front window of an electrical-appliance store, then turned and walked away in the opposite direction. And, with each step, her pace increased, as the urgency of the situation sank in, until eventually she was sprinting.

This time she felt sure she would be in time. Jan had

probably only just got home, so even if he was being attacked, the assault was in its early stages. If she could get there quickly, gain access somehow, there was still a chance she could save him. The thought gave her a boost of adrenaline and even brought a smile to her face. Was this the moment when she broke the curse? When she proved that if you can foresee the future, then you can change it? Was it still possible that she might be saved?

She raised her speed another notch. Though she had never been an athlete at school, she was lithe and swift. Her feet slapped the concrete, her balance constantly shifting as she weaved in and out of the office workers who were beginning to emerge now. She was in the zone, her running rhythmic and intense, never allowing herself to let up, even though every part of her ached. And ten minutes later, she found herself outside Jan's shabby apartment block.

Hurrying to the main door, she yanked at it, but it refused to budge. Turning to the intercom, she ran her finger down the list, until she found Jan's name, next to a buzzer for the third-floor. She was about to press it, when suddenly she paused. If the killer was already inside, was there any virtue in alerting him to her arrival? Instead, withdrawing her finger, she hammered on the main door, pressing her face to the glass panels to peer inside. A gloomy hallway stared back at her, devoid of light, movement or any human presence.

Cursing, she stepped back and scanned the apartment windows, hoping against hope that someone might be standing there, but there was nobody. Immediately she started moving towards the side of the building. Was there an alleyway she could access? A fire escape perhaps? But as she moved off she heard the front doors swing open.

'What's all the banging about? Where's the fire?'

An elderly man in worn coveralls had pushed open the doors. A chipped ID badge on his chest identified him as the janitor, though he could hardly be mistaken for anything else.

Kassie didn't bother explaining, pushing past the startled man and haring inside. Tearing down the dimly lit hallway, she swung round the bannister at the end and raced up the stairs. She took them two at a time, bouncing lightly off the wooden boards as she went up, up, up. In under a minute she was outside Jan's apartment, breathless but exhilarated. She could hear the old janitor wheezing up the stairs below her, but she didn't have time to wait. The door in front of her was cheap and old, the lock rusty. Taking a few steps back as a run-up, Kassie charged at the door, launching her boot at the lock.

She cannoned off it, but the wood split slightly around the lock. So she went at it again. And again. And on her third assault, her heavy boot went right through the door. She was marooned temporarily, almost falling over as she lost her balance, but then roughly tugging her foot back out, she reached an arm through the hole and, finding the latch, turned it quickly.

The door swung open and, as it did so, she saw a flash of movement. A large black shape passed in front of her eyes, darting away to her right. Hurrying inside, her eye was drawn not to this fleeing figure, but instead to the living room. Jan, who was tired to a chair, was staring straight back. He looked confused, stupefied even, and as Kassie took in this appalling vision, she realized why. In addition to the cuts and bruises on his body, there was now a large slit across his throat. It opened and closed hideously, as he moved his head, silently appealing for help.

She had a split second to decide and surprised herself by

tearing after his attacker. She had no weapon, had come ill-prepared for a fight, but there was no way she was letting him get away this time. She reached the kitchen seconds after him, but he was already halfway out the window on to the fire escape. Desperately, Kassie threw herself across the room, managing to grab hold of his left leg, before he made it fully out. She tugged with all her might and to her surprise a large patch of cloth came off in her hand, as the trouser tore down the seam. Suddenly she was unbalanced, but so too was he, stumbling slightly back into the room before hauling himself back out again. Once more Kassie lunged and this time her fingers found flesh, as she grasped his trailing leg. Instinctively she dug her fingers in. Outside, she heard a low grunt of pain, prompting her to increase the pressure. She had him now.

His leg was flailing wildly, as he tried desperately to escape her clutches, but she could sense victory. She could hear shouting outside, the cops would surely be here any second now, then all this would be over. All she had to do was hang on. She raised her head to take in her attacker, to see if he was weakening, but she was a second too late to react to the crowbar that was swinging towards her. She barely had time to jerk her head back, before it struck her a glancing blow to the temple. Suddenly she was flying backwards across the room and a second later her head hit the floor.

Then everything went black.

129

He would keep drinking until he could no longer feel.

Adam knew it was weak of him, that it would end badly, but he didn't care. Oblivion was calling to him and he was happy to accept the invitation.

He had no idea where he was, but that suited him fine. He had roared away from his confrontation with Kassie, his car slewing dangerously back into the traffic, but he was too wired to drive and had abandoned his vehicle a few blocks further on. Stumbling out on to the sidewalk, he had chanced upon a bar. The place was filling up with office workers, who gave him a wide berth, keen to enjoy their Happy Hour drinks in peace. Barging his way to the bar, Adam had ordered a whiskey, then another, keeping his eyes away from the mirror behind the bartenders. He had no desire to see his haunted face.

Another couple of shots followed and eventually he quit pretending, paying for the rest of the bottle upfront. It sat next to him, his only company, as both stools beside him remained resolutely empty. Ignoring the discomfort his presence was obviously causing, he set to work on the bottle, but so far it was having little effect.

Kassie's words continued to spin round his brain, pulling him back to Faith's studio. To that night. Mindless fool that he was, he had been slumbering nearby, but the two women had been awake, staring at each other, as Faith sketched her subject. He could see her hand faltering, could see her chin resting on her chest, could see the tears running off her nose.

Annabelle, she was talking about Annabelle, and her whole body was shaking. Kassie had risen now, was trying to comfort her, placing an arm around her shoulder. But Faith would not be comforted. She wanted to know. And she believed Kassie could tell her.

'Will I ever have a child?'

Faith's voice was shaking, as she wiped her tears away. Her face looked ravaged, suddenly older, as it gazed up at Kassie imploringly. As if she somehow was the seat of all knowledge.

'Will I be a mother?'

Kassie continued to comfort her, but said nothing in response.

'Please, Kassie, I have to know . . .'

And now Kassie was speaking. But it wasn't the teenage girl mouthing the words. Horrifically, it was Annabelle, her dimpled, innocent face perched on top of that gawky torso, who was speaking.

'No, Faith, you will never be a mother . . .'

Roaring, Adam lashed out at this horrific image – sending his whiskey bottle crashing to the floor. Snapping out of his daydream, he realized that pretty much the whole bar was now staring at him. Unrepentant, he threw a fifty-dollar bill over the counter and stumbled to the exit. Fuck them, he thought, his only regret was that so much good whiskey had been wasted.

Barging out on to the street, he tried to shake off the nausea that his hideous daydream had provoked, but it was useless. He was sick to his soul. Because of her. She was selfish and sanctimonious, a spreader of contagion and he now bitterly regretted having let her into their lives. When Faith had invited her to stay, he should have trusted his instinct and asked her to leave. Why had he not listened to the little

411

voice in his head? He had followed its promptings many times before now and been proved right.

This was his fault too, of course. He should have stayed home with Faith that day, he could tell she was in a strange mood. Why hadn't he reached out to her? Why hadn't he insisted that she tell him what was troubling her? He was tortured by the thought of her alone in that big house, while he was running around with the author of their misfortune. His beloved Faith had been alone for her last day on earth, wrapped in silence, consumed by despair. The thought of this ripped his heart out and he knew instinctively that he would never forgive himself, that he would hate himself for ever.

But not as much as he hated *her*.

130

She cut a strange figure in the empty room. Dressed in a paper suit, her hair piled up on top of her head, Kassie sat at the pockmarked table, tearing pieces off a polystyrene cup. She was alone and her constant rip, rip, rip was the only sound disturbing the silence.

She felt like crying – she wanted to cry, for herself, for Adam – but she couldn't somehow. She felt utterly drained by the experience of the last few hours. She had come around in the back of an ambulance, groggy and confused. Once she'd got a handle on her bearings, once she'd recovered her breath, she was suddenly full of questions. What had happened to Jan? Had his attacker been apprehended?

The paramedics of course could tell her nothing – they were far more concerned with whether she had concussion. It was only later, once she'd been passed as fit for questioning, that she began to glean what had happened. She wasn't questioned straight away – her fingernails were swabbed, her clothes taken away for forensic analysis – but during this grim, intrusive process, Kassie had worked out that the news was bad. The faces of the investigating officers said it all.

After that had come the interview, Kassie face to face with Gabrielle Grey, in what was increasingly taking on the feel of a recurring nightmare. Grey confirmed that Jan had not survived and that his attacker had escaped, but had offered little more than that, taking Kassie's statement, then promptly disappearing, summoned away by an urgent phone call. Suarez, a fellow detective, was hot on her heels, leaving Kassie quite alone.

Unsure of what to do, Kassie had risen to leave, but the sight of a uniformed guard standing outside the interview room made her pause. Was she under arrest? She didn't think so, but it was hard to tell. Gabrielle Grey had seemed less hostile, more willing to accept Kassie's explanation for her actions this time, but if she wasn't under arrest, then why hadn't she said she could go? What more did they want from her?

The cup was now destroyed, lying in two dozen pieces on the table in front of her. The sight of it filled her with a sudden sense of her powerlessness. She longed to get out of here, but what could she do? An attorney was on the way but had not yet put in an appearance. So, who else could she call for help? Her mother wouldn't take her call, so the only other person she could phone was Adam . . . but contacting him was the last thing she wanted to do.

Now finally the tears came, Kassie suddenly overwhelmed by the awfulness of her predicament. Her time was nearly up, yet here she was stuck in a festering interview room, while the killer was still at liberty. Was it really possible that this had all been for nothing? That she would die a sudden, pointless death while he continued to stalk the city? The thought made Kassie sick to the stomach and she crumpled on to the dirty table, sobbing her heart out. She had tried her best, risked everything, but she had failed.

She would die knowing that it was not a question of if he would strike again, but when.

131

'Listen up, people . . .'

The whole team turned to face Gabrielle. Having been ordered to attend an urgent briefing, they were curious to find out what was going on.

'The lab has just sent over their results. They ran the skin samples . . . and we've got a name.'

A buzz of excitement rippled around the room. Everyone had been hoping that the skin cells extracted from underneath Kassie Wojcek's fingernails would provide a concrete lead, but you could never rely on these things. If the sample was contaminated, or if the offender was not on the system, then you were likely to draw a blank.

'Take a look at this.'

She handed a sheaf of papers to the nearest detective, gesturing to her to pass the pile on once she'd taken one herself. The single sheets had a photocopied mugshot of a round-faced, white male and underneath it the offender's rap sheet.

'Jan Varga's attacker is a Joseph White, more commonly known as Joe. He's originally from Cicero. His family still live there and Detective Suarez is with them now, but obviously our man is currently in central Chicago.'

The team were already taking in White's 'credentials'.

'He has multiple convictions for trespass and public order offences. He's a Peeping Tom. He also likes to expose himself, to intimidate people, and has been involved in a couple of fights – presumably when his victims took against him. Interestingly, he has been arrested three times on suspicion of burglary, but never charged. Given the MO of our killer, given the fact that his physical description matches the description given to us by Wojcek, I'd say this is our guy.'

A couple of officers whooped a heartfelt 'yeah' and there was a smattering of applause. Gabrielle held up a hand to calm them.

'I've circulated his photo to all the major media outlets. We are naming him as our prime suspect and asking members of the public to be vigilant. I've asked for extra operators to man the hotlines – and I'm pleased to say Superintendent Hoskins has agreed to the request – so your job is to get out on the streets. Talk to community leaders, uniformed officers on the beat, shop owners, bartenders – this guy has to eat and drink, has to buy gasoline, has to take the "L". He was in work today, but left early afternoon, presumably so he could execute his attack on Jan. He probably won't return to work once his name is in the press, but I'm going to send a pair of you there anyway.'

Gabrielle's phone started to buzz, but she ignored it.

'Top priority now is to bring this guy in safely. He has little violent crime on his record, but is clearly highly dangerous and will be armed, so if you spot him, call for backup immediately. I know this is a big case, but I don't want anyone playing the hero.'

Still her phone buzzed and looking down Gabrielle saw that it was Suarez. Immediately she broke off, snatching it up and answering the call.

'What's up?'

'I'm at the family home now,' Suarez replied down the phone, his voice hushed. 'I think I may have an address for you.'

'Go on,' Gabrielle replied, turning away from the team.

416

'It's in the Lower West Side, 353 West Cullerton Street. It's a shared house, I think, mixed tenants. I'm texting you the details now.'

'Why there?'

'His sister says he left it as a forwarding address. Welfare cheques for him occasionally get sent to the family home, though if you ask me the sister hasn't been too diligent about passing them on –'

'When did he give this address to her?' Gabrielle interrupted.

'Six months ago, he moves around a lot.'

'That's good enough for me. Stay with them, get as much as you can.'

Ending the call, she turned back to the team with a broad grin on her face.

'Right, boys and girls, saddle up . . .'

The team rose, grabbing their jackets.

'. . . we've got a killer to catch.'

132

Scowling, he stared at the flickering screen. There was no TV in the communal room downstairs – a tenant disappeared with the last one – so Joseph White had bought a portable, second-hand one, hiding it at the back of his closet in his bedroom. He'd often enjoyed watching *Late Night Live* after a long shift at the Phone Shack, guzzling down a four-pack of Millers and a bag of Doritos, but what he saw now did not please him at all.

His own face stared back at him – his mugshot paraded on the evening news bulletins, as the excited newsreader gave out his name, details of his previous arrests, his family history. Briefly photos of his victims – Jones, Stevens, Baines, Varga – filled the screen, before once more being replaced with his own chubby, goateed face. The fact that he had shaved his beard off, that he had been living and working under false names for months, gave him little satisfaction now. The more people – colleagues, fellow tenants – came to look at the photo, the more they would notice the features that he couldn't change – his piercing green eyes, the distinctive mole on his right cheek, and the thin scar on his neck, the legacy of a childhood accident. They would realize, they would *know,* and then they would contact the authorities. The generous reward being offered by the CPD for information leading to his arrest would ensure that.

Cursing, he switched off the TV and yanked open his closet. Pulling out a battered khaki duffelbag, he started stuffing clothes into it haphazardly. Satisfied, he threw a couple of cereal bars inside, a half-drunk bottle of vodka, a map of the city and, having removed it from his rucksack, the cleaver. He had destroyed everything else he'd taken to Jan's flat and he was tempted to ditch the weapon too, given the potential DNA residue. But he didn't fancy marching into a store and buying a new one, facing unwanted questions, so he'd wiped it clean and kept it. He had a feeling he would be needing it again soon.

Crossing the room, he teased up a loose floorboard. In the cavity below was a roll of ten-dollar bills. It wasn't much – a few hundred bucks that he had squirrelled away for an emergency – but it would do for the time being. Shoving it roughly into his jacket pocket, he left the room and hurried down the stairs and out the front door, leaving his temporary home for the last time without farewells or fanfare.

As soon as he stepped out into the clean, crisp air, he heard them. Sirens, distant but getting louder. Probably some traffic fatality, he thought to himself, but he didn't dawdle, hurrying from the house and away down the street. Remembering his Cubs cap, he removed it from his jacket pocket and slid it on to his head, pulling the peak down. Right now, he wanted to be as inconspicuous as possible.

The sirens were getting louder. White picked up his pace – he couldn't break into a run, but he wanted to put as much distance between himself and the house as he could. He was right to be concerned because, as he reached the intersection, four police cars, lights flashing and sirens wailing, skidded around the corner, racing past him and away down the street. The sight made him stumble to a halt, instinctively following their progress. Thirty seconds later, they pulled up outside his house. Immediately a posse of officers jumped out, removing their guns from their holsters, and hurried towards it.

Joseph White didn't linger to watch the show. A couple of the other tenants were at home and might have seen him leave. It was time to be elsewhere – and fast. Breaking into a trot he hurried away down South Ashland Avenue. His heart was thumping – the sweat crawling down his back, as his eyes examined the street for signs of danger. He knew he'd just had a very lucky escape.

133

He stumbled into the room, colliding with the door frame. Off balance, he lurched to the left – for a moment he thought he might fall – then suddenly he righted himself, taking in the scene in front of him. The whiskey was clouding his vision, everything seemed fluid and shifting, so that even the small, neat room seemed unfamiliar. Stupid really – he had been in their guest room hundreds of times, making the bed for Christine on one of her visits, but today it seemed strange and elusive, as if it were deliberately trying to frustrate him.

Marching forward, he threw the trash bag on to the bed. Kassie had slept in here while she was living with them and her meagre possessions – some old clothes, a battered laptop, a Linkin Park cap – still lay on the floor. Taking in the assorted items, Adam felt a rush of rage, this evidence of her presence in their lovely home underscoring her ruinous impact on their lives. When he'd first met Kassie, he was happy, confident, hopeful. Now he had lost his career, his reputation and, worse, much worse, than that, Faith and Annabelle. How was it possible that he had fallen so fast, so quickly?

Grabbing the cap, he stuffed it into the trash bag. A pair of pants, the laptop and a torn magazine soon followed, Adam ramming them into the plastic sack with venom. He wanted Kassie out of his house, he wanted to obliterate all evidence of her existence, to pretend for a second that this terrible catastrophe hadn't happened.

A pair of shoes. A school textbook. A worn, black hoodie.

In they went, tumbled together in his haste to be rid of them. But, as he tossed the hoodie into the sack, something fell to ground, tinkling gently as it hit the polished wooden boards. Angry, frustrated, Adam bent down to scoop up the offending item, but, as he did so, he paused.

It took him a while to bring it into focus, but . . . it was a key. Kassie's house key, attached to a faded Betty Boo figurine. It caught the light, glinting up at him, urging him to pick it up. He stared at it, transfixed, taking in its golden sheen. For one absurd moment, he wondered if the key had fallen from her pocket for a reason, if he was *meant* to find it. He reached out a hand, even now hesitating to pick it up, wondering what would happen if he did so. But the pull was too great, the key seemed to be calling to him, so, snatching it up, he hurried from the room, leaving the trash bag where he'd dropped it.

134

Kassie stood outside CPD headquarters, a lone figure on the busy street. In the past, she had had the odd friend to run with, plus her mother, and latterly Adam and Faith. But they were gone now and she couldn't even rely on the shadowy presence of the undercover cops for company. She was not a suspect any more, nor even a person of interest. She was a witness, who had grappled with the *real* killer, accidentally harvesting crucial DNA which exonerated both herself and Redmond, but that was all. She had played a valuable role in the investigation, but was no longer useful.

Turning away from the police station, Kassie hurried off down the street. She had never looked cool or smart, but she knew that tonight she looked particularly ridiculous. Her own clothes were still being analysed, so on her release she'd been provided with garments donated by a local charity. The CPD's headquarters was not really set up for juveniles – their Detention Center being across town – so she had had to wear the smallest adult clothes available. They still swamped her and she felt like a kid at a dressing-up party, as she stumbled clumsily down the busy street.

She was gripped by embarrassment and misery. She knew that she had made an important contribution. The police now had a suspect – Joseph White – a name they wouldn't have had without her intervention. Yet oddly Kassie felt no joy, no relief at this development. She just felt empty and rudderless, as if she had been allowed to play her part in this story, without ever getting to see the end.

Instinctively she turned her feet in the direction of home. What else could she do? But it meant nothing. The house was cold and empty and, unless her mother returned, the utilities would soon be cut off. Was that Natalia's plan? To force Kassie to follow her north? Whatever, it was all academic now.

'Hey, watch it . . .'

Kassie thumped into the irritated passer-by and stumbled away, apologizing. He continued to abuse her, but she didn't engage, moving away fast, her gaze glued to the ground. She just wanted to get home now, to find sanctuary for a few hours. For years, she had kept herself apart, reasoning that it was best for everyone, but then, idiotically, she had tried to engage with life, to prove a point. And the results had been catastrophic. Now there was nothing left to do but prepare herself.

She had played this scenario out many times in her head. What to do in her final hours? Sometimes she imagined herself praying, finding God, or something like him, at the very last. Sometimes she imagined defending herself fiercely, miraculously snatching victory from the jaws of defeat. But now she saw only desolation and oblivion. Altering your fate, making a difference – neither of these things seemed possible any more. The best thing she could hope for was to make her peace with the world, smoke a bit of skunk and prepare for the end.

This then was the legacy of her gift. The price of her knowledge.

This was her birthright.

135

'I want everybody looking at me.'

Gabrielle Grey stood outside Joseph White's house, surrounded by an assortment of detectives, policemen and volunteer officers. A few passers-by were loitering, but there was no sign of any journalists, so she could afford to raise her voice. Speed was of the essence and those in front of her needed to know what was required of them.

'According to the other tenants, White left the house roughly twenty minutes ago. His closet is empty, his room unlocked, so we can assume he's gone for good. Our priority now is to find him as quickly as possible. We are going to fan out across this neighbourhood, canvassing local people, looking for evidence of break-ins, automobile theft and so on. We've no idea where he's heading, but let's cut him off before he gets there.'

There were murmurs of agreement from the assembled faces.

'I've spoken to the CTA, who'll be keeping an eye on the transport networks, but it's our job to bring this guy in. Officer Montgomery will organize you into groups. Each of you will be covering four blocks. First sign of a sighting, you call it in. We want White surrounded before we make our move. Now, let's go.'

They swarmed towards Montgomery, who handed them marked-up maps of the area. Gabrielle stepped aside, looking appreciatively at the youthful officer, who was organizing the search parties efficiently and professionally. This case had been so complex, so frustrating, but the fevered activity outside White's former residence gave her real hope that their ordeal would soon be at an end.

136

They were looking at him. He was sure of it.

A man and a woman, no more than twenty-five years old, were sitting together at a sidewalk café, blatantly staring at him. Any minute now, he expected them to point at him, to pull out their phones and raise the alarm. Pulling the peak of his cap down further, he pressed on and, to his surprise, the couple now turned to each other and exchanged a few words, laughing as they did so. Soon, they were engrossed in conversation, with eyes only for each other.

Muttering, he carried on. He was becoming so jumpy, so paranoid, that he risked giving himself away. It was important to remain calm, collected . . . though this was hard to do when you were the subject of a city-wide manhunt. Even so, the authorities hadn't caught up with him yet, and if he was careful, he might still elude them.

If he did, it would be no thanks to *her*. She was the reason they had come to his door. She had haunted his life these past few days, interrupting him before he'd really got going on Varga – he'd had to slit the guy's throat and flee – almost catching him as he tried to escape. Were it not for her bizarre, dogged pursuit of him, culminating in her tearing a chunk of skin off his leg, the police would never have identified him. He had been right to worry about her – she seemed destined to be his undoing.

It was ironic that this slight girl had proved more adept than the professionals in tracking him. The police had cobbled together a rough image of him after the Baines killing – her work again, no doubt – but they seemed clueless in making the connection to someone who had been arrested on several occasions for breaking and entering. That was the thing about the police – they had no imagination. Twice he had dodged charges of trespass and burglary because there was no evidence of a break-in and nothing had been taken – like many others, the police had dismissed him as a confused halfwit, a bumbling idiot who'd stumbled into the wrong house. The reality of course was that he was there to see the owners' reaction when they came face to face with an intruder in their living room and, boy, had it been worth it – the second woman screaming the house down. The police must have seen through his lies, but still it never occurred to them to ask *why* someone might do this. It was principally thanks to their incompetence that he was still a free man.

He had reached the intersection and waited for the Walk sign. As he cast around, he saw that the large screen which blasted out adverts at the passing motorists was now displaying his face alongside the banner headline: 'Quadruple murder suspect at large'. He got a frisson of excitement at seeing himself described like that, but this was swiftly replaced by unease as he lowered his gaze once more. Out of the corner of his eye, he could see an elderly lady, who was waiting nearby, coolly appraising him, before seeming to cast her eyes up to the big screen.

Without waiting for the Walk sign, he stepped down into the road, letting one car pass, before hurrying away. He was hoping the woman was just idly curious or a Cubs fan or perhaps just senile, but as he fled he was convinced he heard her strike up a conversation with the businessman who'd been standing next to her. Were they talking about him?

Debating whether to call the cops or not? Or was she just passing the time of day?

He didn't know and it made him rage. He had no idea how close he was to capture, if he would be frustrated at the last. Though trying to remain relaxed and focused, he was fizzing with anxiety and he saw danger in every face he passed.

He was the one being hunted now.

137

She had been crying, tear stains tarnishing her cheeks. Adam felt torn – guilty at causing this anguish, but furious at Christine for her weakness.

'I just want to understand what's going on. You've been acting so strangely . . .'

They were standing in her spotless front room. She had retreated home following their unpleasant confrontation at his house earlier. She was mad with grief anyway, but had been left badly shaken by Adam's angry refusal to engage with her. Her red, puffy eyes revealed the extent of her distress.

'One minute, you're slamming the door in my face, telling me to mind my own business. The next you're turning up on my doorstep, drunk, asking to come in.'

'I know and I'm sorry,' Adam replied quickly, ignoring the flush of shame at his drunkenness and his clumsy, callous behaviour. 'It's just that things didn't go the way I'd hoped with the Board this morning . . .'

A flash of something in Christine's ravaged eyes – as if she'd known all along what the outcome would be.

'So I had a couple of drinks, more than a couple actually . . . It was stupid of me and I should never have taken my disappointment out on you . . .'

He could taste the stale whiskey in his mouth. He had drunk most of a bottle this afternoon, but still wanted more.

'Which is why I wanted to come around to apologize. I truly am sorry . . .'

Her face immediately softened, further exacerbating Adam's guilt at lying to her. He thought she was about to start crying again, but to his immense relief she managed to retain her composure.

'Apology accepted, Adam. I know things are tough, but we need to stick together . . .'

Adam nodded, shame robbing him of the ability to respond.

'Now how about I fix us some coffee? I'm sure we could both use a cup.'

She bustled off to the kitchen even before the sentence was finished. Adam watched her disappear through the swing doors, then hurried into the hallway. He paused briefly to see if his movement had been detected, but Christine was busy filling the kettle, so he hurried on down the hallway and into the master bedroom.

It was immaculate, like every other room in the house. Crossing the floor, Adam climbed up on to the neatly made bed. The sudden step up made his head spin and for a moment he swayed unsteadily back and forth. But then, placing his hand on the wall for support, he managed to regain his balance, and refocus on the job in hand. First, he removed the portrait that hung above the headboard. Placing it carefully on the bed beside him, he then turned his attention to the wall. A small wall-mounted safe stared back at him. Another quick check over his shoulder, then he began to spin the dial. He had helped Christine install it, knew her pass code was always her date of birth, so the dial clicked easily into place and soon the safe was open. There were numerous documents and keepsakes at the bottom, but perched on top of them was a Beretta M9.

Faith had never liked guns, but had eventually sanctioned her mother getting one, as she lived alone in an increasingly violent city. Christine had never used it of course – but it made her sleep easier at night, which was the point. Eagerly, Adam snatched it up, shoving it into his jacket.

Closing the safe, he replaced the portrait on the wall. It was of Faith as a young woman, painted by a family friend, and the sight made him pause. She looked so youthful, so innocent, so happy. Her eyes sought his out, wanting to make a connection, but he couldn't go there, not now. Instead, he kissed his fingers and placed them on her lips, before stepping down off the bed and hurrying out of the room.

Back in the hallway, Adam could hear Christine humming to herself in the kitchen, the gentle clink of crockery. There was no time to waste, so, easing open the front door, he slipped out into the night, the hard steel of the gun pressing against his chest.

138

The house was cold and empty. Kassie had turned on the heating, but the system was aged, slowly clanking into life, and still she felt frozen to the core. She didn't normally feel the cold, so was she coming down with something? Or was it just her loneliness that was making her shiver?

There was no doubt about it – the house felt wrong. This was her mother's domain, always had been, her constant presence both irritating and oddly reassuring. Kassie now realized that she had seldom been in the house without her mother – she was always the one who was going out, seeking distraction, getting into trouble. Whenever she was here her mother was, fussing around her, spying on her. Even when she did leave her alone, she was never still – always dusting the furniture, cleaning the curtains, rustling up some Polish delicacies in the kitchen.

Kassie opened the fridge, which was empty except for a carton of milk and a mouldy tomato. Closing it, she turned to take in the spotless kitchen. This was the room that felt most odd to her – whatever warmth there had been in this house had been found here. Her mom was happiest when she was cooking, pans boiling, stove humming, the smells of the old country filling the room. When she was young, Kassie would often be given tidbits and treats, which she would devour at the kitchen table, marvelling at her mother's efficiency and expertise. Those were some of her happiest memories, in a childhood which had often been difficult and distressing.

Kassie felt a hollow pit in her stomach. She missed her mother. There was no dressing it up: in spite of everything, she missed her presence. The house felt so lifeless now, a shrine to loneliness, to emptiness.

She felt tears pricking her eyes and, sitting down at the table, tugged her cell phone from her pocket. She started to key in the numbers, her fingers flitting across the screen, until all the digits had been entered. Her thumb moved towards the call button, but now she hesitated. It was such a small thing, but such a big thing too.

What would she say to her? What *could* she say to sum up their fifteen difficult years together? Should she thank her? Berate her for abandoning her? Tell her she loved her in spite of everything? All of these were true, but none of them quite did the job. She knew she had to do – to say – something, but what was the right way to say goodbye?

What, in the end, had it all been for?

139

'Sure, I saw him. He's a big fella, with a Cubs hat on . . .'

The elderly lady said it decisively, even a little triumphantly, as if she was about to win a prize. Gabrielle didn't think this was appropriate, but was not going to censure her. The teams had been doing house-to-house for thirty minutes without success. The testimony of this senior citizen, huddled under her umbrella by the intersection, was their first proper lead.

'And which direction was he heading in, ma'am?' Gabrielle replied, still a little breathless.

'That way,' she answered, pointing. 'Heading south.'

'Can I ask you to look again at the photo. Are you sure it was him?'

'Absolutely,' she answered reprovingly. 'I'm not senile, dear. Well, not yet, anyway . . .'

'That's not what I meant, ma'am.'

'He looked nervous, shifty. Marched across the road on a Stop sign, had to dodge the cars.'

'And can you describe what he was wearing?'

The woman – who had identified herself as Esme Perkins – thought for a moment.

'White sneakers, I think. Blue jeans for sure . . . with a khaki jacket and a Cubs cap.'

'Was he carrying anything?'

'A duffelbag perhaps . . . I can't be sure . . .'

'And was he with anyone?'

'No, he was alone and he seemed in a hurry to be

somewhere. I wouldn't walk across this intersection on a Stop sign if my life depended on it.'

Nodding to a junior officer to continue taking her statement, Gabrielle thanked Esme and pulled out her radio. Holding her ID aloft for all to see, she plunged across the road, her radio clamped to her mouth.

'The suspect has been spotted in the last ten minutes, heading south on South Damen Avenue. Repeat, suspect heading south on South Damen.'

With that, she lowered her radio and started to run. They were close now, she could smell it. And she was determined to be in at the kill.

140

Kassie walked along the dingy hallway, tears filling her eyes. Having plucked up the courage to make the call to her mother, she had pressed the button, bracing herself for a frosty reception. But the call had gone straight to voicemail and Kassie had hesitated, then panicked, before hanging up without saying a word.

Hesitation proved fatal and Kassie had tossed her phone on to the table in disgust, knowing full well she lacked the resolve to try again. She desperately wanted to be reconciled with her mother, but Fate was working against her. Her mother had cut the cord and maybe that was the way it was meant to end. Abandoning her plan to say her last goodbye, Kassie instead hurried to the back room. There was a small stash of skunk there, hidden in an old tin of silver polish, and it was calling to her now.

There was no denying it – she was scared. Scared and upset. It could only be a matter of hours until Adam ended her short life, and there was no one around to comfort her. She had known this moment was coming, but now it was here she wanted to run from it, to hide from her destiny. There was no way she could do this – she had been heading inexorably towards this sudden, brutal end since the day she was born – but still she longed to. She could see Adam, see his anguished face, his finger squeezing the trigger . . .

Leaning down, she yanked open the cupboard under the sink, searching frantically for the small tin. If she couldn't be at peace, she could at least be numb. With her mother gone, she was now at liberty to smoke whenever, wherever she chose and she grasped the tin eagerly. Some things are too ingrained, however, and Kassie now found herself directing her steps to the back door. Smoking in the house had always been strictly forbidden, even for her father, who smoked forty a day, and she couldn't bring herself to pollute her mother's prized curtains. Whenever things got too much, Kassie had always sneaked out into the backyard, hiding the telltale butts in a broken flowerpot.

The yard was a small, scrappy affair, having fallen into neglect since her father's death. Kassie had some fragmentary memory of a strip of grass, of rolling on it as a child, but it was a dirt square now, full of the junk that could not be squeezed into the house. Even so, Kassie wanted to be out there at this moment, medicating herself against the anxiety that was steadily growing inside her.

But, as she approached the back door, she suddenly slowed. It appeared to be closed, but actually was slightly ajar. Kassie stood still, casting a quick look behind her, then ventured forward. Her eyes were fixed on the lock, which she now saw had been forced. She paused, easing the door open carefully, scanning the yard feverishly for signs of an intruder, but could see nothing but darkness and shadows.

Creak.

Kassie spun round. The room was empty, but her ears had not deceived her. Someone was in the house with her. It could be a burglar of course, or a junkie seeking ready cash, but she dismissed these thoughts instantly. The stealth of his entry, his ability to blend into the fabric of the house, provided a pretty clear steer as to who the intruder was. Suddenly fear ripped through her. This wasn't the way it was meant to be. This wasn't how it was supposed to end . . .

She took a step forward, but the ageing floorboards groaned, announcing her progress. Sweating, she considered her options. She could slip out the back, make a break for it, but that didn't appeal. The high chain link fence that enclosed the backyard was padlocked shut – the key hanging on a hook in the kitchen – and beyond it lay a large expanse of scrubby wasteland. No, she needed to get out the front, on to the street, where there was a chance someone might spot them and raise the alarm.

She could rely on stealth or speed. The former was fraught with peril and she wasn't sure her nerves would take it, so she opted for the latter, bursting forward and sprinting down the hallway as fast as she could.

If he wasn't expecting this move, if she took him by surprise, then she stood a chance of getting to the front door. She pounded down the hallway, careless of the noise she was creating. She passed the door to her mother's bedroom, then her own, powering forward. She was nearly at the end of the hallway, could see the living room. She accelerated, speeding on, on, on . . .

Then suddenly she lurched sideways. Something had cannoned into her – bursting from the closet – and she slammed into the corner of the hallway wall. Bouncing off it, she fell into the living room, her head hitting the exposed boards hard. She tried to scramble to her feet, but now a large weight bore down on her. She was knocked on to her hands and knees and, even as she tried to lever herself upwards, she felt an arm slide around her throat. Now, it was pulling tight, choking her, starving her of oxygen.

She was already starting to feel faint, to lose focus, so in desperation she pivoted, driving an elbow backwards into her attacker's groin. It connected and her attacker emitted a deep, low groan. Momentarily his grip loosened and Kassie shrugged him off. Scrambling to her feet, she sprinted towards the front door, screaming for all she was worth.

She made it there in seconds and yanked the latch. Thanking her lucky stars that she hadn't double-locked it, she threw the door open. The cool air caressed her face, but as she stepped outside, a savage blow hit her in the kidneys. Her screaming was immediately stifled, as the breath was knocked out of her and a searing pain flared up her torso. Vomit rose in her windpipe and she felt horribly dizzy. She wanted to keep going, but that was impossible and now she felt herself being yanked back inside. The door was slammed shut and her legs were suddenly swept from under her. She had no time to brace herself and crashed to the ground like a sack of potatoes.

Disoriented, breathless, she tried to fight back, but it was hopeless. The man in the ski mask bent down and, clutching a fistful of auburn hair, dragged her towards the back of the house.

141

She fought him with everything she'd got, kicking and screaming as he hauled her along the hallway. Her arms flailed desperately, smacking into the walls, searching for purchase. She was nearly at the end of the hallway now, but suddenly her fingers found the radiator pipe and she wrapped them around it, arresting their progress. Instantly, a heavy boot slammed down on them. Howling in pain, she loosened her grip and was yanked unceremoniously into the back room.

She landed in a heap, but as she tried to rise a fist connected with her stomach. Gasping, she bent double, then felt his fat hand on the back of her neck. She heard a chair being dragged across the floor and moments later she was deposited on to it, her backside connecting sharply with the seat. Another hard slap stunned her – she was seeing stars now – then her arms were jerked behind her. Her resistance was feeble and she was soon bound to the chair. With her last vestiges of energy, she tried to scream, but a rag was shoved forcefully into her mouth. She gagged, but didn't vomit, the dirty fabric tickling her larynx.

Her attacker paused for breath, his chest rising and falling, clearly exhausted by his efforts. He took a moment to gather himself, then hurried out of the room. She heard his progress, as he returned to the closet. Moments later, he re-entered the room carrying a shabby duffelbag.

Ignoring her, he put the bag down and unzipped it. From it, he removed a large cleaver. Turning, he walked over to

Kassie, the weapon gripped in his fist. Having been a bundle of nervous, adrenalized energy, he now paused, catching his breath once more, looking at the helpless girl in front of him. Kassie thought he was about to speak, to taunt her, but instead he walked straight up to her, grasping the sleeve of her shirt. Raising the blade, he slit along the seam, until the fabric parted, revealing her bare arm beneath. Kassie started to struggle, to rock backward and forward in the chair, but White ignored her, opening up her other sleeve in similar fashion. Now he teased the point of his blade between the buttons on the front of her shirt, before suddenly ripping sharply upwards. Buttons flew everywhere, then the devastated shirt fell open, revealing her bra and the bare flesh of her torso.

Exhaling heavily, White surveyed his victim.

'Ready to play?'

Kassie said nothing, glaring at him defiantly. To her surprise, her captor pulled off his mask, revealing his sweaty, pink face. With a gleam of triumph in his eyes, he stared at her, a thin smile creasing his lips. She had seen his face before of course, but now in close-up it seemed even more repellent. The pale, flaccid skin where the goatee used to be, the cold, dead eyes, the thin folds of fat on his forehead and chin. He looked like a slavering hog, one who was looking forward to a good feed. Lowering himself to her level, he looked her in the eye and whispered:

'On the count of three. One –'

He ripped the blade fast across her stomach. Immediately Kassie was gripped by an awful, burning sensation. Looking down, she expected to see her guts tumbling out . . . but it was just a nasty flesh wound. Was this it then? The beginning of a prolonged, abominable desecration?

Sensing her anxiety, her attacker locked his eyes on to hers.

'I'm going to make you beg, girlie. I'm going to make you *beg* for mercy . . .'

His tiny eyes blazed at the prospect, the veins on his neck bulging.

'I'm going to make you wish you'd never been born.'

142

'Talk to me, people. Where is he?'

Gabrielle tried to keep her voice calm, but the anxiety punched through. Dozens of officers had descended on McKinley Park, fanning out and sweeping the blocks. White might still be on the street, but he might also have gone to ground, finding a derelict house or empty commercial property to lie low in. So every doorway and alleyway had to be checked. But a quarter of an hour had elapsed since Esme's sighting and with every passing minute White's chances of eluding them increased.

'Nothing here, boss. We'll keep at it.'

The voice of Detective Suarez clicked off. He was to the north of McKinley Park, with the majority of the officers. If he was going to hide out anywhere, Gabrielle reasoned, it was around there. He could try to hide out in the shadow of Interstate 55, disappear into the Lower West Side or even, if he was really desperate, plunge into the river. Yet still there had been no sightings of him.

'How about you, Robins?'

There was a moment's silence. Detective Robins and his group were to the east, cutting off the route to Bronzeville and, beyond that, Burnham Park.

'Nothing yet, boss,' Robins crackled back.

'Shit,' Gabrielle muttered, realizing too late that she was still transmitting.

She radioed Albright, who was to the west in Brighton Park,

but the result was the same. That left one possibility – that White had headed south. That route would have led him to Back of the Yards and to the South Side. But surely he wouldn't have gone there? To head there at this time of night would be dangerous, possibly suicidal. Even though White was probably armed, the numbers counted against him – he would be the gangs' plaything within minutes of entering their territory. Even CPD patrols only ventured down there when they really had to. No, it was crazy to think he would have headed that way, however desperate he was. And yet . . . unless he had been extraordinarily lucky, or they extraordinarily careless, he must have headed south. But why? Why on earth would he be willing to head through Back of the Yards to the South Side into certain danger and . . .

And now a thought started to take hold of her. An insidious, insistent thought that rocked her back on her heels.

Suddenly, Gabrielle knew exactly where he'd gone.

143

Adam marched down the road, his eyes set dead ahead. Back of the Yards was unfamiliar to him, but Kassie's house lay in the shadows of the Union Stock Yard and everybody knew where *that* was. It loomed over this part of Chicago like a shadowy phantom, a faded monument to the old Chicago when life was good and work was plentiful.

As he walked, his hand strayed to his jacket, sliding inside to grip the butt of the Beretta. It was solid and powerful in his hand and Adam felt a surge of adrenaline, powering him forward. Even if he had wanted to stop himself now, he wasn't sure he could. This journey – perhaps the last he would ever make – seemed to have a momentum of its own now.

'First, do no harm.' How easily that oath was forgotten. Adam had never hurt anyone in his life – had never wanted to – but now it seemed logical, even inevitable. Someone had to pay for all this misery, all this suffering. And that someone had to be Kassie. He would be deaf to her pleas, to his own conscience – all he wanted to do now was obliterate the contagion that had destroyed his life.

He pulled the handgun from his jacket, flicking the safety catch off before dropping it to his side, careless of detection. He was only a few minutes from Kassie's house and something told him that nothing would impede him.

Kassie had been right all along. He laughed bitterly at the thought, but it was true. Kassie had foreseen how this would end, she had foreseen *everything*. Despite all his doubts, all his alternative theories, she had been telling the truth from the start. She was at home right now, waiting for him, waiting for the promised end. He could see himself raising the gun, pulling the trigger. It was as if a higher force was guiding him, propelling him towards the final act. Perhaps this was why his stride was so confident, his nerve so strong. Kassie had foreseen that he would kill her.

And that was precisely what he intended to do.

144

She howled in pain, the gag muffling her agony, but still he didn't relent. She was at his mercy now and he was determined to enjoy himself. Raising the blood-stained cleaver, he dragged it over her exposed shoulder, once, twice, in a neat criss-cross pattern.

Her body reacted, bucking vigorously, as a low moan stole from her lips. Pausing to catch his breath, White surveyed his victim, pliant and bloodied on the chair in front of him. Her torso, shoulders and arms were covered in deep cuts, yet to her credit she had never hung her head, nor asked for mercy. This one had a bit of steel, for sure, which both excited and unnerved him.

Casting his eyes down, he gripped the fabric of her pants, pulling it up to get a bit of air above flesh, then slid his blade through. The fabric tore easily and her left thigh was now exposed. He ran the blade over her pale, freckled skin, then placing the tip of the blade on top of her thigh, he slammed his fist down on the butt of handle. The wide blade slid two inches into her flesh and then, using all his strength, he started to drag the cleaver towards him, slowly splitting her thigh open from top to bottom. A muffled gasp, followed by a howl, then the girl's body seemed to spasm with pain. Wiping the sweat from his forehead, White took a step backwards, keen to admire his handiwork, to revel in her anguish.

The girl had her eyes tight shut, trying desperately to swallow down the pain, but now to his surprise she opened them again. Instead of imploring him to stop, she gathered herself, looking calmly at him, as she ignored the waves of agony still rippling through her body.

Marching forward, he held the blade up to her face, smearing her cheeks with her own gore. She blinked back at him, repelled, but defiant. Without warning, he pulled the gag from her mouth. The girl gasped, opening and closing her mouth like a fish, as she desperately drank in fresh oxygen. But he gave her no respite, holding the sticky cleaver up to her throat, resting the steel on her carotid artery.

'I was going to take my time, but maybe I should just end it now. What do you say?'

Her eyelids flickered, as he dug the blade into her flesh.

'One cut and that's it. You'll bleed out in front of me, like a stuck pig . . .'

He ran a finger across his own throat.

'What do you think? Should I do it now? Should I?' he continued, raising his voice steadily. 'Or do you want to live?'

He let his words hang in the air.

'I *am* prepared to let you live a little longer. But you are going to have to beg. Can you beg, Kassie?'

This was it. The moment he craved. Despite the trauma of their ordeal, all his victims pleaded at the finish – desperate to live, regardless of how deformed and bloodied they were. That was when he let them know that there was no hope, that they *were* going to die. It was the most delicious sensation, one he had fast become addicted to.

To his surprise, the girl continued to stare at him.

'What's the matter, honey? Cat got your tongue?'

Still she didn't respond, her eyelashes barely moving as she raised her gaze to meet his.

'Fine, have it your way,' he raged, making as if to slit her throat.

She didn't move. Didn't react in any way. And now he noticed that the girl seemed to be looking beyond him, *within him* almost, as she stared into his eyes. Even as she did so, a faint smile seemed to crease her face.

Confused, enraged, White roared his displeasure, brandishing the cleaver above him. But still she refused to be cowed. And now, for the first time since he'd started his campaign of violence, Joseph White was suddenly lost as to what to do. This girl clearly felt pain – she was sickened by the sight of her own body and disgusted by him – but there was one emotion she seemed incapable of. The one emotion he craved above all others.

Fear.

145

Gabrielle flung open the car door and leaped inside. She had left it parked on a side street in Bronzeville, some distance from her search zone, and had sprinted there, cursing her stupidity every step of the way. She had radioed in and squad cars were now racing to Kassie's house, but they were approaching from the north and west, fighting their way through traffic. If she was quick, there was a chance she'd get there first and every second counted now.

She slammed the driver's door shut, just as Montgomery slid into the passenger seat. Without a word, she punched the sirens and slid the flashing light on to the roof, as Gabrielle fired up the ignition. The car leaped forward, both driver and passenger deftly clicking their belts in with one hand, as they roared off into the night.

'He's heading for the Wojcek house,' Gabrielle breathed.

Montgomery didn't need to respond, she seemed to get her line of thinking instantly. There was no reason for White to head through Back of the Yards unless he had a visit to make. And Kassie was the obvious target. Though it shamed them to admit it, nobody had done more to stymie White's reign of terror than the fifteen-year-old girl. Perhaps White wanted to revenge himself on her, to commit one last orgy of violence before he fled Chicago for good?

'You ready?' Gabrielle continued, shooting a look at the junior officer.

She nodded, sliding her firearm from its holster and resting her finger on the safety catch.

'Obviously, I'd prefer to take White alive, but if there is any danger to us, to the girl, we take him down.'

'Sure,' Montgomery responded, gripping her weapon a little tighter.

'This has to end tonight. We may not get another chance.'

They fell back into silence, both reflecting on what lay ahead. Up in front of them, Gabrielle could see roadworks and a long line of traffic snaking back towards them. Assessing her options, she ordered Montgomery to raise the volume of the siren, then mounted the kerb, driving up on to the sidewalk. Cruising along, she gestured frantically at the pedestrians to move aside, and they obliged, ducking into doorways and leaping off into the gutter. Moments later, Gabrielle and Montgomery passed the roadworks and, wrenching the steering wheel to the left, Gabrielle guided the car back on to the tarmac.

The road ahead was clear now and Gabrielle didn't hesitate, ramming her foot down on the accelerator. The car leaped forward with a squeal of tyres, then sped down the street. Gabrielle gripped the wheel a little tighter, sweating, as the adrenaline started to flow. This was it then, this was what the last few days had been inexorably leading to.

This was the endgame.

146

'Beg!'

He roared at her, flecks of spittle landing on her face.

'Beg, you fucking bitch!'

They were so close that their noses were nearly touching. But still the girl didn't respond, didn't react, despite the furious barrage of abuse aimed at her. Enraged, he stepped back and slashed at her thigh repeatedly, ripping the blade back and forth, until her taut flesh was a bloody mess. She looked an abomination – lacerated shoulders, arms cut almost to the bone, blood smeared all over her ravaged face – yet she refused to give in. She refused to be beaten.

He jabbed the point of the blade into her cheek.

'I'll cut your eyes out, unless you give me what I want.'

There was a moment's confusion in her expression but, as she raised her eyes to his once more, a calm seemed to steal over her. She seemed relaxed, a half-smile still seeming to tug at the corner of her mouth.

'Don't you smile at me. Don't you *dare* smile at me.'

But his threats seemed empty now. She had no fear of his blade. She had no fear of *him*. Cursing violently, he turned and walked away. He couldn't stand the way she was looking at him, as if *she* were the one in control.

He marched down the hallway to the front of the house, muttering angrily to himself. Nothing was going as planned, but . . . if he kept his cool, then everything would still be ok. He would start on her limbs. Sever her arms first, then her legs. Then she'd lick his boots for the chance to be put out of her misery. But there was no chance of that – this one had to be made to *suffer*.

Buoyed by this thought, Joseph White stepped confidently into the living room. To find a man with a gun standing right in front of him.

147

Adam Brandt hadn't known what to expect, but it wasn't *this*.

Approaching Kassie's house cautiously, he'd slid her door key into the lock and slipped inside. In the gloom, it had taken him a moment to get his bearings. The living room was empty, but there were noises coming from the back of the house. A voice, but was it Kassie's? It sounded too deep, but who else would be here? Surprised, unnerved, he'd fingered the trigger of his weapon. Moments later, he'd heard movement in the hallway and then, without warning, Joseph White stepped into the room.

Adam recognized him immediately – his face was burned in his memory from that night at Lake Calumet. But what the hell was he doing here? White looked as confused as he did and, for a brief moment, neither man moved. Then, without warning, Adam raised his gun and fired. But White was already on the move, darting back down the hallway, as the bullet slammed into wall.

Adam hurried after him. The man who had been the architect of so much misery, so much bloodshed, was right here. Creeping up to the hallway entrance, he arrowed a look down it. The hallway was gloomy, but appeared to be empty. Adam thought about flicking on the lights, but deciding that that would make him an easy target, pressed on through the darkness. His gun was raised and he was ready to shoot again if necessary, though he could see his hand was shaking slightly.

The floorboards creaked ominously beneath his feet, setting his nerves jangling. He assumed the man was in the back room, but there were doors off to the side before that – fertile territory for an ambush. The house was deathly quiet now, there was no sign of the fugitive. Adam expected him to leap out at him at any moment, to slit his throat . . .

Screwing up his courage, he reached a door on his left. He eased it open with his foot, and, seeing that the bedroom was empty, spun round, expecting to be attacked from the rear. But the door opposite was still closed, and as he pushed it open, he discovered it concealed only another empty bedroom. Turning his attention to the back room, he took another couple of steps towards the mouth of the hallway.

Reaching the end, he counted silently down from three, then launched himself into the room. Yet again he received a nasty surprise. The intruder *was* in the room, as he'd hoped, but so was Kassie, standing by an upturned chair and some severed rope. Her clothing was torn, her bruised face smeared with blood, her arms riven with cuts. Worse still, her left thigh had been cut open almost to the bone, blood oozing from the gaping fissure. The man was standing behind her, a huge cleaver pressed to her throat.

'Take a step closer and I'll slit her throat.'

Adam stared at him, stunned. He had come here intending to take the girl's life and now *somebody else* was threatening to do it for him.

'Don't listen to him,' Kassie suddenly cried, but White dragged the blade down the side of her neck as a warning.

Kassie broke off, gasping.

'Lower the gun and back away,' White continued, edging himself and his captive towards the back door.

Adam kept the gun pointed in White's direction. He was

suddenly a riot of emotions – confusion and doubt the principal among them.

'Not another move,' White intoned, fumbling for, then opening, the back door with his free hand.

A rush of cold air filled the room, as the darkness beyond was revealed. Then, tugging Kassie roughly with him, White disappeared from view.

148

They stumbled across the yard, locked in a hideous embrace. White angrily kicked away the junk that littered the ground as he dragged his captive towards the back gate. Kassie's gaze immediately darted to the house, searching for Adam. She had no idea why he had turned up at her home – had he come to help her or *harm* her? – but she needed him. She couldn't bear to be abandoned to White's cruelty.

And now he appeared, stepping purposefully into the yard, his gun pointing in their direction. White reacted immediately, quickening his pace, as he marched Kassie away. Every step was agony, her mutilated leg threatening to give way at any moment. She groaned in pain, but White showed no mercy, clamping his hand over her mouth, as they continued their clumsy dance.

But Adam was gaining on them. He was twenty feet away, his weapon raised.

'Don't do it, man,' White shouted. 'Think of the girl.'

But Adam kept marching towards them.

'You really a killer? You *really* want her death on your conscience?'

White's tone was mocking. It was true Adam made an unlikely killer – with his smart suit and clean-cut features. But it was an image that Kassie was familiar with, one which had haunted her waking hours for years.

'You haven't got it in you,' White continued. 'Nice college boy like –'

But he didn't get to finish — a bullet ripping over his head. It missed the retreating couple by a foot or so, but still made Kassie jump. The sound was deafening, the sensation of the bullet flying past terrifying.

'That was a warning shot,' Adam said grimly, lowering his gun to their level.

He sounded shaken, but determined. And now for the first time White paused, arresting their progress, wondering perhaps if Adam really *would* shoot. The gunshot was still echoing through the night air and, as it did so, Kassie saw lights coming on in nearby houses. Lights, accompanied by worried voices. And, as the curtains began to part, as the hubbub of voices steadily grew, Kassie noticed something else.

Sirens. The night sky was suddenly filled with sirens. Instinctively, she knew they were coming to her aid — multiple vehicles speeding towards *her* home. White seemed to sense this too, resuming their urgent retreat towards the back gate. Suddenly Kassie was filled with hope. If she could release herself from his grip, if she could buy herself some time, then maybe everything would still be ok. She could escape, White would be captured . . .

'Not another step.'

Adam's instruction was clear, but his voice was shaking.

'Pull the trigger if you want to,' White responded grimly, pulling Kassie closer to him. 'But you'll have to kill both of us.'

Adam was ten feet away now — he could hardly miss — but suddenly he looked uncertain, as if, at the very last moment, pulling the trigger on another human being would prove too much. This gave Kassie an opportunity, but the pair were only a couple of feet from the back gate, so Kassie sank her teeth into White's sweaty hand.

Her captor roared, withdrawing his hand and loosening his

grip on her. Immediately, Kassie lurched forward, breaking free. Adam was within reach now and was already lowering his gun to receive her. If she could fall into his arms, she would be safe . . .

Suddenly her head snapped backwards. The impact took her breath away, her vision blurring. She felt as if she might black out for a second, even as she fell backwards, away from Adam. And now she became aware of White's hand gripping her hair, pulling her towards him.

'No . . .'

White ignored her protests, tugging her back, back, back. Adam looked wrong-footed, his gun still pointing at the floor, but White knew exactly what to do. They had reached the back gate and he kicked out viciously at it. The rusty padlock capitulated, crashing to the ground and the chain link gate lolled open.

And now, too late, Kassie realized how it would play out. Beyond the yard was open wasteland. If White could make it there, he would be free and clear. There was plenty of cover and numerous escape routes – endless tracks and alleyways he could scurry down, even as the police sped to Kassie's front door.

'Take the shot,' Kassie gasped.

Adam reacted, raising his gun. But Kassie's head, her body, were directly in front of White and this seemed to make him hesitate.

'Don't let him get away –'

White's fingers dug into her open mouth, but she shook them roughly away.

'Do it!' Kassie implored.

Adam looked as if he was in pain. If he *had* come here to hurt her, he certainly didn't look as if he wanted to now. But

Kassie knew what he *had* to do, how he could end White's reign of terror. So, even as her captor loosened his grip on her, preparing to make a break for it, Kassie raised her eyes to meet Adam's.

For a moment, time seemed to slow – a silent charge passing between the pair – then Kassie screamed:

'Do it now!'

Grimacing, Adam pumped the trigger – four crisp, clean shots ringing out in the cold spring night.

Epilogue

149

A dull shaft of sunlight illuminated their faces. It was just after dawn and Gabrielle Grey stood in her untidy office, staring down at the photos on top of her scattered case files. Everyone else had been sent home – it had been a gruelling night for all – but Gabrielle had returned to headquarters, to gather her thoughts. She had meant to start by putting her case notes in order, but had been stopped in her tracks by the faces – Jones, Stevens, Baines, Varga, and White and Wojcek too – that stared up at her.

She had never known a case like it and she sincerely hoped she never would again. Perversely, in the final analysis, it had been a personal triumph for her. She had already had a call from the Mayor – he more than anyone was pleased the case was now closed – and Hoskins had hinted at promotion. She hoped to use her elevated status to push for changes in the department – promotion perhaps for Suarez and Montgomery – but still Gabrielle wished the last two weeks could be erased and events rewritten. A city had been terrorized, blood had been shed and many, including members of her own team, had been left traumatized. Nobody should have to endure what they'd been through over the last two weeks. It would stay with them, with her, for ever.

It defied belief that a human being could behave as White had done. Gabrielle had met many unpleasant characters in her time, but this guy was something else. An animal, who showed no empathy, no compassion, who thrived on his victims' fear.

It was some consolation that he would never trouble anyone else – hopefully he was burning in sulphur right now – but that was no help to the bereaved families, who would never be able to rid themselves of those awful images, the knowledge of what their loved ones had endured at his hand.

Gathering up the photos, Gabrielle placed them neatly in their files and ordered her desk. She had intended to write up her report now, while events were still fresh in her mind, but suddenly she felt dog-tired. Now she just wanted to go home and embrace Dwayne and the boys. The last few days had been tough beyond measure, sickening and troubling, but it was over now and it was time to embrace life once more. She was, Gabrielle knew, one of the lucky ones.

She had someone to go home to.

150

He had been in these cells many times, but they looked very different from the inside. The stench was familiar, the graffiti the same, but these holding pens seemed somehow smaller today, as if the walls were crowding in on him. Adam Brandt had thought he'd known what it was like to be a prisoner in Cook County Jail, but now he realized he knew nothing at all.

He was once more in the bowels of the vast prison, but this time he was not wearing handmade shoes or designer clothes. He was in prison fatigues, his possessions, his clothes and his belt having been removed from him, lest he be tempted to take his own life. The irony of that, given all he'd been through, was crushing, but it was one of many body blows he'd had to endure today.

Grey's questioning of him was interminable, a source of slow torture, as was the undignified strip search when he entered the prison. The catcalling he'd received from the other prisoners – some of whom he recognized – was to be expected, but the abusive comments, or worse the silence, from prison officers he'd worked with for years cut deep. Worse still was having to complete the mental health assessment, a procedure he himself had devised.

But none of this hurt as much as the knowledge of what he'd done. He had had no choice of course – he couldn't let White escape – but, still, he had taken two lives. And that was something he would have to live with for ever.

In his mind's eye, he could still see Kassie's body jerking

as the bullets ripped through her, could hear White's startled groan as the bullets struck *him*. Instinct had made him pull the trigger – instinct and Kassie's urging – but still he had been shocked by the scene of human carnage in front of him. Before the gunshots had even faded, White had crumpled to the ground, gasping greedily for the air that would not save him. Kassie followed suit, collapsing on top of the prone figure, her ashen face pointing up at Adam. Her eyes were wide but calm, and a thin trickle of blood slid from her lips. Adam hurried over – too late remembering his real vocation – but his concerted attempts to revive her proved futile. He was still bent over her, exhaustedly pumping her chest, when the police arrived at the scene.

Two charges of homicide now awaited him. These would need to be confronted head on, for there was no doubting his guilt. The question was whether the case would go to trial and, if so, whether the jury would believe his assertion that Kassie had *wanted* him to fire. Or would they see him for what he now felt he was – a trigger-happy, blood-soaked killer?

Time would tell. There was nothing he could do now but wait. Hanging his head, Adam Brandt sat on the prison bunk, staring down the barrel of his guilt. Kassie was gone, Faith and Annabelle too, and now, for the first time, Adam realized that there *was* a fate worse than death.

Life.

151

The old lady stared into the distance, watching the sun creep above the horizon. She was never usually up this early, but today was not a normal day.

The nursing staff had grumbled when she'd summoned them to help her. She knew they dismissed her as a mad old Pole who'd long since checked out of the real world, but she still had some steel about her, insisting they dress her and wheel her down to the water's edge in time for sunrise.

They had lingered, of course, fearing perhaps that she intended to throw herself into the lake, as if she would have the energy for such a thing.

'Are you sure there's nothing I can bring you? A blanket? Some breakfast?'

'No, thank you. I have all I want.'

Still the nurse hesitated, clearly unnerved by Wieslawa's lucidity and sense of purpose. They were more used to her singing nursery rhymes, or muttering to herself, than issuing orders.

'Go, child. I'm quite all right.'

Reluctantly she withdrew, leaving Wieslawa alone. And now the old woman returned her attention to the lake, drinking in the sight of the sun's rays stealing across the huge body of water. She knew she should feel sad today, but somehow she couldn't find it in herself. It was true that she had lost her only visitor, that she would never see her little *babcia* again, but both of them had known this moment was coming. And wasn't it true that it was the ones left behind who really suffered?

What would Natalia be feeling now? Had the authorities already delivered their grim news? Despite their many troubles, the old woman's heart bled for her daughter – she knew from bitter experience what it was to lose a child. But Wieslawa herself felt no pain. Kassandra's gift had always been a curse, as it had been for her, and the poor girl had been tortured by life until the end. But it was over now.

Would they come to tell her the news today? Or would they think the old goose was too senile to understand, too fragile to endure another bereavement? The thought amused her. Most days she was lost in a haze of painful memory and fanciful abstraction, but today she could see clearer than anyone. Today she could see all.

A beautiful, tortured soul had departed. Wieslawa mourned her passing, but would lay eyes on her again soon enough. Indeed, she was already looking forward to night-fall, when she would drink in the sight of a new star in the heavens. That would have to wait, however. For now, she had to content herself with the sight of the vast, golden lake and the happy, carefree birds who called to each other, as they circled above. Looking out at the majestic scene in front of her, Wieslawa felt a smile spread across her face.

At long last, her beloved Kassie was free.

Acknowledgements

Many people contribute to the making of a book, but there are a few I would like to single out for heartfelt thanks. Dr Susan Buratto was incredibly generous, giving up her free time to educate me on the intricacies of mental health provision in the US criminal Justice system and beyond. Many of the characters and locations featured in this book sprang to life during our unconventional tour of Chicago. Back in the UK, Dr Lisa Barkley was equally generous and insightful – thanks to her I now have a much greater understanding of child psychology in general and distancing techniques specifically. I would also like to thank all the great people at Michael Joseph, especially Chantal Noel and Rowland White, who has been an outstanding editor and guide on this book and many others before it. Thanks must also go to my amazing agent, Hellie Ogden, for being a brilliant sounding board, inspiration and friend. Finally, my deepest thanks and love to Jennie, Chloe and Alex, for encouraging (and enduring) me as Kassie came to life. Chloe, I'm sorry the heroine isn't called Ruby, as we'd discussed, but, hey, that's the editorial process for you.